SHE'S MY WITCH

STEWART HOME was born and lives in London. He is the author of twenty-five books and has been translated into many languages. His works include *69 Things To Do With A Dead Princess*, *Tainted Love*, *The 9 Lives of Ray The Cat Jones* and *Re-Enter The Dragon: Genre Theory, Brucesploitation And The Sleazy Joys Of Lowbrow Cinema*. Home has also worked as an artist (including visual work in the Arts Council England Collection), an art class model, a shop assistant, a typist, a factory labourer and a ventriloquist.

STEWART HOME

SHE'S MY WITCH

LONDON BOOKS BRITISH FICTION

LONDON BOOKS
39 Lavender Gardens
London SW11 1DJ
www.london-books.co.uk

A catalogue record for this book
is available from the British Library

ISBN 978-0-9957217-4-6

Printed and bound in Great Britain by
CPI Group (UK) Ltd, Croydon, CR0 4YY

Typeset by Octavo Smith Publishing Services
www.octavosmith.com

'When you love a witch magic happens.'
Pagan proverb

The cards illustrating the chapter headings in this book come from the Swiss *1JJ* tarot deck. They were derived from the *Tarot de Besançon* which was in turn based on the *Tarot de Marseilles*. This pack substitutes Juno and Jupiter for The Popess and Pope in the *Tarot de Marseilles*; these became The High Priestess and The Hierophant in the *Rider-Waite-Smith* tarot and many other occult decks. The Swiss *1JJ* tarot was first produced between 1831 and 1838 in the card factory of Johann Georg Rauch. The Fool is unnumbered and here represents both 0 and 22. The tarot, like this novel, is the story of The Fool's journey to wisdom through endless rebirths, and so the book begins with chapter 0 and ends with chapter 22, both of which unfold beneath the image of The Fool.

THE FOOL

LE MAT.

I was the last person you'd expect to end up involved with a witch and her coven, but the heart follows its own path. I'd been a personal trainer for more than twenty years, and while the job didn't pay too well, it's satisfying to see my clients work their way up to fitness and good health. Before I found my vocation in life, I was a skinhead involved with Red Action and Anti-Fascist Action. I was a real skin, not some numbskull Nazi bonehead. I even wrote a book about my time fighting Nazis and racists entitled *Stand Up & Spit*.

In 2011 my past and my present conspired to bring the world's most beautiful witch my way. I wasn't looking for love. I'd only just got out of a disastrous relationship with an alcoholic. When my ex-wife Petra was sober she was sweet, but when she was drunk she was destructive and violent. She never attacked me but she screamed a lot. She'd moved into my housing association flat, and I didn't have the heart to throw her out, so I left after getting the tenancy transferred to her name. I thought I'd only be kipping on my cousin's sofa for a few weeks when I left in February 2011, but unforeseen circumstances prevented me from getting my own pad for a very long time.

Maria Remedios Varo Uranga contacted me through my professional page on Facebook a week or two after I left Petra. She'd chosen not to showcase her full beauty in her profile picture, and at first I didn't know she was a witch. The initial message I got asked if I'd be interested in her helping me make some videos to promote myself as a personal trainer. She'd noticed I'd stopped posting new material on my YouTube fitness channel. I said I couldn't afford to pay for videos but making them myself bored me. Maria said she'd work for free. We just kept messaging, and our talk moved away from videos to more personal matters. When I revealed I was kipping on my cousin's sofa I got a fast reply.

Maria: I know Manor Road. Some cunt tried to steal my bag there on 6 December last year. I kicked him so hard that I fractured a bone in my foot. I had to use crutches for a while but the bastard went away bruised. Moving on to more pleasant matters, do you ever spend time in the cemetery behind your cousin's house?

Me: I prefer to use Clissold Park for training, and so I don't go to Abney Park Cemetery much.

Maria: That's a shame. Abney Park is very peaceful.

Me: How are your toes now?

Maria: My foot has healed thank you. The muggers, my assailant was with three others in a stolen car, managed to nick four other women's bags that night. I was the lucky one who successfully defended herself.

Soon I found myself messaging Maria several times a day. I really looked forward to hearing from her. She was entertaining and seemed to know a surprising amount about me. She'd obviously done some serious background research before contacting me. I checked out her Facebook profile. There weren't many pictures, but in those she'd put up she was pretty despite a habitual 'I take no shit' look on her face. I liked the long dark hair she had in the few recent photos I could see. She'd grown up outside Valencia and moved to London in the mid-1990s. According to her profile, Maria was forty-two years old and into movies and music. She worked as a video editor for a company in Hackney. When she told me she'd had a painful session at the dentist, I messaged to say I hoped her tooth was better. I also sent a tune I liked, an old mod classic from the swinging sixties in

London, 'Any More Than I Do' by the Attack. There was a fast reply.

Maria: You are such a gentleman Martin Cooper. It's always a pleasure to talk to you. And on top of that you actually know what you're talking about. Now I sound like I'm licking your ass. But I'm not. 'Any More Than I Do' is brilliant. I could spend hours and hours listening to amazing tunes like that with you.

Maria liked northern soul, but she'd been through the Spanish punk scene and was still very involved with three-chord rock. So among the tunes I posted her were Los Rockin Devils' version of 'Gloria', 'Hammersmith Guerrilla' by Third World War, 'Let's Get Rid Of New York' by the Randoms, 'Alcoholiday' by Kaos, 'You've Heard These Chords Before' by the Nervous Eaters, 'Don't Gimmie No Lip Child' by Dave Berry, 'Savage' by the Fun Things, 'I Love A Russian' by Blonde Waltz, 'Bondage Boy' by the Sick Things, 'Gatecrasher' by the Gorillas, 'I Can't Wait' by the Jolt and 'Dr Rock' by Apple. I knew these tunes would appeal to Maria's punk side, a mixture of obscure seventies punk, proto-punk, sixties garage rock, freakbeat and even eighties garage rock revivalism in the case of Blonde Waltz. It turned out Maria didn't know a lot of this stuff but she was well up for getting into it. On the soul side I sent her tunes like the Vibrations' 'Ain't No Greens In Harlem' and trailers for movies like *Dolemite*.

Maria: Before I go to bed I want to tell you a little story. A few years ago I met this guy who was selling hundreds of B-movies on eBay. I wanted to buy a load of them and a few books too. I'd been living with my then boyfriend for six years and he got very upset because instead of this guy sending me the VHS tapes, the seller arranged to meet me in a pub to hand them over. He said he didn't trust Royal Mail to deliver them, and in any case, meeting him would save me the cost of postage. When I arrived at the pub the guy I was meeting said he hadn't brought the movies that day but he had a present for me. It was your book *Stand Up & Spit* with a dedication inside that read: 'To Maria, look forward to introducing you to some TWISTED cinematic treats...' I don't need to tell where this went. The eBay seller just wanted to bring me one movie at a time and give it to me for free. But I wasn't interested in him. After reading your book I checked you out online and found all your fitness videos. I split up with my ex a few months later and I think he still hates you. He didn't mind the eBay creep hitting on me because I wasn't interested. But he got mad at me for looking at your YouTube channel and going on about your book. I read online you were just a poseur and you'd never been a true skinhead. And I wondered whether your taste in music was a pose too. I'm so glad that's not the case. Don't hate me for this, but I used to hang out with skinheads and Hells Angels in Spain. If you look at their photos now they look terrible, just fat middle-aged men. I don't recognise them any more.

Me: Posing is great. But taking skinhead or punk subculture too seriously is silly – and you gotta stay in shape to pose.

Maria: I guess I'll have to work out like you then. I've had a gym membership for two years now, and I've only been there ten times. I have to go more. And now I'm going to bed coz it's very late. Night.

The next morning when I looked at my account there was another message: one Maria had sent after waking up.

Maria: I know from reading your book that you've got left-wing views, but I didn't read it for the politics, I was interested in what you had to say about skinheads and street fighting. I'm radically apolitical – that doesn't mean that I'm not interested in what's going on in the world. It's just that I don't believe in politicians, even if my brother-in-law is a local councillor for the Communist Party in Valencia. The only thing I totally believe in is fighting against animal cruelty. That was one of the reasons I came to London from Spain. You know how they treat animals there. It makes me sick.

Me: I don't mind if you're apolitical as long as you're not racist. It's great you care about animals. I've been vegetarian all my adult life. How a society treats animals reflects the way it behaves towards its own members.

Maria: I was born to be vegetarian. I can't even sleep if I start to think about poor defenceless animals suffering. Even when I was a baby, meat wouldn't go down my throat. It got stuck, and I had to spit it out. Until I was five I lived in a little village were my parents kept pigs, chickens, rabbits, a dog, a few cats, a horse and a donkey. I will never forget the squealing of the pigs when they were slaughtered. It was so distressing to hear them. I cried and cried with them. I think I'm still traumatised.

Me: I was forced to eat meat as a child and I hated it. But if I didn't eat the food put before me I was beaten and badly.

Maria: Guauhhhhh. You always surprise me. We could be brother and sister. I always wanted to have a super-smart older brother who could teach me everything better and faster than I could find it out for myself. To save me wasting my precious and limited time. It's not that I'm complaining about my family, but imagine having an illiterate mother who instead of encouraging me to learn got upset coz I spent my time reading books. She used to get mad and tell me to master things that would help me get a good husband.

When I replied to that message, Maria asked me: 'What are you doing still awake? I thought I was the only insomniac here.' I didn't tell her the truth. That I'd stayed up hoping for a reply from her. The next morning, after putting my first two clients of the day through their fitness paces, I checked my Facebook account on my phone.

Maria: I was beaten very badly when I was a teenager – from fourteen to seventeen years old. That's when I left home for the first time. And I was beaten with everything my mum could find. Big leather belts were a favourite, also the plastic sole or the heel of any shoe she happened to be wearing. I don't know how many wooden-handled broomsticks she broke in half on my back, shoulders or legs, wherever the pole fell. I usually started to run around the flat the moment I opened the front door after being away for several days and I saw my mum waiting for me in the hall. Mostly this was around 7am on Monday morning. But the worst beating I ever had was when she tried a method my uncle recommended. She came to wake me up, and because I'd been deeply asleep I didn't suspect anything. My mum took the rubber hose that comes with Spanish gas bottles and unleashed the orange beast on me. It was like forty thousand bees had stung me at the same time. It woke me up quick. It has an ultra-fast invigorating effect that lasts the whole fucking day!!! You should try it – on someone else. I did. But that's another story. Too soon to tell.

It was only later – after we'd met face to face – that I discovered what a private person Maria was and how little most of her friends knew about her. She was looking for her soulmate, and it took me quite some time to really understand why she believed this to be me and why she'd taken so much trouble to reel me in with her stories. She was like a modern-day version of the narrator of *The Thousand And One Nights*, always looking for ways to keep me interested in her. Maria may have needed someone to talk to but she'd have rather remained silent than tell her secrets to just anyone. Going back to the beatings, I told Maria they sounded really ugly.

Maria: It wasn't ugly in the way I thought it was when the beatings started. I did boxing for two years, and one of the exercises was to get beaten up by two people at the same time – so that you'd lose any fear of being punched all over. But you must know that from your street fighting. I needed the boxing after spending, or rather I should say wasting, four or five years of my life in a very dark place. But even after that I fucking lost a massive six-bedroom flat in the centre of Valencia, near to where the Science Museum is now. The day of the fake auction that wasn't an auction at all because the fucking bank got hold of the flat, I took a plane and I came here to London. And can you believe that sixteen years later I still dream of that fucking flat? No distance in km or in years can make me forget the biggest mistake of my life. Yes, I learnt from it, but I would still like that flat back.

I told Maria what she said made me think she was my psychic twin – coz I was beginning to really regret losing my housing association home. After I left Petra she started running up huge debts in my name. I could have reported her to the cops, but I wasn't the sort of person to do that. I'd pay off the debts, but that meant I'd little chance of getting my own place in the immediate future. I was gonna be sofa surfing for a while. Maria's response was swift.

Maria: I'm gonna freak you out. I know you'll think this is bollocks, but I've got tarot cards. Lots of them, dozens of different decks, mostly presents from people who know I like them. My favourite deck is the *Baphomet Tarot* also known as the *Shadow Tarot*. It's a pity it's only the twenty-two cards of the major arcana and not more. Anyway, the artwork is by HR Giger and the interpretation by this guy called Akron, whose real name is CF Frey. Everyone has heard of HR Giger, so I guess you have too. His cards are special, they're completely different to all the other decks, and they're my favourite tarot.

Me: I know Giger, not Akron. I don't know much about tarot.

Maria: The *Baphomet Tarot* is great coz you can pick just one card and it tells you so much. Last night when I was choosing mine, I pulled one for you too. I won't tell you my card, but it relates me to your mother. And your card was number IV The Emperor. The explanation of the card in Akron's book begins with this quote: 'If a man hasn't got the guts to screw his mother, he should at least do away with his father!' Heinz Sobota in his autobiography, *The Minus Man*, K&W 1978.

As far as I could make out *The Minus Man* was the autobiography of a Viennese pimp who recounted tales of manslaughter, rape, human trafficking and spells in the slammer. I checked online and the book only seemed to be available in German, so I figured that, like me, Maria couldn't have read it.

Me: You know my mother is dead, so I can't screw her.
Maria: That card The Emperor really describes a lot of true things about you. The explanation is very long, but part of it reads like the status update you posted two nights ago: 'Martin Cooper is a bitter abscess on this wounded planet...' I know you have a lot of self-knowledge, but there are parts of your shadow side that still need releasing. You're already unstoppable, but if you unleashed what's still repressed you'd be impossible to beat.
Me: I'd certainly like to be invincible. If you can help me with that then we should arrange a time to meet up.
Maria: What about meeting on Saturday? Can you come my way? For coffee we could go to Fixx on Whitecross Street, or for a wider choice of drinks to the Masque Haunt near Old Street roundabout, which is a Wetherspoon's pub. I like the pub best coz they don't play music, so you don't hear shit tunes. And you can get coffee there too. So what about I meet you there at 2pm?

I confirmed Saturday at the Masque Haunt was good; after three weeks of flirtation online I wanted to meet Maria. Nevertheless I wasn't sure whether I'd just found a fabulous new friend or I was about to embark on a serious relationship. I didn't think I was ready for the latter. I'd only just left Petra.

Maria: I can't wait to meet you tomorrow.

The next day it was me and not Maria who did the waiting. I rode my Vespa down to Old Street. The scooter was my standard transportation when I was going to see my clients, and I'd just been with one. I had a TRX suspension trainer and a rip-trainer that were easy enough to carry in the storage box on my scooter. Unless I was seeing a client at a gym I didn't use barbells or dumbbells, just bodyweight. I was early for our meet. I checked my phone as I drank my second espresso, there was a text from Maria: 'Can you believe I overslept? I have to do my hair, so I'm gonna be late.'

The pub belonged to a big chain offering cheap booze and nosh. The décor was cheap and old fashioned. The carpets and fake natural 'wood' framed windows were truly horrific. But the place was friendly, quiet and exuded an ersatz charm. I checked my phone. There was another text from Maria: 'I'm still colouring my hair. I'll be five minutes. Please, please, please wait.'

Five minutes turned into seventy-five minutes. I'd already convinced myself Maria was worth waiting for, which was lucky, as over the following months she often left me hanging around. When she finally showed up she drank coffee too, cappuccino to my espresso. It took me months of observation to figure out Maria didn't drink. Petra's alcoholism had put me off booze, and having a six-pack stomach – hard to maintain if you keep six-packs in your fridge – helped convince my clients I was worth hiring. Downing beer was the royal route to a floppy gut.

'Sorry,' Maria apologised after we'd made our hellos. 'I just couldn't get my hair right. And I can't go out until it's right.'

'No worries,' I assured her.

Maria looked great. She was skinny and more than a few inches below average height for an Englishwoman of her age. She seemed small even by Southern European standards. She'd obviously spent a lot of time dolling herself up. Her shoulder-length jet-black hair was teased out. When I got to know Maria better I discovered that when her naturally straight hair had these textured waves she'd achieved the look with Mark Hill Zebra Bad Girl Glam Wicked Waver curling tongs. She was wearing tight purple trousers, ankle-high black leather boots, a T-shirt for the band Johnny Throttle and a black flight jacket. She had a studded leather belt around her waist and studded leather bands around her wrists and ankles too. There was plenty of carefully applied make-up on her face, including black eyeliner. In short, she was a super-hip rock chick. I could have eaten her up then and there. But although I found her immensely attractive, after the bad trip of Petra's binge drinking I wasn't sure I'd ever be ready for another relationship.

At first we talked about ourselves. Maria said her video editing job on Mare Street bored her because it was mostly for corporate businesses. She did it for the money. That was why she'd like to help me create fitness videos for my YouTube channel, it would put her skills to better use. Our conversation turned abruptly when Maria pulled what turned out to be tarot cards wrapped in black silk from her bag.

'Hey! I almost forgot to show you these, my *Baphomet Tarot*.'

'Wow!' I said. 'They're big. They must be more than twice the size of ordinary playing cards. I wasn't expecting them to be silver either. They look seriously gothic. I don't know what tarot cards are supposed to look like, but I'm sure it's not like this.'

'Turn them over, shuffle them, then pick a card.'

I did as Maria told me and picked The Lovers. She was smiling but said nothing, so I asked: 'What does it mean?'

'I know what it means. You have to work that out for yourself. It isn't difficult.'

'Why don't you pick a card?' I suggested.

Maria shuffled the deck and pulled out The Lovers. The smile on her face extended from one ear to the other. But she remained silent, so I repeated my earlier question: 'What does it mean?'

'You'll find out.'

Maria was pressing herself against me; she felt soft and warm. I wanted to put my arms around her but didn't. I was tempted to stroke her pale cheek, which was set off perfectly by her jet-black hair. But after the nightmare of Petra I was frightened of getting involved with anyone. It also felt like Maria was testing me, and that having made me wait ages for her to turn up was a part of that.

'I'm the girlfriend from hell,' Maria assured me. 'I've been horrible with all my recent boyfriends. The older I get the more selfish I become and I think that's something we have in common.'

What was she trying to tell me? I was sure she wasn't looking for casual sex, so why say this? Our conversation ceased being perplexing when it turned to music.

'I wish I'd had your luck to see all those great punk bands in the 1970s,' Maria told me. 'I'm so jealous that you saw Radio Birdman in 1978. I was only nine years old. I didn't even know that music existed then.'

'An accident of birth,' I said. 'I was lucky to be born in London in the early sixties. There was very little interest in the Birdmen in the UK in 1978, but when they came here to support the Flamin' Groovies I made sure I caught them because I liked them. They only got a cult reputation later on.'

'You make me so envious. I saw the Birdmen when they reformed and came to London a few years ago. They were still good even if they were old. I can only imagine how good they were in the seventies.'

We talked about music for a long time. Eventually I walked Maria around to her council flat on Fortune Street, her leg repeatedly brushing against mine. When we said goodbye Maria threw her arms around me and kissed me full on the mouth, her whole body stretching upwards so that her lips could meet mine. I didn't want to go home, I wanted to go up to Maria's flat, but she didn't invite me in. I returned to my scooter on Old Street and rode back to Stoke Newington. I felt confused. I was attracted to

Maria, but at the back of my mind there were nagging thoughts about how it had all gone wrong with Petra. What if Maria had some addiction too? If she could sit in the pub for hours with only a coffee she sure as hell wasn't an alcoholic. When I got home and checked my phone I found a message.

Maria: It was great to meet you. You have such a cheeky face. I was so comfortable with you that I didn't want you to leave. I hope I didn't intimidate you. Sometimes it happens when I meet guys alone. And in case you're wondering why your new friend has black teeth... it was the botch job of a fucking dentist – how I HATE HIM – doing a composite on my front teeth instead of using veneers. What I actually needed was classed as a cosmetic treatment and not a necessity, so not available for free on the NHS, and at the time I was skint so couldn't pay for it. Now the composite is wearing off and it looks like I've got black teeth. I'm going to Budapest at the end of the year to have implants. In London it costs £2,000 per tooth to have this treatment, but in Hungary it is much cheaper. I get very annoyed about my teeth.

Me: I'm sure you're more self-conscious about your teeth than you need to be. My teeth ain't great either, sorta off white and yellow. Don't know why as I've never smoked. And they're crooked too. But our bad teeth are just something else we have in common.

Maria: I'll only believe you didn't notice my teeth and weren't intimidated by me if you agree to meet me again very soon.

So I spent the following afternoon with Maria in Coffee@Brick Lane. This was one of a small chain of London outlets that catered to hipsters in a postmodern approximation of a late-1950s beatnik café. The space was long and narrow, the furniture was grotty and the toilet just about worked. For our second meeting Maria was only half an hour late. She'd donned a Bruce Lee T-shirt, done as an Andy Warhol-style repeating print.

'Do you know how much I love Bruce Lee?' I asked Maria.

'Yes, way more than you love me unfortunately. Your love of Bruce is all over your Facebook pages.'

'But do you like Bruce Lee?' I asked.

'He was my hero when I was five years old thanks to my big brother. I wanted to be like my sibling. He showed me how to ride motorbikes when I was nine and I was barely big enough to get on one. And he taught me how to shoot a gun.'

'You told me I was the intelligent older brother you always wanted, who could teach you things faster than you could learn them for yourself, but it sounds like you already have one.'

'I love my brother, and when I was small I really looked up to him. I still appreciate all the things he did for me. But as I got bigger I realised he wasn't as smart as me. I wanted a big brother with a brain like yours; there's so much going on in there. You learn the most from people who are really smart. Sure I learnt a lot from my brother, but he could have taught me so much more if he'd been as clever as you are.'

'He sounds like a great guy.'

'I wish he'd had a better life than the one he's had. He had a shotgun marriage and he's not happy in it. And he's got so fat too, but that's because he's unhappy. He wouldn't have got married if his girlfriend hadn't been pregnant. Sorrow changes people, but it is rare for it to improve them.'

'I'd be happy enough if everyone who'd ever been a cunt to me was filled with sorrow,' I replied.

'Hey,' Maria said as she rummaged in her bag, 'I brought a different tarot deck to show you. This is a *Rider-Waite-Smith* pack.'

The cards she handed me were wrapped in black cloth. I took them out and looked at them. Maria told me to shuffle the deck, divide it into three and pick three cards from the top of one pile and lay them out in a row. The first was The Emperor, the second was The Empress and the third was The Lovers.

'Incredible!' From the way Maria pronounced the word and the look on her face I could tell she was really happy.

'What does it mean?' I asked.

'The first card represents your past and that's you in unhappy relationships. The second card is your present and that's me. The third card is your future and that's the two of us together. But we can expand that by looking at how the cards interrelate to each other.'

'How does that work?'

'Check the direction in which the figures on the cards are facing, to see how they interlace together. Here you are facing forward so you have to face this square on. My face looks straight ahead but my body is angled towards the future. On the future card we face each other as The Lovers, but the angel of the air, Raphael, looks forward from behind us. This is a happy hand indeed.'

'But isn't it just chance I picked these cards?'

'You chose these cards because of who you are even if you don't know it yet. The deck has seventy-eight cards in it. Only twenty-two of them are major arcana, so the odds against picking three trump cards as you did are massive.'

'It might be unlikely but it isn't impossible, after all I did just pick those cards.'

'Yes you chose those cards. The real you chose them.'

'What do you mean?'

'With the minor arcana you learn about things in your life and yourself that you can change. With major arcana or trumps you are looking at your fate, something you can't change. Eventually you'll come to realise who you really are and what your destiny is.'

We talked about the tarot for quite a while and then the conversation drifted back to Bruce Lee and martial arts films we both liked. I was looking at Maria and thinking that I'd never had a girlfriend who dug kung fu films. In fact I knew very few women who liked that particular cinematic genre. When we had a wander around Brick Lane, Maria kept brushing against me. I wanted to grab her hand and hold it but resisted the urge. Maria was giving me the kind of attention I craved from a woman, something I'd got from Petra when we first met but that had subsequently faded away. That had been the pattern of all my relationships to date, and I didn't want to start another in which it happened again. I had a fabulous afternoon with Maria, and once again the so hard to say goodbye concluded with a long embrace and kiss.

THE MAGICIAN

I

LE BATELEUR

Once Maria had friended me on my private page she was scrutinising me there as well as on my professional profile. She'd comment in public but also sent many private messages.

Maria: I wasn't gonna say anything about meeting you just in case you didn't like it. I always try to be very discreet if something involves people I don't know well. But I'm glad you said we met. Your friend Marshall then wrote to me saying: 'Martin Cooper = severely nice.' Ah. You know what? Tonight you're gonna have the most groovy dreams you'll ever have. Trust me. But you won't remember them when you wake up...

I later discovered that aside from tarot Maria did a lot of astrology and she cast the runes as well as practising magic and spells. She was using white magic and dreams to bind us together – but she didn't really need to put a spell on me. I was just naturally attracted to her. And I could see Maria found me irresistible. She messaged me constantly, and for every word I wrote her she sent a hundred in which she confessed her faults and recounted her life story.

Maria: I went to college as a mature student. In my second year at film school I was asked to do a montage with different clips to demonstrate my skills at editing with Adobe Premiere. My theme was death. Most of the material came from Spanish movies and horror films like *Driller Killer*. But the last piece I used was a suicide from a live newscast on American TV. The politician R Budd Dwyer sticks a gun in his mouth and blows his brains out after protesting he didn't accept a bribe for awarding a contract. He'd been found guilty and would have been sentenced the next day. This was my farewell to all the twats in my class. I didn't warn them about what was at the end of my tape.

I didn't see Maria for some time because I was abroad. I had a gig working for a rich American couple who owned a vineyard outside Toulouse in the south of France. They hired me a few times a year to work with them and their friends who stayed with them when they were in Europe. They had a professionally equipped gym in their chateau and a swimming pool in their garden, and when no one wanted any training I could just lounge around and do my own thing. I got paid for a full day but mostly I'd work no more than four or five hours, and if I was lucky only two or three. I'd focus on my own fitness, listen to music and read books. I'd give my regular clients in London routines for while I was away and used my work in Toulouse as an opportunity to take a break from doing much on the internet. I told Maria I wouldn't be online often and I didn't particularly expect to hear from her – but I was pleased that I did.

Maria: I didn't want to send you another message until you were back, but I'm missing you. I'm having breakfast in Bunhill Fields all alone and in peace. Yesterday I was supposed to attend a barbecue, two birthdays, five different gigs – I know so many people who play in bands – and go to Brighton with a psychobilly friend who's a fireman. I got so stressed about having to do so much that I sent everyone a text saying I was ill and stayed in Islington on my own. You said something about the Knights Templar when we met. Are you really interested in the Templars or was what you said just a joke?

Me: I'm not deeply immersed in Templar folklore, but I'm interested in history so I find them curious.

Maria: I was very into the Templars for a while. I lived close to some important Templar sites. Most weekends I'd go to Montesa Castle with friends, where we'd play really loud music, get stoned and watch the sunrise. The castle is at the top of a hill. Really high up, and there'd be so much fog, it was like something out of *Tombs Of The Blind Dead* when the sun rose. I enjoyed looking down on the world from that great height while remembering that we were both Templars there in the twelfth century. Anglo-Saxons always talk about a few Templars escaping to Scotland and transforming their occult knowledge into freemasonry, while seemingly forgetting that our monastic military order survived in Valencia and Aragon, even if it was renamed the Orden de Montesa. We were the lucky few who inherited the true secrets of the Templars. It's a myth the Freemasons have them.

The following day Maria posted 'What's This Shit Called Love' by the Pagans on my private Facebook profile.

Maria: I left a long comment on your wall but I can make it an 'invisible hit' if you think I went over the top. I can make it disappear. I'm becoming a master at this. Sometimes I talk with friends and then make our conversations evaporate. Just for the hell of it. When I posted the Pagans I could hear your heart singing along but your mouth was closed. You don't know your own feelings yet, but you will. After you posted 'Danger Heartbreak Dead Ahead' by the Marvelettes I had that tune running through my head for days.

What Maria said about deleting things she posted and making the comments underneath them disappear was true. She did it to me endlessly. Later I learnt that before Maria deleted anything she'd print it out alongside any conversation beneath, so that she had a record of it.

Maria: Someone at my work is spying on me. At first I thought it was a side effect of spending so much time talking to you. But then I saw the fucker behind a door looking at me as I was checking your stuff on social media. No matter what I did this cunt kept spying on me. Later I got an email from my boss saying that I could only look at Facebook on my break. Unbelievable. The fucking twat spying on me was like a three-year-old kid, he was so bad at it. I'm speechless and increasingly paranoid. This is your fault, Martin. I wouldn't bother with Facebook if you weren't on it. You have to help me.

To make up for what had happened I posted Maria some very old live footage of the Buzzcocks with Howard Devoto covering the Troggs' 'I Can't Control Myself' at the Manchester Lesser Free Trade Hall. I heard from Maria when she'd finished work.

Maria: You always post me great tunes. Please don't stop. I like this one because of the 'fuck it' attitude. It's a good laugh. I like the way Reg Presley sings the original too. You know, Martin, with you I really can't control myself. Maybe I shouldn't ask this, but do you ever wear dresses? I love men in dresses. They're so hot. Which reminds me I have to do the laundry. I only wear dresses at home. I'm like that with high heels too. Often I'm more dressed up at home than when I go out. When I lived with my ex I used to dress him up in my clothes. We both loved it.

Me: I've never worn a dress. I've never even thought about it. Do you think I'd like it? There are no pictures of me in dresses, so I'm going to send you a picture of me sitting in a ridiculously ornate chair in Toulouse.

Maria: I can tell that at the moment you think the tarot is bollocks. But your card was The Emperor, and there you are in Toulouse sitting on your throne ready for whatever comes your way. You don't know who you really are, but you're gonna find out, and when you do you won't think the tarot is shit. Even if you don't know it, you're still the greatest person in the world, at least for me. I'm not able to endure pain the way you can. I wish you were here coz I HATE ALL MY OTHER FRIENDS. I told you I have this bridge on my teeth. Well, had. Yesterday I went to take it out, and now I can't put it back in until my gum is healed coz I got an infection. So when my friend Richard called me and invited me to his gig tonight, I told him I couldn't go because of the gum infection. Do you know what he did? He came to my flat with three other musicians and they drugged and kidnapped me. Then they left me at a bar because they had to do their soundcheck. Now I'm finally back home but I'm alone and really really high. I'm sure you can tell I'm high from what I've written so far. I'm so pissed off and angry. I can't go anywhere until my teeth are done. It's too embarrassing. I just want to cry. Sorry about all this rambling. But what are old friends for, eh? And you are an old friend even if you don't know it. You can complain to me about anything you like too. I know English people love to complain. So don't be shy. Or tell me a story to make me laugh.

Me: Okay, a story. One of my clients is an artist. Recently he was interviewed by Nat Hynde. She's the daughter of Chrissie Hynde of the Pretenders and Ray Davies of the Kinks. In itself that isn't too interesting. What makes it curious is that a week or two before the interview the X-Ray Spex singer Polly Styrene died from cancer at the age of fifty-three. Nat Hynde had been close to Polly and was very upset about her death. My client told me that for some reason Nat recorded her interviews on old-fashioned cassette tapes, and before she asked him any questions insisted on playing a recording she'd done with Polly just before her death, the singer's last ever interview. Nat felt she needed to erase the tape because it was painful for her to hear it, so she recorded my client over the punk singer's final words. My client told her not to do this, but Nat insisted it was fine, she'd started working on a biography of Poly Styrene and she'd already transcribed the interview.

Maria: Your client did an interview with Nat Hynde, WOW! I didn't know Chrissie Hynde had a daughter with Ray Davies. I met Chrissie at the Garage when I was working there as a barmaid, and she was super nice. She gave me tips when I wanted her to have drinks on the house. That's ten years ago now. Did your client say what her daughter was like? I'm sure she must be pretty hot with that pedigree.

Me: My client told me Nat had a fabulous handbag, which she said was a present from her mum. He didn't say anything about her looks, but I think he's more interested in men, although he presents himself as straight to the public.

Maria: Why the fuck didn't Nat use a new tape? Maybe it freaks her out to listen to Poly now. I want to know if Nat is hot. I don't care about her handbag.

Maria and I exchanged more words about the Pretenders and other bands, but eventually the conversation moved on.

Maria: Facebook really is a plug-in drug. How many likes did you get from me today? I had to like all those great things you posted. There are many things I want to tell you and ask you. But I'd like to ask you face to face. Now you're home can we meet again soon please?

It was nearly eight when I called on Maria. As I waited for her at the bottom of her block it felt like way too long since we'd last been together – I'd been away for a month. But when my girl came down and she kissed me, it felt like we'd never been apart.

'Where are we going?' Maria asked after we'd been in each other's arms for ten minutes.

'It's Friday night and all the pubs will be packed.'

'Shall we go to the Slice Of Life?' Maria asked. 'It's a café by Smithfield Market.'

'If there's a free table outside that'll be great.'

We got what we were looking for, one of the two tables outside the tiny café which mostly catered for a takeaway trade. I got a tea because I wasn't sure if I could trust the coffee; Maria got a cappuccino.

'Can we do an experiment?' Maria asked.

'Sure.'

'Let's not talk, let's try to communicate telepathically while we're here.'

'That's crazy.'

'It's not. I'm sure we can make it work.'

'Okay, we'll try. I'm happy just to look at you.'

So we sat for an hour not speaking, and all the while it seemed to me Maria repeatedly told me: 'I love you, I love you!' Was I imagining it?

* * *

Maria: You know when I first came across you I really thought you were gay or bisexual. I didn't know what to think. I couldn't reconcile how bright and happy you are on your fitness videos with the anger in your book about being a teenage red skinhead. I thought only somebody in the closet could be that angry about racism when they weren't even a victim of it. Not that you being gay matters to me as I've got loads of gay friends. But after meeting you I know you're straight. And you wouldn't believe how many gay friends – not lesbians – tried it on with me. I guess sometimes I'm more masculine than them. One of them stopped his car, made me step out and pinned me to the ground at the side of the road. Just like that. He told me his lust for me was driving him crazy. I never saw him again.

Me: I've never been with a guy, but I guess our sexualities flip easily. That said, there has to be consent for two people to have sex. If there isn't consent it's rape.

Maria: My gay friend got deep scratches all over his face when he tried to rape me. Someone told me he looked an absolute mess for weeks afterwards. I never go easy on aggressors. He'd tried it on before, but he'd never taken it that far. It was 10am on a Sunday. There were loads of cars going past and no fucker stopped. That scumbag would have raped me if I'd let him. I agree consent is the ONLY way to have sex. Another time I went to stay with a gay friend in Madrid. I'd known him for years. We were watching a movie, and out of the blue he touched my hand. I just looked at him and moved it away. We didn't need to say anything. I really liked that. Such subtlety and a man who was man enough to accept rejection.

Me: When you're telling me stories I like them to have a happy ending like that. Whereas when I'm watching movies I don't like it if they finish on an up stroke.

Maria: You've lifted up my life. I can't imagine my world without you now. Before I got my Facebook account I was a bit depressed. I could only speak to people about music and silly stuff. There wasn't anyone I trusted enough to talk about how I really felt or tell stories about my life before I came to London. After my mother died in 2008 all the fun went out of the world. Then I found you on here. That was the best thing to happen to me for years. I haven't been able to stop laughing since.

Me: Life's a riot. Enjoy.

Maria: I just came home from the shops. It's so nice to walk the empty city streets at night. I was reading what I wrote yesterday and please PLEASE never take me too seriously. Sometimes I exaggerate on the spur of the moment. Did I tell you about my last boyfriend? He was from San Francisco, we were together for a few months, but luckily he had to go back to the States and that's when I joined FB coz he wanted to be friends with me here. The day I split up with him was the day I found your profile. Sometimes I think I know everything about you and at others you leave me really confused. Are you who I think you are and more like me than either of us know? I guess we'll find out in due course.

I've always hung out with punks, skinheads, bikers and people from other subcultures, but I didn't belong to any specific group. I think you're the same. But I don't understand what's happening between us, or more to the point what's not happening. If I really am right about who you are, why aren't we so much more than just friends?

Me: Who am I? I'm not sure I can answer that.

Maria: I can, but it would be meaningless if I told you. You have to discover it for yourself. But here's a clue. When I was a kid I wanted to be an archaeologist. BTW, I didn't feel like going to work today, so I lied and wrote on my FB wall I was dying from pain – to prime my spying boss for a call saying I was sick.

Me: I'm impressed by your ruse to bunk off work.

Maria: I do stuff like that all the time. I always have. If you think hard you'll remember times I pulled things like that in our past lives together. But how cute and handsome you are in your old fitness videos. You must have had a thousand girlfriends just in this life and I'll bet many at the same time.

Me: Two girlfriends at the same time sounds like really hard work to me. More than two, frankly impossible to manage.

Maria: I'm sure you could manage half a dozen girlfriends at once if you put your mind to it. I'm always a bit grumpy in the morning and with you I'm jealous too. So I'm probing to see if you're seeing anyone. Later today I'll have to apologise for all the horrible things I've said to people on FB – although of course they're true. It's just the way I tell home truths sometimes. I can be very mean, especially in the morning when I feel like shit. But then, while you're nice most of the time, when you put people down you're really vicious. And I have to confess I like it when I see you do that, as long as you never do it to me.

Me: How could I be mean to you when you're always so sweet?

Maria: I want to take you to a good club. Will you come? I know we live in two different worlds. You with your health kick and me with my drugs. But we can still have a lot of fun together.

Me: I'd like to see you soon. Let's go clubbing this weekend. Friday would be best, but I've got clients in the evening. I don't think I can meet you before 10pm or maybe even 11pm. On another track, I just heard my ex is in hospital. She was drunk and fell down the stairs in the block where I used to live. I had to leave her because of her drinking, but now I feel guilty because maybe if I'd still been there she wouldn't have hurt herself.

Maria: This is typically Spanish, but I'm gonna light a little candle for her. Both my parents died without me saying goodbye. No one thought my mum was very ill, so I didn't rush back to Valencia, and now I carry the weight of not having said farewell. But about going to a club, that's great. I don't like to go out early anyway. Friday is great. I'm very fussy about clubs. Most just play rubbish. But there are some old school ones with no metal or indie shit, just garage rock and punk. We'll have ourselves a ball. I'm gonna go to get something for the weekend. And no it isn't contra-ceptives. I don't have a boyfriend and I'm not a quick-fuck kind of lady. I like a steady relationship and I don't have sex on the first date. I've got four days in a row of gigs lined up. I'm sure I'll lose weight with all the whizz I'll be snorting. Do you ever take speed? We can do lots at Garageland on Friday, it's near to you.

Me: I haven't taken any recreational drugs since I was a teenager and even then I wasn't really into them.

Maria: Meet me at the Hackney Trashbar in Stoke Newington Road on Friday. I'll text you if I'm gonna get there late so you don't have to be there alone.

* * *

Before I got on my scooter after training my last client on Friday, I checked my phone. There was a message from Maria saying she wasn't at Garageland yet and would be late. I went home and waited for more texts. One said Maria was still doing her hair, another she was on a bus. By the time we hooked up the bands had finished, but there was still a punk rock disco until 2am. Maria drank lime and soda, and I downed mineral water.

'I usually carry tarot cards with me, but I forgot to take them out of my other bag and put them in the one I'm using tonight,' Maria said.

'I don't need a reading, I just wanna be with you.'

It was just as well Maria hadn't brought her cards because she wouldn't have had the time to use them. She seemed to know everyone at the event, and I hardly got to speak to her, although she introduced me to dozens of people. Mostly her friends were Spanish or Italian; there didn't seem to be anyone from London on the capital's punk rock scene any more. Maria disappeared into the toilets for quite some time, she was super animated when she came back, clearly high from something other than the soft drinks she'd consumed. When the venue closed Maria wanted me to go to an after party with her, but I had clients in the morning and went home to sleep. I didn't hear from her again until Monday.

Maria: How is my favourite Mean Machine doing? You make me laugh so much tearing into those yoga people who say lifting weights is dangerous. You're so rude and yet it seems like you're not even that angry. You know what, I JUST WOKE UP and the first thing I saw is the first three sentences at the beginning of this message. WHERE'S MY HEAD? I fell asleep while writing that to you seventeen hours ago. Fuck. I didn't sleep AT ALL from Friday morning until last night. You could say I had a very social weekend. So many gigs and so much speed. I hope I didn't say anything too crazy to you on Friday night. Everything is a blur, and I'm not very sure what I did. I still have so many things to tell you and questions to ask you, but I need another coffee.

Me: Hey, hope you got enough sleep. It ain't healthy to stay up days on end. You didn't say anything crazy on Friday, unless you count offering me drugs as mad coz I haven't taken amphetamines since I was a kid. Exercise is a good enough buzz for me. But, as you know, a lot of people were doing gear around me when I was growing up, so it doesn't freak me out. Whatever turns you on... as long as you're not forcing anyone else into doing something they don't wanna do. You already know my mother shot shit and died of an overdose years ago, so I don't do drugs.

Maria: Tomorrow I'll tell you lots of things, but now I have to sleep. I can't believe I slept so long and I still feel so tired.

Me: Get lots of rest. I wanna hear your stories, but they'll wait until tomorrow.

Maria: I've had another long sleep. I'm feeling good coz I just had a bubble bath, not the rhyming slang type, a real bubble bath in lovely hot water. I was lying there thinking my job stresses me too much. And I never have any money at the end of the month. When I first came to London I used to manage very well on benefits. With a few jobs on the black to make extra dough. Now I don't know how I did it, but I survived for years without much income. And I was always doing loads of courses: mental health advocacy, care work, HD film-making, Final Cut Pro and Avid at Four Corners. Loads and loads of education, and it was all free if you were on benefits. Now every month it's the same, I never have enough money. I need to start saving money right now, and I can't because I don't have any spare cash.

I shot back an answer and was checking for messages all day but Maria replied in the middle of the night.

Maria: I just woke up. My sleep pattern is fucked. This is not good. I came home at 10pm and fed my cat. Then I sat down on the sofa thinking I'd rest for a few minutes before writing to you, but I fell sleep until 3.30am. My cat Sidney was still on my lap when I woke up. I'm gonna go to bed. I can't think straight and my whole body hurts.

Me: Hey, hope you're feeling good by the time you read this. I get my sleep out of sync sometimes too.

Maria: I still feel horrible. Today I'm supposed to go to this BBQ where some bands will be playing. My ex is gonna be there. I haven't seen him since 2004. We spoke on the phone when he got married. He's getting divorced now. We also talked when my mother died. He really loved my mother. I've run out of excuses not to meet him, so I have to go.

Me: It's seven years since you split up, it ought to be okay. Would it help if I came with you? I'm sure I can find a bit of time between clients – there are some gaps in my schedule and seeing you would be better than filling in time by going to the cinema on my own, which is what I was planning to do. Is the BBQ in the evening? I'm free from 5pm until 8pm, but I have a last client at 9pm.

Maria: I feel so anti-social today, but I don't want to take any more shit just to feel normal. Sometimes I wish I could go back in time. Today I don't give a fuck about anything. While I'd love to see you, I don't want you to see me when I'm so anxious. I've been sweating and had a touch of diarrhoea. I'm in withdrawal and there's no shit in the house because I've been cutting back. Unless I get some gear I don't think I'll make it to that BBQ.

Me: Hopefully tomorrow will be better.

I didn't get a message from Maria for another thirty-six hours. I never worried too much about whether it was her or just the drugs talking when I did hear from her, because if there was a message she was alive.

Maria: *¡Hola Martin!* I wanted to write to you last night when I came home from the BBQ. I was out for nearly twenty-four hours. I'm off to work now. What a life. I had a great time. The only way I could face my ex was to do some shit, so I got skagged up and had a ball.

Me: It's great you had a good time and got along with your ex after not seeing him for so long. And that picture your friend just posted on your wall, I love it. Wow you look so cute I could eat you up.

Maria: I look anything but cute in that picture. The sun was in my eyes so they're half shut, and I only had two hours' sleep the night before it was taken. And I've been without my phone for nearly two weeks now. When I came home from a Parkinsons gig the battery went dead, I took it out and now I can't find it. To be honest I haven't even looked. I wanted a break from my friends. My laptop packed in this morning, so I need to buy a new one. I want a used Mac so I can edit films with Final Cut Pro. I've stayed at work so that I can use a computer here. When I go home I'll have no phone or computer. I can watch trash or the French channel Cinémoi. Unless I've fucked the TV too.

Maria didn't get the Mac she wanted, but a few days later she'd acquired a laptop PC for £30. I really missed Maria when I didn't see or hear from her. I knew I wanted more than just a friendship with her, but I'd also learnt from experience that you can't force someone to stop using booze or recreational drugs. I was wary of taking things any further than flirtation because of Maria's addiction issues. At the same time there was so much more than drugs to Maria. Her messages constantly surprised me.

Maria: I don't know if I told you about the flat above mine. An old man and his adult son have lived in it forever. The father was an artist but suffered from agoraphobia and didn't leave that flat for thirty years. He just painted and wrote and drew comics. I was the only person he would see. At first I just used to see his son coming in and out of the block, but one day I had to go upstairs coz water was running from their flat through my ceiling. The son was out and the old man had to let me in to switch off their stopcock. After that we became good friends. His name was Arthur Cohen. He was obsessed with aliens, spirits and ghosts. He just died. I'm still dealing with the ambulance, the coroner, the police and his son. I'm feeling so sad. The son doesn't want me to see his dad the way he is. He told me his old man was in love with me. Of course he was. I was the only woman he saw for decades. Poor Mr Cohen.

Me: I'm sorry to hear that. Ask the son if he's gonna preserve his dad's artwork, and if not maybe you can save it. They were lucky to have you going up to see them.

Maria: There are six cops here now. The cops have been asking me when I last saw Mr Cohen. He's been dead for days. I just saw the corpse. I don't think I'll sleep tonight. He was mummified. Sitting down and with a glint in one eye. Like he could see me. Oh God.

Me: Are you okay? That sounds horrible. Was the son away or had he stopped living there? Please try to get some sleep no matter how difficult that is.

Maria: Oh Martin, I feel so bad. I can't get the picture of Mr Cohen sitting there mummified out of my head. When you see someone you know dead, it stays with you, especially if you weren't prepared for it. The cops kept me up until 4am, when the undertakers took Mr Cohen away. I feel so sorry for his son. He doesn't really have a proper life; his dad was his whole world. He only left him to go to work. About him being mummified, I think that was happening while he was still alive. For the past month he'd looked like a living corpse. It was terrible having to look at him and not being able to do anything. The last time I saw him I wanted to call an ambulance and have him taken to hospital, but he refused. He wouldn't even let me call a doctor or get help from social services. He just showed me the last drawing he'd made and told me he was okay. Yesterday I was trying to comfort his son. He didn't have anyone to turn to. His mum left when he was four or five years old. His sister went with her, and he doesn't know where she is. The only person he could call was his aunt in Glasgow. They came to London from there, I think, and the funeral is gonna be in Scotland.

Me: What a shock. I'm glad it's the weekend and you can get some sleep now. I really hope you're able to work through all your feelings about this – but it can really take time. Can I come and see you?

Maria: Thanks for your kind words. I slept from 4.30am to 2pm. I just wish the cops had closed the door yesterday and I hadn't seen Mr Cohen. I must remember all the effort he made for me when he knew I was going up. He always wore a toupee to cover his baldness. I'm going to Garageland at the Stag's Head, so I can have a good time with my friends. I'd so like to meet you, but I don't want you to see the amount of drugs I'll be taking to make sure I'm swinging, so let's hook up another day.

Me: I don't wanna intrude on your drug use. I know you need a groove after all the trauma you've just experienced. Have a ball tonight.

Maria: You know what, Martin, I'm already high, and I haven't left home yet. And I just wanted to tell you that you don't know what you need but believe me I do, because I know who you are. I'm a witch, and you've been a witch in previous lives. I know you'll think this is bollocks, but it's true. I belong to a coven. I've studied Wicca and learnt about it from other initiates. You'd be surprised how many people have seen my witch powers work.

Me: I don't care if you're high, I think you should meet me at the Masque Haunt for a quick drink before you take even more drugs with your friends. You're gonna go right past the pub on your way to Hoxton, and I can get there easily enough on my scooter.

Maria: Let's meet. I'm very happy coz I've missed you. I've been missing you all my life. I don't even know where the Stag's Head is. Are you saying it's near Old Street? It's in Orsman Road. Can you get to the Masque Haunt in the next half hour? We can go somewhere else if the Wetherspoon's closes before you arrive.

Me: I'll be at the Masque Haunt in time for last orders. Text me if you're running late, and I'll get you whatever you want to drink. Orsman Road runs off Kingsland Road between Shoreditch and Dalston Junction. It isn't close to the Masque Haunt. It's a twenty- to thirty-minute walk if you move fast like me.

When I got to Old Street I checked my phone, and there was a message from Maria. She said she was running late and she wanted an orange juice with ice. I ordered it and a mineral water for myself. By the time I'd finished my water there was another text from Maria: 'I'll just be five minutes.' I hung around until I was slung out of the pub. I stood outside the boozer for fifteen minutes before Maria showed up. She'd taken more than enough drugs to flip her mood.

'Sorry,' Maria said as she threw her arms around me and our lips met.

'It's okay,' I reassured her when we'd finished kissing. 'Mr Cohen dying must have been such a shock. It takes a while to get yourself together after something like that, so I can't expect you to be on time.'

'Thanks,' Maria replied. 'But let's not talk about Mr Cohen now. I wanna have a good time tonight. Where are we gonna go?'

'I don't want to drink beer, so a café is fine.'

'Let's go to one of the all-night greasy spoons in Smithfield Market.'

'Sure,' I agreed.

Maria held my hand and tottered on her high heels during our ten-minute walk in the opposite direction to her gig. She was gorgeous with her hair teased out and her zebra-print trousers. I couldn't see what was on Maria's T-shirt because her black flight jacket was zipped up.

'Your hands are beautiful,' Maria observed as she squeezed one of them, 'they're in much better condition than mine. I fucked mine up not wearing gloves when I was doing manual labour. They look like a man's hands now.'

'Why do you always point out what you see as your flaws when in sum total you're sex on a stick?'

'I don't feel like sex on a stick. I wish you'd met me when I was younger. Then I really was hot.'

'You're stunning now. If you looked any better when you were younger then it's too much for me to deal with.'

'Fuck off.'

'You know it's true.'

For the rest of the walk, Maria traded an affectionate insult for every compliment I paid her. By the time we reached Smithfield Market we were laughing so much we could hardly stand up. Once again we found an empty table outside the Slice Of Life on Charterhouse Street. The café was open 24-7. We went to the chilled drinks cabinet, and Maria got a bottle of orange juice while I chose water. Maria paid, and we sat down on metal chairs on either side of a small silver table in the street. There was another identical table opposite us taken by a couple of guys wearing high visibility jackets. The café was small, and the only other seating was on a handful of high stools placed beneath a bar table that ran around one corner of the establishment.

'You make me laugh so much I need to sit down,' Maria said breathlessly.

'That means we've got something in common,' I shot back, 'because you're so hot you take my breath away, and I need to rest too.'

'I've been laughing so much it hurts,' Maria giggled. 'And hey, I've got another tarot deck to show you. This one is a modern Spanish tarot. It's the first tarot I ever owned. A friend gave it to me a long time ago.'

As she spoke Maria pulled the deck wrapped in a piece of black Spanish cloth from her handbag. Her vanity was black too with silver studs and clasps. As Maria unwrapped the cards I clocked the cloth was see-through in places and decorated with a repeated flower motif. She handed me the tarot. The cards were almost as long as the *Baphomet* deck she'd shown me in the

Masque Haunt but not nearly as wide. I could see they'd been well used because they were very battered.

'They don't look anything like the other two decks you showed me,' I observed.

'It's a modern version of the *Tarot de Marsella*, the standard traditional deck. It's based on woodcuts from a Renaissance Provençal tarot game, and these are copied from a now vanished Gothic Catalan prototype. What do you think of it?'

'I love the crude drawing and wild colours.'

'Spanish decks tend to be more colourful than those from other parts of Europe. Turn the cards over, shuffle them and pick one.'

I did as I was told and couldn't believe it when I drew The Lovers again. The cards had Spanish wording at the top and English at the bottom, so the one I'd chosen was also Los Enamorados. It featured a man and two women with Cupid floating above them about to shoot his arrow, and the sun behind him.

'I don't believe it,' I said.

'What do you see in the card?' Maria asked.

'Two women. Does that mean I'm gonna have a threesome?'

'Ha, ha, ha. You still think the tarot is bollocks, don't you.'

'Not if it's telling me I'm gonna have a threesome. I really wanna believe that.'

'When you remember who you are you'll also recall the evolution of this card. In the early Italian tarots it featured a man and a woman with a blindfolded Cupid, representing the blind nature of love. The French changed all that. They removed the blindfold and added a third figure; at first it was a priest over-seeing wedding vows, but it evolved into a second woman. One of the women represents virtue and the second represents vice. In the early modern world love was no longer blind, it became a conscious choice.'

'Is the hotter chick on the right vice?'

'Yes, virtue is on the left, wearing a crown. The idea is that you have to choose between virtue and vice.'

'Well if I can't have them both then I'm definitely going for vice.'

'That's me. I'm vice with my vices.'

'Is witchcraft a vice?'

'No. My vices are sex and drugs and rock and roll.'

'Is tarot how you figure out your future?'

'There are lots of ways to learn about the future. I use everything from the I Ching to runestones, but alongside the tarot I like astrology the best.'

'The astrology columns in magazines are silly. A forecast for the week ahead divided by twelve signs, each representing millions and millions of people.'

'That isn't serious astrology. To do it properly you have to know where and when someone was born.'

'Is that why you asked me what time I was born the first time we met?'

'Yes, but I can also work backwards from what I know about you to your exact time of birth, and I'd say you gave me the right time.'

'Are we a good match?'

'More than good, we're perfect together. And I don't just mean on the level of you being Aries and me Sagittarius, fire signs that work well together.'

'Can you fill me in further?'

'I have a Scorpio ascendant first house, so most of what I do is initiated with Scorpio energy and often I start things before I consciously know what I'm doing. I can charge ahead and think later. Of course I'll always be impulsive, but now I'm in my forties I can channel myself better. My strength is the shadow side – sex, death and regeneration. I've looked at your chart, and your Scorpio moon needs and craves the nourishment of my first house Scorpio energy, which is fiery like your Arian Mars temperament. Your moon in turn can nurture my ascendant – how I bring things into the world and what I choose to show to the world. We have so much in common, and each of us will bring out what is repressed in the other. We make each other complete.'

'I hear what you're saying but I don't understand it.'

'You don't need to understand it now, you'll understand later, once we've worked with it.'

'Do you want another drink?' I asked Maria because I couldn't think of any other way to keep the conversation going.

'No, let's go for a walk.'

So hand in hand we wandered around the city for hours laughing and joking. There was no more talk about the tarot, astrology or who I really was. Our focus was the music and movies we both loved. For much of that time I was semi-consciously wondering whether Maria was going to invite me back to her place. At about 4am I figured she wasn't, so I told her I was tired and needed to go home. She walked me to my scooter, which I'd parked by the Masque Haunt. When we kissed goodbye I was wishing we could have woken up in the morning wrapped in each other's arms.

JUNON.

THE HIGH PRIESTESS

I'll fast forward through the weeks that followed our trip to the Slice Of Life. Summer is the best time for me because I mostly work outdoors with my clients. Those that just want a companion and a pacer I take running. Others I drill through complex moves in parks. I did my work well and I enjoyed it. The big thing in my life was Maria. We'd message each other repeatedly during the day, and I'd dream of her at night.

Maria suggested we meet in nearly every message she sent. I wanted to see her, but I was frightened of starting a relationship because of her addictions. I knew I'd succumb to Maria's charms if I saw her. Her gorgeous arse and skinny legs were always on my mind. What Maria wanted wasn't in doubt by this point, and I wanted the same thing, but my rational side told me I ought to be wary. In retrospect I was stupid to resist Maria. She was the girl for me, and once we'd met it was inevitable we'd become lovers. Maria was incredibly persistent, and eventually I'd have to confront the fact that my feelings for her were overwhelming.

On the surface during the months that followed everything seemed the same, but underneath they changed. It didn't matter that I repeatedly excused myself from seeing Maria, the more we messaged the more deeply we were bound to each other. I'll skip over a lot of what we said about love and magic and movies and music because it becomes repetitive. This is just a snatch of our exchanges.

Maria: I have a dilemma. You know I'm a good person, don't you? A few weeks ago when I took a cab I was involved in this little accident. An old woman hit the cab from behind and now the lawyers I contacted about it are sending me forms to claim compensation. I don't know how my claim will impact the old lady. Obviously her insurance will pay, but will it make her insurance prohibitively expensive in the future? On the other hand, if she's no longer a safe driver is it better she quits before she seriously injures herself or someone else? I really don't know whether to pursue the claim or not because I don't know what the consequences will be.

Me: Were you hurt? If you were you might need the money.

Maria: That's the thing. In 1988 I had an accident going to Marbella. I broke a cervical bone, the last one in my neck, but I've got an extra bone, which is very rare. I had to wear a collar the whole summer and take four months off work – and I wasn't paid for it. But I didn't get a penny compensation coz the drunk driver was a bitch. She told us she had no insurance but we found out later she claimed lots of insurance money for herself. Every time I think about that accident I get upset. Since then I've been unable to carry heavy weights or do much exercise. I had to give up boxing. So this recent accident feels a bit like karma. I do get pain in my neck, but I'd feel bad if I exaggerated that on my compensation claim. But it hurts sometimes because I've never fully recovered from the first accident. I really don't know what to do. What would you do? You're my psychic twin...

Me: I think you should go for the insurance money now or you might regret it.

Maria: I've been at the riots in Hackney. You were so funny when you claimed on my wall yesterday that I orchestrated the riots, when all I said was I'd been up to Dalston to get some shopping – groceries are so much cheaper in Ridley Road than around Old Street. Today I got nine bottles of Tropicana and one of wine. But better than that I shot loads of footage of looting and burning cars, vans, bikes and rubbish bins. Dozens of cars and even a taxi were smashed up. What an evening. I felt like I was fifteen again. But listen, I didn't want to steal anything. In fact I was there for hours filming people running out of shops with their arms full of looted booze. But after three hours of excitement I was thirsty. All the shops were closed, so the only way to get a drink was to loot it. I made my way inside a mini-market and took all the Tropicana that was intact. I gave three bottles to someone outside, and the bottle of wine I'm gonna give to a friend. It's not like I was greedy. And why I'm justifying myself to you I don't know.

Me: You don't need to justify yourself – we're psychic twins. It's okay.

Maria felt guilty because it wasn't any old mini-market she'd obtained the Tropicana and wine from; it was the Clarence Convenience Store. The shop and its owner – thirty-nine-year-old Siva Kandiah – became a centrepiece of reporting about the 2011 riots. Kandiah was a poor immigrant who'd spent eleven years building up his modest business, and it seemed that not only was he going to be ruined because he didn't have contents insurance but it was kids he'd showered kindness on as they grew up who were responsible. As well as the looted stock, the fittings were stripped from his shop. Fortunately there was a happy ending as a community whip-round raised more than £30,000 to keep Kandiah in business and out of the bankruptcy courts. What Maria eventually gave to the Save The Clarence Store Fund was way more than the value of the goods she'd taken.

Maria: You're always extremely nice to me, but you're being even nicer than usual tonight. Can I take advantage of it and ask you anything I want?

Me: I'm going to bed and yes I sleep in the nude.

Maria: Ha, ha, ha, ha. In the summer I sleep in the nude too. I can't believe I'm still awake. I wasn't gonna ask you whether or not you wore pyjamas. Stop teasing and don't give me ideas unless you want an incestuous psychic twin. It would be nice to see you again soon. But you're always busy training someone or going abroad with your clients. Doh. Usually when I wake up I'm grumpy, but finding you've posted me a comment makes me smile. I'm sure I'd be happy if I woke up beside you. Why don't you dress like a skinhead any more? It would suit you as you've slagged off every tune anyone has posted on your private wall for weeks now. You're so mean when you don't like something. Those poor people who make all that effort just for you, and what do you do? But I have to confess I love it when you're like that. It makes me think you're still a skinhead at heart. And it also put this wonderful tune 'Mean Man' by Betty Harris in my head. I'm going to three gigs and after parties at the weekend, and you know I'd like you to come too. But if you have to be with your clients or sleeping to get up early for them, you know my spirit/psychic side will be with you. And, tiger, while you're getting fresh air and training people I'm stuck inside a stuffy edit suite. Are you gonna meet me for a drink soon? And what are those ropes you have in those pictures you just posted on your public profile? Are you into bondage? Coz if you are I can help you with that.

Me: What you saw were battle ropes, they're just exercise equipment, they're not supposed to be anything kinky. I wouldn't bother too much with them, but some clients like to use them. I've got this seventy-year-old guy who saw some stuff about them in a magazine and insists on doing battle-rope sessions with me. He told me he was a big fan of the Velvet Underground and he felt like he was Gerard Malanga doing the whip dance as part of an Exploding Plastic Inevitable show while I had him working out with battle ropes. Then he gave me this really dirty laugh and said – 'My wife better watch out tonight.' Well I wouldn't do that to you. I'd be way more tender.

Maria: Is that an admission you find me irresistible? We have to celebrate that as soon as possible or I won't see you until next year. Maybe you could have a coffee with me on your way to see one of your clients. I just want to talk to you about music and movies. That's all.

Me: Today my clients have all cancelled, so I get to do my own thing. I went to the gym early in the morning – well it didn't open till 9.30am coz its Sunday and I woke up at 7.30am. And you know I train clients all week and then when I get a day off what do I do? I go to the gym and I love it. I must be the saddest guy alive.

Maria: What have you done to me, tiger? Jung said: 'The meeting of two personalities is like the contact of two chemical substances; if there is any reaction, both are transformed.' I don't think you've changed at all, but I started laughing much more after I met you. My life is so dull when I'm at work. I feel bored a lot of the time. I've got a bit of a fever and my stomach is upset too, but I have to go and edit corporate crap and porn.

Me: I hope you're feeling better by the time you read this message.

Maria: I feel like shit. I need a break from work or I'm gonna have a nervous breakdown. And you know it breaks my heart when you kind of say we shouldn't see each other. If we go to a movie together we don't have to look at each other, just the movie. That said, it would be hard for me to have you sitting next to me and for me not to look at you. Now I have to go back to work. But first I want to tell you something that you don't know about me. I've got a vast collection of semi-precious stones and some other rocks that aren't so precious.

Me: The problem for me is you're so super attractive and I won't keep my hands off you. That's why I won't see you. I need a bit more time to recover from my last relationship. At least when I'm ready for another one it will be an improvement. Nothing could be worse than Petra. But I'm not ready yet. I'm so into you but I'm so afraid of fucking up.

Maria: Just give me a chance, tiger. Show me your bright stripes. I'd like to see that little tail of yours bobbing about. Don't forget I'm highly skilled in the art of scrying and that I'm a witch. I knew you weren't pissed off with me. You'll never ever be pissed off with me. Even if I push you a bit too hard sometimes. Don't you know that every time I suggest we meet I'm just having (half) a laugh? I like it best when you go all quiet and don't know what to say to me. That's so cute. Knowing what a beast you can be when you want. Before I forget, the other day you posted something about *Django*. I always had a crush on Franco Nero. My dad was a spaghetti western fanatic. I used to watch all those films with him when the other Franco – the dictator – died, and they finally got to show them on Spanish TV.

Me: Franco Nero is great. You must have been quite a small kid when you were first watching those movies with your dad. What else do you remember from then?

Maria: I was sexually abused when I was five and a half years old. I don't tell many people about this. It happened in an orange grove and lasted more than four hours. I kept screaming I wanted to go home to my mamma, and my attacker just told me to shut up and slapped me. I don't want you to see me as a victim coz I never felt like one. I just learnt very early on that bad things can happen to good people and children.

Me: You definitely don't come across as a victim. But that's horrible and I'm sure not typical of what happened during your childhood and teenage years.

Maria: Before I say goodnight to you, tiger, I just want to tell you a quick story. Before I lived with the bikers and Hells Angels, I hung with the skinheads in my village. They weren't too bright so they'd do what I told them to do. I wasn't as big and strong as they were, but I had more than enough brains to lead them. One day one of them got a VHS tape of the Tinto Brass film *Caligula*. We all started watching it and because of the sex scenes they became very excited, so they asked me to leave. They told me I could stay if I wanted, but things might get out of hand if I did. So I left and they told me later they'd had a circle jerk while they were watching the film. And this wasn't just a couple of guys. It was twenty-one young skinheads.

Me: I think leaving was a smart move.

Maria: Definitely, because they'd have wanted to gangbang me if I stayed, and I've never been into that even if I'm a bit feral. I'm glad I left. They gave me the tape later so that I could see the whole movie. Tonight I'm tired and sick and have to go to bed. Night, tiger.

Me: Hey, I'm having breakfast. What's up?

Maria: I'm still missing you. Today I was thinking about a shop that sells lots of martial arts movies. It's called Umit and is on Lower Clapton Road. Maybe you know the place. I'm sure the guy that runs it can get anything you're into. He has lots of old movie equipment and cameras too. Which reminds me one time I was in Dundee with a friend who was studying at the art school there. We went to see a dealer, and the fucker had three CCTV cameras on the stairs leading up to his flat and a big screen in the living room. We could see everybody who was coming to buy smack. We were there for hours. You know what else happened in Dundee? I have two whips I bought there. They were only a pound in a shop near the bus station. It was a pound store but it was selling really weird things. I got three whips and gave one to the friend I stayed with. I also bought two porcelain dolls from the same place, and we transformed them and now they're called Justine and Juliette in honour of the Marquis de Sade. I still have the dolls. How many people need whips? It was strange seeing them in a pound shop among cleaning products and packets of food. It made wonder if BDSM is really big in Dundee? I'm gonna sleep now. I haven't slept for twenty-four hours and I'm very tired. I don't want to start writing things that I might regret telling you later.

Me: I'm sure you'll feel great when you've slept. I like Dundee.

It's a very compact city with everything near the water – unless you're going to the Hill Town of course.

Maria: I woke up half an hour ago and I still feel numb. I didn't know if it was Sunday or Monday, so I was late for work. I need a holiday, but all I can do is snatch a break by sitting on the toilet and sending you a message.

Me: Tell them you're sick and go home to sleep. I'll message you again when I can, but I'm doing a training session with a client in ten minutes. I'm at Highbury Fields waiting to start the workout.

Maria: You always make me laugh. Highbury Fields sounds like a good place to get high. I just sat down to eat some cake and fell sleep again. Now I can't think straight. I know this week is gonna be very intense coz of the full moon. You know you're the greatest legal high in the world. I want you to shag me, really fuck me hard and make love the way we did in our previous lives.

Me: You're very naughty and seem to know my secret desires. More reasons to love you.

Maria: I'm so embarrassed. I have never ever said anything like that to anyone in my whole life unless I was in a relationship with them. I can't believe I said that to you. What was I thinking? Well I know exactly what I was thinking, but I won't say because it will only make things worse. Now I won't be able to look you in the face if I see you. That was so out of character for me. I'm not saying I'm not naughty sometimes, but I just keep it to myself. Do you see how dangerous you are? I can't stop laughing now over the way you make me lose my cool. Nobody else can.

Me: It's alright. I'm sure you know I want to shag you, but I think I shouldn't. If I'd got over the anger I feel about my last relationship I'd happily fuck you several times a day, seven days a week. But my head is a mess so I think I'd screw things up if I started seeing you.

Maria: Some friends invited me to Frieze Art Fair. Unless I'm high I don't like art openings or the people you find at them.

Most of them are so pathetic, but if I'm off my box I find it hilarious. The last opening I went to I was so bored I sat by the entrance – coz that was the only place I could find a chair – waiting for my friends to come out. Everyone who filed past said nice things because they assumed I was the gallerist. I laughed so much that evening. But I can't go to Frieze because my cat Sidney is going blind again. Seeing her unable to do anything breaks my heart. So I want to stay home with Sidney. I can't leave her all day to go to an art fair. A few hours would be okay, but my friends will want to be there longer than that.

Me: Sorry to hear about Sidney.

Maria: Thank you. Not everything in my life is bad. Sometimes I have great days. I just had dinner with my crazy Catalan friend Olga and Billy Rath from the Heartbreakers coz he's over from the States. I have to find Billy a pick-up band. Olga kidnapped him yesterday. She took him to her place because she wanted his company, as a friend not a lover. Billy had been staying in some shithole, so he was glad to get away. This afternoon she came to my flat. She hadn't slept and was buzzing. She'd left Billy sleeping so I had to go and rescue him and make dinner. When I got to Olga's flat Billy didn't want to go anywhere, but now that I've charmed him a bit he'll do whatever I want. So we're going to the Stag's Head to see the Toyotas from Germany and two other bands. He's such a nice guy. He's sixty-something but shows no signs of slowing down. It would be great if you came along too, but I know you won't.

I knew the Heartbreakers from when I was a kid in the seventies. They were very overt about their use of heroin and described their music as 'love songs for objects'. Many saw the Heartbreakers as 'too much junkie business' and blamed them for introducing smack to the London punk scene when they relocated here from New York. Billy Rath had been the bassist and unlike singer Johnny Thunders and drummer Jerry Nolan wasn't in the pre-punk glam rock band the New York Dolls. Johnny Thunders had died in 1991 and Jerry Nolan the following year. Guitarist Walter Lure had left heroin chic behind him to work as a stockbroker on Wall Street, so Billy Rath was almost the last man standing for those that dug the Heartbreakers' drugged-up punker attitude. And he wasn't even the band's original bassist, but he'd replaced Richard Hell before they came to London and inked a contract with Track Records.

Maria: I just woke up half an hour ago. I really needed to sleep. Last night I came home early by my standards, at 3am, but I'd been out all day with Billy. I only left him coz I was worried about Sidney. She's okay, but her eyesight hasn't improved. Last night after we'd finished dinner I asked Billy if he wanted anything else? Coffee? Beer? Maybe speed? He wanted all of them and then asked for crack too. At first I thought he was joking, but he wasn't. God, he's an old man in his sixties and he's got a wooden leg and walks with a stick. What a pirate. I told him he wouldn't need anything coz when we got to the Toyotas gig he'd get high on all the admiration he'd receive from my friends, who are all huge fans of the Heartbreakers. We didn't get to the Stag's Head until after the bands had played, but everybody was there. They were all screaming Billy's name and telling him he was their hero. When Olga suggested we go back to her house, a small army of punks followed us to the bus stop. I took the first bus that came so that I could go home alone. I could see Billy through the window. The expression on his face said 'Bitch, why have you left me here?' He wanted to be with me, but I wanted to go home. I'm gonna take a bath. I feel like shit today, and I need your help. Olga just called me and she wants me to go and do smack with her and Billy. I want to be strong and not fuck up. I made myself a promise that I wouldn't touch heroin again. I still get high on speed, but I want to stay away from skag. Now I feel so weak and the temptation is so strong. PLEASE HELP ME.

Me: The best thing is not to see Olga and Billy. If you go you'll do the smack. Just get some sleep and stay with Sidney coz she needs you. And if you do that I'll meet you on Saturday.

Maria: I think Sidney knows what you're saying to me. She was sleeping, but as I read your message she got up and sat next to me. So thank you for your support. For a moment I was going to go and shoot up with Billy. You know Billy Rath doesn't matter any more because I'm not gonna break my promise to myself, and now it's a promise to you. It's Halloween today, and I'm sure Johnny Thunders' ghost will come to possess Billy on the one night a year he walks this earth again. But not even Billy and Johnny together can break my resolve now I've got your support. About meeting me, I know you're frightened of starting a new relationship because your last one went so badly. Well I'm gonna invite my friend Neil Savage to meet you with me. Then you'll have a guy around who is totally in love with me to protect you from yourself. And just for the record I'm absolutely not sexually attracted to Neil. He is a beautiful friend, but I don't want to make it anything more than that. All I want from you is a great big hug.

Me: Individually we're both weak, together we're strong. Sidney will keep you at home while I'm rushing about. I've got to see a client in Green Park in fifteen minutes. Glad you're staying clean. And you'll get a grin with that hug when I see you on Saturday.

Maria: I hope you have a great Halloween. In Spain everybody lights candles for their dead loved ones because when you fall asleep they come and sit on your bed. I'm gonna light a candle for my mum. You should light one for yours. Then your mother will sit beside you tonight.

Me: I'd love to see my mother tonight. I hope you see yours.

Maria: Just light a candle and you'll see her. I'm gonna light an extra candle for your mother too. I'm about to watch Jess Franco's *Mansion Of The Living Dead*. I've never seen it. I hope it's better than all the other movies he made after

1980. Mostly they suck. Did I tell you a friend of mine worked with him on *Killer Barbys*?

Me: I can't remember if I've seen *Mansion Of The Living Dead*. I've seen dozens of Franco movies, and the lesser ones all get mixed up in my mind. I thought *Killer Barbys* was one of his superior late outings. I like his stuff from the sixties and early seventies best. But great that your friend got to work with him. You hadn't told me about that.

Maria: My friend also worked with Santiago Segura who made the *Torrente* flicks, and he still rants about how lousy the experience was. But he really liked acting for Jess. I'm off to work. Trust your day is great.

That was Tuesday morning and I was counting down to Saturday. So I'm gonna forget about Wednesday, Thursday and Friday. We'd arranged to meet in the Masque Haunt, and I arrived early. Neil had got there before me and introduced himself. He became agitated as the appointed time for Maria's arrival came and went. I checked my phone and found a text from her. It said she had a slight fever but she'd be along soon. Maria was so late that we only had time to drink one coffee as she pressed herself against me. We were seated at a table with a bench sofa on one side. Neil was on a chair opposite us. Maria pulled out a tarot pack. I could see from the box it was called *El Gran Tarot Esoterico*. Maria handed the cards to me. I shuffled through the pack; it was crudely drawn and wildly coloured.

'It's the astrological sigils on these cards that make them really interesting,' Maria said. 'I want both of you to shuffle the deck and pick a card.'

I handed Neil the pack, and he took first turn. His card was the five of swords. It showed five swords in the shape of a Star of David. Above was an All Seeing Eye in a triangle within an orange sun. Beneath the swords and rising up to their level on the right side were waves.

'Every tarot has its own meanings,' Maria told us. 'In most packs this wouldn't be a good card and might signify failure. But in this deck it represents spiritual insight. The water making up the waves signifying the emotions, the Star of David represents the spiritual, the All Seeing Eye represents logos and this card shows the integration of these things. It's a great card. Neil, it means you're really going places both emotionally and spiritually.'

I took the deck and shuffled it. My card was Death. It showed a skeleton in a wizard's black cloak – with stars and crescent moons on it – holding a scythe and riding a dog. Yes, a dog not a horse. The ground beneath Death and his dog was green and littered with crowns, a shepherd's crook and other items. In the background was a classical temple with an Egyptian cross at its centre. There was what I took to be a Hebrew letter in the top right-hand corner and the Arabic numeral forty bottom left.

'Martin's gonna die,' Neil laughed. 'It's the worst card in the deck.'

'You never predict death for anyone during a reading,' Maria chided. 'Besides, the Death card doesn't mean death, it represents transformation. Martin is changing because he's finding out who he really is. He's gonna be an even better version of himself when that process is complete. This is a great card for Martin. I'm really happy for him.'

It was wonderful to feel Maria's body pressing against mine and so much more than great to smell her. She was both bitter and sweet, her breath was fresh, but the aroma of Drum tobacco pervaded her body and clothes. I was sorry I had to go and train a client, but Neil was pleased as punch about this. Maria and I got up for a hug and a kiss. Then I got on my motor scooter and slipped away. I was in love with Maria but felt really conflicted about whether I should risk another relationship in which an addiction was constantly threatening to tear it apart.

III

L'IMPERATRICE

THE EMPRESS

Maria: I hope you had a good time at the Masque Haunt yesterday. I did despite feeling very ill. You're so handsome. I can't stop thinking about how good those hugs we had felt and how much I enjoyed touching the back of your head. Your hair was really soft and your eyes looked bluer than ever before. Neil was a bit jealous. He said that he'd never had a hug from me like the ones I gave you. I've known Neil fourteen years. I told him that I hugged you the way I did coz you were my psychic twin, and after looking at me for a bit he said you were a 'lucky sod'. I laughed so much at that. But even if he was jealous, Neil is a nice guy and he liked you. Who doesn't when they actually get to meet you? I'm still sick. I only got up and went out yesterday because I really wanted to see you.

Me: So you haven't seen anyone else over the weekend?

Maria: I didn't tell you yesterday but on Friday Olga brought Billy Rath over to see me before he went to play a few songs with Walter Lure at the Purple Turtle in Camden. I'm not sure who else was in his pick-up band that night. I got a load of texts saying it was a really good set. Billy came to see me again when I came back from the pub yesterday. I've been a good girl and I didn't take the heroin he offered me. Billy told me stories about the old days. He talked for ages about how hard it was for him and Thunders to move Walter to the bath when Lure overdosed because he was so big and heavy. He had so many really funny drug stories.

Me: Wow. For someone who's sick you had a really sociable weekend. You have all the gossip.

Maria: I do. Billy's extremely angry. He was gonna play some gigs with Steve Dior. They managed one at the 100 Club on 22 October and another at the Boston Arms on 26 October. Billy came to England to play with Dior as the Broken Hearts. They were supposed to be a twenty-first-century Heartbreakers, but they had to cancel two gigs because people were being unreliable. You probably know that in the late seventies Steve was in the Idols with ex-New York Dolls Jerry Nolan and Arthur Kane. Billy's take was that Steve was not Johnny Thunders, though. Billy's so fed up with not getting to play proper gigs in London that I've put together a one-off band for him until he goes back to New Jersey in a couple of weeks. I know so many musicians it wasn't hard. On Tuesday they'll jam together for the first time. We'll see what comes of it. I just want Billy to enjoy himself from now on, so he can forget all the bad stuff.

Me: I hope Billy gets to play some gigs. It's great you can help him out. And I'm so proud of you for staying away from smack too.

Maria: Now I have a problem, Martin. I've got four drummers and three bassists, none of the bassists will be needed as that's Billy's thing. Billy playing bass and singing is the whole point of this one-off band. I've got six guitarists. Yeah six or maybe seven, as I've got an extra one who isn't sure he can make it. They are all good and already in more than one band. I've also got a girl who really wants to play keyboards. As if. The Heartbreakers never had keyboards and Billy's not gonna want them now. I sent an email to all the musicians I know asking if they could help Billy out by being his pick-up band. Everyone wants to play with Billy. Somebody help me please. It won't be long before all hell breaks loose. But it's gonna be a laugh. It's not my fault there are so many musicians. I just couldn't say no coz I was feeling too sick to be tough with anyone and all of them are good friends. So we'll see how it goes. BTW: I really want to see you naked. Rorrr. So many reasons to love you. My feelings for you are a curse. I finally meet the man I've been searching for all my life, and he's so upset about his previous relationship he doesn't even want a little bit of fun with me. Fuck it. I need to run to work. Today is my first day back. Ah.

Me: I'm sure you'll sort it out. And you don't know how in love I am with you, but yes I've been hurt and need to recover. And you should complain. What about your huge army of male admirers? Seeing the effect you have on other men makes me chuckle. I even laugh about the effect you have on me, but maybe I shouldn't.

Maria: But I thought I didn't have any effect on you whatsoever. I looked so horrible the other day. All sick and without any make-up because I was too tired to put it on. Neil said I didn't need it, but he's so sweet and in love with me that he can't judge. I'm stuck in bed again. I went to my doctor and he told me I wasn't fit to go to work. I've got a chest infection. And no I'm not smoking much, I'm just taking antibiotics. When my fevers come on I see your face and sometimes I think it really is you in my flat with me, then I want to go outside coz I'm too hot and sweaty. And did you notice I didn't smoke at all last Saturday? I didn't want to smell like an ashtray – although I always have strong mints with me to counter that too. I want you to know I make an effort for you because you seem like an angel to me. I'd really like us to dance together with you laughing in my ear. I can still hear you laughing in my ear when we hugged, and you know I'm deaf in the one your face was pressed against. Martin, I'm so sick I really don't know what I'm saying to you. And I wish, I so wish I could be with you right now. I've got to go back to bed, but I want you to know I'll be thinking and dreaming of you.

Maria was sick for more than a week. I got regular messages about her health and how the pick-up band with Billy was shaping up. She also banged on about how terrible she'd looked when I last saw her. My endless reassurances that she radiated beauty made no difference. Another subject Maria wouldn't leave alone was her desire to tickle me. I told her I'd heard a BBC report about a tickle therapy from Spain and it seemed she was going to use it to help me get over my terrible relationship with Petra.

Maria: Oh you know how much I'd like to put my hands on your soft hair and wiggle my fingers into your tummy, tiger... But are you the ticklish kind? I'm feeling much better, but I still don't understand what you're doing that makes me say all these things. I'm trying to send you this message – I started more than an hour ago – and although I'm hidden in a corner with Olga's laptop, she and Billy can't stop talking to me and trying to get my attention. The only thing I want to do right now is to talk to you. Doh. The second jam with Billy went better than the first. Chris Low came along to play drums, and he is so much better with Billy than the other drummers. But the guy who owned the studio we rehearsed in got pissed off with Chris hammering his kit. I shouldn't say this, but I miss you so much, blue eyes. I know I've said that to you before, but I haven't said this. I want to see you every day. I want to wake up in the morning with you beside me.

Me: You don't know how much I want to see you and how much I think I shouldn't because if I keep seeing you something is gonna go wrong like it did with Petra. I'm conflicted. Sorry. I'm glad Billy's pick-up band is coming together and that you're feeling better.

Maria: I just woke up and it's 8pm. My sleep is really out of whack. Billy's backing band aren't communicating with each other. If things don't improve I'll wash my hands of it. One of the guitarists is being a complete twat. He's thirty-one but acts like a baby. He's upset coz I told him some home truths. He's always disliked Olga but all of a sudden he wants to be her friend coz Billy's staying at her house. When it comes to Billy he's a real ass licker. It's embarrassing to see it, but it's not just him. I got so pissed off with everyone but Chris that I told them to get the band in shape without me. Although we didn't go out last night, I didn't get to bed until 4am. And I found some girl online claiming that one time she saw you with Leo Sayer curly hair. Is it true?

Me: What the girl says is true. My hair is naturally very curly. You just can't see it because I keep it cut short, but every now and then I get the urge to let it grow.

Maria: I haven't told you this but when I was ten years old I got it into my head that I wanted to have an Afro. Back then I'd never met a black person, but I saw them in films and wanted hair like that. My mum said the whole village was gonna laugh at me if I had a perm, but I didn't care and I cried and I cried to get what I wanted. But not even that worked. When my sister Esther was getting married I was sent to the hairdresser on my own, and I lied that my mum wanted me to have a perm for the wedding. I was beaten when I got home, but I was so happy with my new hair. And last week I found the family photo of that day.

Me: You'll have to show me the picture and I'll show you one of me with grown-out hair.

Maria: Yesterday Billy asked me why I didn't have a boyfriend. I told him that I was lucky because all the men I liked had been in bad relationships and were afraid that if they started a new one it would go wrong, so there was no chance of me ending up tied down. We couldn't stop laughing. And finally something has come together with Chris Low, a guitarist called Nuno Viriato and Billy. Tomorrow they're playing at the 12 Bar in Soho. Will you come if I put you on the guest list? We can have fun teasing each other.

Me: I'm training some clients in the early evening, but I guess

Billy isn't on early so I can make it when I finish work. I could get there for nine. What time are the bands on?

Maria: That'll be so great. I'll send you more details later. You'll be in time for Billy. The place might be quite empty coz the Dwarves are playing somewhere else and they're sold out. Most of my friends will be at the Dwarves. We only confirmed the gig yesterday, and it is hard to do effective publicity with that kind of time frame.

Me: I can't wait to see you tomorrow.

Maria: The idea of seeing you tomorrow makes me happier than knowing I'll see Billy play. I'll let the boys set up and do their soundcheck without me, so I'll aim to get there between 8.15 and 8.30pm. I don't think Billy's set will be before 9pm, but I'll tell you more tomorrow when everything is confirmed. And don't worry. I'll be good tomorrow, unless you want me to be bad. Just teasing again.

Me: I can't remember the last time I was in the 12 Bar, but I know Denmark Street well. And as ever you'll tease and please, and I'll love everything you do.

Maria: Morning. If you can post this information on your private Facebook wall that would be great. Billy Rath's Street Pirates will be playing at 10pm, but there are three support bands on before that. There's a secret place upstairs that looks like a balcony. We can see all the bands really well from there without anyone bothering us or pushing us around. I'll be there by 8.30pm. You don't need to rush. As long as you're there by 10pm you'll see Billy play. If we get fed up we can always go and get a drink from the Intrepid Fox next door. There's a girl from my village called Carolina who works there. Last time I saw her she was doing a porno movie for *Playboy*. Yeah. There weren't many bad girls in my village, but those that were tough were very hard indeed, like me and Carolina. But really she's lovely and sexy and very small. You'll like her. I'm gonna bring my Afro hair photo to show you. That'll give you a good laugh. It's gonna be a great night, you'll see.

Me: I'm all set then. If you really want to surprise me maybe you can get a perm this afternoon.

When I got to the 12 Bar at 9pm there was no sign of Maria. I checked my phone, and she'd sent texts to say she was running late. I was on my own for an hour, and the support bands didn't interest me. The 12 Bar was a rock-and-roll toilet, rather like the clubs I used to go to as a teenager in the late seventies, a total dive. But by 2011 scummy clubs, which were once a dime a dozen, had become an anachronism in Soho. When Maria arrived an hour late we kissed, she introduced me to her friend Olga and left us together while she went to the bar.

'Have you heard of the Heartbreakers?' Olga asked me.

'Yeah. I got their album *LAMF* the week it came out in 1977, although I haven't seen Billy Rath play in a long time. The last time I remember seeing him was when he was part of Iggy Pop's backing band at the Lyceum here in London back in 1979.'

'Wow,' Olga replied, 'you don't look old enough to have been going to punk gigs in the late seventies. Did you see a lot of bands?'

'It ain't worth talking about the UK bands I saw coz I saw so many, but I also made sure I caught the acts who only came here on tour, like the Dead Boys, the Dictators, Destroy All Monsters, Pure Hell, Radio Birdman...'

'Did you see the Lurkers or Slaughter And The Dogs in the seventies?'

'Of course,' I replied. 'I saw the Lurkers' last ever gig with Howard Wall fronting them at the Electric Ballroom on 31 December 1979. It was a funny night coz they played with Adam And The Ants who also underwent a radical line-up change after that show.'

Olga told me she was a total punk rocker, although she was clearly too young to have got into it before the 1980s. She said that like Maria she'd moved to London 'for the punk rock scene'. That kinda amazed me coz aside from a few English musicians it seemed that for the past decade or two it had been made up mainly of people who'd come to London from southern Europe. As far as I could see they could have stayed where they came from and had a punk rock scene there. In London punk had been a fashion; people like me got into it when we were kids and left it behind as we grew up. In socially conservative southern European countries kids used subcultures like punk to break away from traditional values, but it meant that if they wanted to maintain that break they tended to remain punks or whatever for the rest of their lives. Aside from being a punk rocker, Olga told me she was a painter and decorator with a very artistic approach to her work. When Maria returned she handed me a large whisky.

'Hey, I wanted water. You know I hardly drink.'

'C'mon, live dangerously for me tonight,' Maria shot back. 'One drink won't kill you.'

Moments later Billy Rath's Street Pirates took to the stage, and the volume of the music made it impossible to talk. So I downed the Scotch. Maria grinned and pressed herself against me. The band started with 'Pipeline', the tune that opened Johnny Thunders' solo album *So Alone*. The Street Pirates were rough and ready and in true punk style sounded extremely sloppy. They ran through half a dozen familiar songs – most of them twice – 'Pirate Love', 'Born To Lose', 'Chinese Rocks' and 'Do You Wanna Dance'. The audience was ecstatic. Maria's friend Carolina got up on the tiny stage and spread her legs wide across the boards before proceeding to make erotic dance moves. Carolina was wearing tightly fitting cropped shorts, black stockings, knee-high boots and a Sex Pistols shirt.

Billy Rath lost his left foot some time before this gig and had a prosthetic leg. It was a real effort for him to stand upright while wielding a heavy bass guitar on stage – he needed both hands to play so he couldn't use his walking stick. Carolina clearly didn't know this and arched over backwards with her legs spread to grab Billy's right calf with both hands. She then mimed giving Billy a blow job with her face inches from his crotch. Billy accepted the situation and treated it with good humour, but the girl didn't want to let go of him. I was amazed and impressed that

Rath managed to stay upright. Afterwards people were laughing about this and imagining Carolina's shock if she'd grabbed Billy's other calf and discovered that Rath had a false leg.

'Can you believe Carolina French kissed Billy on stage at the end of the set?' Maria asked when the show was over.

'I saw it,' I replied, 'but I didn't think anything of it.'

'Billy has hepatitis C.' After a pause and almost as an after-thought Maria added: 'And AIDS too. I love Billy, but I wouldn't kiss him like that.'

'I think she'll be alright.'

'I wouldn't do it. But c'mon, let's go find Billy. I want to intro-duce you to him.'

Billy was in a courtyard behind the club with the other musicians and various hangers-on. Maria told him I was her friend Martin.

'Are you Maria's boyfriend?' Billy asked.

'It's complicated,' I replied.

'That's not an answer. Are you Maria's boyfriend?'

Maria looked like she was gonna die of embarrassment. It was clear that most of those present including Billy knew she was madly in love with me and this was totally humiliating to her.

'Maria told me she's spent six months chasing you and she won't ever stop trying although she never gets anywhere,' Billy persisted. 'So I'll ask you again, are you Maria's boyfriend?'

'We're really close friends. And I enjoyed your set tonight.'

Maria ducked out of the courtyard and back into the club as I said this, so Billy changed the subject.

'I fuckin' love rock and roll,' Billy boomed. 'I wanna die on stage rocking out!'

As Billy warmed to his subject and told me about his times with Johnny Thunders, he became very likeable. He'd disappeared from public view in 1985 – when he'd stopped playing with the reformed Heartbreakers – only to re-emerge on the music scene after a twenty-year gap. In the meantime he'd done both rehab and university. Psychology at graduate level and post-grad in theology. Billy told me about that too. He'd had two decades off the music scene and wanted to make up for lost time. I guess he knew he didn't have long to live, and he died less than three years later, at the age of sixty-six on 16 August 2014. He wasn't on stage, but his body was completely wasted from a life of rock-and-roll excess. When Maria reappeared, Billy dropped his nice-guy act and returned to bullying.

'Are you Maria's boyfriend?' Billy didn't say this just once; he endlessly repeated it.

I took Maria's hand and suggested we go outside. Maria told everybody she'd be back soon, and we left. We walked across the road to the Intrepid Fox. We didn't make it into the bar; we sat down on a cantilevered bench that ran around the inside of a curved wall marking the outer limits of the pub's concrete beer garden. Within seconds of parking our backsides we started to kiss. I felt so sorry for Maria, and I had no idea whether Billy had been trying to provoke me into doing something sexual with her or was just being cruel. Very quickly I was enjoying the sensation of my tongue in Maria's mouth too much to really care about the musician's intentions. I slipped my hands under her T-shirt and massaged them into her back. We kissed for a long time before Maria unzipped the flies on my jeans and slipped her hand inside my pants. It felt incredible when she clasped my erection and massaged it very gently, repeatedly running her thumb over the tip. I started to squeeze one of Maria's small firm breasts.

'You know,' Maria said after pulling her lips from mine as she continued to caress my dick, 'I was beginning to think I was wrong about you. That you weren't who I thought you were.'

'I still don't understand this.'

'You will. Let's kiss a bit more and then go back to the 12 Bar. I can't abandon Billy for too long. And I want to introduce you to some more of my friends.'

Somehow a few kisses turned into many and my cock was no longer in my pants but out in the open where Maria continued to caress it. This foreplay only stopped when Carolina came past and said hello. She was going into the Intrepid Fox to collect some things she'd left there, then going back to the 12 Bar. When we returned to the courtyard behind what was still at the time London's premier rock-and-roll shithole, Billy boomed at me: 'Are you Maria's boyfriend?' I decided I didn't want to hang around for too much more of that, so I told Maria I was gonna go. She understood why, especially as Billy just kept repeating his question. I got on my scooter and sped home. I crawled into bed around 2am, and I was tired the next morning. Nonetheless I found time to send Maria a quick message before going off to train a client.

Me: What can I say? Thanks for such a great night.

THE EMPEROR

IIII

L'EMPEREUR

Maria: I Just woke up. My head hurts. All I want is to be with you. I didn't go anywhere last night. On Thursday when you left, we all went Olga's. I came back home to take a bath and went straight to work without any sleep at all. I came home, and I couldn't sleep or write or think or do anything at all. I took two temazepam and just woke up so now I need to get ready to go out. My phone has fifteen missed calls and I've loads of unanswered texts. But none from you. Ha, ha, ha, ha. Tonight I'm having dinner with Chris Low, Olga and Billy. Why don't you come too? It's gonna be very quiet. Ah.

Me: I can't come out tonight. Please be careful with the temazepam, it's only suitable for short-term treatment of insomnia. And there are loads of people who shouldn't take it ranging from anyone with depression to those with liver problems. It is very easy to get addicted to it and not so easy to have it prescribed – but then I'm sure you'd have no problems getting it on the black market.

Maria: Hey, I'm being a good girl. I told you that. I've been to my doctor about my insomnia. Let's talk about something else. I just remembered Carolina grabbing Billy's leg. I'm laughing so hard tears are coming from my eyes. Poor man. He finds it extremely difficult to stand up without using his stick, and when you add in the weight of the bass. So it was really hard for him when Carolina kept pulling at his leg. And guess what? Carolina thought Billy had been in the Sex

Pistols. The whole thing was so surreal coz the longer the Street Pirates played and repeated the same songs, the worse they sounded to me. I got this text from Chris and it says: 'Tell Billy everyone's raving about last night and saying they thought it was the best of the shows he's played since he's been over. I couldn't hear A THING where I was so please apologise for any fuck-ups.'

Me: The Street Pirates were very rough, but I'm happy I saw the best of Billy's shows. If that was the best I wonder what the worst was like?

Maria: They were terrible. It was so bad I wanted to cry. But still it was funny to watch it. I hope you enjoyed your night out. I hate the Intrepid Fox, it's an awful tourist trap, but from now on I'll think of that place where we sat down outside as one of my favourite spots in London. You were so cheeky and so naughty. I can't stop thinking about what we did. There are two things we can do. First, we can stop, and I don't want to do that. Or we can keep driving each other mad, which is what I want to do. I really really like you. And now I know for sure you really desire me too.

Me: I told you I wouldn't be able to behave myself if I kept seeing you. I enjoyed Thursday night very much and mostly because I was with you. The Street Pirates were a laugh and definitely got worse when they repeated songs.

Maria: I'm going to pick Billy up. I'm his minder today. I have to take him to a load of places. It's Billy's last night in London and everybody wants us to go to their gigs, so we're on three guest lists tonight. All I want is to be with you. Can you believe it? Everyone keeps going on about Billy, but I'd rather talk to them about you.

Me: Have fun with Billy tonight. But it makes me happy you'd rather be with me.

* * *

Maria: Do you think the evening is a good time to wake up?

Every weekend it's the same. After hardly sleeping or staying up all night on Friday and Saturday, I sleep through Sunday to make up for it. I HATE myself for always sleeping through so much of the weekend. I've never done a fraction of the things I want to do. Sometimes I would like to close my eyes and never wake up again. It would be so easy and painless to die by taking just one great big shot. I'm a bit depressed right now. Give me half an hour and then I'll be normal again. What have you done in the last few days, tiger? Has everything been good for you? Have you thought of me even if it was just for a few seconds? I've been thinking about you coz everything else in my life sucks. I'm gonna have a strong coffee and I'll be back. Sorry for my dark mood... if I'd woken up with your arms around me I know I wouldn't feel as shit as I do now.

Me: I'm sure you're gonna blush when I tell you what I've been dreaming about you. I can't write it down, I'll have to whisper it in your ear. And you know how sad I am. I just spend hours on my days off in the gym coz I enjoy it. I hope I'm not gonna lose any clients coz I'm going away with the rich Americans again. I give them workout plans for while I'm gone and don't charge for them. If they'd stick to the routines I give them they'd get fit and save a bundle of money. Of course my clients never do what I tell them to do when I'm not there – they don't like exercise and pay me to force them to do it. I guess that's why they're not too bothered when I go away. It's an excuse not to exercise. And this time the Americans are taking me to a sports resort in Lanzarote called Club La Santa. I don't know why they're paying me to go with them when there are great trainers there, but I'm not complaining. It's money for old rope and the place is great. It has world-class training facilities. It's very popular with triathletes.

Maria: I'm late for work. But today I feel much more like myself. Will you tell me about your dreams? I'm sure you wouldn't want Carolina saying anything online about what we were doing outside the Intrepid Fox, but you don't need to worry about that. Yesterday we talked on the phone. I've known her since she was a child. I was her older brother's best friend. He's dead now. He ran out of petrol one night and was walking down the road to get some when a passing lorry ran him down. Carolina laughed and told me she got a good look at your cock before I put it back in your pants. She's a total slut but also a great friend. She even checked if it was okay for her to shag Leonidas two years after we'd split up. She didn't want to upset me. So you can see how much she cares about her friends. Hope you have a great day, tiger.

Me: Carolina sounds great. I hope your day was good. Mine was average, but at least the clients I saw are coming along. Apart from one who drives me nuts. He just seems incapable of doing what I tell him to do. It's a problem I often encounter. He thinks because he's exercising he can turn off his mind, but that's not true. You really have to think about what you're doing when working out, putting maximum effort into it and getting into the zone. Exercising well means thinking with your muscles coz that's the only way to totally control them. And it isn't just those who over intellectualise in their daily lives who suffer from such mind–body dualism. I've seen it in yoga instructors too. Some of those New Age types will be teaching asanas and tell their students the last adjustment is the mind. That's such bollocks. You don't and can't adjust the mind after the body coz they're not separate things – they're in a feedback loop.

Maria: Does that mean when my muscles ache I'm thinking? Just kidding. You know how much I'd love to see you. I won't see you for ages now. I can't believe you're going away and to Lanzarote this time. Maybe next time we meet you could come to my work. Then I won't have to run any-where and I won't arrive late. I have a set of keys and lock up when I'm the last to leave. You could bring any film you want and we could watch it on the big pull-down cinema screen. We wouldn't have to go anywhere to watch movies and there are comfortable chairs. Or we could spread rugs out on the floor and roll around a bit as we're watching a flick. Sorry I'm a bit high. I know it's Monday, but I went to see a friend whose mother had surgery for uterus cancer, and we had to celebrate coz the doctors say the operation was a complete success. So we snorted some whizz.

Me: When I'm back I'll come to your work with a film. When I go to Club La Santa in Lanzarote I'll be offline most of the time. I really need to get away as much as possible because I feel I'm imposing on my cousin. She's great but has a young baby, and I'm on the sofa in the living room. Although her husband is out at work all day, she does the housewife thing with the kid. I know she's glad to have my company if I'm there in the day, but even so I can't bring anyone around coz they might disturb the baby. I didn't think I'd be staying long, but as I told you I discovered my ex Petra ran up debts in my name. So either I have to get her done for fraud or pay them off. Well I'm not reporting her so I'm stuck with the payments. It does make me regret letting her have my flat coz I can't find anywhere I can afford while I'm making the repayments.

Maria: That really sucks. I miss you so much when you're out of London. I'll find something good to post for you before you go. Now I'm gonna get something to eat. Although you know what I'd like to eat if you were near me. LOL. I thought that after last Thursday I'd feel closer to you. I'm thinking I'm fooling myself about that coz I'm not expecting anything from you. But I wonder if you regret what happened? If you do then tell me, and I won't mention it again. It will be as if it never happened. Okay?

Me: No I don't regret Thursday. I really enjoyed it. I don't want to pretend it didn't happen. It's just I don't know if I'm ready for my next relationship and I don't want to fuck you over.

Maria: I'm going to Neat Neat Neat. Johnny Throttle are

playing there to launch their first record, and the club is closing because it's been losing money. Tonight everybody will be there. The atmosphere will be electric. It's a pity you're in Lanzarote. You should be at this gig. You'd enjoy it much more than Billy Rath. Still, there are many things we can do together if you're up for it. I don't know what to say to you. I think of you and I want you so badly. I don't even know when you're back. Do you love me? It just felt so right for me that night we went to see Billy. I was so comfortable in your arms – because I've been with you before — and at the same time it was all so exciting and new. What I remember the most is how warm your skin felt when it touched mine. Your hands on my back... Mmmmmmmmmm. And something else – the shape of things to come. It may be a while before I let you take things any further. When I love it is very intense, but it builds slowly. When we can't stand it any more then we'll see what happens. There's nothing I like more than to play. I'd love it if you begged me to fuck you. I'd keep telling you no, until one day I'd surprise you by saying yes – but only after making you wait a very long time. But tell me what you feel about me, about you, about us you know. I want you much much closer to me.

This was one of a series of messages I didn't read until I got home from Lanzarote. The majority – like the one I've just reproduced – were about us, but there were also several about Maria's health and hospital appointments. She said she had stomach issues but was vague about what was actually wrong.

Me: Hey, Maria, I just got home, and I've been reading through your messages. It's best if you let the doctors check your stomach with the camera. I've a very low opinion of most hospital mental health, but the straight biological stuff I think is generally pretty good. You must get it checked out. I'm concerned and hope you're okay. Also about you bringing up the time in the Canary Islands, it isn't odd it is the same as in London and two hours different from Spain. Franco changed the time in Spain to be in line with Hitler and the Nazis, and this has never been corrected. Fascists are insane. Spanish time really ought to be the same as in London coz both places are on the western side of Europe. Didn't you ever think it odd that when you go over the border from Spain to Portugal there's also a two-hour time difference?

Maria: I'm glad you're back safely. But I'm so afraid of medical procedures. Am I gonna see you soon? BTW: I didn't know that about Franco and Spanish time, but let's not talk about him or his dictatorship.

Me: I could come round to your flat next week and we could take things from there.

Maria: Don't get me wrong, I'd love to invite you in but I can't yet. I'd have to tidy up a bit and hide a few books and records that I know you won't like. Meeting at my work is best. Hey, handsome, I can't wait to see you even if it's only for five or ten minutes. But longer would be better because then you'll have time to show me how real communists make love. I just got home from work, and although I didn't want to go out this weekend, Jack Oblivian is playing at the Boston Arms tonight. Do you wanna go?

Me: I've been a bit sick today, just a light fever. I can't blow out my clients after being away but I need to spend as much time as I can lying down.

Maria: I'm sorry to hear you're ill. You seem so healthy all the time and have all that energy. I'm always under the weather. But that's coz I don't sleep enough, I don't exercise, I eat so much shit, I don't drink enough water and I smoke. It's lucky I don't like alcohol, isn't it? I know I have to do something about my lifestyle very soon. Sometimes I get really paranoid when I think of cancer and all those other illnesses old people get. In Spain people eat more healthily than here. I'm always getting fevers, I'm sure you'll get over yours soon. I can get you some really good black-market painkillers if ibuprofen isn't enough to see you through your sickness.

I didn't tell Maria I avoided stuff like ibuprofen when I could. If I took something it was a last resort to ensure I could work. Too much medicine weakened the body, and in my view painkillers were to be avoided outside of exceptional circumstances. All I told Maria was I had a cold and would be better soon. After all it was December; it wasn't unusual to be sick in winter.

Maria: I intended to message you last night, but I fell asleep at the computer. I really needed the kip after spending less than three hours in bed the night before. I wanted to tell you about the first time I came to London in 1991. I spent the first few days in Talbot Road. The woman we were staying with was a retired prostitute. She'd been a call girl in the 1970s.

Me: I guess you were only in London a week or two that first time?

Maria: Yeah not long. I'm gonna tell you something funny that happened today. This morning I was really rushing to get to work, so I got out of my bath and dressed very fast. When I got to work I realised I wasn't wearing a bra. And you know what happens to women's nipples when it's cold, don't you? Luckily for me my shirt had two big breast pockets and I could put my phone in one and credit card in the other to cover them up. I felt really free, and when I was alone I was touching my breasts. Please don't think I'm a pervert. I don't touch myself up at work all the time. But it really made my day.

Me: You should do it more often. You sound really happy.

Maria: I'm still not wearing a bra. Now that I'm home why bother? And you should see how many bras I have. For a while I was obsessed with lingerie and bought some every week. How are you, guapo? Are you going to meet me?

Me: Monday or Tuesday would be the best days to see you. I've got no clients either of those evenings. And I'm good.

Maria: It's my birthday on Tuesday, but I always try to avoid celebrating it. You should meet me then coz that's the only thing that will stop me indulging in a heroin fiesta. I'm gonna take it easy this weekend. Instead of going out tomorrow I'm gonna start fixing things in my flat. I never find the time to do that.

Me: I'll definitely see you on Tuesday. Hope you get your flat sorted.

* * *

Maria: I just woke up and I'm very depressed. I hate Xmas. It's less than a week away, and I turned forty-three today. The only things I'm happy about is that I don't have to go to work and I'll see you. Coz I'm not working let's meet in Stoke Newington. You pick a restaurant. I really haven't managed to do anything at home. I need to paint the bathroom. I also need to pull down a half wall in the kitchen so I can get a washing machine in there. It's a fucking pain going to the launderette every week, and I have so many clothes. Sorry. I'll stop moaning and tell you something else instead. When I moved to London in 1995 I came with ten packets of Marlboro cigarettes, no return ticket and with £25 in cash – it was £24.78 to be exact. And I couldn't speak a word of English. It was a crazy thing to do. I had the address of a friend who lived here and no other contacts. When I called my friend she asked me where was I gonna stay coz she lived with her boyfriend in a studio flat. I got to sleep on her kitchen floor in Baker Street that night but had to find somewhere else the next day. I ended up in hostels for the homeless but not for too long.

Me: Wow, I wanna hear the rest of that story. Do you want to meet at Rasa? It's a south Indian restaurant at 55 Stoke Newington High Street? 7.30pm?

Maria: I'm not very well, but a meal would be good. In fact I'm very depressed. I got my period an hour ago. The most unwanted present of all time. It's not fair. I was going to surprise you and shag you, but I can't have sex when I have my monthlies. It's too messy.

Me: You're the only person capable of seducing me, but it's at your own risk. I have at least warned you that in my present state I'm not good boyfriend material because I'm still brooding on my last relationship. The restaurant is pink on the outside. You can't miss it. But there are two Rasa restaurants opposite each other, one for meat eaters and the other for vegetarians. We're going to the vegetarian one obviously. See you in about ninety minutes.

Maria was sitting in Rasa waiting for me. The pink exterior suggested that inside the restaurant might be more exotic than your average English curry joint. It isn't, but the waiters are very friendly, which is one of Rasa's strong points. I was less interested in the interior than I was in Maria, and she was more interested in me than anything else around us. Her hair was teased out into waves, she sported a William Burroughs T-shirt and her jacket was hung over the back of her chair. I'd got her some presents: a couple of books on punk, two Eurosleaze horror DVDs, a few northern-soul compilation CDs. And a birthday card too of course.

'You shouldn't have bothered.' But the broad smile on Maria's face and the way her eyes drank me in told me the presents were well worth getting. 'You know I hate my birthday.'

'You might not want to celebrate, but I do. Did you get any other presents?'

'Yes, this miniature edition of the *Rider Waite Tarot* from my friend Ainhoa.' Maria rummaged in her bag, pulled the gift out and said: 'You should pick a card.'

The cards were still in the box. There was a reproduction of The High Priestess on the front. The pack was much smaller than all the other tarot decks Maria had shown me.

'I don't need to pick a card, that's my card on the front.'

'Why's The High Priestess your card?' Maria asked.

'You know BJ stands for blow job.'

'Sure.'

'Well look at the pillars on either side of The Priestess, the one of left has a B on it and the one on the right a J. That must mean I'm gonna get a blow job.'

'You really think the tarot is bollocks, don't you. You'll change your mind when you see the things it predicts come true. You can jest about it, but what it says is gonna happen will still happen.'

'I'll be super happy if they do. So what do the B and J mean if they don't stand for blow job?'

'They represent the inscriptions on the entrance to King Solomon's Temple. B is short for Boaz or "God's strength" and J represents Jachin or "God founds". But the B pillar also symbolises King David, and the J King Solomon. Notice too that one pillar is black and the other is white. In The High Priestess we see the union of opposites, yin and yang, male and female, passivity and aggression. The previous card in the major arcana, The Magician, is nominally male, while The Priestess is nominally female. But ultimately all the cards are both male and female. And that's our task in this world, to realise ourselves in the union of opposites.'

Our conversation was interrupted by a waiter bringing starters to the table. Masala vadai or deep-fried patties made from mixed lentil batter laced with fresh curry leaves, ginger and green chillies. Rasa idli or steamed black-lentil cakes topped with vegetable masala. Both dishes were served with coconut chutney. Maria told the waiter to give me the rasam – a peppery lentil soup made with garlic, tomatoes, spices and tamarind.

'But I haven't ordered my food yet,' I said.

'I ordered before you got here. I'm psychic so I knew what you'd want. You have the soup, we'll share the other starters.'

I couldn't argue with Maria, although the personal trainer in me was particularly horrified by the masala vadai. No one but Maria could have got me to eat something as unhealthy as that. I also drank the salt lassi Maria had chosen for me – of course hers was sweet. If Maria hadn't used her psychic powers I'd have been drinking water. With Maria rubbing her leg against mine underneath the table, I just wanted to please her, so I ate food I'd have normally avoided. Our conversation shifted from tarot to music.

The conversation was interrupted again when a waiter brought our main courses. Beet cheera pachadi with brown rice for me. This was beetroot and spinach blended together in a yoghurt sauce with roasted coconut, mustard seeds and curry leaves. Maria was having cheera curry with lemon rice. The paneer (curd cheese) and spinach cooked with garlic, peppers and tomato in a creamy sauce, was possibly even less healthy than my dish. She'd also ordered a Kerala salad and paratha bread for us to share. I was too engrossed in Maria to reject this food as incompatible with my sports diet. I couldn't really blame Maria. I'd picked the restaurant, but then I generally avoid eating out because I like to rigorously control my food intake. I just had to write off what I stuffed into my face at Rasa as a cheat meal. Maria asked me if I could speak anything other than English, and I had to tell her no.

'I've been in London so long sometimes I can't even speak Spanish like I used to,' Maria said. 'Now I mostly talk and think in English. And when I came here I didn't have a word of English. I put so much effort into learning it. And of course my English is far from perfect, I have such a strong Spanish accent.'

'You're accent is really sexy.'

When the bill came Maria wouldn't let me pay it. I couldn't believe it. After all it was her birthday. But she was so insistent I had to back down. Maria told me in Spain it was always the person with the birthday who paid for drinks and food. We kissed and cuddled one doorway down from the restaurant. It wasn't long before Maria's hand was in my pants, but things didn't go any further there, we just kissed and cuddled for a long time. After a while we went looking for somewhere a bit warmer to hang out, but we couldn't find anywhere suitable. After some discussion I agreed to take Maria home on my scooter. We went to get my bike and a second crash helmet. Everyone was asleep in my cousin's flat so I had to tiptoe around while Maria waited outside. My own helmet was chained to my bike.

When Maria rode pillion behind me, she pressed her body hard against mine, and it felt just great. I parked in Golden Lane, and we walked along to her tower block in Fortune Street. At some point that evening I'd told Maria I was allergic to cats and got bad asthma if I was in close proximity to a feline in an enclosed space. I didn't know whether or not Maria was gonna invite me into her flat, but I thought it best she know in advance there was a potential problem if I ended up in there with Sidney. Maria had told me her place was a mess and she'd be embarrassed to let me in. She took me into her block, and we went back to our kissing and cuddling, but this time on the stairs close to her floor. We had to stop when people came down the stairs from higher up. Maria was biting me all over, leaving little marks. Before long she had her hand in my pants, then she pulled my lower garments down my legs. At first she frigged me with her hand, then she began to run her tongue along my erection. When she put my meat in her mouth I could have come, but with a great deal of effort I held back and luxuriated in her sucking and blowing. When Maria took my length out of her mouth and began to work it hard with her right hand, it only took a few strokes before I was spent.

'It's so nice, it's so nice,' Maria whispered as she dipped her fingers into the spunk that was splattered all over my stomach.

Maria pulled out her phone and took a photograph, but it was what happened next that really surprised me. She took a tissue from her pocket and wiped me down, using it to remove all the stickiness from my abdominals and manhood. Once my pants and trousers were where they should be in a public place, we kissed and cuddled some more, but I didn't get invited into Maria's place. She promised she'd let me into it soon but right now it was too messy to have visitors. By the time I crawled into my own bed it was 4am.

Maria: Hello there. I don't know what to say about last night. That's the first time I've used the stairs in my block for something like that. There's always a first time for everything. I hope you'll see me again soon. I've no idea what you were thinking coz you didn't say much once we got to Fortune Street. Thank you for taking me out and all the presents.

Me: I was very happy. Sometimes I'm just quiet. Of course next time we should go to the top of the stairs, coz there'd be less people to interrupt us.

Maria: You weren't quiet all the time. I really liked it when you were screaming and moaning with pleasure. And there was a moment when I was so close to telling you: 'Come on, let's go up one flight of stairs and into my bed.' But then I thought what if his cat allergy kicks in and he has to be rushed to hospital? And do I have to get rid of my cat if I'm ever gonna take him home? Luckily we still have the stairs.

Me: You can't get rid of Sidney, she's your best friend. I just thought you ought to know I had a cat allergy.

* * *

Maria: Martin dear, I wish you would remember your previous lives. We are meant to be together. You are so good for me. You make me so happy. But I'm sure you'd be happier if I got a boyfriend to take the pressure off you. Then you'd be able to relax and stop worrying about getting into another relationship like your last one. If I was seeing someone else you wouldn't make such an issue of your commitment or lack of it. I don't really want to go out with anyone else, but if you get down on your knees and implore me then I might consider finding myself a boyfriend.

Me: If you had a boyfriend would you tell him about me?

Maria: Beg if you want to find out. Billy Rath emailed to wish me happy Xmas and to ask how things were. You know Billy is a bit like me. It took him half his life to find his wife and he's so in love with her. I wish I could have seen you on my lunch break. It gets lonely working all day on your own in a big office. Everyone else is taking their holidays, but at least I'm getting overtime. Tonight when I came home Mr Cohen's son gave me some of his father's drawings.

Me: It's great you got some of Mr Cohen's art. I'm not gonna see you until after New Year now. Bummer. I hate seeing my family at Xmas, but they expect it. And it will give my cousin a break from me. Wouldn't be so bad if most of my relatives hadn't left London. I'd rather be with you than them. What we did on your birthday was such fun.

Maria: I can't help thinking we're both sick in the head. Tonight I'm having dinner with friends, so Xmas won't suck that much. And guess what? My brother and sisters gave me £6,000 to get my dental implants. I can't believe it. It isn't a present, it's the money all four of us get from renting out the family house in our village. My oldest sister said take the money and pay it back when you can. No interest or pressure. And because we're always getting rent from the house, some of what I owe will be paid off automatically every month. I'm so happy I don't have to take a loan from a bank, which would have been hard because I have so many debts. My horrible front teeth are coming out. No more fucking cheap shit composites or bad bridges. I want nice, even, white teeth but with enough variation to look natural. My teeth were making me miserable and angry. I stopped smiling in order to hide them. I'm so HAPPY.

Me: Hey, Maria, that's great, but really other people don't notice your teeth so much – but if they make you self-conscious then it's good to have them fixed.

Maria: Listen, I don't care if people notice my teeth or not. I'm doing it for myself. If I don't have them fixed soon they'll fall out and I'll have to wear dentures, and then I'll feel like I'm eighty years old. Although the health service say it's cosmetic dentistry I'm not doing it for purely aesthetic reasons. My front teeth are horrible and don't dare contradict me coz I see them every day. But the problem is the two bridges I have that keep coming out, so I can't even eat properly. But let's not talk about this. Did I tell you when I first came to London I had a cleaning job in Penge for a woman called Alice Noon. I couldn't speak much English, but Alice and her family really loved me.

Me: You've never told me about Alice. After New Year I'm going to work with my rich clients in Toulouse. I really wish I had a place of my own and wasn't still sofa surfing. But until I've paid off my wife's debts I can't afford my own pad, and I don't want to impose too much on my cousin. I'm going to be with my American clients until the middle of March. But I'd like to see you before I go. On Thursday I'm catching Andy Milligan's *The Body Beneath* at the BFI. I'm going with friends and it would be great if you came too. We already have tickets, so can I buy one for you? It's my last chance to see you. I'm going to France the next day.

Maria: I'm not going to the BFI. I tried to book a ticket online because I didn't want you to pay for it. There were hardly any left. What's the point of meeting you to see a movie if I have to sit down next to someone I don't know? I want to be beside you so that I can slip my hand inside your pants during the sex scenes. It's a shame coz I really wanted to see that movie. It isn't often you get a chance to see one of Andy Milligan's films on the big screen.

Me: Doh.

Maria: I'm not going to see you for months, tiger. Noooo. And the last gig I went to was totally fucked up. A young plumber wanted to take me home. He just couldn't believe I was twenty years older than him and still looked so good. And this guy Patrick who's been going to the same gigs as me for a while was there too. He's from Ireland and very handsome. He left his girlfriend dancing and followed me around. If I'd met him before I'd met you maybe I'd have been interested. I've always been very fussy about boyfriends but now I compare all men to you and no one comes close. Damn. As the club was closing, Patrick's girlfriend started shouting at him that he was a jerk for harassing a girl who clearly wasn't interested. He was so embarrassed he walked off fast, and his girlfriend tried to follow him. She was wearing high heels and fell flat on her face. She was too drunk to get up unaided and nobody went to help her. Patrick didn't even notice coz his back was turned. I had to tell my friend Danny and the young plumber to pick her up. And to put a proper damper on the night, my ex Leonidas told me if I didn't take someone home I'd end up with cobwebs between my legs. Fucking jerk. I was so pissed off I told him some choice things, and he was upset too.

While I was in Toulouse I thought about Maria a lot. I realised there was nothing I could do about her drug use other than accept it. If I loved her enough maybe she'd stop using, but that was all down to her. I could offer support, but Maria would have to fight incredibly hard to get clean. It would be difficult no matter how committed she was. As a process it wouldn't ever be completely resolved either. There would be relapses, but if Maria was going in the right direction then the gaps between them would get longer until there was finally blue water between her and smack. And I knew relapses were more dangerous than regular use coz tolerance went down. That's how my mother died, overdosing after relapsing, coz she wanted to get clean. Returning to Maria, I'd slipped into a relationship with her and discovered she made me very happy. Now I was away I was missing her badly. I was on a long trip, which was good because I wasn't sofa surfing. What wasn't good was that I couldn't see Maria.

Maria: 2012 really sucks. I'm not surprised it marks the end of the Mayan calendar and maybe the world. So far I haven't been anywhere or seen any of my friends. It's all work and no play. At least it's Friday and maybe I'll get some rest. Tomorrow the Cannibals have a one-off reunion of their

1984 line-up. I can't miss that. I wish I was in Toulouse with you. My favourite place in the whole world is Lake Avernus. It formed inside a volcano in Campania, southern Italy. I'd like to take you there. And if I'm ever rich I'll buy a big house by the lake and retire there. I just want you and my cat with me. I love volcanoes and rocks. I've been collecting rocks since I was a child and I'm completely obsessed by volcanic rocks and lava.

Me: I'd like to go to Italy with you and visit volcanoes. And I want you to tell me more stories about your life before you came to London.

Maria: I'm feeling a bit depressed so I'm gonna tell you a sad story. My best friend ever was Diego. He was even more of a brother to me than my big brother. He took me everywhere when I was a teenager, to all the best clubs. I was everything to him. I valued his friendship, but I didn't want anything more than that, so I ended up treating him badly because he was so in love with me. As a result he began to drink heavily and was nasty to people. Then he cut his wrists. He spent weeks in hospital coz he lost so much blood. I abandoned him when he needed me most because I didn't want to deal with the mess in his head. He wanted to come and see me in London, and my last words to him were: 'No, you ain't coming Diego! Don't you dare!' And that was the final straw for him. He cut his wrists a second time and made sure he was alone so nobody could save him. I can't stop crying when I think of him.

Me: I'm gonna post a tune to your wall to cheer you up. You know you shouldn't blame yourself. That's so sad, but you're not responsible.

* * *

Maria: I've got so many things to tell you, Martin. But don't panic. Today I'm coming to my senses again. You really are my psychic twin. Are cosmic twins and psychic twins the same thing? Or are they distinct? I know soulmate is something different, but we're soulmates too. Sometimes I doubt you, but then I have to remind myself that the last time you died it was very suddenly in a car crash. The shock of sudden death has made it hard for you to remember who you are in your current incarnation – but you are you, there's no denying it.

Me: I guess cosmic twins and psychic twins are the same thing.

Maria: I'll be your psychic sister as well as your cosmic twin. But I can only be your sister if there's some incest in it. Don't take me seriously please. My head has been clear for the last two days so I guess I should tell you about some of the shit that's gone down and why you haven't heard from me in more than a week. I got to the Cannibals gig late, but if I had known what was gonna happen I wouldn't have gone at all. As soon as Neil Savage's wife saw me she went apeshit. She hustled him outside, where she wailed like a banshee and made a drama out of nothing, screaming I was trying to steal her husband. As you know I'm not interested in her husband or anyone else apart from you. This incident really fucked the night up. Neil had to go home, but I stayed for a bit. I was just so sad that when I saw your message asking me to tell you a story I told you about Diego. And then because I couldn't cope with all the drama I took a shedload of shit. Every night this week I got completely off my box on smack. Now I'm gonna stay clean and work through any emotional problems I encounter rather than using shit to block them. I hope this doesn't put you off me.

It was too late for anything to put me off Maria. I couldn't wait to get back to London to see her. She was sick a lot of the time I was away and signed off work by her doctor. I got constant updates about Maria's dizzy spells and the heavy cold she had until she told me she needed a break from social media.

Me: Get well! That's the important thing. At least I won't waste time on Facebook if you're not here.

Maria: You're such a liar. But I like it when you say things like that to me. Now I'm feeling a bit guilty coz I'm a liar too. I didn't have a cold. It's my fucking teeth playing up again. I'm gonna have to have the composite on the front one removed because it's such a mess. I can't stand it any more. That's why I really need my implants done. But it seems there was some misunderstanding between my older sister who said I could have the money and my other siblings. So now I don't know when I'll get the money I need. And I can't get a bank loan because of my debts. I shouldn't have told you anything about my teeth. I don't want you to think of me as having really bad teeth. That's why I didn't go to the BFI. I'm finally having my bad tooth removed tomorrow, and there was no way I was gonna see you until my teeth were fixed. So I missed the Andy Milligan film and I really wanted to see it. I just want to cry and cry and cry.

Me: You'll have it all fixed soon. I hope you feel alright. So painful having all that work done. But you'll be fixed up before I'm back in London. Please don't make me wait to see you once I'm home.

Maria: I just came back from the dentist. Things are looking good. Stage one done. Still four or five more to come. Everybody wants me to go to Garageland tonight – four bands are playing. I could go and celebrate, but I'm not in the mood. I'll celebrate when my teeth are properly fixed. It's so cold outside I don't want to go anywhere. I wouldn't even go to see Billy Rath if he was playing. Which reminds me of a funny story. Two days after the 12 Bar gig Olga wanted to go out but Billy and me wanted to stay home. We were watching *Jaws*, and Olga kept standing in front of the TV and changing the channel. We were shouting at her: 'Leave it, leave it and fuck off.' The last time she blocked our view, I picked up Billy's wooden leg – he'd taken it off and it was resting beside him – and I chased Olga into the hallway swinging it at her while singing the *Jaws* theme. We couldn't stop laughing.

Me: This might be my last message to you from Toulouse. Can we meet in the Masque Haunt on Monday about 8pm?

Maria: Better if we make it 8.30pm just to make sure you don't have to wait for me. I can't wait to see you.

I trundled to Old Street on my scooter. Maria was only ten minutes late. After a long kiss I ordered drinks, and we snuggled up against each other on a sofa. Maria had a cappuccino and I had a mineral water. Maria smelt so nice I wanted to drink her. She was wearing her Bruce Lee T-shirt. She knew how much I liked it.

'You look fantastic,' I told Maria.

'I don't feel fantastic. I won't feel good until I have some implants to replace my temporary dentistry.'

'You're too self-conscious about your teeth. I'll never convince you they don't matter. So before you contradict me on that, let's talk about something else. Have you got a tarot pack to show me?'

'I've got one but I don't wanna do tarot now. I know you think the occult is bollocks. So what's the point of doing fortune cards with you?'

'Just show me the pack. I don't need to pick a card.'

Maria handed me a small black bag with a drawstring. I opened it up, and inside was a miniature *Tarot de Marseille*. I pulled the cards out and saw it was major arcana only. The titles of the cards were in English.

'It's a modern interpretation of the *Tarot de Marsella*,' Maria explained using the Spanish name for the second biggest city in France. 'I like the way that on The Magician the table is squared up rather than at an angle to the viewer. The figures are all quite simplified but more realistic to a modern eye than the way they are depicted on older cards.'

'Yeah,' I agreed.

'The animals pulling The Chariot are small enough to be

Shetland ponies, but they're relatively realistic. The thing I don't like about them is that they're coloured in a similar way. I prefer it when one of the creatures is dark and the other light, the contrast making them yin and yang, male and female.'

'I don't know if I've looked at enough decks to have an opinion on that. What else is special about this one?'

'The Fool is numbered XXII, rather than unnumbered, which is how you find him in the traditional *Tarot de Marsella.* Modern occult decks generally give him the Arabic numeral 0.'

'Where did you get the cards?'

'They came out of a book I found when I was at the recycling centre. I still have the tome, it's called *Tarot: Reading The Future* by Didier Colin. It's translated into English from German. I had to tear the cards out of special sections sewn into the book. If you run your fingers along the edges you can still feel the perforations.'

'Yeah I can!' I exclaimed.

'You know you mustn't buy tarot decks for your own use; they need to be given to you. This one was given to me by fate, I didn't pay for it. I find loads of new books and DVDs at the recycling centre. I was lucky to get Didier Colin's book with the cards still in it.'

Maria had a lot to say about tarot, but the conversation flowed on as our hands wandered all over each other. We stayed in the pub until it closed. Then we went our separate ways because Maria said after I'd been away for so long she wasn't gonna bring me off the moment I got back. We agreed to meet again in a few days. Maria wanted to take me to Umit & Son in Lower Clapton Road, so that I could choose some martial arts movies for my birthday.

Maria: You're gonna love Umit & Son. If I was rich I would pay the owner Ümit Mesut to screen *Enter The Dragon* on Super 8. It's his most prized possession as there were only twenty copies. As I'm not rich, I can only buy you three or four DVDs. I'm sure you're gonna get on very well with Ümit. If you don't know much about Turkish cinema (I don't) he'll introduce you to a few forgotten gems. The store is open until 8pm, so if you can get to my work by 7pm we'll have enough time. Just next to the Ümit's shop they do the best pizzas in Hackney, and they're very cheap too. You probably don't eat pizza, but these are really special. If you let me buy you a pizza for your birthday it would make me very happy.

Me: Of course I don't eat pizzas, they're so unhealthy. But I'll eat one for you. Just once. I'll come to your work at 6pm.

V

JUPITER.

THE HIEROPHANT

Star Video Productions was just a few doors down from the railway bridge at the top of Mare Street. When I arrived Maria was wearing a beige 1970s trouser suit with huge flares. After a long kiss she led me up some stairs to the company's editing space. Watching her move got me all sexed up. Inside the edit suite there were desks along three walls with two dozen high-end Apple Macs standing on them. The wall without a desk had a pull-down cinema screen; there was a projector screwed into the ceiling. The company had other space in the building, but this was the heart of their operation.

'Everyone wants to get off early on a Friday if there's no rush job on,' Maria told me. 'We can come back here to chill once I've bought you some birthday presents.'

I couldn't believe I'd just turned fifty since Maria made me feel like a teenager with a serious hormonal imbalance. It didn't take long to get to Umit & Son in Lower Clapton Road. Ümit Mesut was slightly older than me and clearly a film nut. There were signs about the superiority of celluloid to digital all over his shop, alongside a lot of old projectors and reels of film. I had a quick rifle through the Turkish cult cinema DVDs but spent more time on the martial arts section. Maria gave all her attention to the old projectors.

'Have you picked something out?' Maria asked.

'*Enter The Seven Virgins*,' I told her.

'What is it?'

'It's a German/Hong Kong co-production from 1974, the

first kung fu comedy sexploitation crossover movie.'

'Well I'm gonna buy you more than one movie. Choose another.'

So I pulled out *Kung Fu Mamma* from 1974, but Maria said two movies were not enough. So I picked *Avenging Angels* with Moon Lee and Cynthia Khan from 1988, a Far Eastern *Charlie's Angels* rip-off, and 1979's *The Crippled Masters* too. Maria chose some sweets for herself, and Ümit charged her fifteen quid for everything. Maria told Ümit the films were my birthday present.

'So you like kung fu films,' Ümit observed. 'Have you got any favourites?'

'So many,' I said. 'Of course I love Bruce Lee and Sonny Chiba, but I'm also a big fan of Jimmy Wang-Yu, particularly *Master Of The Flying Guillotine* and *The Man From Hong Kong*. But as you can see I like battling babes too.'

'I projected *The Man From Hong Kong* when it was shown at the Rio,' Ümit told me. 'It's a great film.'

He went on to describe his Super 8 copy of *Enter The Dragon* and spoke of much else to do with movies and martial arts. Maria tried to chip in to the conversation, but Ümit seemed more interested in talking to me because I had a greater knowledge of fu flicks. We left when Ümit had to deal with some customers who wanted to buy soft drinks. We scooted around the corner to Pizza Man. Maria bought two Vegetarian Hot Pizzas with mushroom, green pepper, onion, sliced tomato and jalapeños. She got a seven-inch version for herself but insisted I have a ten-inch pizza. I drank mineral water and Maria drank Lilt. I tried to pay, but Maria wouldn't let me.

'It's your birthday treat, I'm buying.'

'But you insisted on paying when we went out on your birthday and told me that's how it's done in Spain,' I shot back.

'You don't argue with a lady,' was Maria's retort.

'And you don't argue with my regular customers,' the guy serving us told me. 'If she says she's paying I won't let you pay.'

There were only a couple of tables as the pizzeria specialised in takeouts and home delivery. Not only did Maria insist I eat all of my pizza, she made me eat half of hers too. That was one hell of a cheat meal to celebrate turning fifty.

'I've got such a small stomach and it gets full so quickly,' Maria told me, 'so I waste a lot of food. But you're fit and healthy so I want you to eat, eat.'

Maria looked at the covers of the films she'd bought for me before handing them over. Then she talked about the places she liked to go in London. Umit and Pizza Man were both high on her list. I felt stuffed by the time we'd finished. I wasn't used to eating such heavy food. No one else would have got me to eat that way. We held hands as we walked back to Star Video Productions. Maria went up the stairs ahead of me, and the way her legs and arse moved made me want to melt. She arranged some beanbags on the floor and put my copy of *Enter The Seven Virgins* into a Mac that was linked up to the projector. The film started, but I wasn't ready to sit down. I grabbed Maria and kissed her. She reciprocated and before long her hand slipped into my pants. I squeezed Maria's breasts, then slid one of my hands down her belly and undid her flies.

Maria unzipped my jeans and pushed so that they and my pants fell down around my ankles. I worked my fingers around Maria's clitoris and then into her hot creamy slit. Next I pulled the front of her pants down and pushed my cock through her fly. I experienced mild pain as Maria pulled the zip up. I buckled briefly, but shortly afterwards I got the tip of my knob inside her. It came out again after a couple of seconds but Maria quickly got the head of my tool back inside her. With her zip pulled up around my throbbing gristle I had little room to manoeuvre. I was unable to get anything more than the tip of my length into Maria and from the way she was moaning and groaning she obviously liked it that way. After a while Maria pulled me down to the floor. We writhed around on the beanbags she'd scattered in the middle of the room until the film finished. The sound was loud, but I wasn't really taking it in. I just caught odd glimpses of the visuals, copious nudity and fights. Maria gave me a blow job and eventually got me to come with her hand. Once again she used tissues to clean me up. After that we cuddled on the floor.

'There's so many things about me you'd never guess,' Maria whispered in my ear. 'But you won't have to coz I'm gonna tell you.'

'Surprise me,' I said.

'I used to work as a dominatrix. First of all with this black lady Cindy in Mayfair, and then at the London Dungeon near London Bridge – not the tourist place, a BDSM operation.'

'I was training a woman who worked as a dominatrix for a while. She told me mostly she just tortured guys, but if she found them attractive she might give them a blow job.'

'I wouldn't do that,' Maria told me. 'I started working as a dominatrix when I was with Steve. I was so angry with men at the time it was great to go to work and hit them, especially when I was splitting up with Steve.'

'How did you get the job?'

'I heard about the vacancy and told Cindy I'd worked as a dominatrix in Spain. It was a lie, but she believed me. I just winged it on the first day. But it was easy to pick up. Cindy was just into money and she was so cynical. She'd advertise herself as a blonde and just put on a wig. She'd be so cruel to men too. She'd get a huge strap-on and fuck a guy up the arse, and although he'd be screaming and begging her to stop she wouldn't.'

'What happened when guys wanted a straight fuck at the end of the session?'

'I said I didn't do that. Cindy would fuck them. She didn't care. I would fuck guys with a strap-on. It could be such a turn on pushing it around their mouth or making them take it up the arse. I was being paid a lot of money to do things to guys and often it was boring, but fucking men with a plastic cock was something I really liked. It was a way of opening up their feminine side, so to me it was spiritual as well sexual. And they were always naked but I never took my clothes off.'

'So why did you stop working as a dominatrix?'

'After I'd been with Cindy for a few years there was an idiot who really complained about me not letting him have normal sex at the end of his domination sessions. He wanted to have penetrative sex with me so badly. He kept coming back and paying and demanding straight sex after the kinky stuff. Cindy would screw him after I'd punished him, but in the end she got fed up with it and told me if I wouldn't do what he wanted I couldn't work with her any more. But she couldn't find a girl to replace me and she had too many clients to deal with all by herself. So she phoned me up after a couple of weeks and begged me to come back. We'd sit around all day waiting for guys to come for punishment. I was doing heroin in the toilet one day when there was a police raid. I flushed my gear down the lavatory so the cops didn't find it. Cindy said I was just her friend. We both told them I wasn't working there although I had all this fetish gear on. After that I was too scared to work at the place. I didn't want to be nicked. I'd been working with Cindy for about seven years by then.'

'So you got a job some other place?'

'Yeah, I went to the London Dungeon, the unofficial one. But I wasn't there for so long. They said I had to have straight sex with guys at the end of the sessions, and I didn't want to do that, so I left.'

Maria continued regaling me with tales of how she'd tortured various men. Being told how turned on she became towering above a guy on his knees and forcing a strap-on down his throat made for compelling listening. From what Maria said I concluded she occasionally had orgasms doing her dominatrix work. Eventually I had to leave. There was no way of explaining what I was doing in the office if someone turned up early for work. Maria said it wasn't worth her going home.

I decided to try and grab a couple of hours sleep at my cousin's flat before I saw my first client. I urinated before going to bed and my tool hurt. When I looked at it I could see there was a two-inch scab that had been made by Maria's zip. If she hadn't told me she'd worked as a dominatrix that night I'd have assumed it was an accident. Given her liking for kinky sex I suspected it was deliberate. The scab was gonna take weeks, if not months, to heal. And my whole body was covered in bite marks. I was so sexually aroused by Maria that I'd felt relatively little pain when she zippered my cock.

Me: I saw on your wall that a friend of yours died. I'm sorry. On a different tack, I can't believe the scabs you've left me with. It hurts a bit, but it's your mark, which is groovy too.

Maria: What scabs? Did I hurt you? Oh no!

Me: There are scabs all along my cock from where you pulled your zip up over it. Real zip track marks. They make a lovely pattern. Two inches of them. Because you told me you'd been a dominatrix and mentioned the cock-and-ball torture you did on clients, I assumed you did it deliberately. How the fuck do I explain that when someone asks about it in a gym shower? Do I lie and say I was careless doing up the button-down flies on my 501s? LOL. Or do I just say my girlfriend used to be a professional dominatrix and she likes to keep her hand in with me?

Maria: I guess either you're gonna run away from me or I have you trapped. The scab is a couple of inches, wow! Why didn't you complain when it was that bad? In BDSM if it's too much you're supposed to say red light for stop. If you're liking it but it's on the edge of being too much then say amber light, meaning we need to talk about where this is going before continuing. If you're happy, say green light for go go go. And if you learn to like being hurt just a little, then, tiger, I can really give you the time of your life. And unlike the guys who used to pay me to torture them, I'll give you such great release after I've had some fun teasing you. I really want to see the scab I made and run my fingers along it. I'm such an animal. That was just a little tease because I like you too much. Imagine what I do to men I hate. I thought I was being gentle. I just wanted to stimulate you by torturing your cock a little. Did I give you that scab when you managed to slip inside me for just a few seconds? Or was it the second time when I wanted to feel you inside me and I trapped you in there with the help of that zip? I want to take control of you and your cock because you've been a bigger sadist than me. You teased me for a year without giving me any release. That's pure torture. You don't know how much you've made me suffer. So I do hate you a little bit, and I'm gonna use a few tricks I learnt when I was a dominatrix to make you squirm, if you let me. If you're man enough not to run away then you'll quickly grow to like it and you'll end up begging me to give you my special treatment. Have you got the balls to meet me again? I promise I'll never chop off your bollocks, but I might pull them so that you scream, or once I've got your pants down spend ten minutes slapping your testicles with my fingers and palms.

Me: Let's meet on Tuesday at Baxter's Court, the Wetherspoon's on Mare Street. I'm sure you know that pub. Is 8pm okay with you? I can't get there earlier. And as for my cock, the damage was done before I slipped in, or the worst of it anyway. It was so nice to see you last night, and I like the fact that you always surprise me. I didn't complain about your heavy-duty cock torture because I thought it was an accident – so what was the point? But what you told me about working as a dominatrix later on made me realise the scarification was deliberate. By then it seemed pointless to say anything about it.

Maria: It serves you right for putting it there. I hadn't had sex without a condom since I split up with Steve and that was in 2004. Having so many friends with serious illnesses doesn't help. So when you put your cock inside my fly I freaked out and switched to dominatrix mode. I've also been wondering how many girls you're sleeping with. I know I'm too paranoid. And actually I loved the sensation of your cock inside me so much I nearly took my trousers off. Nobody else would dare go as far as you went. They wouldn't even get the tip of their donger into me. Do you have any disease you should tell me about? I did all the tests two months ago and everything was negative. Now I can't stop thinking how good it felt without a fucking rubber being in the way. And yes I know Baxter's Court. I'll see you there. If I finish work much before 8pm I'll fill in my time by going to Umit.

Me: I haven't had sex with anyone since I split up with Petra. We didn't even have sex the last year we were together. My rich clients are a bit paranoid too, so they make me have tests once a year; and don't worry, all I do is train them with exercise techniques, not BDSM. I last had the tests in October and got the all-clear.

Maria: I'm very glad to hear that. You do look very healthy, so I figured you were probably disease free. But I know some people who look as if they're in good shape and they've got AIDS and hep C so you never really know. I think it is important to take this very seriously. I get tested every year and not coz I'm having lots of sex, far from it. But coz you can catch these diseases in all sorts of ways. I always get clean needles from a needle exchange and don't share them, but it makes me feel more relaxed to have the tests and get the all-clear. I know I should have trusted you and maybe I shouldn't have asked. Next question. Why me and why now? I'm sure you have lots of opportunities with women who are much younger and prettier than me. I'm just curious.

Me: That's cool – if you're worried you should ask – coz worrying is unhealthy. Why is harder to really put my finger on. I like the way you move. I can't explain everything, but I think you're fantastic and I find you way sexier than any of the younger girls I meet at the gym. I find it hard to relate to twenty-something girls, they have so little experience of life.

I got to Baxter's Court before Maria. It was generic but then that was one of the things I liked about Wetherspoon pubs, the others being that they were cheap and didn't play music so you could hear yourself think and what your friends said. By chance a group of people I knew were drinking at the bar. I chatted to them as I waited for Maria. When she arrived I got her a cappuccino, and we went and sat down at a table away from my acquaintances. We were on a bench facing outwards with chairs on the other side of our table.

'Hey, you didn't tell me you were meeting other people in here too.'

'I didn't know they were gonna be here.'

'Bad timing.'

'We can go somewhere else.'

'I'm not feeling so well. Let's stay here, coz it won't be for so long. And I wanna feel your scab.'

'It's a shame you're not feeling well. The scab belongs to you. I think my cock does now too.'

Maria put her coat over my crotch and worked her hand beneath it. She unzipped my fly and took my manhood out of my pants. She stroked my erection.

'I like the way your scab feels, but I have to look at it too. I'm gonna drop a pen so I've got an excuse to go under the table. I can put my head beneath my coat and use my phone as a light.'

Maria did just that. She wasn't under her coat for very long, but she found time to give my scab a couple of licks. I wondered if she was using her phone as more than a light. If she took photographs and the sound was on I would have heard clicks, but video was silent, and in any case the phone could have been in quiet mode. I could have asked Maria if she'd taken video or stills, but somehow it seemed better to leave my question unasked.

'The scab is wonderful,' Maria said when she was sitting up beside me. 'I can't believe I did that, but it's really beautiful.'

'I'm marked as your man.'

'You'll always be mine.'

Maria's hand was back under her coat and working my length. After I'd come, she dried me off with a tissue and put my tool back inside my pants. We talked for a while about movies, music and books. Too soon Maria needed to get home to lie down. I said goodbye to my friends and walked Maria to a bus stop. We had a long kiss while we were waiting for the bus. I wished I'd brought a spare helmet so I could have taken Maria back to Fortune Street on my scooter.

Me: It was a shame you weren't feeling well and had to go home so quick. I wanted to run off with you.
Maria: You know I'd go to the ends of the earth with you. Why don't we meet today? I'm feeling better.

So that's what we did. We met at the Rochester Castle, another Wetherspoon's pub, but this one was on Stoke Newington High Street. We went there because Maria was going on to the joint birthday party for two friends at the Hackney Trashbar afterwards. It was great to cuddle up tight against Maria.

'Did you like that Scabs track I posted the other day?' Maria asked.

'"Leave Me Alone"?'

'Yeah.'

'It's a lot better than the song of the same name by the Angelic Upstarts, but I figured you'd posted it because of the name of the band.'

'If I'd been posting purely for the band name it would have been a tune by the Scars, but I like the Scabs better. And I bet you saw the Upstarts back in the seventies.'

'Yeah, and they gave me a headache.'

'The first time I saw the Upstarts was in the mid-eighties in Spain. I was fifteen, and I went to this club the Isla with the skinheads from my village. We used to get in lots of fights. Mostly I'd tell the boys in my gang who to attack. I'd pick someone out, and they'd beat them up. That time we saw the Upstarts I just remember it was a hell of a night and that I ran really fast into a fat guy and I knocked him over. I was so proud that I'd really contributed something to the fight. I don't remember much about the gig. Just the fights we had there.'

'Who did the skinheads attack when you weren't directing them?'

'It's embarrassing. I grew up with them. That's why they were my friends. I didn't agree with their beliefs, and I was just a kid.'

'So what you're saying is they weren't redskins?'

'They were racists. I wasn't. But everyone in and around our village was Spanish so their racism was meaningless in terms of who we attacked. That said, if someone was from the south then the skinheads would pick on them.'

'I'm not gonna argue with you about it. I know you're not racist.'

'They looked after me because we were from the same place. I'd have been sexually assaulted and beaten up loads of times if it hadn't been for them. They'd always step in and help me when they saw I was in trouble. No one else did that for me then.'

'That makes sense.'

'Let's talk about something else. You only seem to like old punk bands from the 1970s; maybe that's why you never want to go to gigs with me.'

'I was going to see riot grrrl bands in the 1990s – and not just British acts. I saw the likes of Bikini Kill too.'

'The only post old-school punk bands you like always have lots of chicks in them. I think you're just more tolerant with women.'

'It's because I like women so much, especially you.'

'If you like women so much why don't you learn to love the things they love?'

'Like what?'

'Women's shoes and clothes. I'd like to see you dressed up in drag. You'd look great in stockings and a skirt.'

'I think I'll learn to love the tarot before I learn to love that.'

'I've got a tarot deck with me. Do you wanna see it?'

'Yeah.'

Maria took the cards from her bag. They were in a red velvet drawstring bag with a mandala embroidered upon it in gold thread. She spread some cards on the table.

'This deck is the *Sheridan Douglas Tarot* from 1972,' Maria explained. 'The images are quite plain because the men who made it drew inspiration from the simplicity of early printed tarot decks. The drawings are basic, but the solid colours make them special.'

'They're groovy,' I said as I admired the cards.

'The thing that is amazing about this deck is that while image wise and in terms of card names and ordering it goes back to the *Tarot de Marsella*, the guys who made it were very interested in the way the Hermetic Order Of The Golden Dawn understood tarot too. So when putting it together they've used insights from AE Waite, Paul Foster Case, Aleister Crowley and others, who were all part of that order. The minor arcana are illustrated, but many of them look quite different to the *Rider-Waite* deck. Nonetheless, if you understand that deck you can get it on with this one really easily. It's like you get the best of *Rider-Waite* and the *Tarot de Marsella* in one pack, with a great seventies vibe thrown in too.'

'What do you like about the art?' I asked.

'I'll start at the beginning with The Magician. His table is lined up straight to the viewer's perspective and not at an angle as you'll find in most decks. Then look at what he has on it, artefacts from the four suits of the minor arcana rather than cobbler's tools or whatever. And he's still got the infinity symbol floating above his head.'

'Yeah. The suits being on the table is a nice self-referential touch. Why don't you shuffle the cards and pick one?'

'Okay,' Maria agreed.

She pulled out the two of swords. By this time I'd seen the garrote Maria carried around in her handbag – it was a length of fishing wire between two plastic handles that could be pulled apart and used to strangle someone. It was clearly deadly, but Maria felt she needed it for protection when she went to buy drugs. What I hadn't yet seen was her extensive collection of knives; she'd show them to me in due course. Maria loved knives, and the two of swords in the *Sheridan Douglas* deck featured a naked woman swinging short swords that looked like knives to me. Beneath the woman's spread legs was water representing the emotions and intuition, behind her was fire representing violence and beyond that a black sky.

'I'm glad I'm using the *Sheridan Douglas* deck,' was Maria's response to the card she drew. 'This is a much better card in this system than it is in the *Rider-Waite* deck.'

'What does it mean?' I pressed.

'That I've worked hard on correcting my past.'

'Is that the literal meaning of the card?'

'No, the card means equilibrium. Everything is in balance, and creation is both possible and happening. Look at the fire and water. They're opposing forces, but we need both, even if we're fire signs. There was a time when this card would always appear reversed in my tarot spreads representing my love of discord and uncontrolled passion for violence. It's what we were talking about earlier when I said I'd tell the skinheads from my village who to beat up.'

'You're beyond that now.'

'Only by effort. I'm still attracted to violence, which is why whenever I hear there are riots in London I go and film them. It's why I'm attracted to you too, the violence in your past which you now have under control.'

'I hope I do.'

'I still feel guilty about the people I had beaten up. Most didn't deserve it. With you it's different. You thought those you targeted were scum and you still do.'

'They were fascists.'

'See. That's why you don't feel my compulsion to give money you don't have to charity. I have to give it. I have to make up for my past.'

'It doesn't sound that bad.'

'There were worse things than the stuff I've told you, but I'm not gonna tell you about those other things yet.'

We carried on in this way for a while. Then we walked arm in arm around Stoke Newington. Eventually I took Maria down to

175b Stoke Newington Road. She wanted me to go into the Trashbar with her, but I needed to go home and sleep. I had to get up early for my first client. Besides, I just didn't dig watching punk bands play any more. I still loved music, but my tastes had changed over the years. I heard from Maria the next day.

Maria: The bands at the Trashbar were great. Afterwards we went to some guy's place to carry on with the party. There were so many of my friends in every room it was ridiculous. I can't remember the name of our host. It was fantastic to see everyone, but it was so much better to see you. I hope I didn't freak you out by telling you about the racist skinheads I grew up with. I know we really love each other and always will. But you need to know everything about my life this time around if our love is to remain true. And parts of this present incarnation really aren't very good. I'm sorry.

Our communications and meetings went on in much the same way for weeks. That was until Maria's past in Valencia popped up again and threatened to bite her on the arse.

Maria: Martin, I'm so scared. On Sunday Matias, the biker I lived with for five years, sent me a message. He just got out of jail. He served seven years of a fourteen-year sentence for drug dealing and wants to come to London to live with me. I was so shocked I switched off my computer and didn't put it on until today because I didn't want to reply to him. I told him he couldn't live with me and moving to London is a bad idea as far as he's concerned. He wouldn't get a job here, so to make money he'd have to join the Hells Angels and that would entail the risk of going back to jail. At least in Spain he could get some shit legal jobs. I haven't seen him since I moved here seventeen years ago. Surely he can't expect anything from me now? Today I got three more messages from him. Never mind the Hells Angels, I need a guardian angel.

Me: If you've told him he can't live with you and you're not interested in him, you should ignore him from now on. Anyone reasonable wouldn't expect anything, but guys who've just got out of jail are often desperate.

Maria: Don't get the idea that I'm reasonable – and I'm not just out of jail. You wait and see what happens if I catch you with some other girl. I'll sharpen my ninja stars and coat them with poison. Just kidding. You always make me laugh with your combination of stupid jokes and completely sensible advice. Just this afternoon I was thinking you're the cutest man I've ever met. I've met English guys and thought I could swim in their blue eyes, but when I look at yours I think I can fly. And moving from fly to flies, I was very impressed by the power of my little zip. You know I sometimes fantasise about getting some pretty young girls together and training them in the ways of the dominatrix just like you train your clients into fitness. After showing them the ropes I could have them working for me in a new dungeon, and I could give my ex-Matias a job keeping an eye on the punters. Everyone would be happy and with all the money I'd be making I could travel the world first class. If only.

Me: You couldn't trust Matias to keep an eye on the girls – that would be my job when you weren't around. Hey, can we meet on Friday at the Masque Haunt?

Maria: 9pm. Unless you wanna go somewhere else. Otherwise we could eat at a restaurant or there're some gigs on.

Me: Let's meet at the Masque Haunt and then move on if we feel like it. I don't wanna see a band. I'd rather talk and at gigs it's always too loud for that.

So we met, cuddled up and drank coffee. The few hours we had together seemed like two minutes to me. Before we parted Maria walked me to my scooter where we kissed. It wasn't long before she plunged her hands into my trouser pockets. I got all excited because she'd grabbed my manhood. I knew the stairs were waiting for us, and that's where we went for some more fun. She still wouldn't let me into her flat. I wanted to try love in a lift, but Maria said someone was bound to call it and catch us in flagrante. I got home in the small hours and didn't get enough sleep before my first client.

THE LOVERS

VI

L'AMOUREUX.

Maria: Often I don't send the messages I write after I've just seen you. They're too over the top. To summarise the last one, you're always a pleasure to be with. I also suggested we meet in a dark alley. I told you I'd wear a skirt but no knickers and I wanted a fast and furious fuck against a brick wall. I haven't done much today. I went to see Leonidas, and then Olga's ex came to my house to sell me some shit – yeah, I know, but I'm cutting back and only doing a little. I'm gonna stop completely soon. You'll see. I just ran my fingers under my bra thinking it was you, and ohhhhhh boy.

Me: I wish it had been me with my fingers on your perfectly formed tits.

Maria: Where is my tiger? I want to try something I haven't done yet in this life. Tonight is Walpurgis Night, and if you get this message in time we could have some magickal fun. And coz I don't want you to think I'm even more crazy than I am, until you remember who you are I won't tell you about it. I'm gonna take a nocturnal walk coz I need tobacco. You know even when you're absent you accompany me everywhere. How is that? You know already. You just need to remember, that's all. I'm restless tonight, damn. On Tuesday I went to the dentist, and afterwards I was in so much pain I had to stay off work. I'm feeling better today. I wish I'd seen you yesterday as you suggested. Unfortunately pain makes me bitter so I turn off my computer and forget about the whole world.

Me: Hey, I wouldn't expect you to like pain. You were a dominatrix. You dished it out, you didn't receive it.

Maria: I hate to sound like I'm always complaining so I'm gonna tell you a story that'll make you laugh. I became friendly with this guy Manuel who came to live and work in my village. He got fed up with his girlfriend Carmen and wanted to end their relationship. Unfortunately he didn't know how to tell her they were over. Then they were in a car crash, and Carmen was badly injured. Manuel blamed himself and felt really guilty about what had happened to her. He still wanted to leave her, but when he suggested they break up she cried and said now she was all smashed up she'd never get another boyfriend. So he stuck with her. A while later when Manuel was in the local bar, a Mercedes with a camera crew pulled up. His girlfriend had handcuffed herself to the iron door of the central market in Valencia and refused to move until he promised to marry her. The camera crew took him to her and filmed him promising to get hitched. It was on TV, so after that he couldn't back out.

Me: A bondage wedding rather than a shotgun wedding. That's funny and crazy.

Maria: It makes me sad that before my dad died I never told my parents I loved them. It haunted me for years, and I made sure my mum knew how I felt about her. I find it hard to say I love you. So when I whisper it in your ear you need to appreciate how much I mean it. I really wanna see you somewhere private. We can't do what we want when other people are around. I wish we could be rolling around in the grass somewhere. I really would like that. I've got some really nice corsets and suspenders and many other really sexy things. Even if you don't like fetish I'm sure just seeing me in them will give you a massive hard-on.

Me: I get an erection just from hearing your voice or reading your messages. Imagine what it will be like when I see you in your sexiest clothes.

Since Maria wouldn't let me into her flat and I couldn't invite her round for sex where I was sofa surfing with my cousin, we had regular hook-ups at her office. I'd get there when everyone else had gone. Our kissing very quickly turned into penetrative sex, and the issue of prophylactics just didn't come up. When we had sex it was always unprotected sex. I guess we both liked it that way. I could have come quickly, but I always held myself back because both Maria and I had a better time that way. That's the overview, now I'll fast forward to one specific night.

'Can you stand on your hands?' Maria asked after endless panted sweet nothings. She'd had at least two orgasms, and I wanted her to have more.

'Yes.'

'For how long?'

'Against a wall for ages but I'm not so good freestanding.'

'I wanted to give you a blow job and make you fall over from a handstand but you won't fall if you're leaning against a wall.'

'I can stand on my head for a long time without using a wall.'

'Then stand on your head in the middle of the room.'

We stopped fucking and got up. I'd never done a naked head-stand before, but it didn't feel any different to doing one with my clothes on. Maria ran her tongue over my manhood. What she was doing felt great, but I remained upright, so after a few minutes she sucked my erection into her mouth. When this didn't cause me to fall she started to work me with her hand as well as her mouth.

'It's not fair, you haven't toppled,' Maria mock-chided me after taking my meat from between her lips. She was still massaging my length with a firm hand. 'But if I carry on like this you're gonna come all over your own face. It will be auto-bukkake. I'm so tempted, so you better get out of that headstand and lie on the floor.'

I did what Maria told me to do, and once I was on my back she jerked me off and then wiped my stomach clean with a tissue.

Maria: I really regret not making you come all over your own
face when I had the chance last night. Doh. Now you'll have

to meet me again this evening so that I can realise my fantasy or I'll die. Your eyes were so amazingly blue yesterday. For me everything was wonderful. I really loved it when I got you to stand on your head , in fact I can't stop thinking about that. You'll have to do it again coz I don't give up easily. I can't believe you didn't fall over. I'm gonna make you fall, I just need to work on it...

Me: We can work on it together.

Maria: And what have I done since I saw you? Well I spent the last two days entertaining a Basque couple who came to London for a holiday. Last night we saw a friend in Amhurst Road, and at 5am we were standing outside number 359 with me telling them it was where the Angry Brigade used to live and were busted. They knew about Stuart Christie coz of his failed attempt at assassinating Franco. When I told them the cops believed Christie was part of the Angry Brigade and the group were Britain's most progressive urban terrorists in the 1970s, they got so emotional. You know how Basque people are. Later I took them to Clissold Park and told them about Astrid Proll working there as a gardener. I didn't have to tell them about her involvement with the Red Army Faction. They knew all about German revolutionaries. I also spoke to them about Mary Wollstonecraft and Edgar Allan Poe's connections to the area. I was tempted to take them around to meet you, seeing as we were so close to where you live. I would have done if I'd been able to contact you, but I'd left my phone at home. As you can probably guess I'm very tired because I've hardly slept all weekend and for once I'm gonna tell you the truth. It isn't that I hate politics, I just know that if I involved myself with the issues of the day I'd end up becoming a terrorist out of my frustration at the way the world is.

Me: It would have been great to see you but chances are I was out with a client. Can we go and see a movie on Tuesday night? I wanna see this new martial arts flick *The Raid*. But if you'd prefer something less mainstream then *Barbaric Genius* is on for another week in Panton Street. It's a documentary about John Healy, a homeless alcoholic with a history of petty crime who discovered in prison he was brilliant at chess, so he sobered up but failed to make it as a grandmaster.

Maria: Let's see *Barbaric Genius* first and *The Raid* another day. Please wear a Brutus Trimfit for me. That's the shirt you were wearing the last time we were in the Masque Haunt. It really suited you. Can we meet in front of the Jean Cocteau mural in the church next to the Prince Charles cinema? It will only take a couple of minutes to get to Panton Street from there.

I didn't check my phone until I got to the Church of Notre Dame de France in Leicester Place, just off Leicester Square. Rather than going in I stood outside waiting for Maria. She was an hour late. It wasn't worth going to see *Barbaric Genius* as we'd missed most of this short feature, so we went in the church to look at the Jean Cocteau mural. Maria seemed so happy and at home inside – I knew that before she'd got into punk rock she'd gone through a heavy Catholic phase, and I could see some of that would always be with her. Cocteau's murals were in his instantly recognisable style. In 1957 he'd done a triptych showing the Annunciation, the Crucifixion and the Assumption. Maria enjoyed pointing out the self-portrait Cocteau included in the piece. She looked radiant, and at that moment she might have stood in for the Virgin Mary, or at the very least Mary Magdalene.

From the church we moved on to Waxy O'Connor's in Rupert Street. The pub was named after a Dublin candlemaker with a reputation as a hard drinker. Inside, the establishment was carved up into a series of odd spaces. There was even an Irish tree dating from the early part of the eighteenth century as an interior decoration. It had died towards the end of the twentieth century and in 1995 was moved in pieces to this central London pub where it was now a feature. I got Maria a lime and soda and a mineral water for myself. We sat down. Maria was to my right, and she draped her left arm over my shoulders and turned towards me. She threw her jacket over my lap, slipped her hand underneath her coat and, after undoing my flies, extracted my manhood from my pants. Maria proceeded to jerk me off. As she did this I looked directly at the people across from us, they were too absorbed in themselves to notice I was getting a hand job. Once I was spent Maria used a tissue to clean me up as best she could without actually being able to see what she was doing.

'I love doing really naughty things blatantly but secretly in front of other people,' Maria whispered in my ear.

'I just love what you do to me,' I told her. 'What tarot deck do you have to show me today?'

'Some say that what I have in my bag isn't a tarot deck,' Maria whispered. 'I think it is, but it's a curious variation called the *Minchiate*. There are forty-one trump cards, which with the suits makes for ninety-seven cards rather than the seventy-eight we're used to. The expanded nature of the deck means it's great for insights and divination.'

'Are you gonna show me?'

'Although on a conscious level you think tarot is bullshit, deep down you're desperate to get into it because you yearn to really know yourself. We just have to drag that knowledge back to the surface of your mind.'

'You love riddles. Show me the cards.'

When Maria took the deck out of her handbag they were in a black silk drawstring holder with a beetle embroidered on it. She pulled the cards from this protective covering and handed them to me. I flicked through the modern reproduction of eighteenth-century engravings.

'You'll find the suits no different from other decks, but the trumps include all seven virtues rather than just three, the four elements and all twelve signs of the zodiac.'

'They're really curious, but is this The Lovers?'

'Yes,' Maria confirmed when I showed her the card.

'I prefer it when there is a man and two women on this card.

There's only one woman here, and worse yet the man is kneeling and Cupid is very definitely aiming his arrow at the man.'

'Shuffle the deck and pick a card.'

I did what Maria told me. I pulled out trump twenty-nine, Sagittarius. The image on it depicted a figure that was half man and half horse with a bow and arrow that looked very much like the one Cupid was wielding on The Lovers. My card depicted the centaur Chiron, who mentored Achilles in archery.

'What does it mean?' I asked.

'Curious, isn't it, that you'd pick my star sign. Not only that but the knights in *Minchiate* decks are often either centaurs or sphinxes. You're gonna discover your secret affinity to the tarot before long, I just know it. The strict meaning of the card is that you possess an extraordinary mind and rise above the commonplace. Something we both know is true.'

'You must be able to tell me more than that.'

'I could say a lot more, but I don't want to bore you. In case you're interested those half-man, half-beast creatures like the one on this card are all about integrating the rational mind with the physical and carnal aspects of ourselves. Other cards are about merging the emotional with the logical, the former represented by the feminine and the latter by the male. You see it most obviously in The Devil, who on many tarot cards has female breasts but obviously male features too. In this pack The Devil is quite masculine but has beautiful small tits just like mine. In any good tarot The Devil will be a hermaphrodite because the emotions and reason must be integrated before our final spiritual evolution begins. We find the spiritual by realising ourselves as simultaneously physical, emotional and rational beings. That's what real witchcraft is all about.'

'But that's also the process of disalienation as described by Marx. You see it very obviously in his first full laying out of historical materialism in his introduction to *The German Ideology*. It's the fisherman quote.'

'Tell me exactly what Marx says.'

'I'll have to look it up because I can't remember the exact

words.' I searched for the quote online using my phone. 'Here it is: "In communist society, where nobody has one exclusive sphere of activity but each can become accomplished in any branch he wishes, society regulates the general production and thus makes it possible for me to do one thing today and another tomorrow, to hunt in the morning, fish in the afternoon, rear cattle in the evening, criticise after dinner, just as I have a mind, without ever becoming hunter, fisherman, herdsman or critic." It's great because he's saying we have to realise every aspect of ourselves and for us vegetarians we can just take the hunting bit as a metaphor. It's exactly what you say you're doing with the tarot.'

'Am I starting to convince you that tarot isn't bollocks?'

'Why don't you pick a card?'

Maria took the pack and shuffled it. She then cut the deck and the card that was revealed was trump twenty-seven, Aries. The engraving showed a ram standing on its hind legs imitating the stance of an upright man.

'I can hardly believe it,' Maria exclaimed, 'I've picked your star sign! That's more than coincidence.'

'Please elaborate.'

'It's proof that you are who I think you are. Not that I need proof, I know. We've been together before and we'll always be together. We belong to each other and we aren't complete until we come together in our different lives.'

'And the strict meaning of the card?'

'Courage and audacity. Being able to face any situation like a brave knight.'

We spent another thirty minutes looking through the *Minchiate* cards. Then we moved on to Gaby's in Charing Cross Road. It was an unpretentious Israeli restaurant that had been under threat of closure due to the machinations of developers. Somehow a massive public outcry had saved it, for the time being at any rate. We ate hummus and falafel and sat around until we were thrown out.

We messaged endlessly and met up again soon after missing *Barbaric Genius*. Maria amazed me by being on time, so we didn't miss the flick we'd planned to see. Before the movie we went to the 101 Snack Bar on Charing Cross Road. I drank tea, and Maria had orange juice. I ate a mushroom omelette, Maria skipped food. She said she'd eaten lunch a couple of hours earlier. *The Raid* was an action roller-coaster, and we both enjoyed it. I was a little distracted in the early part of the movie as Maria jerked me off in the darkness. She did her usual trick of throwing her jacket over my lap. She whispered she wanted to give me a blow job but said she'd be pushing her luck if she did that.

Me: Why don't we go and see the new David Cronenberg movie *Cosmopolis* either on Tuesday or Thursday next week?

Maria: All the reviews say it's terrible. Online nearly everyone says they left before the end coz it was the most worthless and pretentious piece of shit they'd ever seen. Of course there is a tiny minority who say it is a little masterpiece and that Cronenberg is back on form. If the film is boring we can amuse ourselves in other ways. Thursday is better for me. This time I'll buy the tickets, okay?

Me: Do you wanna go to Curzon Soho or Islington Screen On The Green?

Maria: Screen On The Green coz we can get one of the sofas at the back and be very naughty if the film is a turkey. Lydia Lunch is playing in London on 1 July. Do you want to go and see her again? I was so shocked when you told me you went to her last gig in the Elephant And Castle because I was there too. That night I was really bored. I went with a Colombian punk girl, and she wasn't much fun coz she was seriously depressed. If only I'd known you then we'd have had such a fun night together.

Me: That Corsica Studios gig was just a few months before we first met.

We'd planned to get into *Cosmopolis* early, but in the end I stood in the street for thirty minutes because Maria was late. When she finally stepped out of a taxi she looked stunning, and any anger I harboured over her timekeeping just evaporated. We only missed the ads and still managed to grab a sofa at the back of the cinema. After Maria bought food and drinks we had a few seconds to spare before the film started. Word of how poor the movie was seemed to have got around because the Screen On The Green was very empty. The flick was tiresome and based on a premise that didn't seem too far removed from the 1975 sexploitation feature *Rolls-Royce Baby* helmed by Erwin C Dietrich and starring Lina Romay, but minus the frolics and nudity. *Cosmopolis* featured a financial speculator riding around in his stretch limousine and talking shit. That was it. Maria told me it sucked a few minutes in, and we started making out on our sofa. The cinema staff behind us paid no attention to what we were doing.

A woman a few rows in front kept turning around to look at us. She was probably bored by the movie too, and she was on her own. I glared at her whenever I caught her gawping, and eventually she kept her eyes on the screen. Maria lost no time in getting my cock out, and after massaging it with her hands for a very long time gave it a good suck. She was wearing a skirt, and after I'd pulled her knickers off she sat on my lap and we had penetrative sex. We fucked until we'd both come. After that we just went back to kissing and cuddling.

Me: I'm gonna meet some people I know in the Betsy Trotwood in Farringdon Road tonight. Why don't you come along too? We could sneak off to a different pub – there's a Wetherspoon's, the Sir John Oldcastle, down the road near Farringdon Station. Neither pub is very far from your flat.

Maria: I'm in agony. I haven't been to work today. One of my back teeth is playing up again. Tomorrow morning I have to go to the Royal London Hospital in Whitechapel. I'm in so much pain it's driving me mad. What I'd give for half an hour with you, but I'm not up for it. Doh.

Me: That's a shame, but I understand. I really hope the pain eases off. Can we meet on Friday? Hopefully that will give you enough time to recover. I wanna see you now, but if you're sick I'll have to wait a few days.

Maria: Let's meet on Friday. I said I'd go to Garageland too, but I can pop in there to see my friends after I've seen you. This dental shit really sucks.

Me: Some say Friday the 13th is unlucky, but it ain't for me if I'm going out with you. If we met at the Dove on Broadway Market it would make a change from Wetherspoon's.

Maria: Okay, it's Hackney. I don't want to keep telling you how sick I am, but I've never felt as bad as I did yesterday. Today I'm a bit better, but I don't want to push it. I'll be at work tomorrow so let's meet at 7pm. I may not be able to stay out long if I'm still in pain.

I got to the Dove on time despite road closures for the London Olympics making it much harder than usual to get around. Maria was more than an hour late. We decided the pub was too noisy and went to a coffee shop that was still open on the other side of Broadway Market.

'Have you got any tarot cards with you?'

'Yes. I have the *Crowley Thoth Tarot*.'

'You mean a tarot by Aleister Crowley?'

'Yes and no,' Maria said as she got one of the now familiar pouches from her handbag and pulled a deck from it. 'The pack was painted by Lady Frieda Harris under the direction of Aleister Crowley. But Crowley just wanted to make a few revisions to the traditional tarot; it was Harris who insisted they remake it.'

The cards had a greenish tint to them. The trumps used geometric patterns that gave them a modernist vibe along the lines of cubist or futurist art, but the figures were stiff and looked like outsider art. The overall effect was surrealism as filtered through the mind of a hippie stoner. The pip cards weren't illustrated with scenes like most modern tarot decks, but they were more elaborate than those found in the *Tarot de Marseille*. And every pip card had a keyword at the bottom.

'The *Thoth Tarot* is the most widely used and influential

modern tarot after the *Rider-Waite-Smith* deck,' Maria told me. 'And isn't it interesting that in both cases the visuals are the work of women directed by men who held high rank in the Hermetic Order Of The Golden Dawn. Crowley and Harris worked on the *Thoth Tarot* during the Second World War, and although the cards appeared as illustrations in Crowley's 1944 book about tarot the world had to wait until 1969 before they were produced as a deck.'

'You're very into them, aren't you.'

'Not as much as the *Giger Tarot*, but the *Thoth* deck did influence my favourite pack,' Maria said. 'This deck deviates from the tarot norm even more than the *Giger*. In the trumps as painted by Harris, Justice becomes Adjustment, The Wheel Of Fortune just Fortune, Strength is transformed into Lust, Temperance becomes Art, Judgement is The Aeon and The World is The Universe. In the *Giger Tarot* Temperance becomes Alchemy rather than Art and The World is The Universe. So you can see the influence of Crowley there, but the changes aren't as extensive.'

'So why do you prefer the *Giger*?'

'I think the art is better but also the system is simpler. In the *Thoth Tarot* Crowley overlays so many different magical systems and sets up all these correspondences between them, resulting in intuition being overrun by rational organisation. Rather than going for a pictorial narrative, the *Thoth Tarot* abstracts everything into symbols and mashes up alchemy, astrology, the cabala, high magick and various mythologies including those of the ancient Celts and Egyptians. It's a good shadow deck, but some aspects of it are too intellectual and too male despite the amazing input of Frieda Harris.'

'So you're not a fan of Crowley?'

'I have a lot of time for Crowley, and I'm not saying his work on the tarot wasn't important, it was probably the last really significant contribution made by a man. The spread of the tarot over the last fifty-plus years has really been down to women, and that's the period in which it's become a massive phenomenon. The big revival of interest in the cards started with the publication of Eden Gray's *Tarot Revealed* in 1960. And other women writers like Rachel Pollack and Mary K Greer played a huge role in spreading tarot through their books from the 1970s onwards...'

I got in an hour of tarot talk with Maria. But she wasn't feeling well and needed to go home. We kissed before Maria got into a taxi.

Maria: I'm feeling better today. I went to see Olga in Stoke Newington and had a great time. We ate in the Rochester Castle. Then we went to Clissold Park to see the animals they have there and for me to take pictures of Olga. She just loves to pose. Her boyfriend was away with his friends so we were a bit naughty. We ended up at her flat smoking crack. I know what you must be thinking of me now, but I haven't had any crack since Billy Rath went back to the USA and that was at the end of last year. Anyway Olga says she'd love you to come around to her house for a coffee or a meal. She has a two-bedroom flat, and we could go to one of her rooms after a bit of socialising with Olga and spend some time in bed.

Me: Hey, let's go round to Olga's house soon. What about next weekend?

Maria: My period is next weekend. The weekend after that?

Me: I don't mind if you're bleeding.

Maria: I can't have sex at the end of my power cycle, but let's meet at the weekend anyway. We can still go to Olga's for more teasing than pleasing.

THE CHARIOT

I met Maria outside the Daniel Defoe pub so she could direct me to Olga's pad. The flat was in a hard-to-find cul-de-sac. Maria had keys, and we were able to get in despite Olga being out. Maria wanted to cook for me, but I only needed coffee. She made it on the stove. She heated milk for herself, I had espresso. Olga came home while we were sitting at the kitchen table drinking coffee and holding hands.

'¡Hola!' Maria and Olga seemed to say the word at the same time.

'Hey, great to see you again,' I said standing up.

'Good to see you,' Olga shot back before we kissed.

'Do you want coffee?' I asked.

'I've been up all night doing speed,' Olga told me, 'didn't Maria tell you? I don't want coffee. I need to go to bed.'

Olga and Maria exchanged a few words in Spanish and then our host retired to the bedroom at one end of the flat. The kitchen and bathroom were in the centre with a living room cum bed-room at the back overlooking a small garden. Maria and I got more coffee and went into the back room, where the double sofa bed had already been unfolded.

'Let's put some music on,' Maria said. 'What do you want? Choose.'

I looked through a bunch of music DVDs. All punk and mostly bands from the eighties onwards. There was one of Eater, but it was a comeback gig, not the band when they were young kids in the 1970s. In the end I picked the Lurkers, not the classic line-up but a later version of the band without original singer Howard Wall.

Maria pulled our clothes off but kept her pants on. She said I couldn't fuck her because she had her period. She scratched me a lot, then got me to massage her neck and shoulders. We wrestled around and engaged in some serious frottage. After a couple of hours Maria gave me what she called the exquisite brush off. She tickled my balls with a make-up brush, moving it around in circles. It felt divine. She used the brush on me for a long time because she liked the squeals of delight it elicited. Eventually Maria dropped her brush and gave me a blow job. I didn't get to come in her mouth, after taking my meat from between her lips she jerked me off for about thirty seconds. I shot my load over my own stomach. Maria wiped my spunk up with some tissues. Afterwards we cuddled and whispered in each other's ears.

'You drive me crazy,' Maria panted.

'I could say that to you too.'

'You do know that my favourite sessions with my subs was when I used the strap-on?'

'You told me you'd make them give you a blow job or fuck them up the arse.'

'I've never felt more powerful in my life than when I was doing that. I should have been paying the subs, but they paid me.'

'It was a win-win situation,' I observed.

'Have you ever been fucked up the arse?'

'No.'

'You have but you don't remember.'

'I don't remember?'

'In some of our pasts lives I was the man and you were the woman,' Maria told me. 'Sometimes we were both men and some-times both women. When we were Templars it was always me who sodomised you. Our genders in any given life don't matter. There'll always be both spiritual and physical love between us because we belong together. We aren't complete without each other. We'll always be an item, and we'll always meet in future lives.'

'I don't understand this.'

'It's because you need to be opened up.'

'And how do you propose to do that?'

'Eventually I'll use a strap-on, but we'll build up to that slowly. I'm gonna get an anal training kit. I won't hurt you. I'll stretch you out a little at a time. When I open up your more feminine side you'll have better recall of your past lives.'

'I don't know about the strap-on.'

'You'll learn to love it if you let me do it.'

The conversation continued online.

Maria: Don't worry, I don't have a strap-on at the moment and I won't buy another until you're ready. But I do have a cane and three whips. And handcuffs. And lots of rubber clothes.

Me: In that case the only other things we need are talcum powder and northern soul to go with it. We can wrestle to see who gets to use the handcuffs on who. I'd quite like to tie your hands behind your back and have you at my mercy.

Maria: I'll let you do that one day, but I'm not ready yet. I've just been to the dentist to get my back teeth back – we'll see how long this new bridge lasts. It was agony. I had to come home and take super-strong painkillers. At least my teeth look good now. So I'm happy.

Me: Great your teeth are looking how you want them to look. I hope the pain goes soon.

Maria: It isn't just how good my teeth look – it's also being able to eat properly and without pain. So what about meeting tomorrow?

I couldn't believe that Maria was actually sitting in the Rochester Castle waiting for me when I arrived. She'd got one of the little booths against the wall all to herself. We kissed, and as Maria's lips met mine it was as if she'd sent an electric shock through my body. Maria sat down, and I got coffee.

'Hey, I came early,' Maria told me as I returned, 'because I wanted to be able to snuggle up to you in one of these booths. You see they've all gone now.'

'You really look after me. I've got you some presents. A few DVDs. But don't look at them now. Check them out later.'

'You're always giving me films,' Maria said as she took the bag I gave her.

'I like giving you movies because you appreciate them. I like old films as a way of winding down after work too. I watched *Murder In A Blue World* last night. It's Spanish. Do you know it?'

'Who's it by?'

'Eloy de la Iglesia.'

'Your Spanish pronunciation is beyond terrible. It makes me laugh. Say it again.'

'Eloy de la Iglesia.'

'I'm sorry, but the way you say Eloy de la Iglesia is so funny.'

'Do you know the film?'

'I know the director. Tell me the plot, then I'll know what it is.'

'It's set in the near future. There's a nurse who seduces young men, and after she's fucked them she plunges a surgical scalpel into their hearts. The cover said it was the Spanish *Clockwork Orange*.'

'*Una Gota De Sangre Para Morir Amando*. That flick is fantastic. I love Eloy de la Iglesia's movies period. You ought to see *El Pico* and *El Pico 2*. *The Needle* would be a literal translation of those titles. They were big movies in Spain in the eighties. I'll try to find English versions for you.'

'A lot of his stuff isn't available in English. I've tried to track it down. *Cannibal Man* was banned in the UK as a video nasty, but of course it's easy enough to get now. I'd love to see more of his movies, but I've only seen that and *Murder In A Blue World*. Oh, and *The Glass Ceiling*. Some were released in English in the seventies, but I never saw them at the cinema and they didn't get video releases here. His more obviously gay flicks were released in the USA on VHS, but I haven't bothered tracking any down.'

'Do you know which titles?'

'*The Priest*.'

'*El Sacerdote*,' Maria answered.

'*Pals*,' I said.

'*Colegas*,' Maria replied.

'*The Deputy*.'

'That's *El Diputado*, you might like it although it's probably too much of a drama to ring your bell.' Maria looked me dead in the eye as she said this. 'It's about a gay left-wing politician in trouble with the Franco regime. It was based on a true story.'

'I don't like dramas. De la Iglesia's last movie *Bulgarian Lovers* was issued on DVD in the USA, and the reviews make it sound like a porno flick.'

'The first Eloy de la Iglesia flick I saw was *Navajeros*. It translates as *Knifers*, but that sounds crap in English; it works in Spanish. To really understand his movies you'd have to think about what Spain was like at the end of Franco's dictatorship.'

'And you say you're not into politics. Both *Murder In A Blue World* and *Cannibal Man* are clear but understated critiques of Francoism.'

'Let's change the subject. Another Spanish director I really like is Jose Antonio de la Loma. You should see his trilogy *Perros Callejeros*. That's *Stray Dogs* in English.'

'I don't think I've seen anything by him. I've heard he's a hack. A few of his action movies came out on VHS in English, but they never made it onto DVD. His thriller *Target Eagle* used to prop up bargain bins, but I was never tempted to pick it up.'

'I like Loma a lot. Eloy de la Iglesia's work and *Perros Callejeros* are the most famous cine quinqui movies. It's a Spanish genre of juvenile delinquent films. These flicks often used kids who just acted out stories about their real experiences of drugs and prison in slightly fictionalised settings. The genre was popular immediately after Franco's death, in the seventies and eighties. Many of the actors suffered drug-related deaths, AIDS or an overdose.'

'I don't think I've seen any of 'em.'

'I'm sure you'd love them. They're always sensational with close-ups of needles going into veins and lots of sex and violence.'

'I wish there were English versions of those films. With all these directors it's the movies that fit into niche markets like horror, action, gay or art house that find an international audience.'

Maria got more coffee, and we pressed against each other in our little booth. She threw her coat on my lap to hide the fact that she was grabbing my manhood. We had a great time. I could have gone on to Olga's pad with Maria, but I felt it best not to get in the way of what they wanted to do there. Not that Maria told me they were doing crack, it was just that my intuition said that was what would happen.

Maria: It was so nice to see you the other day. Too nice. I needed to stay away from you for a few days, but I've been watching the films you gave me. *Tokyo Decadence* brought back so many memories. I got very nostalgic about my old life in the sex industry after seeing the dominatrix scene near the end. Sometimes I really miss doing domination coz I would be paid to be really nasty. Maybe it's better that I'm not doing that any more – at least I've got a punch ball at home.

Me: I thought you'd dig *Tokyo Decadence*. I saw it when it came out but I haven't seen it since. I understand the attractions of your old life in the sex industry, but obviously it had its downsides too.

Maria: I liked *Tokyo Decadence* coz as you know I'm a voyeur. I really like to watch people having sex. I'd much rather watch than be watched. And I could never be a sub, not even in mild role-playing. I would hate it. But now I'm thinking maybe I AM a submissive at work. Although I make the decisions about how to edit, I'm still told which videos to make by someone else and what I do has to meet with his approval. You don't know how lucky you are being your own boss. Although I guess you have to keep your clients happy.

Me: No one is really free in this world, certainly not me.

Maria: Well you've really done something by bringing me back to life. For several years before I met you I might as well have been dead I was so unhappy. You give me so much joy, and it's very hard for me to keep my hands off you. You must have noticed I keep jerking you off in public places. It makes me look like a pervert or a slut, and I'm not. I'm shy and coy. I've never done those things with any of my other boyfriends. I can't believe I wanked you off in public yet again last time we met.

Me: I like you doing those things, and I find your shyness really sexy. Your reticence is irresistible.

Maria: I love to see and feel you getting erect. That change from soft to hard seems like a miracle to me. Enough because I have to go to the dentist again. But before I leave do you wanna see *Somi: The Taekwondo Woman* at the Cinema Museum in Kennington on 14 September? I'm sure you'd love it.

Me: I really wanna see *Somi* with you. I'm going to a birthday party for my friend Pete in the Eagle on Farringdon Road this Friday. Can you meet me there? I'm not waiting until the middle of September to see you. I'll be at my mate's drink-up about 7pm.

When I arrived at the Eagle there was no sign of Maria. I checked my phone at 7.30pm and found a text saying she was running late but would be with me soon. Maria appeared an hour after that. I was waiting outside when she turned up because I was fed up with the party.

'Hey,' Maria shouted the moment she saw me. She dropped the aitch but sounded Spanish not cockney. 'I got held up at work and had to feed my cat.'

'I'm just happy to see you.' I couldn't say any more because Maria pressed her lips against mine.

I got Maria a cappuccino. I'd already had a long conversation with my mate Pete, but when he saw me with Maria he broke away from the group he was with and made a beeline for us.

'Who's the lady?'

'Maria,' I replied.

'Hi,' Maria said.

'Hi,' Pete replied. Then he lent in and tried to kiss Maria on the mouth, but she turned her face so he got her cheek.

'I don't know how you do it, you know all these beautiful ladies,' Pete sighed. 'And this is the most beautiful one I've seen you with so far.'

'Like attracts like,' I told him.

'Are you one of his clients?' Pete was addressing Maria. 'Are you free and single?'

'No, Martin's my boyfriend.'

'You're gorgeous.' Pete was too drunk to accept Maria was committed to me.

Maria put up with five minutes of Pete's treatment as she finished her coffee. Then she turned to me and said: 'I have to go, I just came in for a quick chat. Walk me home, Martin.'

'You can't go yet,' Pete complained to Maria rather than me. 'I've only just met you.'

'I'm sorry, but I really need to go. I'm tired.'

'Let me get you a proper drink,' Pete tried.

'That would just send me to sleep.'

Pete leant in and tried to kiss Maria on the lips again, but she was too fast and he only got her cheek.

We thought it best not to go in the Betsy Trotwood since it was so close to the Eagle, so we walked down Farringdon Road to the Sir John Oldcastle. Maria was wearing high-heeled leopard-print shoes, and she held my arm and leant against me laughing as we wandered away from my friends and into a more private adventure. Despite it being a Friday we somehow managed to get a booth to ourselves in a far corner of the pub. Maria was drinking orange juice, and I had a pint of tap water.

'I loved that Dead Boys footage you posted the other day,' Maria told me. 'I wish I'd seen them back then like you did. But I wasn't as lucky as you. I saw Stiv Bators fronting the Lords Of The New Church in Valencia. It was one of the first gigs I went to and it changed my life. I never lost my belief in the spiritual side of things, but I decided the church was too conventional and rule-bound to allow me to become truly illuminated through my faith. After that gig I gave up the vague idea I had of becoming a nun to pursue punk rock and inner knowledge by other means.'

'Tell me more.'

'You're not ready for all of that yet. I'll tell you this instead. My friend Luis Ferroa used to bring the best bands from around the world to Valencia. He was one of the top DJs in Spain at the time. When the Lords played I'd only just met him, but later we became close friends and he took me on tour with all the groups he sent around Spain. I went everywhere with the bands he was promoting but never as a groupie. I had really great times. And Luis was also really good with whips. He taught me how to do loads of tricks with them.'

'Wow, I wish I'd known you then, and I'd like to see what you can do with a whip.'

'Don't wish for anything you don't want. It might just come true. Back then what I did with whips was just rock-and-roll fun.'

I pulled Maria closer to me and started to kiss her. Maria responded as she often did by throwing her flight jacket over my lap and jerking me off.

'I've got my period,' Maria explained after I'd shot my load. 'Otherwise I'd have dragged you into the toilet to fuck me.'

Maria: Last night was great. You looked like you were seventeen. You ought to grow your sideburns again. They look so sexy in the photographs I've seen of you with them. Your friend Pete sent me a friend request today and he wants to meet me for a drink. I can't believe the way he's hitting on me. You told me he was married. Although I'm not the good Catholic girl I was before I got into punk rock, I'm not a slut or a home wrecker. When I was young I was very pious. I never rejected my faith, I simply added to it, that's why I became a witch. That's why I know we're fated to be together, because witchcraft enables us to recall our past lives.

Me: It was fantastic to see you yesterday. And you made Pete really happy on his birthday. He just instantly fell for you. It seems love begins at fifty. And guess what, I have to see a client near Old Street tomorrow. Why don't we meet in the Masque Haunt afterwards? About 4.30pm. I won't have too long, but it would be great to see you.
Maria: Great.

I got to the Masque Haunt before Maria. I stood up to greet her, and she was on her tiptoes as we kissed. We talked about music and movies until the conversation turned to another familiar topic.

'I've got a really nice tarot deck in my bag,' Maria told me.

'What is it?'

'It's the *Tarot Balbi* by the Italian artist and occultist Domenico Balbi.' Maria was getting the cards out as she spoke. 'Balbi is a really ancient name. It means master.'

She handed me the deck. The images were brightly coloured drawings. The pip cards were relatively plain. The pack was in the style of the *Tarot de Marseille*. I laughed when I saw that The Fool was being chased by what looked like a tiger rather than the more traditional dog. The creature was orange with some black and some white stripes. It could definitely be read as a tiger even if it was a dog.

'You see,' Maria said, 'this is our pack tiger. El Loco is unnumbered but goes between card twenty, El Juicio, and card twenty-two, El Mundo. Some people believe the animal chasing El Loco is a tiger. Both Antoine Court de Gébelin and Louis-Raphaël-Lucrèce de Fayolle de Mellet provide eighteenth-century sources for this. Balbi will be drawing on these or other authorities in his depiction of El Loco. Comte de Mellet saw the card as representing madness and the tiger as a symbol of remorse slowing El Loco's descent into crime. I don't agree, but it's an interesting interpretation.'

'The trumps are in English at the top, but what's that underneath?' I replied. 'Is that Spanish or Italian?'

'It's Spanish.'

'Well that doesn't make much sense if the artist is Italian.'

'Yes it does. The cards were published in Spain by Fournier who are based in the Basque Country.'

'No wonder you like this deck,' I said as I pulled out The Magician. 'El Mago is standing behind a round table, and on it, in his hands and around his neck, are the suits of the pip cards.'

'This tarot illustrates that spiritual development comes about when we explore our shadow and flip sides. Look at the figure of El Mago, and you'll see he or she is very feminine despite The Magician being a man. The face and hands are feminine, but the body is more male since there don't seem to be breasts on the torso. Here El Mago is a hermaphrodite, and that's what we all become when we develop ourselves spiritually. El Mago is the first card and our first manifestation in the world. We develop from wholeness by splitting into male and female: La Sacerdotisa, La Emperatriz, El Emperador, El Sumo Sacerdote. But as we progress through the trumps we become hermaphrodite again, but at a higher level of consciousness.'

'The Magician's hair is pretty wild. The green is really punky.' I said this to avoid bringing politics up by pointing out again that what Maria was telling me sounded awfully like humanity's journey from primitive communism to mature communism via class societies in Marxist discourse.

'Some people say The Magician's hair is green because Balbi is linking El Mago to the Green Man, but if he's doing that then he's making a link to the Goddess as well – because ultimately the Green Man must become the Goddess, and vice versa.'

'Do you think Balbi believes that?'

'In a sheet that comes with the deck El Mago is described as an image of absolute unity. That relates to the alchemical insight that the two sexes of male and female travel in the company of a third and superior sex, the hermaphrodite. Man is a microcosm of the universe, so man must also be a woman and a herm-aphrodite. Even in the *Thoth* deck The Magician connects to Mercury because the pure spirit of The Fool is now manifested in matter. The Fool has no sex, and El Mago cannot be placed within the binary opposition of male and female.'

'So where do these ideas come from?'

'It's the perennial philosophy, but Balbi's deck is specifically based on the writings of Eudes Picard, whose late-nineteenth and early-twentieth-century tarot research forms a distinct and separate line from those of his fellow Frenchmen who influenced the cartomancy of the Golden Dawn. Of course both camps related the trumps to the twenty-two letters of the Hebrew alphabet and the signs of the zodiac, but Picard and the likes of Joseph Maxwell use a different system of alphanumeric relationships to those found in the *Thoth Tarot* and its clones. Picard's influence can be seen in a number of Spanish decks, so it makes sense that Balbi's was also published in Spain.'

'You've lost me.'

'When you understand what I'm telling you about the tarot you'll have fully regained your knowledge of who you actually are. But I'm gonna have to use some sex magick to open you up as well as the cards.'

'I'm up for anything. And I'm sure you know that I'd like to go back to your flat with you right now.'

'You can't go into my flat. Nothing can be moved in it. Sidney is blind and can only navigate her way around because she knows where everything is. If I move anything then Sidney can't get to her litter tray and shits on the floor. I can't let anyone in my flat in case stuff gets moved and it upsets Sidney.'

We snuggled up close and kissed. The conversations stopped for a while. In fact it stopped for a long time because we got up from the table, locked ourselves in the disabled toilet and had sex. At first Maria was pressed against the wall, then I was seated on the toilet and she was on top of me. We were having such fun I was nearly late for my final client of the day.

JUSTICE

VIII

LA JUSTICE

Maria: I have the key to a flat in Hoxton that belongs to a friend. They can't move in for a while coz they're working in Germany. I don't know if it's furnished. I'll check tomorrow. Can you meet me there soon?

Me: What about tomorrow?

When I next checked my phone there were texts from Maria saying she'd taken bedding to her friend's flat and she'd found builders working on the kitchen. I called her and insisted we meet the next day anyway. She said she'd like to come my way. I suggested we rendezvous at Nar, a café in Stoke Newington Church Street. Maria's hair was freshly dyed when she arrived late; it was this colouring that had held her up. I'd already had a double espresso so I ordered another and cappuccino for Maria.

'This place is nice and the coffee is good, but I'd prefer to have a sofa so we could snuggle up against each other,' Maria said.

'I just wanted to go somewhere different, but you're right, we can't get up close to each other in here.'

'You're the biggest loser coz I can't get my hand down your pants without somebody noticing.'

'I should have arranged to meet in the Rochester Castle. And I'm wearing my new blue jeans too.'

'I'd really like to see you in a pair of tight white trousers.'

'I don't think I've ever worn white trousers, but I would for you.'

'You'd look great in them and even better in a short skirt.'

'You're the one who looks great in anything. You'd look much better in a skirt than me.'

'My legs are too skinny for short skirts; they're matchsticks. Yours ain't bad at all. And I really wanna see you wearing a dress.'

'We could work on your legs and build them up with lots of squats and lunges. I could give you an exercise routine.'

'I've got something to show you,' Maria said changing the subject. 'I've brought an early occult tarot with me, well, a reprint of it, the *Grand Etteilla* or *Egyptian Gypsies Tarot*. You know originally tarots were made for gaming, it wasn't until the eighteenth century that occultists started designing special packs for divination, and this was the first.'

Maria took the cards from her bag and handed them to me. They didn't look anything like the decks she'd shown me before. The designs were crude and the cards were numbered one to seventy-eight with the twenty-one trumps at the beginning followed by the suit cards and finally at the end Madness or The Fool.

'Are these new?' I asked.

'No, why?'

'They're in order.'

'I was looking through them recently and sorted them out. Etteilla's tarot system is totally different to all others. He really shifts the order of the trumps from the traditional *Tarot de Marsella*. And he removes the names from the major arcana too – the words on the cards represent their meanings. Some of the interpretations are changed as well. El Mago becomes card fifteen and is illness rather than skill and resourcefulness.'

'This pack is really crazy.'

'It makes sense as you work with it. Shuffle the deck and choose a card.'

I did as I was told and picked card thirteen. It showed a man and a woman being joined in marriage by a priest with a beard. The man had a feminine appearance.

Maria drew the same card. I was looking at it upside down so that I saw the meaning for the image when it was reversed was a love affair. That's the way Maria would have seen it when I drew the card. We both laughed.

'There's definitely a marriage and a love affair going on here,' Maria observed. 'This would be The Lovers in a more traditional deck.'

'Is this the only deck with this order of cards?'

'Etteilla had followers, and they created some variants. As a consequence this 1788 pack is now known as the *Grand Etteilla I*. The *Grand Etteilla II* was designed by Simon Blocquel around 1838. That version is similar to the original, although some of the images are completely overhauled. The *Grand Etteilla III* appeared around 1865 and takes its cue from Blocquel's version but reworks the graphic elements in a neo-gothic style. However, once the *Rider-Waite-Smith* deck appeared in 1909 Etteilla style cards lost favour with those wanting an occult rather than a gaming deck.'

I paid for our coffee and we wandered down Church Street. We soon found ourselves in Lucky Seven Records. It was a garish secondhand shop with a good stockpile of books, comics and DVDs, as well as vinyl and CDs. I spent a long time looking at records but didn't buy anything. When we left we walked arm in arm around Clissold Park taking in the animals and other idlers as well as stopping to kiss.

Maria: While you were looking at the records in Lucky Seven, I went to see if we could get more intimate in the basement where they have all the bargain vinyl. Someone came out of a back room to say there'd been a flood and they needed to lock up that part of the shop. I wanted to pin you down on top of the cheap vinyl and fuck you until the records were smashed to pieces. Now I'm gonna go check whether the builders are still at my friend's place in Hoxton. It's really empty, sofa in one room and a bed in the other. I can take sheets and a duvet. I don't know if you'd really want to go there. We could get lost in the cemetery or find some hidden spot in a park. It feels like we're cursed and we can't get privacy. How fucking long is it gonna take you to pay off your ex's debts? I know I shouldn't say this, but I really wish you'd report her for fraud.

Me: You know I won't report Petra. Can we meet later today?

Maria: Can you come to my flat? Ring up for me when you get here. I'm having some hassles. I had a gas inspection today. The guy doing it detected a leak. He didn't know where it came from and had to disconnect everything. Now I can't cook and don't have hot water. My neighbour said I could use his bathroom, so I'm going there for a shower right now.

I pressed the entry buzzer at the bottom of Maria's block. She appeared fifteen minutes later. We kissed, and as we walked hand in hand to the Masque Haunt for coffee we chatted about what we'd done that day. Once we were sitting entwined on a sofa, Maria took a tarot from her bag.

'What are these?' I asked.

'It's a *Bosch Tarot* created by Atanas Alexandrov Atanassov. The deck incorporates elements from Hieronymus Bosch paintings, and the cards are styled to look like his work. I use it a lot, that's why the cards are mashed up.'

'I can see its shadow side and a bit surrealist, but it's also quite funny.'

'Not everyone can see humour in it.'

'I like the way The Fool is dragging a dinosaur dog along.'

'You're no longer El Loco. You're beginning to remember what you always knew, and you were a very good tarot reader.'

'But everything I know about tarot I've learnt from you.'

'In this life yes, but you know about it from previous lives too.'

'In that case if the tarot is the story of The Fool, I must have progressed to being card two, The Magician.' I hunted through the deck and found it. 'He looks comic here too with that out-of-perspective table he's reaching towards as if he's gonna correct its distorted proportions.'

'You've embodied El Mago, now you need to go further.'

'Let me find the High Priestess,' I said. 'Here she is. She looks ridiculous. Is she practising her deportment with that book on her head? It's crazy. Given the angle of her neck that tome should have fallen to the ground.'

'I'm happy the *Bosch Tarot* amuses you. Some people think it's dark – but to really see darkness you need some light. Now I want you to shuffle the whole deck and pick a card.'

'Ain't that great,' I said after I pulled the ten of pentacles. 'I've got money falling out of my arsehole.'

'See, you understand the tarot.'

'But what else would I say when I get a picture of a midget crouched over an open treasure chest and with a coin half in and half out of his bum. I'm just having a laugh.'

'Your intuition has kicked in. The ten of pentacles, or coins to give it a more traditional name, means wealth and prestige. It's a visual symbol, and you correctly interpreted it. What you say is spot on because you're in touch with your real self.'

'Why don't you choose a card?'

Maria pulled Strength. On it a half-naked woman wearing a soldier's helmet was using one hand to hold open the mouth of a beast that was half dragon and half dinosaur, while stabbing its brains with a small sword. We didn't get to discuss the meaning of these symbols because Maria leant in against me and whispered in my ear.

'The guy at the next table has been staring at us the whole time we've been here. Do you know him?'

'No, I don't,' I whispered back. 'I think he fancies you. Shall I tell him to piss off?'

'Don't do anything to cause trouble. He might be an undercover security guy for the pub.'

'Surely he can't be, he's drinking a pint.'

'It could be alcohol-free lager. Don't cause any trouble, I don't wanna get banned.'

'Shall we go to the disabled toilet instead?'

'I'm worried that guy will clock us. I think he's a spy.'

'Shall we go somewhere else?'

'It's cosy here. I just want to cuddle up to you, but I can't put my hand down your pants until that creep goes.'

We cuddled and conversed, but the spy didn't leave. Eventually I had to go and meet a client. We kissed by my scooter.

Maria: I wish I hadn't looked so tired today. I was afraid to turn my head directly towards you because if I did I knew you'd see all the crow's feet around my eyes. When I haven't slept properly I look ten years older than I am. But you looked so hot and handsome. I had to restrain myself the whole time we were together. The stalker sitting opposite us stopped me doing what I wanted. I felt a bit frustrated. But it was still great to see you. Your short hair really suits you, and it's lightened up in the summer sun. That really brings out the blue in your eyes. Sorry about there being no flat to go to and that I can't let you into mine because of my blind cat. I'm gonna make it up to you as soon as I get the chance. You won't believe how much I'm gonna make you moan and groan.

Me: The guy doing the reckless eyeballing was a saddo pain in the ass. I can't wait to see you on Friday for *Taekwon-do Woman*.

Maria: Do you ever get unbearable cravings for me like I do for you? I get them all the time, especially when I'm messaging you. Doh. I'm about to watch Jess Franco's *The Inconfessable Orgies Of Emmanuelle*. Would you like me to wear some dominatrix underwear when we see *Somi*? We've been so restrained lately that I'm shocked at my own good behaviour. Donning sex clothes will bring out my dominant side, and I'm sure I can teach you to enjoy a little submission. I'd never be really nasty with you, I'd just like to tie and tease you. I really want to have you helpless and squirming before me for a few hours or, if you can find the time, a few days. I'd also love it if you were a little bit rough with me sometimes. You're my tiger, ain't you?'

I got to the Cinema Museum on time. Half an hour later Maria sent a text saying she was running late and I should ask for the tickets she'd booked. I explained the situation and got the tickets. I was then able to have a look around the museum. There were movie posters, signage, cinema seating, old projectors and even attendant uniforms on mannequins. I heard the opening speech for the Zipangu Japanese Film Festival and watched three shorts before Maria showed up. She didn't miss much. She had her hand down my pants for all of *Somi: The Taekwon-do Woman*. It was set in the medieval precursor to modern-day Korea, with farmers revolting against their corrupt rulers. The parents of Somi are murdered as an uprising is suppressed. Somi and another boy from her village end up being raised by a martial arts master, and the skills they learn in his fighting school come in handy when it's time for their revenge. This 1997 martial arts epic was directed by Chang Yong Bok and had been co-produced between North Korea and Japan. It had only been screened once in Korea and once in Japan, so its first London showing was the international premier, even if it came fifteen years after the film was made. For me the movie was too much of a drama and not enough of a fight flick.

Our tickets entitled us to free popcorn. Maria collected this after the film was over. We also got coffees. Since it was the opening night of a festival people didn't rush off after the movie but hung around to chat, which meant I was able to canoodle with Maria. Eventually we walked together to her bus stop, holding hands and laughing all the way.

'You know what I was wondering all night?' I said.

'Of course I do, we're psychic twins. You wanted to know if I was wearing my dominatrix pants.'

'That's right. I was also pondering what they're like?'

'Have a guess.'

'Soft black leather, I'd imagine. And I figure you've got an ordinary pair of knickers on beneath them.'

'Good guess.'

'Are you really wearing dominatrix pants?'

'You should have put your hand down there to find out.'

'I don't think you are because you said they make you act very dominant.'

'I can be very dominant without them.'

'And very naughty. Tell me a story about being bad.'

'The worst things I've done have nothing to do with sex,' Maria replied. 'For example, before I was with Matias I wanted to be the barmaid for the Hells Angels in Valencia. They had a small bar so it only needed one person to run it. A friend of mine called Lobo had the job. He wasn't a biker, but he knew how to look after the place and he wasn't gonna give up the work any time soon. So I came up with a plan to get him to leave. Me and my boyfriend went to see Lobo with some really good smack and tempted him to do it with us instead of opening the bar. The next day we went around to his flat before he opened up and told him the Angels were really pissed off about the bar being closed the night before and he better stay away if he didn't want to get beaten to a bloody pulp. Then I went to the bar, and because there was no one to run it I told the Angels I could do it. I'd done bar work before so I got the job. That's also when I started dating all those bikers before settling down with Matias. I was such a junkie then. I wouldn't take a job from a friend in that way now. I was so bad back then.'

We'd reached the bus stop so we kissed, and Maria thrust her hands deep into my pockets. I had my arms around her. I worked one hand under the waistband of her trousers because I really was curious about her underwear. Her pants weren't made of leather. She had on a comfortable cotton pair. The bus came too soon, and I had to retrace my steps to get my scooter. Maria was going on to a gig, but she'd missed most of the bands. I didn't wanna go coz I had to get up early for my clients.

Maria: I had a great night yesterday. You left me feeling so high that I didn't need anything else when I went on to Garageland. I've become a good girl since I met you. On the bus I couldn't stop laughing about what an animal I am. I just love to grab your cock, and I really don't care if it's in a public place like a bus stop. I'm sorry. I just find you so adorable and irresistible.

Me: You're welcome to stick your hands in my pockets any time you want. I love it.

Maria: I just took some DMT. Don't worry, it's not something I do regularly.

Me: DMT ain't so bad. There are far worse things you could have taken. I bet you had a good time.

* * *

Maria: Sometimes Facebook really sucks. A few days ago a friend posted some photos of the Hells Angels bar I used to work in. We got a bit nostalgic and started talking about all the baseball bats, knuckle dusters and other weapons stored in there for when the gang needed them. We didn't do it to cause any trouble, but the Angels and their mamas saw it and were really pissed off. We had to delete everything. I'm getting messages from people I don't even know telling me I've really upset them. They say an Angels barmaid ought to know to keep her mouth shut and if I can't do this myself then they'll help me with my problem. Things are getting out of hand over an innocent comment. I know the two top Angels are in jail for murder and they have problems with the authorities, so I won't say anything more about them. But I was talking about what their bar was like more than twenty years ago, not now, so there's no need for people to threaten to kill me.

Me: I'm glad you're in London and not Valencia. I assume you've apologised and agreed with whatever they said even if it was complete bullshit. You know well enough that's the best way to avoid the trouble this could bring.

Maria: I did what you said. Now tell me your troubles.

Me: I'm not seeing enough of you. Can we try and meet tomorrow afternoon? I have some time between clients.

Maria: Of course. My friend with the flat in Hoxton told the builders I may go there to take showers. So we've an excuse to go in, and if no one's about we can have some fun. Do you wanna see if you like the empty flat? I'll bring lots of duvets and clean sheets and a CD player. If we're enjoying ourselves it won't matter where we are. I'm going to a gig tonight, no idea what time I'll get home.

Me: All I want in that flat tomorrow is YOU. Just by turning up you'll make me twenty years younger. 2.30pm? I can meet you outside the Masque Haunt and we'll walk there together.

Maria: I just got in from the gig. 2.30pm outside the Masque Haunt is great for me. I can't wait. When you leave for Old Street send me a text so I know you're on your way. Don't expect too much coz the flat is empty. I'll bring some CDs, but you should bring some too. I can't wait to wrap my arms around you. If you don't like the place we can go somewhere else. I won't get angry.

Me: Any flat with you inside it has gotta be great.

Maria: Hey, tiger, I'm getting everything ready for us. No builders today. I wanted to clean the place up a bit and run the hoover over the carpet. Sure is a lot of dust and shit around. And I have to do the laundry coz I want our sheets to be fresh. I don't know if you're gonna read this message before you leave, but what if you came at 3pm instead of 2.30pm? Please. If you want you can stay with me all night. Just blow out your client. I know you won't.

I arrived at the Masque Haunt at 3pm. There was no sign of Maria. I got an espresso and sat at a table outside the pub. Traffic was thundering along Old Street. After ten minutes I sent Maria a text asking where she was. I got one back saying didn't you get my message? Her message had gone astray. When Maria showed up I instantly forgot I'd spent forty minutes waiting for her. We walked hand in hand to her friend's flat. It was as Maria had told me: bare. We went straight through to the bedroom. I took off my clothes and Maria put some up-tempo soul music on a portable CD player.

'You look so nice. Can I restrain you with these?' Maria asked as she pulled a pair of handcuffs from a bag.

'I dunno,' I said. 'I've never done any bondage or anything like that.'

'Are you afraid I'll make you my prisoner and won't let you go?'

'It's not that, it's just a bit weird not to be able to use my arms if we're having sex.'

'You'd get used to it. We'll do it another time. Let's play a game instead.'

'Okay.'

'I've got a pack of cards, and you have to pick three at random once I've blindfolded you. The cards have the names of body parts on them, and I'll put sticky food on myself in the places indicated. You have to find the food and guess what it is.'

Maria blindfolded me then took off her own clothes. I picked three cards without knowing what they were. I heard Maria opening containers but I couldn't see where she placed the food she took from them. She lay down beside me and told me she was ready for the hunt. I figured there couldn't be anything on her back because she was lying on it. The first thing I licked was Maria's pussy. I'd missed my targets, but I got to massage her clit with my tongue. Food was getting into my hair, there was something on Maria's inner thighs.

'You're not playing the game,' Maria half laughed and half chided. 'There isn't a card for my cunt, so stop licking it.'

'But your bits taste better than food,' I protested before getting back to my meal.

'You can do that later. Play the game properly or I'll get angry.'

I turned my attention to Maria's thighs and guessed correctly that she'd put honey on them. Then I ran my tongue down her legs and tried sucking her toes. There wasn't anything there so I moved back up, giving her clit a sneaky lick before moving on to her belly button. Still I found nothing. Moving up to Maria's breasts I guessed correctly she had whipped cream on her nipples. I ran my tongue around her armpits but there was nothing there. I kissed her on the mouth, then licked the edges of her eyes but still found nothing. It wasn't until I got to her earlobes that I discovered the maple syrup she'd smeared there.

'We're both filthy, we'll have to have a shower,' Maria said.

We had sex in the shower, and once we'd cleaned ourselves we had sex on the bed. I regretted not cancelling my client as I didn't want to leave. I kissed Maria and went.

Me: I love the way you taste. And I can't believe you've got me digging the smell of Drum tobacco, coz you smell of that and other things – bitter and sweet together. I know you don't smoke when I'm with you, but the smell is always in your clothes and hair, and I love it because it's a part of you.

Maria: I can't stop thinking about you going down on me. I love the sensation of your tongue flicking over my clit and running into my slit. I can't believe I stopped you the first time you did it. The second time after we came back from the shower, once you'd been down there for ten minutes, I couldn't stand it any longer which is why I made you put your cock inside me. And that amazing piece of ass you got. God, it is so firm and smooth. Let's meet tonight. I know I saw you yesterday, but I can't get enough of you. I wanna fuck your brains out.

I was waiting for Maria in the King Charles I pub on Northdown Street in Kings Cross. When Maria turned up I bought her an orange juice. It felt great to breathe her scent, and I loved what it did to me when she touched me.

'I'm not even gonna tell you what a bad day I had at work. It left me so stressed,' Maria sighed. 'My boss is giving me a hard time for being late most days. I've got a doctor's note explaining my health problems, so he should leave me alone. I don't want to think about my job, I want you to look at this instead.'

She pulled a tarot deck from her bag and handed it to me.

'What's this?' I asked as I flicked through the cards.

'It's the Jean Noblet tarot of 1650, the oldest known deck in the Marsella tradition. It's the first in which Death is actually named on the thirteenth card rather than represented by an image with no wording, which is how the Italians originally did it. Here Death is rendered as La Mort.'

I flipped through the cards, and some of the images really looked like they came from another world, a medieval set-up rather than a modern capitalist society. It was a full deck of seventy-eight cards, and it was the trumps and royals that caught my attention.

'Look,' I said as I held up the only unnumbered trump, 'that's not a dog at the legs of The Fool. It's a cat.'

'It's related to you, tiger, but now you've looked at the cards shuffle them and pick one.'

I did as I was told and pulled out The Hanged Man, or Le Pendu.

'Is something wrong?' I asked Maria as I took in her face.

'That's a bad card in this pack. The Noblet emerges from medieval traditions where hanging from the leg was a punishment given to traitors. The victim would be taken to the outskirts of town and hung by one leg with their hands tied behind their back. They'd be at the mercy of passersby and wild animals and weak from all the abuse they'd already suffered because they were tortured first. Sometimes they lived and sometimes they died. Being hung by the leg rather than the neck was agonising but wasn't a death sentence even if death was very often the outcome.'

'But what does it mean in relation to you and me?'

'I hope you're not gonna go off with some other girl. This card is too much after the day I've had. I'm gonna go out and have a cigarette to cool off. You stay here with the drinks.'

I handed Maria her cards, and she put them away before making herself a fag with a liquorice rolling paper. A few minutes after Maria went out a friend of mine called Helen walked in. I'd known Helen for ten years having met her through her uncle. She was a pretty English girl of about thirty whose life was one drama after another.

'Hey, Helen,' I shouted to her.

'Hi,' Helen shot back. But she didn't come towards me. She went to the bar and asked for a cigarette.

'You won't get anything from me,' the barmaid screamed at her, 'you're already banned.'

Helen responded by spitting in the barmaid's eye. Seconds later she was surrounded by bar staff and customers, all of whom were telling her to get out. Helen hurled abuse at them. She was clearly spoiling for a fight. I didn't think about what I should do, I got up and walked over to her. I put my arm around Helen's shoulders and as she screamed vitriol at everyone but me I slowly turned her around. Eventually I managed to walk her to the door of the pub.

'C'mon, let's go, we can get you a fag someplace else. You ain't gonna get a smoke here.'

As soon as we were on the street we ran into Maria who took one look at us before turning and walking away fast. I was in two minds about what to do next. I could tell from Helen's movements and the smell on her breath that she'd been drinking. She was too pissed to run after Maria with me, and if I let go of her I figured she'd head straight back into the pub because she was spoiling for a fight.

'Come back,' I shouted after Maria. 'This isn't what you think.'

'Fuck you!' Maria screamed without even turning her head.

I decided the best thing to do was to get Helen somewhere safe and then call Maria and explain the situation. I persuaded Helen that I should take her home, which wasn't far, just a walk up to the Angel. On the way she told me that her boyfriend had just died. We stopped in a shop to get her some fags, so all in all it took about twenty minutes before I left her at her doorstep. Once I'd walked onto the main road I called Maria but she didn't pick up. When I got home I sent her a message.

Me: The girl I came out of the pub with is Helen, I've known her about ten years, she's just a friend, there's nothing between us. Helen's boyfriend died two months ago and she is in a right state about it. She was drunk when she came in the pub. She spat in the barmaid's face coz the landlady wouldn't give her a cigarette. I had to get her out of the pub without her starting a fight and then take her home. I wanted to run after you, but if I'd let go of Helen she'd have gone back in the pub. She's got a death wish right now. You had a bad day at work and I can see how things looked, but now I've told you what happened can we just forget it? It's just a misunderstanding. I tried to call but you didn't pick up. I can see why you reacted as you did. I just wish I'd had a chance to explain before you ran off.

Days later I got a reply.

Maria: Before I had a chance to light up Helen asked me for a cigarette. But I offered her tobacco and she wanted a ready-made fag. Now I know why her eyes looked so sad. I'm sorry to hear about her boyfriend. And just two months ago, that's hard. How did it happen? Were they together for a long time?

Me: I think her boyfriend overdosed. Helen wasn't too explicit about it, but that was definitely the drift of what she was saying. I hadn't seen her in months. She was very cut up and emotional after drinking with friends earlier in the day.

Maria: I want more details about what happened. You don't just spit in someone's face when they don't give you a fag even if you're drunk and upset. And how did you stop the fight from happening? Did you have to hold her very tightly and perhaps even give her a few kisses?

Me: She was too drunk to tell me the details, but she'd already been barred from that pub. The barmaid knew her as a troublemaker. I just put my arm around her shoulder and slowly guided her outside saying c'mon let's go. I figured with my arm around her if she lunged at someone I could hold her back, and gradually I just turned her while she screamed abuse. Once I got her away from the pub I took my arm off her shoulder.

Maria: She's a very pretty girl. Are you sure you aren't interested in her?

Me: She's beautiful, but it's only you I'm interested in. And she's not ready for another relationship. She needs to get over her dead boyfriend first. She was angry about his death and looking to get in a fight. If I hadn't intervened she'd have wound things up until she'd provoked some violence.

Maria: Anything else you want to tell me about last Wednesday? Did anything happen – or did you want anything to happen – when you took her home? I don't like lies and I don't like it when you tell me only half of the story either. I shouldn't have to ask you to tell me everything. Tell me the truth about this and then we'll try to forget the bad bits. I'm feeling very grumpy at the moment and I've been nasty to all my friends.

Me: This is making me cross. Of course nothing happened with Helen and I didn't want anything to happen. She was obviously very drunk on Wednesday, and I don't exploit vulnerable people. All I wanted to do was stop her getting into a fight. That's because I'm her friend, and I'd have tried to do the same for any friend of mine – young or old, male or female, pretty or ugly.

Maria: I've been very upset, but tonight I don't feel sad coz I stayed home and had three speedballs on my own. I know it's stupid, but it was the only way to cheer myself up.

Me: Please let's forget about this. We're not meant to be like this with each other, we're psychic twins.

Maria: I just woke up, and I'm very cold.

Me: I hope you get warm – the weather has got colder.

Maria: Hey, my new boiler is being installed. At last... And listen, I'm really sorry for being so jealous. Will you forgive me?

Me: Of course.

THE HERMIT

Maria: I'm so happy because I've got heating and hot water. All the time I went without made me realise how many things we take for granted.

Me: I'd never take you for granted. You make me feel like I'm sixteen again. We really are like a couple of kids when we're with each other. What are you doing tonight?

Maria: I was gonna watch a Jess Franco movie I got from LoveFilm. They come from a collection, and I never know which flick I'm gonna get until it arrives. They've just sent me *Downtown Heat*. The reviews say it's very bad, but I'm gonna check it out anyway. I could sit through endless bad movies if you were beside me. I'm sure you remember that when we saw *Cosmopolis* I was wanking you off with both my hands. For a while I twisted my right hand around your dick, working it like I was using a screwdriver, while with my left I made gentle circles around the tip of your knob. If I got to do that every time I saw a crap flick how much I'd love seeing them. Can we meet tomorrow?

I parked my scooter outside Maria's block and called up for her. She told me she'd be down in five minutes. I sat on the low wall in front of her tower for twenty minutes. When Maria appeared we kissed and then made our way to Fix Coffee on Whitecross Street. As usual, I got espresso, Maria had cappuccino. We sat on a sofa and snuggled up to each other. I could see that under her flight jacket Maria was wearing a Screaming Lord Sutch T-shirt.

'I haven't listened to a Screaming Lord Sutch tune in a long time,' I said, 'but there's some great footage of him performing in the early sixties on YouTube.'

'I know. I love the way the girls scream and pull back in fright when he jumps off the stage and approaches them. I met Screaming Lord Sutch at a gig in the mid-nineties. He gave me lots of signed currency from the Bank Of Loonyland and tried to tell me about his Monster Raving Loony Party. I couldn't understand much of what he said. I think he just put that down to the fact we were at a noisy gig, but I could hardly speak any English then. He kept asking me where I was from. He was one of the nicest rock and rollers I ever met. The other old rocker I really liked when I met him was Link Wray. They were both really friendly guys.'

'I've never met either of 'em.'

'Lord Sutch was so nice. We were hugging all night like old friends. When I heard about his suicide I couldn't believe it.'

'He was manic depressive. You must have met him when he was up.'

'He was definitely up. I just wish I could have been in London in the sixties. I could have seen Lord Sutch on stage in his prime, and so many other great bands too. I came here way too late.'

'I was around London then, but I was just a baby and kid. I never saw any bands until I was a teenager. The seventies started less than a year and two weeks after you were born. We were never gonna see those sixties bands at their best.'

'Do you know who we should have seen instead of arguing about your friend Helen? We should have gone to GBH. It's been uploaded to YouTube. I watched it, and it's really terrible but in a so bad it's good way. I really wish we'd gone to that.'

'We should definitely go to some gigs. But what about what you usually do when we meet. Where are the cards?'

'I'll show you a tarot deck today but I'm not sure about picking any.'

'Why?'

'Last time when you got El Colgado I was right that meant traitor, but I applied it to you and it was me who became the traitor by doing that.'

'Let's forget The Hanged Man. Show me the pack you've got with you.'

Maria extracted the deck from her handbag. It wasn't a standard tarot. There were extra cards, and the pack was almost square in shape rather than the more usual rectangular cut. I could see why Maria was attracted to the deck; many of the human figures were a little androgynous, and that was her thing, the merging of male and female energies. But the pack was hard to handle; the cards were not only very big they were also printed on thick card.

'What is this? There are more than seventy-eight cards here, this isn't a normal deck.'

'It's the *Deva Tarot*. There's an extra suit called Triax to represent the spirit. Of course there are also cups, discs, wands and pentacles too. The trumps have an extra card as well numbered twenty-two, The Separator. The design and card assignments are inspired by the *Thoth* deck, but it also focuses on nature spirits or the Devic Kingdom, hence the name of the pack.'

'Does the connection to Crowley's tarot explain the number of cards too? Doesn't the number ninety-three have some special significance to Crowley?'

'The two central tenets of Thelema, the religion founded by Crowley, can be reduced to the words Love and Will.'

'Do what thou wilt shall be the whole of the law and love is the law, love under will?' I replied.

'Indeed. And in Greek with *thelema* for will and *agape* for love, numerologically these two words add up to ninety-three. So Crowley and his followers would greet each other by saying "ninety-three".'

'Do you need to know all that to read these cards?'

'No, you can just use your intuition. But you're making me happy because I think you're recalling lots of things you knew in your past lives.'

'I read some stuff about Crowley when I was a teenager, but I never took him too seriously.'

'You still made the connection between the number of cards in the Deva pack and his magickal system.'

'It wasn't difficult.'

'What do you think of the deck?'

'They're colourful and their art nouveau symbolism is amusing.'

'You're holding back. Tell me what you really think.'

'There's a feeling of trickery about this deck. I don't trust it.'

'You're right, there're always risks when you go to the shadow side, but you have to embrace that. Now I'm thinking you should pick a card and tell me what it means. This deck is about allowing the meanings to bubble up from the bottom of your mind. What it says is very free-floating. That's why you think it's tricky. You just have to let something surface.'

I pulled The Lovers. A dark-haired lover faced a light-haired lover, with their legs and hands they touched each other. I didn't need to say anything. Maria threw her arms around me and we kissed for a very long time.

Maria: I finally got around to watching Jess Franco's *Downtown Heat*, and there's a scene where a guy goes looking for a punkette and is ambushed by a gang. Two of my friends are in the gang. And they're in some other scenes too. It was such a surprise. I knew they were in two Jess Franco movies, but I didn't know that *Downtown Heat* was one of them. You told me you'd seen *Downtown Heat*, the other Franco flick they're in is *Killer Barbys*. One of them, Gonzalo, was my boyfriend for a while. He wasn't happy when I dumped him, but when we made up we became like brothers.

Me: I'll have to watch that Franco movie again. I like his earlier stuff best. All the later flicks just get mixed up as one big movie in my mind.

Maria: If you watch *Downtown Heat* again beware coz my friends didn't look too good when it was shot. There's a hippie vibe about them. My skinhead mates would grab them and ask if they were bothering me whenever they came near. I saved them from a good beating more times than I can count because the skins didn't like long hair. I knew Gonzalo for a year before he got rid of his freak stylings, and it was only then that I noticed how attractive he was, so I thought I'd give him a try. I lived with him and his friend Pedro for six months, but as a boyfriend Gonzalo didn't work for me. Sometimes I slept in Gonzalo's bed because Pedro was a sex beast and couldn't keep his hands to himself. But I never let Pedro screw me. Most of the time I slept in a secondhand coffin they had in the living room. The coffin was a stage prop and had never had a corpse inside. It was a present from a magician they knew. When the Cramps came to Valencia, Lux Interior had a nap in my coffin. Don't think badly of me for sleeping in a coffin. I was young and I needed somewhere to live.

Me: Hey, I couldn't think badly of you if I tried. That's a funny story, but I never wanna see you in a coffin. I want you to live forever.

Maria: I wish so much we had met seventeen years ago when I first arrived in London. I was such a bad girl then and so much younger. You would have liked me more.

Me: How could I have liked you more in the 1990s than I do now? I love you so much, liking you more isn't possible. Let's meet at the end of this week.

Maria: I was looking through my books, and I found one from 1973 called *Biografia De Las Perversiones* by Paul Reader. It gave me some ideas for things I wanna do with you. Let's meet on Friday, and perhaps we can go to my friend's empty flat.

Me: I've got a cold. I hope it's gone by the end of the week.

Maria: I could teach you a simple spell to make you better. You should try it coz even if it doesn't work you won't lose anything. Magic is all about the power of auto-suggestion, and if you really believe in it then it will work. I can do the spell for you if you want. As you know I'm a witch – but a good one. I never make bad things happen, I only help people. If you do black magic you pay a price for it eventually.

Me: Let's try some magic. Can you do the spell?

Maria: I'm gonna need a lock of your hair or some nail clippings. Then I can do the magic. I can take them on Friday, but maybe you'll be well again by then. I'll take them anyway in case I need them in the future.

My scooter got me to Old Street in no time. I parked near Maria's flat and rang up for her. She was still doing her hair. By now I was used to that and I'd had the foresight to bring a book with me. I was sitting on the low wall in front of her block so absorbed in rereading my copy of *Science And Practice Of Strength Training* by Vladimir M Zatsiorsky that I didn't hear Maria walk up to me. She put her arms around my neck and kissed me on the top of the head.

'You're so adorable,' Maria told me.

'Not as adorable as you,' I replied.

We walked hand in hand to the Masque Haunt where I ordered coffee. We found a sofa and snuggled up, my espresso went cold as we kissed. When we'd drunk our cold brews Maria got more.

'I just love the way you move. You look great,' I told Maria when she sat back down beside me. 'But you know you could look even better if you worked out at the gym.'

'My problem is I can't stand all that horrible techno music they play in gyms.'

'There's good and bad techno.'

'We love so much of the same music but we'll never agree about techno. You do know that Valencia was the centre of rave culture in Spain? Lots of illegal clubs were running right across the weekend just south of the city. People came from all over the country for the good times, but I lived there. The drugs were great, but the techno music sucked. Often I'd go to the car park with my friends so we could play punk rock on the sound systems they had in their wheels. If you'd been to all the raves I went to when I was young, you'd hate techno.'

'I've heard about that scene. The media called it Ruta Destroy. They say Spain and its remaining colonies had the equivalent of London's swinging sixties in the eighties after Franco's totalitarian rule ended. I've been told the rave area is now part of a national park and that there are still many bodies, not to mention loads of cash and drugs, hidden in the forest. A Spanish guy told me Valencia in the late eighties and early nineties made Ibiza's nightlife look like a Salvation Army bingo evening.'

'That's true. I ought to know. I was at the centre of it and many of the drug dealers and DJs were my friends. I went to lots of clubs including Spook Factory and ACTV but I liked Villa Adelina best. Everyone was off their box in all those places.'

'Some say Ruta Destroy created a huge drug problem in Spain.'

'It's more complex than that; the media always wanted to make it into something negative.'

'There isn't too much about Ruta Destroy online in English.'

'If only you could speak Spanish you'd have no problems learning about *Ruta Del Bakalao*. There's a really great documentary, *72 Horas: La Ruta A Valencia*. And I could tell you a lot that isn't in films or written down. I will in time, but right now I don't want to speak about that because I've got the *Morgan-Greer Tarot* in my bag.'

I could see immediately that the *Morgan-Greer* deck was inspired by *Rider-Waite-Smith* but took a close-up approach and avoided much background detail. The colours on the cards were rich and the look was influenced by superhero comics.

'Wow,' I said. 'These must be the work of some hairy hippie.'

'Why do you say that?'

'They're so seventies.'

'That's when they were created. Do you like them?'

'Not sure. The Empress doesn't look at all like you with her fair hair and buxom appearance. You have beautiful tits, but they're small. I'm not that white-haired Emperor either. And look at The Lovers. The guy is a dark-haired hippie; that's not me. The women has natural red hair, which ain't you either. Coz your hair is dark unless you dye it lighter.'

'They're just symbolic representations of us. They don't have to be a physical match. The way colour is used in the deck draws heavily on what Paul Foster Case has to say about the matter. But do you know what I like best about this pack?'

'No.'

'Find The Page for each suit of the minor arcana.'

I did as I was told, and after shuffling through the pack a few times had them laid out on the table in front of us. Rods, cups, swords, pentacles.

'All the Pages are completely effeminate,' I exclaimed.

'They're androgynous,' was Maria's take on the matter, 'and that's what we have to learn from each other and the tarot. We need to merge to become complete. I like the fact Bill Greer does that with the Pages. I don't know if it was his idea or came from Lloyd Morgan who was his art director.'

'You know what, that gives me an idea, let's lock ourselves in the disabled toilet?'

'Hell yeah.'

Maria put the cards in her bag, and we went over to the loo. It was locked. A guy at a nearby table saw us and laughed. He told us that due to the toilet being misused, anyone wanting to get inside needed to go to the bar for the key. He also told us not to bother as we wouldn't be allowed to misuse it again. Maria and I went back to the sofa we'd been seated on and canoodled instead. She slipped her hand down my pants, but she didn't jerk me off. When I asked about going to the empty flat, Maria said she'd forgotten to bring the keys with her and anyway she wanted to drive me insane with desire. She said she'd take me to Hoxton the next time we met.

Maria: Hey, I think we've got satyriasis, but our sex addiction is only for each other. I'm watching *Island Of Death* on the

Horror Channel. It's from 1977, you told me you'd seen it. I'm messaging you now coz the guy is gonna fuck the goat, and I don't want to see her killed, which I know will happen.

Me: It's ages since I saw *Island Of Death*, so I don't remember everything with crystal clarity. But don't the nympho tourist couple turn out to be brother and sister, and they spend their time shagging everything in sight and then killing those they've had sex with? It's a crazy movie that made me laugh a lot. The gore scenes are really ineptly handled.

Maria: You've got such a great memory. But let's discuss something serious. Do you like me shaving my pussy? Or do you want me to let it grow a bit?

Me: I like you shaved.

Maria: One day I want all my body hair removed with a laser. It's really expensive but well worth it.

It was dry when I parked my scooter in Hoxton Square. There were spits of rain by the time Maria turned up ten minutes later. We French kissed and then walked the short distance to her friend's empty flat. Within seconds of getting through the door we were rolling around on the floor. Maria dragged me through to the bedroom. There were no curtains in the flat, but Maria had draped a sheet over the bedroom window. We didn't rush into sex, there was a lot of playing around first. After we'd both come, we lay in each other's arms and kissed.

'We didn't even manage to put any music on.' It was getting dark by the time Maria made this observation.

'We can put some on now.'

'Have you brought anything?'

I put on a funk compilation I'd made years before. Maria flicked the light on before going to the living room and returning with a bag. She pulled a deck of cards from it.

'I'd planned to show you these before we had sex.'

I looked at the box. It said it was the *Tantric Sex Deck*. I took the cards out. On one side there were illustrations in a pseudo-

Indian style showing strong influences from both European art and Japanese manga. The flip sides held text. These included words on the spiritual nature of sex and how intercourse was a merging of the masculine and feminine. There was plenty about slow sex too and multiple orgasms for men.

'Curious.'

'Have you found the card about it being normal for straight men to be anally pleasured by their woman?'

'No.'

'Well it's in there. And I really want to fuck that arse of yours. I'm not gonna rush it, but when you're ready it will really open up your feminine side, and that will give you access to your past lives.'

'It won't.'

'It will. I'm an expert at anal training. I can just slip a lubricated finger up there to start with. If I stimulate your G-spot, which is reached through your arse, it'll make you come.'

'Are you sure?'

'I know what I'm doing and it's necessary. We have to reverse roles sometimes so that we can merge and fully realise ourselves by becoming each other.'

We started kissing again and that led to more sex. After lying in each other's arms we took a bath together.

The next day, after seeing clients, I went to meet Maria in Coffee@Brick Lane. She was late. She handed me the *Barbara Walker Tarot* to check out while she got coffees. The deck was really far out, a feminist reading of the tarot with the royal cards in the suits represented by gods and goddesses from different pagan traditions. Kali was the queen of swords, and she was depicted eating the entrails of a corpse. I could see why this tarot appealed to Maria, after all she loved the shadow side.

'What do you make of the cards?' Maria asked me.

'They're a trip. And your favourite magical lesson about the merging of male and female is a prominent part of them. The Magician is deeply androgynous.'

'Androgynous in the picture. Barbara Walker makes it plain El Mago is a man when she writes about him. But curiously La

Fuerza is wearing the same hat as El Mago. La Fuerza is feminine but represents what some take to be a masculine quality.'

'I hadn't noticed that.' I riffled through the deck and found the Strength card. 'But you're right. Here she is.'

'Check out Los Enamorados, that's always a really interesting card but it's particularly fascinating in this deck.'

'You mean The Lovers?'

'Yes Los Enamorados.'

'Here it is. I like this version of The Lovers, it's another one with two women for the man to choose between.'

'Look at it closely. The man isn't choosing between two potential lovers, the older woman is a priestess marrying him to the woman on the right. In her book *Secrets Of The Tarot* Barbara Walker explains that for a man to grasp reality requires physical union with a woman. Los Enamorados must be merged with a metaphorical pouring of water into water. That's why I keep telling you that to realise ourselves sexually and spiritually we must become each other.'

Our talk of the tarot and the mystical marriage of the masculine and feminine continued after we finished our coffee and wandered down Brick Lane to get curry at Sweet And Spicy. Since the coffee was rarely good in curry houses, after eating we moved on to Café 1001 in the Truman Brewery complex. We went upstairs and sat on a sofa. We placed our coffees on a table in front of us. Maria took her coat off and threw it over my lap. Once we'd finished our coffee, Maria took my cock out of my flies and jerked me off. As she did this I was looking directly at some of those seated around us, mostly they were absorbed in conversations or their phones, two guys glanced back at me.

Maria used a tissue to wipe me down and she put my manhood away before lifting her coat from my lap. Despite her hatred of techno music, she didn't seem to notice that it had been the soundtrack to our naughtiness.

Maria: I really enjoyed our weekend together. We've never had
  better sex. It was more than great. I loved how you grabbed

and touched me. It's so wonderful to be close to you and not talking at all. When you left you were so naughty telling me all the things you'd like to do with me. Afterwards I couldn't stop thinking about the filthy shit we're gonna do to each other. Sadly I just got a message from my friend who owns the empty flat. She's coming back to London at the end of the week and will move straight into it. So we can't go there any more. I also wanted to say Happy Halloween! I'm lighting candles for my dead loved ones, so that they'll come and sit on my bed while I sleep. It's a special night when the veils between worlds are thinnest. I'm not allowed to tell you anything about it, but I did a ritual with my coven earlier this evening. Once you reconnect with your past lives you can join the coven too.

When the weekend came around again I met Maria at the Royal Indian Restaurant in Stoke Newington High Street. I ignored the menu and waited for her so that we could order together. Maria looked stunning in an Ossie Clark Kensington trouser suit. The outfit was black with white trim, and while Maria doubtless acquired it for free or at a knockdown price, I'm sure she could have sold it for a lot of dosh. We kissed before sitting opposite each other.

'Did you ever see the movie *Live And Let Die*?' Maria asked me.

'Yeah, when I was a kid I'd see all the James Bond movies as they came out. I don't think I've seen *Live And Let Die* since it was on first release when I was eleven years old.'

'Do you remember the tarot pack in it?'

'No.'

'Well there was a tarot pack used in it, and I have it here, it's reproduced from original oil paintings by the Scottish artist Fergus Hall.'

I flipped through the cards Maria handed me. The artwork appeared somewhat naïve, with a dash of surrealism. I liked the brightness of the colours, but the draughtsmanship was too sloppy for me. The suit had pip cards and I rather liked those but wasn't so keen on the illustrated royals and trumps.

'This one is funny,' I said as I flashed Strength at Maria.

'Why's that?'

'Well he's used the traditional numbering for the card as its eleven here and not eight as in most occult decks. But the image is of a strongman tearing a book in half and not a woman holding open the jaws of a lion like you'd see in the *Tarot de Marseille*.'

'You're rediscovering who you are. Look at how much you know about the tarot. Before long you'll be ready to accompany me to my Witches' Sabbats.'

'You taught me about tarot.'

'No, I'm just helping you remember what you already know.'

'Wouldn't you prefer a woman for Strength because that's a role reversal?' I asked.

'On the physical level yes, but La Fuerza is also about mental and spiritual strength. We have to merge and become each other in all those ways to truly realise ourselves.'

The conversation was interrupted by the arrival of our starters. Coconut samosa and paneer kastoori. My cheese came on a skewer and was marinated in masala sauce. We'd barely finished this when the mains arrived. Paneer tikka and jalfrezi, a hot dish with shallots, green pepper and green chilli. We were drinking lassi. My diet went to pot when I saw Maria, and looking at her I really didn't care. The only thing I cared about was Maria.

Looking at her I knew I wanted to live with Maria but that she needed to quit street drugs first. I wasn't gonna tell her what to do, that was pointless, she'd only get clean through her own efforts. It wasn't gonna be easy coz I knew Maria had been trying to give up smack for a long time. She didn't use as much as she had in the past, but it was obvious she was still indulging herself at least every week or two, and sometimes more frequently. I wanted the gaps between when she used to get longer and longer until she wasn't doing anything any more. Until I'd paid off my wife's debts the only way we could shack up together would be by me moving in with Maria. That felt to me like it could work, but if we had to wait until I could afford some place bigger so be it.

'We've known each other eighteen months now and we've been lovers for a year, but I've never been inside your flat,' I said.

'You've got a cat allergy, but there's the other problem. If anything is moved Sidney can't find her way around. She's blind, poor thing, and I can't let anyone in my pad in case they disturb something.'

'I'd really like to have sex with you on your bed. Imagine how good that would be.'

'I'd like it too. But because of Sidney my flat is a real mess. I couldn't let you see it. I'd be too embarrassed.'

'What about if you blindfolded me outside the flat and then led me to your bed?'

'Sidney isn't used to people coming into the flat. Hey, I saw that post your Italian friend made of early-twentieth-century Spanish heroin ads. They claimed smack was a cure for coughs and colds. That's crazy. Is it for real?'

'I think so. There was a time in Europe when smack was an over-the-counter medicine and people would use it for minor ailments.'

I could feel Maria's leg pressing against mine, and it felt just perfect. I walked home dreaming of a future in which I'd wake up every morning with her lying beside me. I didn't care if it took five years. We had plenty of time to sort out our problems. When everything was right I'd live with Maria.

LA ROUE DE FORTUNE

THE WHEEL OF FORTUNE

Maria: Today I'm feeling bored and depressed. That's what happens when I've got no one to answer to. Whenever I get a day off work I start suffering from angst. I think I'm just wasting my life. You seem so settled and happy being a personal trainer. I wish I felt as secure as you do.

Me: I hope you're feeling happier. You looked so great yesterday. I loved that sixties trouser suit you were wearing. There's no room in my life for an existential crisis, I just don't have time for one. But I need to see you.

Maria: I just fell asleep watching a zombie movie. Let's meet tomorrow. Where do you wanna go? Brick Lane?

I got to the Coffee@Brick Lane before Maria. Although on a superficial level we seemed to be repeating what we'd already done, deep underneath our relationship was evolving and growing. This showed itself in subtle ways. As time went by Maria was less telling me about the tarot than testing me on it.

'This is the *Haindl Tarot*,' Maria told me as she gave me the deck in Coffee@Brick Lane.

I looked through the cards and picked up the *Thoth* vibe immediately. Among other things the names of the major arcana gave it away. The pack was thick with symbolism and heavily influenced by the Hermetic Order Of The Golden Dawn's tarot interpretations. The trumps featured Hebrew letters, runes and astrological symbols. Many of the minor arcana were overlaid with material from the I Ching. The royal cards in the suits invoked Hindu, Egyptian, Norse and Native American gods and goddesses. With its gothic feel I could see this pack appealed to Maria.

'Wow, this is really unorthodox,' I exclaimed.

'Elaborate,' she replied.

'Hard to know where to start, so I'll begin with The Fool. Rather than the usual dog chasing after him, or even a cat or a crocodile, it's a swan.'

'That's because The Fool in this deck also represents Parsifal from the Grail stories. The dying swan not only reminds us that Parsifal wounded a swan but simultaneously references the way in which European colonialism laid waste to much of the world.'

We snuggled up on a battered sofa, and Maria spent quite some time pulling cards from the deck and explaining them. We moved on to Sweet And Spicy and then Café 1001. When Maria threw her jacket over my lap and jerked me off, my orgasm was even better than during our previous visit to the Truman Brewery complex.

Maria: If we're not careful we're gonna get caught when I'm jerking you off. But you don't complain and I shouldn't either. I can't stop thinking about what you said to me. I know I usually wear trousers but you're right, if I was wearing a skirt we could do all those things you suggested, and if we were subtle no one around us would notice. I'd really like to sit on your lap and fuck you in Café 1001.

Me: Can we meet on Saturday at 6.30pm? There's a talk at Housmans Bookshop in Caledonian Road. It's about the beat poet Allen Ginsberg.

Maria: I don't want to sit through a talk. Why don't we do something on Sunday? A walk in a Regent's Park would be nice.

I wasn't expecting so see Maria, so it was a great surprise when she turned up at Housmans. We sat holding hands through Steve Finbow's presentation. He'd grown up in London but had been one of Allen Ginsberg's assistants in New York for a few years. Finbow wasn't afraid to address controversial subjects. He explained that he and others had tried to persuade Ginsberg not to support kiddie-fiddler organisations like the North American Man Boy Love Association but to no avail. Ginsberg, Finbow explained, was a massive supporter of free speech, and it was impossible to get him to view NAMBLA from any other perspective.

After the presentation we headed round to the King Charles I pub on Northdown Street. We'd decided to override our bad memories there by creating some good ones. We snuggled up on a bench. Maria showed me an Italian tarot deck. It featured Egyptian characters. There were Hebrew letters and other symbols on the cards. The suits had been cut down to two royals and four pips but there was a full set of twenty-two trumps.

'That's the occult influence at work with The Fool as number twenty-one and featuring a crocodile,' I said.

'How do you know that's El Loco?'

'It's obvious Il Pazzo means The Madman, that's El Loco to you and The Fool to me – although I know the card is Il Matto in most Italian decks.'

'I didn't know you knew Italian.'

'I don't, but I'm getting to know the tarot.'

'You're remembering so much, it's fantastic.'

'You've taught me.'

'You knew it all along, you'd just forgotten.'

'How do you know there aren't any minor arcana cards missing from this deck?'

'Because I have the box and booklet that came with it. The cards fit perfectly in the box and the booklet says there are twenty-four suit cards.'

'I've heard about these cut down tarots being issued for gaming but this is the first occult deck I've seen with only twenty-four pip cards.'

'What does this deck make you think of?'

'The Great Belzoni is the name that springs to my mind because of the Egyptian connection.'

'Who?'

'Giovanni Battista Belzoni.'

'Who's that?'

'He was a circus strongman at the start of the nineteenth century. He was very tall, about six and a half feet. After moving from his native Italy to Holland, he wound up performing at Sadler's Wells Theatre in London in 1803. He was just twenty-four years old when he began his run there. He had a weight-lifting act that included a contraption that allowed him to carry around seven adults on stage.'

'What's that got to do with Egypt?'

'I was getting to that. Belzoni left England in 1812 and toured Spain, Portugal and Sicily, as a strongman. In 1815 he went to Malta and got involved in discussions about irrigation and reclaiming land for farming in Egypt. Belzoni was interested in hydraulics and thought he could help with irrigation schemes. In the end the powers that be weren't interested, but he travelled around and did a lot of archaeological work. He organised the shipping to the British Museum of a huge granite bust of Ramesses II that weighted seven tons. The Great Belzoni was the first European to visit many important Egyptian archaeological sites, and he sent many antiquities back to London.'

'Wow,' Maria sighed as she stroked my hair. 'Now I know why my tarot deck makes you think of the Great Belzoni.'

'I only know about him because I'm interested in strongmen. I got taken to the British Museum as a kid, but back then I had no idea how all the Egyptian stuff ended up there.'

Maria: I hope it was a nice surprise for you to see me. I know I said I wasn't going to the Ginsberg talk, but I wanted to see you. Your hair felt lovely. Kinda velvety and peachy. I could have played with it all night. There were other things I would have liked to touch a bit more too.

Me: It was fantastic to see you.

Maria: Are you still going to Toulouse on Friday? I want you to take me inside your suitcase coz my passport is out of date. Doh.

Me: I'm leaving for the Pink City as planned. Sorry.

* * *

Maria: There you are in your rich client's huge chateau and I'm
in a little studio flat off Old Street. My place is better than
a bedsit, at least I have a separate kitchen and bathroom.
But I'm sick of having a combined living room and
bedroom. I really need to get a transfer as soon as I can so
that I can have one more room.

Me: Hey, I'm back from Toulouse. Sorry I didn't message while
I was away. They worked me hard this time. Can we meet
tomorrow?

Maria: Let's go to the free horror screening at the Horse
Hospital. I'll see you at the tube station at 6.30pm.

I got to Russell Square a few minutes early. Maria was thirty
minutes late. We headed straight to the Horse Hospital for the
screening of *Shiver.* There were free beers and Horror Channel
coffee mugs. Maria and I accepted the mugs and handed our
beers to others who wanted to booze. I didn't care that the seats
we got were to the side of the screen coz I had my arm around
Maria, and her right hand was creeping up my left leg.

The official entertainment began when Emily Booth and Billy
Chainsaw introduced a trailer of upcoming Horror Channel TV
premiers. Then it was on to the main feature, a special preview of
Shiver directed by Julian Richards. It was a low-key comic police
procedural about a goofy psychopath who 'terrorises' the city of
Portland. Franklin Rood (John Jarratt) is the Griffin, a serial
killer who tape records his female victims telling him how powerful he is before he strangles them with steel wire; he then cuts off
their heads to keep as souvenirs. When Wendy Alden (Danielle
Harris) survives Rood's first attempt to murder her, the Griffin
obsesses over the one that got away. Despite going after Alden
with a vengeance, Rood fails to kill her. Since the cops are a
bunch of bumbling idiots, Alden finally offs the bogeyman after

he escapes from custody. The film was rife with eighties B-movie clichés – so I kinda forgot I was watching something shot in 2010. *Shiver* wasn't anything special, but I laughed along with and at it. I was feeling happy because Maria had her hand in my pants.

Afterwards Maria and I went to the Friend At Hand. I had a pint of tap water, Maria an orange juice with ice. We sat pressed against each other, and the booze-soaked world around us just seemed to melt away.

Maria: When I was walking home a car stopped just ahead of me. I don't know why, but I crossed the road. What followed was just like a scene out of *Shiver*. I was alone, and a guy got out of the car and started following me. He asked how to get to Baltic Street and without stopping I told him I didn't know. Then he asked if I did the business. I'll be forty-four in a few weeks so I should take that as a compliment. Anyway he left me alone when I told him I wasn't a hooker. When I got home I watched two horror movies. I don't know what kind of spell you've put on me, but I find you more handsome every time I see you. How's that possible when the first time I met you I thought I've never seen a better-looking man?

Me: I'm sorry you were bothered and glad you know how to take care of yourself. Do you wanna see the William Burroughs show at the October Gallery?

Maria: Can we go this weekend?

I arranged to meet Maria in Queen's Square. She was late, but I'd brought a book with me. When Maria sat down beside me there was a lot of kissing before we moved on to the show.

All Out Of Time And Into Space was an exhibition of William Burroughs' 'art' that was on for a couple of months in Old Gloucester Street. Burroughs' cultural reputation rested as much upon his biography as anything he actually produced. That ran: rich kid who became a junkie, rich kid who killed his wife in a shooting 'accident' and got off scot-free etc. Influenced by Brion Gysin's ideas about applying collage to writing, in the sixties Burroughs produced *The Nova Trilogy* of experimental novels. Burroughs was a better writer than Gysin and used his friend's notion of cut-up literature to greater effect. That said, Gysin was a gifted artist and Burroughs wasn't, so it was no great surprise that some of the latter's pictures came across as a very poor imitation of his friend's calligraphic painting. Even Maria, who was a huge fan and dressed in a William Burroughs T-shirt, laughed with me at his 'art'.

After leaving the gallery we went to Caffè Nero on Southampton Row. We wanted a sofa to cuddle up on and there was one facing the window.

'Hey,' Maria said as she took a pack of tarot cards from her bag, 'I've got something to show you.'

The cloth bag Maria took the cards from had *Tarot Nusantara* embroidered on it. When I asked if this was the name of the deck, Maria replied in the affirmative. In terms of symbolism the cards were a knock-off of the *Rider-Waite-Smith,* but the art was redone south-east-Asian style and the titles were in a language I didn't recognise – although the alphabet was Roman.

'Are these from Bali or somewhere like that?' I asked.

'They're from Indonesia.'

'Is the writing on them Indonesian?'

'It's Bahasa. What do you think of the cards?'

'They must be easy to read coz they're so similar to the *RWS* deck, but the Indonesian styling makes them cute.'

'You don't think they're a serious deck?'

'Of course it's a serious fortune-telling deck, it's based on the *RWS* which is designed for divination. But at the same time the hybrid oriental visuals and western symbolism make them seem kitsch. But they'll work well enough as a reading deck.'

'You've really regained your understanding of the tarot. Do you remember anything of our past lives?'

'I'm just looking to the future.'

'Then pick a card from the pack for both of us.'

'I don't need to pick it, we know it will be The Lovers.'

'Pick it anyway coz that's not just our present and future, that's our past too.'

I shuffled the deck, cut it three times and turned over the top card from the middle pile. It was The Lovers. I learnt that Sang Pecinita was Indonesian for The Lovers. This card had shifted further from the *RWS* imagery than many of the others. The figure at the top was no longer the angel of the air Raphael but an Indonesian humanoid I couldn't identify. The female lover wasn't looking up at Raphael to receive his blessing but down at her man, who was on one knee and staring at the ground.

'Maybe we no longer need Raphael's blessing,' I said.

'You see,' Maria replied, 'you're starting to remember we've been together before and are already blessed.'

We cuddled up closer and started to kiss.

Maria: I slept for nearly twenty hours. I guess I needed it. Today I only work until lunchtime. I've a hospital appointment this afternoon to hear the results of my gastric endoscopy. I'm not too worried coz I'm not in pain any more.

Me: I hope it's all good news today. I've come home because a client cancelled.

Maria: I got the all-clear. There is just a little scarring on my stomach lining but that seems to be regenerating. Considering I had gastritis for years, it's great it's not degenerating.

Me: I'm so glad you had excellent results.

Maria: My period came this morning. I keep thinking about you standing on your head and me sucking your balls and giving you a blow job. Do you think you could 69 standing on your head? Let's try it – but no pressure if it's too difficult for you.

Me: Wow a 69 on my head! We gotta try it. Whether it works will depend on your body position. But if you kneel hopefully you can suck my cock and put your pussy in my mouth. I'll have to do a basket headstand, not a tripod, so my arms don't get in your way. Once I'm in the headstand I can't really move my head so you'll have to very gently put your slit and clit against my lips. That's such a far out thing to think about. We just need to find somewhere private to do it.

Maria: Can you meet me at Covent Garden tube tomorrow afternoon? Say 4pm?

I got a series of texts from Maria saying she was running late. Once I had my arms around her I didn't care that she'd made me wait. We made our way to Caffè Nero, not the branch on Southampton Row we'd patronised the previous weekend but the outlet on Long Acre – very close to Covent Garden tube.

'Hey,' Maria said as she pulled tarot cards from her bag, 'I was given the *Golden Tarot* as a present. I wanna know what you think of it.'

The cards had flashy gilt edging. The images were collaged into tarot scenes from reproductions of old master paintings. The effect was very limp surrealism that desperately wanted to be high art.

'These are clearly based on the *Rider-Waite-Smith* deck, but I don't get much of a vibe from them. The artwork is too contrived. You'll never get a good reading from this deck but you know that, you're just testing me. The cards are all in order, you haven't shuffled this pack yet, and I don't think you ever will.'

'The deck is very popular with the online tarot community, but they do nothing for me. It feels a bit dead. Do you know what I liked about the pack when I opened it up?'

'That's obvious. The first card we both saw was The Fool and it's a woman.'

'Psychic twin,' Maria said as she kissed me.

The cards were forgotten as we snogged. Then we got more coffee, snuggled up and whispered sweet nothings to each other.

Maria: It was great seeing you but don't go spending any more money on gifts for my birthday. You're my best present, and

I just want you to kiss my neck when no one is looking. I'm always kissing your neck. It drives me crazy. I love your arse too. When I bum fuck you with a strap-on you'll see how good it feels. I'll give you multiple orgasms by hitting your G-spot.

Me: You've got a *One Track Mind*. Are we meeting at Russell Square tube again for your birthday? 7pm would give us half an hour to get a coffee before the Horror Channel screening. Happy birthday! It's after midnight already.

Maria: I'd like a nice Jewish cheesecake with my coffee, and I know you'll need a decent espresso. I just had roasted hazelnut coffee. I need to buy more. It's expensive, but I really love the taste of hazelnuts. I'm addicted to hazelnut coffee, Jewish cheesecake, French meringue macarons, Hungarian smoked cheese, Spanish Manchego. And I can't eat enough rocket salad and pine nuts. I'm gonna dye my hair before I see you. So you've been warned and won't get a surprise. I bought this radiant red colouring for dark hair more than a month ago but got cold feet every time I was gonna use it. My birthday is the day to do it. I haven't had red hair in ages, but in the past I've had so many different shades of red: fire, ruby, copper, wine, burgundy, pink, strawberry, mahogany – *caoba*. All kinds of red. I've bought a black dye in case I don't like the one I'm gonna try. We'll see. Did you know that the Horse Hospital toilet is unisex? If the film is really boring, I'll go and smoke in the courtyard, then you can come out for a piss and if no one else is around we can have a quick shag in there.

I went to the West End early to get Maria more presents. Some DVDs, old Roger Corman films, and some not-so-old Corman-produced movies like *Sharktopus*. I also got a photo book about the LA rock underground of the 1970s, *Live At The Masque: Nightmare In Punk Alley* by Brendan Mullen. While I was shopping for Maria I got a text asking if we could meet at 7.15pm. She needed a little more time to dry and style her hair.

At 7.45pm I got a message telling me to go to the movie on my own and Maria would meet me there.

Christopher B Stokes' *The Helpers* was very average contemporary horror fare. Young friends on a road trip break down near a motel run by a bunch of psychos who are out to have fun murdering them. Torture-porn comedy of this type bored me. I wouldn't have cared if I was sitting next to Maria, but I wasn't. When the film was over I checked my phone, and there was a message from her telling me not to leave, she'd be with me soon. It was her birthday so I couldn't be angry. When Maria arrived we kissed and she apologised for being late.

'I love your red hair,' I told Maria.

'I'm not happy with it,' she replied. 'That's why I'm so late, I kept trying to fix it.'

'It looks great to me.'

'Let's get outta this place.'

'What do you wanna do?'

'Shall we go for a drink in the pub across the road?'

'It's your birthday and I'll do whatever you want, but I'd rather walk around a bit. I've been sitting down for too long watching that movie.'

'Okay let's stroll.'

So we walked hand in hand around Bloomsbury, Maria obsessing about her age and looks, while I told her she was beautiful.

'The darker I have my hair the older it makes me appear. That's why I wanted it red, but I'm not happy with it like this either.'

'You look fabulous.'

'No I don't. I'll never get used to how crap being old is. I've got lots of wrinkles and I look so tired all the time.'

'You don't look tired, you just feel tired coz you never sleep properly.'

'I really need to put on weight so that my face gets round again and my cheeks regain the volume they've lost coz of my teeth being extracted. I've lost so much bone and muscle from my face that I'm considering having Restylane filler injections so that I can look normal again.'

'How many times do I have to tell you that you look fantastic. I love and want you just the way you are.'

'Getting older depresses me. I wish we'd met ten years ago. There's nothing I can do about ageing other than get used to it, but that's really hard for me. I was so fresh and sexy into my early thirties. Of course my life of excess doesn't help. I really should stop doing drugs and make sure I sleep properly.'

'It would be great if you did that, but I can't make you, and I love you regardless. But if you cut the uppers and downers it would make me super happy. It'd kill me if you died the way my mother did. I know you won't OD, but that doesn't mean I don't get paranoid about it sometimes.'

'I'm sorry you lost your mother so young and sorry for moaning so much, but it is my birthday. I'm not really vain, but I'm a woman and I like to look good. I'm seeing my hairdresser on Saturday, she'll give me a great fringe and layers. Right now my hair is too long and looks horrible. You'll see a big difference once it's cut the way I want it.'

'I like your hair now. And hey, it's your birthday so you can moan as much as you like.'

Maria: I've got the keys to another flat, but there's a cat there. However, it's better than my pad coz the cat isn't sick and can stay in the living room. Plus there aren't piles of books on the floor that can't be moved.

Me: That sounds great. Let's go there. Tomorrow?

Maria: I'll send you the address. Yesterday it was the anniversary of my dad's death. This time of year really depresses me. First I find myself a year older, then that anniversary, next its Xmas. My dad died in 1989. I know that's a long time ago, but it still hurts.

I didn't hear from Maria again until early on Boxing Day. Most places are closed on that day but the Highbury Fields local authority gym was open. I did a cardio workout. I liked the Life Fitness equipment, particularly the mountain climber, perhaps the hardest piece of cardio equipment there is, and strangely it wasn't very popular despite the place being crowded with people either avoiding Christmas or trying rectify too much food and alcohol the day before by burning calories. I checked my phone in the changing room and found a message from Maria asking if I could meet her at 3.30pm. At 3.25pm I found myself waiting outside 54a King Henry's Walk. Maria arrived at 3.30pm on the dot, out of breath from cycling.

'I can't believe you're here before me, I so wanted to be first and wait for you,' Maria panted.

'It doesn't matter. We're both here now.'

'Just let me put the bike inside and feed the cat. Then let's find somewhere to eat.'

We went into the bottom half of a terraced house that had been divided into two flats. It was painted white inside. You could tell a woman lived in the place from the shoes lined up in the hallway. There was a living room at the front; the kitchen, bathroom and bedroom were at the back. The cat seemed spooked by me but was happy when Maria put her food out.

'Hey, I brought clean sheets and towels and everything we need when I fed the cat yesterday. Now I'm gonna put the heating on so it's nice and warm for us when we come back,' Maria told me.

We walked hand in hand to Kingsland High Street and found plenty of places to eat. We took in the menus and discussed the merits of the food. Since Maria insisted she was paying I didn't want to go anywhere too fancy, but I needn't have worried coz the places that were open were cheap. We walked north towards Stoke Newington because we'd agreed somewhere Turkish would be best. In the end we hit on the Istanbul Restaurant at the bottom of Stoke Newington Road. It advertised itself as classic Turkish cuisine prepared in traditional ovens. It had a bright interior with brash Turkish murals on the walls. A bunch of Turkish families eating there acted as a thumbs-up. Bread and salad came with the menu. We ordered mixed olives and stuffed vine leaves as starters. These arrived promptly with our drinks – ayran, a cold yogurt beverage mixed with salt, for me and pineapple juice for Maria. Once we'd ordered, Maria pulled a tarot pack from her bag.

'Hey, look at this, it's a Swiss *JJ* pack,' Maria said as she handed me the deck.

'What does *JJ* stand for?' I asked.

'The Roman gods Jupiter and Junon, they've replaced The Pope and Papess in this deck to avoid winding up hardcore Protestants and equally hardcore Catholics. That stuff was still a bit of an issue in the areas where these cards circulated in the nineteenth century.'

'I've found Jupiter,' I said.

The cards were clean looking with crisp figures and bright colours. The titles were in French. They were clearly a *Marseilles* variant that had been souped up and stripped down for a nineteenth-century audience. The Fool, for example, had lost his bundle of belongings and the animal accompanying him. Le Mat looked more like The Joker from a standard pack of cards than the tarot figure he was supposed to represent.

'What do you think?' Maria asked.

'As a pack it's okay, but it's way too masculine. I'm not sure if the third figure beneath Cupid on The Lovers is an old man or an old woman, but the lion tamer on Strength has definitely been transposed to a bloke.'

'You're so funny. Why don't you pick a card?'

'Because I know what I'll get.'

'Do it anyway.'

So I shuffled the pack, and neither of us was surprised when I pulled out The Lovers. I handed the cards to Maria and she shuffled them. We were both expecting her to pull out The Lovers too, but she didn't, she pulled out Death.

'That's what you get for being so into goth culture,' I joked.

'I'm gonna make you love Nick Cave,' Maria shot back.

We were spared further discussion of the card – which never

signifies death but merely change – by the arrival of our main courses. Falafel served with hummus and garlic for Maria. I had türlü tava, which was a mixed-vegetable dish – fried aubergine, tomatoes, potatoes, red and green peppers. It came with rice, salad and sauces. Maria only ate about half of her main course and got me to eat the rest.

'I'm skinny but I'm like a snake; when I eat my stomach bulges out. I can't eat much at once. You have to finish it for me.'

By the time I'd cleaned the plate we both felt stuffed. A total cheat meal. We had a Turkish coffee before we left. The excitement coming off us as we walked hand in hand back to King Henry's Walk must have been visible from miles away. It felt to me like we were burning with electricity. Once we got into the house we went straight to the bedroom and Maria pulled my clothes off as we French kissed. Once I was naked she pushed me down on the bed, whipped her pants off and got on top of me. She was still wearing most of her clothes. Her skirt was hitched up so I could see her stockings and suspenders. I wanted to take things slowly, but Maria was just going for it. It was only a matter of minutes before she had an orgasm. She pulled off her skirt, and we curled up together under the duvet. It felt great being there with Maria, just kissing and caressing each other.

Maria: Sorry I wasn't at my best yesterday. I've been doing lots of shit since my birthday. That's why you didn't hear from me for days and I blew my chance of spending Xmas with you. I didn't see anyone. I just had my own private slumber party. You don't need to say anything. I think you guessed and so didn't ask me why I hadn't arranged to meet on Xmas day as we'd planned. Now I'm trying to be a good girl. I haven't used any smack today and I feel terrible. I'm so ashamed of myself. I've tried so hard to stay clean, especially since I met you, but I never manage at this time of year. I wanted to tell you how great it was seeing you yesterday. With most people I get bored with their company after a few hours, but I could spent days hanging out with you and still really dig it. Tomorrow my mood will improve. I'm going to bed. I just need to take a couple of pills and rest. And don't worry, the pills were prescribed by my doctor.

Me: Hey, don't feel bad. We had a fabulous time even if you'd been naughty. It was great being with you. If I don't hear from you I figure it's best not to ask why. I know getting clean isn't easy, my mother struggled so much with it. I'm just happy and impressed that you're trying so hard to quit. You're doing much better than you think, and I'm super proud of you. But please go to the gym when you feel better. I want to get you addicted to exercise like me. You'll feel much more together when you've slept.

Maria: I feel like I've been living in a cloud. Today I feel a bit more like myself.

Me: You were great on Boxing Day, but you're even better when you're not hopped up. I can't wait to see you again.

Maria: You'll see me when I've totally recovered. This afternoon I went to Beyond Retro on my way to feed the cat in Dalston. While I was there I bought myself another waspie. It's a waist cincher corset that's steel boned. It's really well made with rods that don't bend as you move. I'll wear it for you next time I see you. And I'd really like you to wear it – just once, please – for me. Now I'm straight I can see how selfish I was on Boxing Day. As soon as you made me come I didn't want to fuck any more, and I knew you weren't finished. But I just wanted to take a break. I feel like I haven't given you enough loving, sorry. Can you meet me next week at my work? I'll be fully recovered from my relapse by then. I've found a great new place to eat. They do a fabulous pomegranate, feta and almond salad, and wonderful vegetable quiche too. I'm sorry I haven't been in a good way over the holiday when we could have been together if I'd not been smacked up. People think I'm elusive coz often when I say I'll be somewhere I don't make it. I'm volatile, so if my mood changes I don't show. Sometimes I just need to evaporate and disappear. I can't even explain where I was or why it took me so long to come back. And my mood can flip so easily, so I'll be gone before anybody knows it. But I'll always turn up for you – even if I'm late. And when like now I'm in no fit state to see you I'll tell you and you have to accept that. If you were with me this evening I'd get you to eat twelve grapes at midnight, but I should stay in bed. No more shit for a while. I've had too many friends accidentally kill themselves with an overdose. I want to be fit and healthy in my old age.

Me: Can't I see you sooner? I can come to Old Street.

Maria: I'll meet you in Church Street but not until Saturday. I wanna be at my best when I see you. I need time to recover.

After I'd settled in Naz with my double espresso I checked my phone. There was a text from Maria saying she was running late. Eventually we kissed, and I got more coffees. While I was getting the drinks, Maria had pulled a tarot deck from her bag.

'This is a restored *Jean Dodal Tarot* from 1701,' Maria informed me as she pushed the cards across the table.

I picked them up, and looking through I could see this was a traditional *Tarot de Marseille*. The colours were vibrant but restricted in number to eight if you count black and white as colours, otherwise there were only six. The engravings were expressive with a lot of emotion evident in the faces. Sorrow was more prominent than beauty.

'These cards are great,' I told Maria.

'I knew you were gonna like them. Pick a card.'

'But I always get The Lovers.'

'Well you can't in this deck coz card six is La Movrev.'

'You're right,' I said after I'd flicked through the pack and found it, 'but it still looks like The Lovers.'

'Choose a card.'

I did as I was told and was surprised when I pulled out La Pances – which being card two would more normally be titled The Papess or High Priestess.

'What does it mean?' I asked.

'Nobody knows what La Pances means. But that card isn't me, I'm La Emperatriz. So you'll have to watch yourself or I'll get jealous. I won't allow another woman in your life.'

'Now you're taking tarot no more seriously than me.'

'We both take it seriously. We always have done and always will.'

'In that case you'd better pick a card.'

Maria pulled out trump seventeen, which in this pack was titled Le Toille but to me was The Star. It featured the traditional nude woman pouring water from two jugs onto land and into a river.'

'Don't take it literally,' Maria said, 'use your intuition to tell me what it means.'

'The woman on this card has a distended belly. Does that mean she's pregnant?'

'Yes.'

'But I'm not gonna get you knocked up.'

'It seems unlikely.'

'From my encounters with you I'm gonna become a new man and discover who I really am.'

Maria leant over and kissed me. I was now saying back to her what she'd long been telling me. That we'd always been together. Maria put the cards away and insisted on paying for our coffees. We walked hand in hand around Stoke Newington. We didn't need to speak. We were just so perfect together. My response to the card was purely intuitive but then Maria saw that as a perfectly valid way of interpreting tarot, she wasn't fixated on traditional meanings. My words could have come from Maria's mouth, so we didn't need to talk about the card or what it meant in any detail, we both knew we were intended to be together. Talking about what we'd finally agreed upon that winter afternoon was the only thing that could have undone its magic.

Maria: I asked my friend Lola from Murcia if we could go to her house on Saturday and use her room. She said it isn't a problem. She goes clubbing at the weekend, so it's perfect for us. I want you to stand on your head for me again. I'm gonna make you come upside down. I want to see pearls of spunk run down your stomach and chest. I'd like to see some of that white stuff splatter onto your face too.

Me: That sounds great.

Maria: The house is in Stamford Hill, so we should meet somewhere near you. Lola said her flatmate is going to Edinburgh tomorrow so we'll have the whole place to ourselves coz she'll be out all night. Are you ready to do that nude headstand for me? You can expect a lot of teasing. Before I give you a blow job I'll tickle you to see if I can make you fall over. Judging from what happened last time you're quite strong and will be able to take it and stay upside down. But I'm really gonna have a lot of fun trying to make you tumble. And if everything else fails I'm gonna bite your arse. If you fall over then it's a forfeit and you have to let me sink my teeth into that fabulous firm arse of yours. So whatever happens I'm gonna nip your fine round bum.

Me: Can we meet about 6pm outside the Daniel Defoe? I can come with my scooter and a spare helmet. And I came across this word – candaulism, when a person exposes his or her partner in a sexually explicit manner. I think that's what you do with me sometimes.

Maria: I've never heard of candaulism before, but I don't think it correctly describes me coz I like doing sexual things with you in front of other people but have them not notice. You need a different word for that.

XI

LA FORCE

STRENGTH

Maria arrived in Church Street a few minutes after me. She got on the back of my scooter, and it was great to feel her breasts pressed against my back as she directed me to Lola's pad, which was on a back street behind Stamford Hill train station. The flat was on two stories in a brick terrace. The kitchen was decorated with posters for punk gigs – Rebellion in Blackpool and for acts like Cock Sparrer and the English Dogs. Maria made coffee as soon as we got in. She directed me to Lola's bedroom on the top floor. I stripped off, and when I heard Maria coming up the stairs with our beverages, I got into a headstand.

'Wow! What a great surprise!' Maria laughed as she came into the room.

Maria put the tray she was carrying in a corner, came over to me and licked my erection. She gave me a ten-minute suck. Finally she started to shake my manhood.

'Hey, don't make me come yet,' I said as Maria brought me right to the edge of orgasm, 'I wanna fuck you on the bed.'

'You're so cheeky and such a cheat. I'd really like to see your spunk dripping all over your face, but maybe we can do that later. Before you come off your head, I'm gonna bite your butt.'

So that's what happened. When I got out of my headstand we lay down. At first we kissed and teased each other. Finally Maria let me remove her trousers and panties. When I squeezed her tits I did so through her T-shirt. The skin on Maria's neck was exposed and whenever I kissed her there she went bananas. I didn't bite Maria, but she nipped me and soon I was covered in bruises.

'Hey, don't come, I wanna make you come when you're standing on your head.'

Maria's words came too late. She'd already had several orgasms and I couldn't hold back any longer. Afterwards we cuddled up. Then we slept.

Maria: I really wanted to go to the gym, but it was so cold tonight that I came home. I was frozen from my cycle ride. Yesterday I did some exercises I found in a magazine. They're short intense circuits. I'm gonna show them to you. I wanted to do abs with a Swiss ball coz I get tired doing crunches and I'm scared in case I fuck my neck. But I don't have a Swiss ball at home.

Me: You can get a Swiss ball from TK Maxx or Argos and loads of other places. You'll easily get one for £10. Or I can buy one for you. You need a 55cm ball, a 65cm is too big. But don't be fooled, it's harder doing abs on a ball than the floor coz it destabilises you. And if you do crunches right they won't hurt your neck coz it shouldn't be involved – support your head with your hands if you need to. There's a lot more than crunches that you can do on the ball. I can show you many moves. But also don't forget you're bent over a desk all day editing, so crunches aren't what you need to focus on since they take you into a position you already spend too much time in. I can show you some better abdominal exercises, and I want to strengthen your lower back and all the muscles around it. We won't go crazy on working the back coz you need to be careful with it when it's a bit weak, but give me time and we'll sort everything. I'll balance out all your muscle groups and make your spine super healthy.

Maria: I'm more concerned about how my stomach looks, I'm happy enough with my spine. Can I meet you at the Horse Hospital around 8pm on Thursday? I have to work until 7.30pm. I'll be there before the film begins. I promise. Please go early and get us seats at the back. Now I really have to go coz I gotta get up early tomorrow. Au. That's Valenciano for bye.

I arrived early for the Horse Hospital screening. It was no longer the Horror Club, the sponsor was now *Bizarre* magazine and the event had been renamed *Cut!* I had to sit around for half an hour before the screening, but I'd got seats at the back so that Maria and I could make out rather than watch the movie. My phone was soon buzzing with texts from Maria saying that the burglar alarm had malfunctioned when she was putting it on and she had to stay at the office to sort things out. She promised to get to me soon but wouldn't arrive for the start of the screening.

The preview was for *Wrong Turn 5*, a typical slasher about a bunch of mutant cannibal killers who attack teenagers attending the Mountain Man rock festival. The official UK release of the film was four days after this preview. It was a drag not having Maria beside me during the screening. She finally arrived after it was over. In the free raffle at the end I won a DVD copy of the movie I'd just seen. I offered it to Maria, but she wasn't interested in seeing the film. We quickly moved on to the Friend At Hand. Maria was super apologetic about leaving me to watch a movie on my own again. She was with me now, so I no longer cared and the conversation moved on.

'Kids today are so lucky,' Maria whispered in my ear as she snuggled up against me. 'Imagine if we'd had access to cameras and all the other equipment they've got now when we were teenagers.'

'I didn't even have a stills camera, let alone a movie camera.'

'Me neither,' Maria confirmed. 'And I was always role-playing with my friends and re-enacting all kinds of stuff from movies. Imagine if I'd been able to film it.'

'You'd have made something like *Kárate A Muerte En Torremolinos*.'

'When you say anything Spanish,' Maria laughed, 'it comes out so wrong.'

'I only said that coz I'm pretty sure I know how to say karate and Torremolinos, and I thought I knew how to say *muerte* coz I've seen so many Spanish horror flicks with English subtitles.'

'One day I'm gonna teach you to pronounce Spanish words properly. It'll take a long time and I'll enjoy correcting you.'

'I bet you will. Correction would help. So far you've just got me to say odd Spanish words over and over and laughed at how I pronounce them.'

'I'm laughing with you, not at you. The British are so lazy about languages.'

'My English ain't bad; it's nearly as good as yours,' I countered.

'Hey, did you know that Pedro Temboury, the director of *Kárate A Muerte En Torremolinos,* made another film called *Ellos Robaron La Picha De Hitler*?'

'What does that mean?'

'*They Saved Hitler's Cock.*'

'I know that as a tune by the Angry Samoans.'

'That's where the title comes from. You can see the whole movie online, but it's in Spanish.'

'Looks like you're gonna have to spend a long time teaching me Castilian. There're so many Spanish directors who have a few of their movies dubbed into English, and I'd like to see the rest of what they made.'

'Name one we haven't talked about.'

'Francisco Lara Polop.'

'You make me laugh so much,' Maria was nearly crying, 'your Spanish pronunciation is so bad.'

'But do you know who I mean?'

'Of course I do. Polop was born in the same part of Valencia as me, up in the mountains, away from the city.'

'His first film *Murder Mansion* is really great, a gothic horror with some Italian *giallo* influences. The cinematography is fantastically atmospheric and the old dark Spanish house vibe is a groove.'

'That's *La Mansión De La Niebla*. I like it a lot too.'

'What about his second movie *Forbidden Passion*?'

'You mean *Cebo Para Una Adolescente*?'

'I think so.'

'That's just a melodrama.'

'Sure, but it's simultaneously a critique of Francoism. The fifteen-year-old secretary played by Ornella Muti represents the people and the boss who seduces her the regime. When Muti finds a guy her own age the boss blackmails her into continuing the relationship. It has the feel of Eloy de la Iglesia's *Cannibal Man* without the more gruesome elements. But both flicks are savage critiques of Franco.'

'*Cebo Para Una Adolescente* was very successful. People wanted change, and it came just a few years after the flick was released. I guess the fact films like that even got a release was a sign of transformations going on under the surface. What else have you seen by Polop?'

'Not much. *Christina* with Jewel Shepherd, but that's shit.'

'He only made *El Fraile* after that and then became a tour guide at the El Escorial Monastery. Maybe that was even more of a pact with the devil than the one in *El Fraile*.'

'That last film was released on VHS in the UK as *The Final Temptation* and *Seduction Of A Priest* but I've never seen it.'

'I think you'd like it more than seeing Jewel Shepherd kidnapped and ravished by lesbian separatists. But not that much more. *La Mansión De La Niebla* is his best flick. It's a shame *Cebo Para Una Adolescente* was such a big hit in Spain; if it had flopped he'd have probably gone back to making horror films.'

Maria: Have I told you that at work I often edit porn? Is it normal that porn doesn't turn me on? Am I weird? I don't like all the spitting instead of lube. I guess I'm not punk enough. I've also noticed many of the girls – way too many of them – have really elongated labias. Perhaps it's because huge things are always being inserted into them. And it ain't just cocks. I should know coz I have to edit this shit. I'm very happy with my pussy being smaller, tidier and much more beautiful than any gash I've seen on a porn star. I'm thinking of having IPL laser treatment on my bikini line so I don't have to shave the sides, but I'll still have a bit of hair to play with if I want to. And going back to the porn I edit, just looking at the size of the cocks on most of the guys, I know that if they shagged me it would be really painful. They say size matters. Of course it does, but big doesn't mean better. Not for me anyway. Big is painful, medium is perfect.

Me: You're not weird. The porn you edit is aimed at men. It ain't for you.

Maria: I'm not going to work today. I feel terrible. This afternoon I've got an appointment with a specialist in Harley Street. I need a medical examination so the lawyers can finalise the accident compensation I'm getting. Do you remember me telling you about an old lady smashing into a taxi I was in? I decided I'd make a claim coz I need the money.

Me: I hope you're feeling better.

Maria: I am. I've got the keys to the flat in Dalston. I'm feeding the cat again this weekend. Do you wanna go there tomorrow?

I sent Maria a text telling her I'd be at King Henry's Walk at 5.45pm. I arrived on time and checked my phone. There was a message asking if we could meet at 6.15pm. It wasn't worth going home, so I just hung around. Maria arrived at 6.15pm, but she'd forgotten the keys to the flat. She wanted to go home and get them, but I told her we should get a coffee instead. We went to Beyond Retro.

'It's strange, this is when I'd normally pull out a pack of tarot cards to show you, but I didn't bring any today coz I thought we'd be in the flat fucking,' Maria said.

'But don't you usually carry a pack of tarot cards with you?'

'Yeah, but the two decks I've got you've already seen. Today I'm carrying close friends.'

'Who are?'

'A mini *Tarot de Marsella*. I showed it to you in the Masque Haunt.'

'What's the other one?'

'My Spanish major-arcana-only deck, with the crude drawings and wild colours that you saw in the Slice Of Life.'

'I remember that deck, it's great. I saw that the first summer I knew you.'

'It was 10 June 2011 in Smithfield Market.'

'Wow, you know everything.'

'You do too, you just have to do some more remembering.'

'So you're not gonna show me those decks again?'

'No.'

'Have you got anything else to show me?'

'I'm gonna show you some porno I edited that's up online. You can see it on my phone.'

After handing me her mobile, Maria grabbed my cock. I found myself studying a pegging video, and the guy getting the strap-on up his butt sure looked like he was enjoying it.

'Do you like it?' Maria asked.

'The editing is fantastic,' I told her, 'you're brilliant.'

'Ha ha. But just imagine if I was doing that to you. I know you're gonna love it when I do.'

Maria showed me a couple more porn pieces she'd edited, mainly so that she could point out how the actresses' pussies had been twisted out of shape. I had a hard-on but not from the sex movies; what got me hot and bothered was the way Maria was manipulating my manhood with her hand. One of the women working in the shop started looking at us so we stopped petting and checked out some of their clothes. Maria wanted to buy me a 1960s button-down shirt, but what they had was not great in terms of either design or condition. We looked at some dresses too, but Maria couldn't find anything suitable, so we sat down and had another coffee.

'Don't be too long,' the woman who brought our drinks said, 'the shop should already be closed.'

We started getting intimate again, and the women running the place looked the other way this time. They cleared our cups once we'd finished our coffee. Even after the table had been wiped down there were a handful of other customers in the store, but eventually it was just us pawing each other. So we had to leave. I told Maria to wait for me in the street. I rode my scooter home to get a spare helmet. Then I took Maria to her place to pick up her key.

Maria: I can't believe I forgot the fucking key. When we were sitting on the sofa in Beyond Retro and I could feel how hard your cock was in my hand and you were telling me how much you wanted to fuck me, I nearly dragged you into the toilet. I could have pulled down your pants and sat down on top of you. The only thing that stopped me was how closely the women working there looked at us when we were getting fresh. I'm sure they'd have called the cops if we'd both gone in the loo together. But if we had I'm sure I'd have come as soon as I felt the tip of your dick in my pussy. Good lord look at me thinking of fucking the moment I'm close to you. The effect you have on me is the same as a super-potent aphrodisiac.

Me: Well look what you do to me, you turn me into a sex maniac too.

Maria: Once we got in the flat I thought you were gonna bite my neck, but you didn't. Next time? I'd like a little mark to remind me of you when you're gone. I love it when you surprise me. Like when we've been saying goodbye but instead of leaving you've kissed me, then pulled my shirt up and sucked my tits. Lately I've been having this fantasy about you. You come and grab me from behind, with one hand on my tits and the other on my pussy opening the lips and pressing my clit. I get wet every time I think of it. I like the idea of you being totally in control but losing it completely when you start fucking me.

Me: I always lose control when I fuck you.

Maria: I've been thinking about becoming a madam. I'd really like to host the best bacchanales ever. I'd find the most beautiful girls from the four corners of the earth. I'd treat them fairly and with respect. I wouldn't exploit them. I'd let them keep at least half of the money they made. I'd like to restrict the parties to once a month with a very rich clientele. They'd be themed with all the girls dressed like Vestal Virgins or 1920s style with short wigs like Louise Brooks in *Pandora's Box*, or girls in mini-skirts who look like they've stepped out of a 1970s exploitation movie. I'm sure there are brothels where they are doing stuff like this already, but my bacchanales will be better. I'll spend all the money I make setting up animal sanctuaries in Spain. I'll rescue as many animals as I can and give jobs to my cruelty hating friends. There are hardly any good jobs in Spain now so I know plenty of people who need the work. I've been feverish today but there's nothing wrong with lucid dreaming. I had several delirious encounters with you too. Then I got insomnia again tonight. I went to bed but I couldn't sleep so I watched another movie. It's nearly six in the morning, and I think I'm just about ready to nod off at last. Are you still up for meeting me at lunchtime?

I arrived at Maria's office at 1pm. Before I got up from the street she'd disappeared into the toilet to fix her make-up. Her colleagues were friendly. Once Maria was happy with her face, we held hands as we walked slowly to Brew For Two at 101 Morning Lane. It was a homey place with a mix of dishes from around the world. There was a garden at the back, but we sat by the front window. Maria had baked halloumi on vegetables, while I had warm quinoa and six-bean salad.

'Hey,' Maria said, 'I want you to look at his tarot pack.'

'Ah,' I replied as I took in the Valet de Baton, who was on top, 'the *Oswald Wirth* deck of 1889, which some view as the first in a long line of occult tarots, but only because they've dismissed the various *Etteilla* packs as mere divinatory diversions.'

'How do you know that?' Maria asked.

'Haven't you shown me this deck before?'

'No, not in this life.'

'Are you sure?'

'One hundred percent.'

'You must have, otherwise how would I know what it is?'

'You're remembering from a previous life.'

'Maybe I've seen it somewhere else.'

'You've seen it before alright but before you reincarnated this time.'

I didn't want to argue, so we just discussed the deck. It was basically a modified *Tarot de Marseille*, incorporating occult elements including the twenty-two letters of the Hebrew alphabet on the major arcana as a nod to the theories of Eliphas Levi. The cards were printed in metallic colours because Wirth wanted them to look like medieval illuminations. I knew all this already although I don't know how. We did some readings with the cards over lunch and, naturally, however we dealt them they told us we were destined to be together. Even after we'd finished our meal, the deck had been put away and we were walking down Mare Street, they remained the subject of our conversation.

'The *Wirth* deck always makes me feel a little sad,' Maria told me.

'Why?'

'C'mon, you know why. You can't keep pretending to me you don't remember.'

'Because Wirth when working as a mesmerist put a patient in a hypnotic trance and this subject made predictions about the other man's destiny. That Wirth would receive an invitation from an aristocrat and when the two men met it would change his life. The invitation came, it was from Stanislas de Guaita, and Wirth became his secretary. They became great friends and intellectual companions with de Guaita instructing Wirth to make his tarot. How do I know all this?'

'I'd told you this before you were born this time around. Now tell me what's sad about the story.'

'Stanislas de Guaita was obsessed by the occult and

Rosicrucian brotherhoods. He was the most famous decadent caricatured by JK Huysmans in the novel *Là-Bas*. Like a number of other decadents, de Guaita experimented with drugs and became a morphine addict, dying of an overdose at the age of thirty-six.'

'Which,' Maria said to conclude our story, 'deprived Wirth of his best friend and the only paid work he ever had that he considered a joy rather than a drudgery.'

By this time we'd walked past the town hall and into the main Hackney library. We were able to see into the room that had hosted *Stamford Hill Mods: The Genesis Of Marc Bolan*, an exhibition Maria had so wanted me to visit but I'd missed. The display was in the process of being packed up, but some of it was still visible. From there we moved on to Maria's gym, Energise, which was housed above the library. I showed her how to programme various machines and some moves she might do off them using either free weights or her body weight. Unfortunately we ran out of time all too quickly. I had a client and Maria had to get back to work. That didn't stop us indulging in long lingering kisses before I hopped on my scooter.

Maria: I'm about to watch *Sons Of Anarchy*. I know you think all TV is crap and you don't dig motorbikes and are quite happy with your little scooter. But *Sons Of Anarchy* makes me think of being young coz that's when I hung out with all the bikers in Valencia. I was the only girl who was allowed to ride their hogs. None of them let their girlfriends ride them, just me. They thought I'd return such favours by jumping into bed with them. They were such dreamers. You know at lunch when I felt your cock getting all hard in your pants it really drove me crazy. I nearly pulled it out so that I could kiss it. I would have done if there hadn't been an old guy at the next table looking right at us. Oh boy I want you so much. All this waiting. It's driving me mad.

Me: The waiting just makes it better. You must have been an amazing dominatrix with all that tease.

Maria: It wasn't just tease. I took the virginity of a nineteen-year-old. He was half my age when I did it. But he didn't fuck me. I fucked him. I had a big strap-on. It was his first sexual experience. There were other times when I thought I should have been paying the john because I enjoyed myself so much. But those thoughts didn't stop me taking their money. I'm sure I've already told you how turned on I became when I was giving a guy irrumation. Would you like me to fuck you in the mouth with a big strap-on? Please don't think I'm perverted or I'm gonna regret telling you this. And about your desire to tie me up, nobody has ever done that to me and I'm forty-four. What would you do to me if I let you do that? Think carefully before you answer coz if I like what you say you'll become the only man I ever let restrain me during sex.

Me: I just want to tie your hands and fuck you when you're helpless, make you suck my cock a little while I'm above you.

Maria: If you want to do anything else you better tell me. You're not allowed to do anything we haven't agreed in advance. Today I'm happy coz two of my oldest friends from the Hells Angels sent me emails with plans for when I next visit Valencia. They have a very low Harley Davidson specially customized for a small girl like me. And the reason I took a while to get back to you, I didn't sleep at all at the weekend. I took some really strong amphetamines on Friday night and I was still awake on Monday. I went more than seventy-two hours without sleep. I had to take the day off work yesterday, and I slept for twenty hours without waking up once. Today I feel better, but as soon as I finish work I'm going to bed. You know how I am when I feel anti-social and just have to switch off. Either I sleep or I watch three or four films back to back. This morning the postman brought a card from my gym saying: 'We miss you. Please come back or give us a call so we can book you a free personal training session…'

Me: Hey, I'm so glad you're here now. Please go to the gym and get going with your training. You just need your kit. Pack it the night before like I told you. Towel, shower gel, deodorant, change of underwear and socks, trainers, T-shirt and shorts (or tracksuit bottoms). Then you don't have the excuse of not having time to get your stuff together in the morning or forgetting to pack it. Can I see you soon?

Maria: I'll go to the gym tomorrow after work and book my free personal trainer. Last time I went in the evening it was full of very fit young guys, but aside from me there wasn't a woman in sight. I'll meet you in a day or two, but you can't see me looking like an old lady. After I've stayed up for days I look terrible, and now I'm in my forties my body takes so long to recover. One day soon I want to show you Valencia and the places I grew up. I have a flat and a house just 40km from the city. There isn't a beach but we have a beautiful lake for swimming. There are so many lakes and caves and other amazing places to go. But if you like the beach my sister Esther has an apartment in Oliva. There are plenty of sand dunes there too, so we can easily find a nice spot on a beach that is very private.

Time passed, and I went back to Toulouse for a while. I exchanged messages with Maria, and when she wasn't recovering from a drug high I would get to see her. Usually I'd go to her flat and ring up for her. On the specific night I'm thinking of, she came down after fifteen minutes and we kissed. With Maria in my arms everything just felt right. Soon after we found a sofa to sit on at the Masque Haunt and I got Maria a coffee. I didn't want to drink espresso so late because it would keep me awake, so I had a pint of tap water with ice and lemon. While I was at the bar Maria had pulled some things from her bag.

'I love this *Re/Search Pranks* book,' she said as she handed it to me. 'Don't read it now, I want you to borrow it. It really makes me laugh; it'll make you laugh too.'

Then Maria spent a bit of time showing me a yoga book for

couples. It had various erotic poses, and she pointed out the ones she'd most like us to try together.

'We can work on those,' I said, 'but it'll take a bit of effort to get them right. Maybe we should both do some yoga classes.'

'I get yoga classes included in my gym membership.'

'Maybe I can come and do some with you.'

'I bet it's nearly all chicks at the yoga classes. You better not look at anyone in there but me, even if some of the girls are really hot.'

'No one is as hot as you.'

Maria kissed me and put the yoga book away, then she handed me a pack of cards.

'What are these?' I asked.

'You know.'

'The *Amado 777 Tarot*. But don't tell me I know that because I can remember them from a previous life. There's some crude computer manipulations on these drawings so they were obviously done well after I was born this time around.'

'So you admit it, you do remember your previous lives.'

'If you told me the moon was made of cheese I'd believe it. So how do I know about these cards?'

'We're opened up to each other. What I know, you know. We're psychic twins and you know everything I do.'

'So do you wanna know what I think of these cards?'

'I know you think the drawings are stupid and ugly. And you were humouring me by talking about the look of the cards as a means of dating them. You knew exactly when they were produced because every card has the date 1999 printed on it.'

'So which card do I dislike the most?'

'That's a trick question. There are two cards you particularly hate. The four of cups because it has a large swastika on it and The Lovers because you find the figures on it antiquated and ugly.'

'And why do I find this pack silly.'

'You don't believe the claims of the guy who made it who says he is the illegitimate son of Aleister Crowley, and you think he's bullshitting when he claims it's based on an ancient gypsy pack handed down through his family for hundreds of years.'

'Well you can see the trumps are influenced by the *Rider-Waite-Smith* deck from the beginning of the twentieth century. The suits are less conventional, especially the additional ones of crowns and acorns, and they're also very silly. The five extra trumps vary in quality. I can dig the hermaphrodite figure on Zany even if it is badly drawn, but the Ku Klux Klan figures on the Question card suck.'

'You know this deck is a novelty, don't you,' Maria put in.

'We'll never get a good reading out of it! And 111, numerologically that's overly conventional too.'

'One plus one plus one. It's the trinity,' Maria observed.

'Psychic twin,' I said as I kissed Maria softly on her neck.

We spent a long time laughing at the Amado Crowley cards. After closing time the bar staff had to hustle us out of the Masque Haunt. Maria led me back to her block. I thought she was gonna take me up to her flat, but we stopped on the steps. Maria explained yet again that she couldn't take me into her pad because of her blind cat. We had sex on the stairs then spent a long time talking.

Maria: Can you believe I haven't been to bed yet and I have to go to work. The night before I only slept for a couple of hours. I did some more of the super-strong speed I'm scoring at the moment, that's why I talked so much last night. I hope I can survive eight hours of work.

Me: Please sleep as much as you can. I'll see you in a day or two.

Maria: All the sleep I've been missing really caught up with me. Tonight I got home at 7pm, and as soon as I sat down on the sofa I dozed off. I've only just woken up, and I'm happy coz tomorrow is the weekend. Can we go to the cinema?

I met Maria outside the Vue in Leicester Square. We were there for Quentin Tarantino's *Django Unchained* and were seated before the film trailers started. We held hands and drank the coffees we'd bought with our tickets. Maria, as she so often did, offered me mints and chewing gum. As usual I refused. She used the mints to cover the smell of tobacco on her breath and the gum was just her thing. It was great just sitting there with Maria, so I didn't really care what I was watching. But *Django Unchained* wasn't bad, just not nearly as good as the original *Django* movie from 1966 or its sequels and rip-offs. It dealt with slavery and revenge in the American south before the civil war in a mostly comic book way. It drew on the heritage of spaghetti westerns without being entirely beholden to them. Maria and I laughed hard and long when an aged Franco Nero, star of the original *Django*, asked the Django character in Tarantino's movie his name. A large part of the audience seemed to miss the joke.

'Are you glad you saw *Django Unchained*?' Maria asked as we got up from our seats.

'Yeah, but I enjoyed being next to you more. There were some nice set pieces but the movie was way too long.'

'For sure. Can you imagine a real spaghetti western that went on for two hours and forty-five minutes?'

'It would have been a way better movie if it was shorter.'

'Think how great a real spaghetti western made on a budget of a hundred million dollars would have been.'

'I've no idea what a director like Sergio Corbucci or Ernesto G Castellari would have done with that amount of money.'

'They'd have blown our minds.'

'They managed that with a lot less dosh.'

We decided to get a quick coffee before I headed off to meet a client. I took Maria to Bar San Valentino at 13a Greek Street. Here I'll mention one of her habits that I haven't recorded to date. As soon as we got out of the cinema, Maria rolled herself a cigarette – Drum tobacco in liquorice Rizla rolling papers. She hadn't had time to smoke it all by the time we arrived at Valentino, so she put it out and left it outside on the ledge of the café's window. I knew from seeing her do this before that when we came out she'd pick up the remains of her cigarette and light it again to finish her smoke. The café was tiny but was mostly used by people getting takeouts, so we had a table to ourselves for our coffee.

'You know at work the stuff they give me to edit just gets more and more bizarre.'

'What have you been doing lately?'

'All these sock and sneaker fetish videos.'

'What happens in them?'

'People sniff dirty socks or sneakers – they sometimes put the socks in their mouths. It's really disgusting.'

'It sounds unhygienic.'

'It's filthy.'

'What do you like to edit?'

'Videos of men cross-dressing. Now those turn me on, but not as much as the thought of dressing you up as a lady. You'd look great in a corset.'

'I'm not sure about that.'

'You won't know until you try. You'd be surprised, and it would really get me excited.'

XII

LE PENDU

THE HANGED MAN

Maria: I just crashed out on the sofa again. I was stroking Sidney and nodded off. After leaving you I stayed up half the night to enjoy being in love with you. I wanted to tell you some stories about Josh Collins. In the eighties he used to host sixties nights at the Frat Shack. He'd project hardcore porn behind all these hot chicks he had dancing in Swinging London gear. Sometimes it was gay sex to piss homophobes off. There were always bands there too. I didn't come to London until 1995, but I went to the Frat Shack a lot. I think the club's final night was in 1999 with the Dukes Of Hamburg playing. I wanted to tell you some of the crazy things that happened to me at the Frat Shack. I don't have time to write them down now, so I'll tell you when I see you.

Me: I remember the Frat Shack. A lot of my friends used to go there.

Maria: I've been to the dentist. The treatment hurt. I can't think straight now. But I have good news, I'm feeding the cat in Dalston. I'll message later about when we can meet.

I got to King Henry's Walk ten minutes before Maria. We kissed before she opened the door to the flat. Maria insisted we sit in the kitchen and have a cup of tea before we did anything else. When we'd finished our drinks she filled a pint glass with water to take through to the bedroom. We undressed each other. I left Maria's stockings on but removed her corset. She was beautifully shaved, as she always was when she thought there was a chance we'd get intimate. We rolled around on the bed teasing each other.

'You know,' Maria said, 'I've got some lube.'

'Am I not exciting you enough tonight?'

'The lube is for you, not for me.'

'Are you sure? I hope you don't have some huge strap-on with you.'

'No, tonight I'll just use a finger and maybe if you open up I'll move on to a couple of my digits or my thumb.'

'I dunno.'

'Listen, once you let me give you anal pleasure you'll discover you love it. When you've relaxed a bit I'll use something longer than my fingers so I can hit your G-spot and give you anal orgasms.'

'Are you sure about this?'

'I've done it professionally.'

'I know, but that was on masochists. I don't want to do it if it hurts.'

'It won't hurt, honestly. I'll gently stretch you. I'll build up slowly and you'll love it.'

The conversation went around in this way for a long time. Eventually I gave in and let Maria insert her lube slavered finger into my rectum. I was surprised by how nice it felt as she moved her greased-up digit around my anus.

'Hey, I like this,' I said.

'I told you you'd like it. I've been telling you that for ages.'

'Can you get it in any deeper?'

'No, I'm pushing in as far as I can go.'

'If you could just get it a bit further I'm sure I'd have an orgasm.'

'I don't want you to have an orgasm yet.'

We played around for quite a bit longer. Maria got into some serious frottage. She'd obviously decided I wasn't gonna slip inside her that night. She seemed to want to prove we could have a good time without male-on-female penetrative sex. We were still driving each other crazy on the bed when my ex called me because she was drunk and wanted someone to berate. While I was on the phone, Maria took my manhood in her mouth. I had a hard time doing anything but laugh, which really pissed Petra off. Maria switched from oral to hand stimulation. She'd made me come by the time my ex hung up on me.

Maria: Happy birthday, my boy. I hope you have a great day today and enjoy being fifty-one. Wow. You're not quite seven years older than me, and I can't imagine reaching fifty. It just doesn't seem possible. For most of my life I couldn't imagine being forty either. I always thought I'd blaze like a meteor and die young. But here we are, I'm forty-four and you're fifty-one. Yesterday was great. I love to feel your cock just rubbing against my pussy. That's all I wanted last night. You drive me crazy, but I wanted to prove we didn't have to have a heterosexual hump just because we could. It was great finger-fucking your arse. I'm going to take that slowly coz I don't want to hurt you. You should have seen the way Cindy, the first dominatrix I worked with, fucked guys with a strap-on. She'd tie them up and really didn't care how much she hurt them. It was awful to hear the johns begging her to stop. And the more they beseeched her the longer she kept it up. She was much more of a sadist than me. So don't worry, I'll always be gentle with you. What do you want for your birthday?

Me: All I want for my birthday is you. Why did I schedule clients all day and all evening?

Maria: Yesterday I got in from work and tried to watch a film on cable. I was too tired and fell asleep on the sofa. I woke up at 5am with a horrible feeling of foreboding, so I took a long hot bath. Now I'm getting ready to go to work and all I want is to be with you, preferably in bed with our arms wrapped around each other. You still haven't told me what you want for your birthday. Do you want to go to Ümit's shop and see what movies he's got? Just tell me.

Me: What about the Carter Stevens' *Punk Rock* sexploitation detective movie for a birthday present? It was originally a porno film, but there's a new cut with less porn and more music and that's the version I'd want. Classic 1970s New York punk rock. The more music version is on a double DVD with *The Pleasure Palace* (which doesn't interest me much). If you get it please watch it before you give it to me. You probably need a multi-region player. My cousin has one because I bought it for her.

Maria: Wow that *Punk Rock* movie looks good. I'm gonna get one for you and another for me. I want one of my own. It might be sleazy, but it looks a lot better than so much of the punk rock shit I've already got. Last night I watched *Intrépidos Punks* again. I don't know why because it is so bad and 'the punks' don't even look like punks but are basically bikers. And the actors are so ugly. No wonder I fell asleep before the end. I'm sure you must have seen it, but in case you haven't, it's a Mexican film from 1980 directed by Francisco Guerrero. I want to see you soon, like yesterday, today and tomorrow. We could meet during my lunch break and go to Umit for some extra birthday movies. Or if you can't make lunch meet me after work on a day I can finish early and there will be time to get DVDs. Tomorrow evening I'm gonna get my fringe cut and have the layers done, so once my hair is sorted you can see me any time you want. But not until then.

When I called for Maria at her Fortune Street flat she came straight down. I thought her hair looked fabulous, but I didn't say so as she'd told me in a message she thought the fringe was too short and people could see her eyes too easily. We kissed then walked hand in hand to the Masque Haunt. We found a low table with a sofa beside it. I thought it too late for double espressos, so I drank water but Maria had a cappuccino.

'Hey, I've got something to show you,' Maria said once we'd sat down.

'The lube you told me about in a message?'

'Close,' Maria replied as she pulled a tarot deck from her bag and handed it to me. 'What do you think of these?'

I looked at the cards and somehow I knew they were the *Golden Dawn Tarot* as devised by Israeli Regardie and drawn by Robert Wang. They were based on the no longer confidential teachings of the Golden Dawn, an occult society of the nineteenth century that had sworn its members to secrecy on pain of terrible retribution if they revealed any of its magical methods to non-members. Nonetheless Aleister Crowley and others published its secret teachings on the tarot and much else without suffering death at the hands of a deadly and hostile current of will set in motion by the chiefs of the order.

'You know I'm not convinced by the way in which the Golden Dawn assigned each of the twenty-two letters of the Hebrew alphabet to the major arcana, and I'm even less persuaded you can relate the cards to the tree of life as they did.'

'How do you know this is a Golden Dawn deck?'

'I just do, and I don't like the artwork on it nearly as much as that by Pamela Coleman Smith on the *RWS* deck. I don't even like it as much as the *Thoth* deck because while Lady Frieda Harris comes across like an outsider figure to me, she does at least know something about modern art. Robert Wang's work is so crude it looks like it's been executed by a child.'

'You don't like this deck, do you?'

'No.'

'Nor do I.'

'So why are you showing it to me?'

'You know why?'

'To test me, to see what I remember, to prove that we both know what the other knows.'

'Of course.'

'And you think that if you're gonna use a tarot deck you have to find it attractive.'

'You think the same thing too.'

'You're right, I do. And you really hate The Lovers in this pack.'

'You don't like it either. And without looking at it I already know it shows a woman chained to a rock looking quite happy about the fact that she's about to be embraced by a sea monster, and that rather than having Cupid you've got some guy in armour falling out of the sky.'

'Don't you think that could be a representation of sub-conscious sexual drives?'

'Yes but that doesn't mean it's a good representation of them. And I don't like The Hanged Man being depicted like he's been cross-dressed in a woman's swimsuit while suspended over the ocean. Nor do we like the Egyptian elements brought into The Wheel Of Fortune, Justice and various other cards.'

'So now I'm gonna put the pack away and show you something else.'

What Maria took from her bag was a tube of Durex Play Tingle Lube. That excited me a lot more than the *Golden Dawn Tarot*. I examined the label on the gel as Maria threw her coat over my lap. When she'd got my cock out of my flies, I handed the lube back to her so that she could squirt some into her palm. She proceeded to rub the Play Tingle into my manhood.

'Can you feel anything?' Maria asked.

'Yes, the beginnings of an orgasm.'

'Is that the effect of the gel?'

'No, it's what you're doing with your hand that gets me off.'

'Does the lube make you tingle or even burn?'

'I can't really feel anything more than a bit of moisture. What I'm loving is the feel of your hand.'

'Shit, some of the bar staff are looking right at us.'

'Don't worry about it. Just keep going. You can't stop now.'

'I'm embarrassed. They know what we're doing.'

'Well, we're grown adults, there's nothing wrong with it.'

'Suppose they come over and tell us to stop?'

'Well if they do that we'll stop; there's no need to stop before someone says something to us.'

'Are you sure?'

'Keep going.'

I was enjoying myself so much I didn't go with the flow of what Maria was doing and tried to hold back. When I lost control, I came. Maria cleaned me up with a tissue and put my cock back in my pants. We then spent the rest of the night kissing.

Maria: I had such a great time last night. I hope you enjoyed yourself as much as I did. You're so naughty. I can't believe what you made me do while people were looking. I love doing stuff like that when nobody notices, but you know how shy I am. Last night the staff were really great, not like some of the times we've been in there. I thought they were gonna come over and kick us out, but instead every time they passed our table they just smiled.

Me: I had a really good time. You just leave me wanting more. We're both a bit naughty. And we're gonna keep on having real good times together. I guess they have the sofas in the Masque Haunt so that we can get busy on them.

Maria: I'm watching this series *The Walking Dead* on TV. The plot is shit but the zombies are well made and look very real. There's plenty of gore and violence. I'll be back later.

Me: Enjoy your trash TV.

Maria: This morning my boss called me with some very bad news. Simon the maintenance guy for all the businesses in our building was found dead last night. Either he had an overdose or his body just couldn't take what he'd been doing to it any more. He's dead, and it still hasn't properly sunk in. He was a real friend, someone I saw every day I was at work. I'd told him about you and I knew all about his life. The funny thing is we never talked about doing smack, but I could see it in his eyes every time he took it. I'm so sad and I still haven't cried. I just can't believe it.

Me: Shit, so sorry to hear about your friend Simon. Hope you're okay.

Maria: Jess Franco died today. This is one of the worst days I've had for a while. Fuck it. No wonder I was feeling so anti-social last night.

Me: I can't believe Jess Franco has passed on – you'd had such a great time watching his films recently. I've seen so many of them over the years, more than fifty I'd guess.

Maria: My friend Simon has left two young kids behind that ain't never gonna see their dad again.

Me: Can we meet?

Maria: I need to sleep.

Me: Tonight I'll dream of you. I always do. I hope you don't have nightmares and just dream of me instead. I feel so useless. I should be with you holding your hand.

Maria: I had such troubled dreams last night. Simon's death has brought up lots of memories. Not just of him but of so many missing friends. I've told you a bit about Ruta Destroy. The eighties and nineties were crazy times in Spain. So many people I knew died or got sent to jail. I used to spend my weekends in El Saler and Les Palmeretes and then ended up in La Malvarrosa on Monday morning. But I only went to the beach for the sunset and sunrise. I loved it coz you'd be in a club full of people and everything was a bit claustrophobic but it only took two minutes to walk to the sea.

Me: Can I see you today?

Maria: I've booked a facial to cheer myself up. We can meet after that and hopefully I'll look less tired than usual. It's gonna cost me seventy quid, so it better be good. Come to my flat about 6pm. Please don't be cross, but I've also taken something to give me a boost. I needed it.

Six o'clock finally arrived, and I was ringing Maria's bell. She told me to wait outside and appeared fifteen minutes later. She looked great, but I could see from her face and the way she moved that she was blazing. I assumed Maria had been doing smack and then amphetamines to wake herself up for me. We put our arms around each other and kissed. Five minutes later we unlocked our mouths and walked down the street.

'The facial was crazy,' Maria told me. 'The women in there can hardly speak English. They remind me of how I was when I first came to London. I think they are Romanian. Anyway, it doesn't matter coz the treatment made me feel great. I'm really buzzing from it. Besides, I didn't really let them say much because I just wanted to tell them how shit it is to get old and how much effort you have to put into looking good.'

I didn't get a chance to say much either. Maria just carried on in this way until we got to the Masque Haunt. We ordered coffees and sat on a sofa with a low table in front of it. Maria got out a pack of tarot cards.

'What do you think of these? They're a redesigned full-colour version of CC *Zain's Brotherhood Of Light Egyptian Tarot* created for his Church Of Light. The earlier versions were in black and white, but I like the addition of colour. The cards are a real wonder of occult science because they blend alchemy, astrology and magic. One of the things that really grooves me about them is the way the major arcana have been renamed. Not all of them but most of them. They are: Magus, Veiled Isis, Isis Unveiled, The Sovereign, The Hierophant, The Two Paths, The Conqueror, The Balance, The Sage, The Wheel, The Enchantress, The Martyr, The Reaper, The Alchemist, The Black Magician, The Lightening, The Star, The Moon, The Sun, The Sarcophagus, The Adept, The Materialist…

'Hey,' I said, 'you've memorised these cards.'

'I can remember a lot more,' Maria assured me, 'and you can too. I remember Lemuria, so the Shaver Mysteries are no mystery to me. And you remember all of this too. We can both remember Lemuria, Atlantis, Shambala, Ancient Egypt, Glastonbury, Avalon.'

As she spoke Maria sorted through the cards and created two piles. One for the major arcana and a second for the pip cards. When she'd finished Maria picked up the major arcana and shuffled them. Then she fanned them out before me and told me to pick one. I pulled card fourteen which is usually known as Temperance and featured an Egyptian figure pouring some fluid between two jugs.

'Wow,' Maria breathed, 'you've picked The Alchemist, a card

that in this system represents the unfolding of nature in the endless transformation of male into female and female into male. Androgyny really is the state to which God leads us in both the highest and lowest realms. Everything in the world evolves from the transformations of male into female and female into male. But when male and female become one in spiritual union, as you have been and will be again with me, we achieve the holiest and highest state of being. Now you must take all the major arcana and shuffle them for me, so that I can pick one.'

I did as I was told. Maria pulled card twenty-one, which in most decks is known either as The World or The Universe. Of course in this pack it was something else.

'Far out,' Maria sighed. 'The Adept, the perfect match to your card. The winged linga at the heart of the zodiacal flowers represents our final joining together in perfect union and the attainment of higher consciousness.'

Maria swept up the cards, put them back in her bag, then leant over and kissed me – she also slipped her hand inside my pants. Next she pulled me up, took my hand and led me outside.

'I'm feeling restless tonight. Let's walk for a bit,' Maria said by way of explanation. 'Isn't it incredible how the cards always confirm what we already know. I so need to fuck your arse it isn't true. But I'm gonna work up to it gently. I don't wanna hurt you. I'll do some more finger-fucking to start with, then I'm gonna get an anal training kit. We'll start with a small butt plug, and I know you're gonna love it when I get one of those into you. Then gradually we're gonna move on to bigger butt plugs until finally you're gonna be ready for a good pegging.'

As Maria talked we found ourselves making our way through the city and up onto the Barbican Highwalks. I laughed when I realised Maria was leading me past Speed House. I knew the block was named after the cartographer and historian John Speed, but his name simultaneously invoked amphetamine. As Maria rambled, we brushed against each other. Every now and then we'd stop to kiss, until Maria had the urge to move us on again so that she could continue with her monologue, which went on for hours.

Maria: I hope I didn't freak you out too much. I know I shouldn't take speed when I see you. I had to do some amphetamine before you arrived or I'd have crashed out. I'm sorry I didn't give you a chance to speak. Today I felt much better, but I did really overdo it in the last few days and now I'm old it takes me so long to recover. I don't wanna think about that, I wanna remember being young. I'm sending you a picture of my inner circle from Ruta Destroy. In the middle is my best friend Yelena who was nicknamed Deep Throat. I'm sure I don't need to tell you why. The picture was taken in the toilets at Nivel a long time ago. I'm not in the photo coz I was fixing up in one of the cubicles. Look at Yelena's expression. We were soooooooooo bad. All the other girls were really scared of us. I was the worst one coz I was always coming up with evil things to do, but I didn't do them. Lina always wanted to ingratiate herself with me and show me how tough she was, so she carried out my plans. Although we were young no one dared touch us because we had all the skinheads in Valencia on board with us.

Me: Judging by Yelena's expression rocks melted in her mouth and butter was doomed for sure.

Maria: Yelena was a nymphomaniac and that's the type of woman I like. I needed sex-obsessed close friends coz I got a lot of unwelcome attention. I dealt with it by introducing unwanted suitors to my hot sidekicks. I'd bum gear and money from the boys and my girlfriends would fuck them. That way I'd have my music and drugs and be left alone to enjoy them. Everyone was happy.

Me: Then I'm one of the lucky ones who didn't get palmed off on one of your girlfriends. Will you meet me at the Rochester Castle tomorrow night?

Maria was waiting in the pub when I arrived. She'd come from work rather than going home first. She was sitting in a booth but stood up so I could hug her. Before I arrived Maria had taken an executive decision we were both having a vegetarian roast. Dinner arrived before I'd managed to sit down. When we'd eaten Maria handed me a pack of tarot cards.

'Wow,' I said. 'I wouldn't expect you to have a deck like this. It's a gaming pack with French suits.'

'You can still use clubs, hearts, spades and diamonds for divination. You don't have to have an occult pack. This is a tarot put out by Fournier, a Spanish company, but inside are the official rules of La Fédération Française De Tarot. The publisher has a French name because the founder had a Spanish mother and a father who'd moved to Burgos from France. Burgos really is deep Spain, but the company is based just up from there in the Basque Country. Fournier has been bought out by the United States Playing Card Company, so maybe it's American now. They sell playing cards all over the world.'

'Burgos is where Franco's scum had their headquarters during the Spanish Civil War before the fall of Madrid.'

'That's right, but let's talk about tarot, not those horrible fascists. What do you make of the cards?'

I looked through them. The royal cards were mirrors, the pips looked like those in any old gaming deck, it was the trumps that were odd. They were split into two halves but showed slightly different scenes each way up. Apart from The Fool, which was a true mirror like the royals. Some of the trumps were loosely related to the cards in traditional decks, but they bore little resemblance to what occultists call the major arcana. Rather than boasting Roman numerals, the trumps bore Arabic numbers, aside from The Joker or Fool, which was marked with a star.

'It's obviously a gaming deck,' I said. 'Do you play tarot or do you use them for divination?'

'What do you think?'

'Divination.'

'Pick a card.'

I picked the king of hearts. Maria chose the queen of hearts. I knew what she was gonna tell me, so I said it instead.

'That's us, in this deck the king and queen of hearts are better representations of who we are and how we belong together than the trumps that would normally be the Emperor and Empress.'

'We're psychic twins. When you let go of your preconceptions you know what I'm thinking. And when you don't block me out I know what you're thinking too.'

Maria threw her coat over my lap, slipped her hand under it and into my pants. She wrapped her digits around my erection. I thought she was gonna jerk me off, but she just squeezed my cock gently.

'Hey, aren't you gonna do what you did last time? Or do you wanna see if we can get into the disabled toilet?'

'Tonight I just want to tease you coz you tease me so much. I wanna fuck you in a bed next time we have sex.'

'Is it fair to tease me like this?'

'Life isn't fair. I don't wanna give you a lecture,' Maria said getting serious, 'but you really have to make more money and pay off your wife's debts since you won't report her for fraud. I never had dough until I got my film-editing job, and I'm still using my wages from that to pay off my debts. All the dosh I get goes by the end of the month and then I'm broke. We both deserve a lot more than we see.'

'The problem is the interest. I've paid off all the sodding money Petra had in my name and now I'm just paying for the loan.'

'Money is evil, but in this fucking world it is so necessary. What's really important is what you do with it. If you have any cash then you're a scumbag if you don't use some of it to help others who are less fortunate than you are. That's why I give to charity every month.'

Then we gave up on our serious conversation and went back to petting until the pub closed. I saw Maria onto a bus, which was an effort coz neither of us wanted to stop hugging when it arrived.

Maria: Guess what? Yesterday after work I went to the gym for two hours, and when I got home I was so tired and so sore I instantly fell sleep. But I'm very happy I went. I could really feel my muscles working and today my legs hurt a bit.

Me: Hey, that's great. Are we gonna meet tomorrow? After we both go to the gym of course. Really happy you worked out and slept well and feel so much better as a result.

Maria: Why don't you come to my gym and we can work out together? I'm sure no one will notice you don't have a membership. At the weekends it closes quite early. Maybe we should go to Lola's new flat? Do you remember in the pub I told you she's just moved to Caledonian Road and we can use the place whenever we want? Or we could go to Brick Lane. I really wanna see you coz I've had three horrible weeks. It hasn't been easy for me since Simon died. So please, whatever happens, just make sure you see me tomorrow.

Me: I'll come for you at 4pm or 4.30pm and we'll decide what to do.

Maria: Yes, come for me at 4pm. I'll be home. I don't know why, but I feel a bit sick today. What I do know is that when I see you I won't feel ill. You work like magick on me, tiger boy. See you in a few hours.

I parked my scooter and called up for Maria. She was down about ten minutes later. As she always did Maria shouted 'hey' as soon as we had eye contact. As I may have already said, it sounded like 'hey' to me but the 'h' wasn't really pronounced and she had quite a heavy Spanish accent, so maybe 'ey' would be a better way to render it. We hugged, and I loved the way Maria's head nestled against my shoulder. She frequently rested it against me in this way because she was so much smaller than I was. We started walking towards Brick Lane but veered off course and ended up going to Hamilton Hall on the Bishopsgate side of Liverpool Street station. We found a table upstairs and Maria went to order food. Vegetarian roast again; my eating was always going to pot when I was with her, and I didn't care.

'Hey,' Maria said as she passed a pack of tarot cards across the table. 'Check these out.'

I looked through the deck and I could see it was another French gaming tarot, a reproduction of a nineteenth-century pack. The trumps were mirrors and featured the subject matter you'd expect in the *Tarot de Marseille*; they had Arabic numerals. The royals, like the trumps, were also mirrors. The suites were coins, cups, swords and batons. Traditional pips.

'They're very conventional,' I said, 'but then there's nothing wrong with that. I like them.'

'It's a historical reproduction put out by Fournier. The cards were originally issued in 1860 by J Gaudais of Paris. Pull out the trumps and pick a card from the major arcana.'

'Death,' I said after doing what Maria had told me to do.

'That means transformation. There's gonna be a big change in your life before too long.'

'I wonder if I'm gonna pay off Petra's debts. Once I do that I'm gonna shack up with you, if you'll let me.'

'If I had any money I'd pay off your debts for you, so we could live together sooner.'

'Let's not talk about money. Why don't you pick a card,' I said as I handed the trumps to Maria.

'The Lovers.'

We laughed and kissed. Then our food arrived. Hamilton Hall was a big noisy space. We talked as we ate, but I found it hard to hear Maria. So we headed across the pedestrian square the pub was on to a Caffè Nero. We sat down on a long seat fixed to the wall at the east end of the café. It wasn't quite as comfy as a sofa, but we could snuggle up against each other and drink our coffees. Maria threw her coat over my lap and slipped her hand inside my pants.

'I know what you're gonna say.'

'Tell me.'

'You're just gonna tease me, you ain't gonna make me come.'

'See we're psychic twins,' Maria said before she kissed me.

We continued to make out and talk over a second round of coffees. It was nearing closing time and Nero was pretty empty. We were the last customers and were enjoying ourselves so much we had to be thrown out. Then we walked around for hours, stopping every now and then to kiss.

XIII DEATH

LA MORT

Me: Hey, gorgeous, when we met I would never have guessed you'd felt sick for half the day if you hadn't told me. You looked on top form. It was more than great to see you and almost as good that you've committed to regular exercise.

Maria: If I stick with my gym routine for a month you'll see an amazing difference both mentally and physically. I'll be full of energy and motivated to do the things that really matter to me. I'm gonna start making my own films again. Before I met you I was in a dark place. Now that Simon's dead I've been asking myself what's the point of my life as I live it now. Sure I've got a good job and it pays reasonably well. I've more money than when I was on benefits. But what am I achieving? I edit porn and corporate crap when I could be making art. I'm trying to put things in perspective by asking myself what's important in my life? My job ain't important. You are. Apart from my cat Sidney, a few close friends and my family – who are far away – you're my main source of happiness. I can't wait to get into bed with you again or have a secret quickie somewhere. Just thinking about it gets me all excited. But I'm also gonna tease you a lot because I want you to understand how frustrating this is for me. We should be living together. Do you really need to pay off your wife's debts first?

Me: I haven't even got the money to pay the rent on a room until Petra's debt is sorted. You've never let me in your flat

214

but that's not an issue coz you've told me why. If we're gonna live together we need somewhere bigger than your pad and until I've paid off what's owed I can't afford it. I can't believe my cousin's let me stay at her place so long. I ease the situation by going away for work, but that's a drag coz it means I can't see you. You looked so great today. You just gotta keep that gym routine going. I can't believe you're gonna look even more beautiful. And thinking of being in bed with you or that quickie makes me super excited too.

Maria: Hello, handsome. You'll be so proud of me. I went to the gym and as well as doing a short but very intense workout with a few of the machines, I also did a legs, bums and tums class. It was really hard. Fuck, it nearly killed me. Can you tell me about protein supplements? I want to go and buy some tomorrow.

Me: It's really good to go to classes and learn new exercises. You work your muscles in new ways. Your body quickly gets used to whatever you throw at it, which is why you need to keep up the pace and must constantly swap exercises around. As for protein powders you can get many different types. The most popular are dairy-based and called whey. There are many different flavours, but I think natural is best for all supplements – but I just know you're gonna get chocolate. I won't judge you, although I would judge anyone else. Look for a half-price offer or two-for-one on a big tub. You can get them in Holland And Barrett or GNC or some place like that. If you look around you can usually get a big tub of whey for around twenty quid, or forty quid for two big tubs on an offer together. Otherwise try hemp protein or pea protein and have less dairy in your diet, which is better. If you get pea you'll need a rice protein to mix with it so you get everything necessary. Hemp and whey already have everything in them, so you don't need to mix them with another protein source. Hemp is a bit bitter, so you might not like it. Blend whatever powder you choose with lots of green vegetables, and knowing you some fruit too because your tooth is so sweet. You might also want to use some other supplements, but I can tell you about them later.

Maria: I'm so tired when I get home that I'm taking a nap on the sofa or going straight to bed. But I'm happy I'm doing so much exercise. Thanks for motivating me. On Friday I'm gonna go to a yoga class for the first time. Is that hard too?

Me: Anything new is hard, but it gets easier eventually. When that happens you have to find harder exercises to do.

Maria: Today I was reading about creatine, and I remembered you talking about it once. What do you think of Maxi-Muscle Promax 454g Chocolate Whey Protein Shake Powder?

Me: I knew you were gonna go for a chocolate protein powder. You're gonna do what you're gonna do and it doesn't matter what I think. I'd rather you took creatine than speed, but you don't need either. Don't worry, I won't give you a lecture on these or related subjects. I love you as you are, and I know I can't change you.

Maria: I was so happy today. Lola gave me the key to her new room in Caledonian Road. She told me she goes out every Saturday and she's away from 2pm until late. So we can stay there until 3am tomorrow if we want.

Me: What's the address?

Maria: Lola's house is in Pedlars Walk, but it's tucked away and hard to find. It's better if we meet at Caledonian Road station. Choose a time, but tell me as soon as you can so I can tell Lola. It's her birthday on Saturday, so she'll be out all night. I wanna wrestle with you for a bit and then feel our bodies melt together. I can't wait to be all naked and sweaty with you – but I only like fresh sweat, when it starts to smell I hate it. Your scent with all your pheromones makes me go crazy. I just love having sex with you, and there are still so many things we haven't done yet and so many things we need to try.

Me: 7pm?

Maria: Hey, I'm preparing a suitcase with things we might want to play with tomorrow. I've got blindfolds, handcuffs, two cat o' nine tails whips and lots of sexy lingerie for me. We're definitely gonna have some fun at last. Lola is in a big shared house, so maybe other people will be there. There are Portuguese, Spanish and Italian. So we can't make too much noise.

Me: If we're not gonna make too much noise we'll need gags as well as handcuffs.

Maria: Please don't get upset, but can we make it 7.30pm?

Me: Okay, 7.30pm. And I'm not upset, I'm just looking forward to seeing you.

Maria: You know I've got butterflies in my stomach. Isn't that brilliant. You get me so excited. With everyone else I don't feel anything at all. Please tell me I can do anything I want with you when we meet? That would be so sexy.

Me: Later tonight, just to thank you for letting me know about your butterflies, I'm gonna do anything you want. Whatever you ask me to do I'll do.

Maria: Please don't get upset and please don't say no, but I want you to be my sub. I'm gonna restrain you and make you suffer a little. That's part of what gave me butterflies. I had all my dominatrix gear in my suitcase and I didn't know if you were ready to let me use it on you. But now you've said yes I'll make you regret it just a bit. Let me tell you a secret, when you relax into it you'll love the very light humiliation I'm gonna give you.

I travelled to the tube station on my scooter and had to wait for Maria. We kissed before I pulled her huge wheeled suitcase to Lola's house. The place was a modern brick terrace. It looked like it had been built in the seventies or even later. The front door was open and there were guys in the hallway drinking beer. There was football on in a downstairs living room. They must have been watching the end of Wigan's shock one-nil victory over Manchester City in the 2013 FA Cup Final. I knew the game had kicked off at Wembley – not so far from where we were – at 5.15pm. The guys we passed asked what we were doing and Maria told them we were going to wait for Lola in her room.

Even upstairs it didn't seem like we were alone. Lola's housemates were shouting and cheering in a drunken frenzy. It was a big football night and they were obviously hell bent on celebrating it. Maria pulled lots of lingerie from her case. Then she showed me her whips.

'The cat o'nine tails is quite soft, it feels so nice when you're hit with it. Take your pants down so that I can show you.'

I'd said I'd do whatever Maria wanted, so I complied. I suspected she was deliberately failing to hurt me, but when the tails of the cat lashed against my butt and upper legs it didn't feel like much. Maria struck me repeatedly and I felt nothing more than a mild tingling. She was hitting me across a wide surface area, so that was another reason it didn't hurt. If she'd focused on one small spot with repeated blows it would have been much more painful.

'I want you to take all your clothes off now,' Maria instructed.

When I'd done as I'd been told, Maria spun me around then pulled my arms behind my back and slipped a pair of handcuffs over my wrists. After this she shoved me onto the bed and got on top of me so that we could kiss. We kissed for a long time before Maria got up.

'I never kissed the johns when I was a dominatrix,' Maria told me. 'But I often did what I'm gonna do to you now, I used to leave them tied up and waiting for me. I'm gonna go and have a shower and fix myself up. Before I go I'm gonna slip a blindfold over your eyes, then I'm just gonna leave you here with the door ajar. Maybe someone will come up and look in.'

The bathroom was next to Lola's bedroom, and I could hear Maria running the shower. I was also aware of the drunks downstairs. They seemed to be watching highlights from various European matches and they'd turned the volume up really loud. After a while a woman tried to use the bathroom. She only wanted the toilet, but Maria told her she was washing her hair and would be in there some time. The woman seemed to linger on the landing, so I guess she had a good look at me tied up on the bed. I don't know whether there was another bathroom or toilet in the house. Several people seemed to stop on the landing trying to get into the john.

Maria really took her time coming back. When she did she took my blindfold off – actually a silk scarf – and I could see she was dressed up in a tight leather corset and skimpy black panties. She reached into her suitcase and when she stood up there was a flash of steel and several loud clicks. Maria had expertly opened a balisong, or butterfly knife, with one hand. It was a Filipino weapon that you could legally possess in the UK, but it was against the law to carry one in public. When closed the blade was concealed by a handle that was split in two, these parts rotated around so that the weapon could be fanned open with one hand for effects ranging from terror to amusement. Maria bent down over me and pressed the flat part of the blade against my cheek, while simultaneously kissing me on the mouth.

'I'm gonna cut you up,' she whispered in my ear.

Then Maria ran the flat part of the blade around my cheeks and down my chest. She lightly wiggled the pointed end of the blade in my belly button, without cutting through the skin. Next the knife ran down the outside of one leg and then the other.'

'You're so nice,' Maria hissed, 'I want to kill you.'

Then she was running the knife up the inside of my left leg, followed by the right. Maria proceeded to jiggle my testicles with the flat part of the blade.

'I could cut your balls off if I wanted to.'

'But you won't,' I replied.

'You said you'd do anything I wanted tonight,' Maria laughed as she closed the knife. 'But you're a terrible submissive. I don't know why I'm bothering with this. I've had johns come when I've put a knife against their balls and threatened to cut them off, but you hardly react.'

'You wouldn't like me if I was too submissive, and you know all you have to do is touch my cock with your hand and I'll get an erection. Warm flesh is so much nicer than cold steel.'

Maria put the knife down and whipped off her knickers. Then she wrapped her fingers around my manhood. I wanted to put my hands on her rib cage and hold her tight, but I couldn't move them from behind my back because I was still handcuffed. Moments later Maria eased my cock into her pussy. She'd obviously enjoyed her knife play because she was dripping wet. She jumped up and down astride me, threw her head back and screamed with pleasure. I loved the way Maria's thrusting stimulated my length, but at the same time the movements were painful because they jammed my bound wrists into my lower back. Maria didn't care and just kept thrusting until I shot my load. She'd already had several orgasms by the time I came.

'Hey,' I said, 'please undo the handcuffs, they're starting to hurt.'

'I don't know where the key is,' Maria replied. 'Do you know where I put it?'

'Stop teasing. I want you to undo the handcuffs.'

'I'm not teasing.'

'Okay, you're not teasing, but please unlock me.'

'I will if you can tell me where the key is.'

'I don't know where it is, just look for it.'

Maria made a pretend search for the key. After about ten minutes she acted out finding it in the front pocket of her suitcase. I was happy when Maria released me, but she only unlocked one handcuff, and before I realised what was happening, she'd chained me by one arm to the head of the bed.

'Hey,' Maria laughed, 'I'm having too much fun. I don't want to let you go. You said you'd do whatever I wanted tonight, and you will. I'm really enjoying being in charge of you. I might even ask the drunk guys downstairs to come up here and gangbang you. So you'd better be good to me.'

Maria got back on the bed and kissed me. I responded amorously. I slipped my free hand between Maria's legs so that I could massage her clit. Soon my middle digit was inside her. Maria had her right arm around my neck and was fingering my balls with her left hand. After I made Maria come again, she got up and took another knife from her suitcase.

'I wanted to show you this,' she said as she towered over me. 'It's a *navaja*, a traditional Spanish folding knife. Listen to the beautiful noise it makes when I open it. The clicking sound is very distinctive and for hundreds of years has been associated with violent altercations in Sevilla and elsewhere in Spain.'

I thought Maria was going to run this knife all over me but she just put it away and lay back down on the bed so we could kiss and cuddle. I was enjoying myself, and it was several hours before Maria finally released me. Before she did, she took a lot of compromising footage on her phone and said she'd post it online. In the small hours I helped Maria tidy the room and pack up her stuff.

Maria: I hope you had the fun last night. I haven't done those things to a man for so long and I was really missing it. For me it was easily the best night we've had together. Now I really want to spend a couple of days in bed with you. Imagine how much fun we'll have and all the new things I'll make you do. I so want to dress you up in women's clothes with lots of make-up and maybe a long wig too. With your pretty face and fit body you're gonna be a total sex-bomb. Any boy who sees you like that will be gagging to fuck you. You're gonna look so good on camera. But don't worry, I won't really put anything like that online. All film and photos are simply for me to keep and look at. I just like to threaten you with that kind of exposure because it's part of the game during a domination session.

Me: We had a ball together. But what a horrible house, even if Lola is lovely for letting us use her room.

Maria: Forget that. You left a tiny mark on my tit where you bit me. I love it.

Me: I got some marks on my right wrist, several, but it isn't obvious what from. Unless you knew you'd never guess it was handcuffs.

Maria: I know your back is scratched too but maybe you haven't checked that in a mirror yet? You should, it looks very impressive. My period just started. So penetrative sex will have to wait. But you can be sure that when I tell you it's safe to have unprotected sex, it is. I can't stop thinking about being at Lola's pad. I had such a great time and you were so adorable. You look so helpless in the pictures I took. Do you remember I told you about my friend Lina from Ruta Destroy? I'd love to send her a few of those photos, but I won't unless you say it's okay. And I just got a message from Lola saying she has been kicked out of her room because of our visit. One of the women who lives there saw you on the bed and she sent a couple more chicks to check you out. At least one of them has evidence on her phone. So it really wouldn't matter if Lina saw a few photos too – she wouldn't be the only one.

Me: Shit, poor Lola, what a disaster. Seemed like a really shit house with all that noise and overflowing beer bottles in the bin outside. I can't believe it's already a week since we were there. Can I see you this evening say 5pm or 6pm?

Maria: Sunday is never good for me coz it's the day I start back on the pills for my addiction. I'm okay if I'm sitting down at home, but they knock me out and I don't have the energy to go anywhere. I hope you understand.

Me: I trust the pills are working. I guess you like to party at the weekend, which is why you start the pills on Sunday.

Maria: They work really well, but I'm gonna have to come off them soon. They're opioid receptor antagonists, which means that if I take smack when I'm on them I don't feel anything coz they block the effects. I started taking them when I was feeling very low years ago and I thought I was gonna develop a really heavy shit habit again. Of course it's very easy not to take them for a couple of days and do whatever I want. But I take them during the week to make sure I go to work and don't stay at home doing shit. One of the reasons I don't sleep properly is the pills give me insomnia.

Me: I should have seen you yesterday.

Maria: I'm feeling a lot better now. The tablets really work because as long as you take them you can't do shit. They're very different to methadone. Everyone I know who has a methadone script takes shit on top anyway because methadone doesn't stop you doing anything. Whenever I tell someone on a methadone cure about my tablets they look at me like I'm crazy coz they know that I really want to get off smack. For them taking my tablets would mean getting clean from shit and methadone. But I hate talking about my opiate blockers coz it's like admitting I'm not strong enough to deal with my addiction on my own. I'd much rather talk about something else. Like how I'm gonna put you in a dress and wig and take lots of sexy photos.

Me: What's putting thoughts like that in your mind?

Maria: TV. I'm watching Jess Franco's *99 Women* on the Horror Channel. I've seen it before but in Spanish as *99 Mujeres*. After Franco they're broadcasting *Dead Hooker In A Trunk*. I haven't see that, and I got quite excited coz it's listed as being from 1967. Checking online it seems it's from 2009. I'm sure the Horror Channel listing is wrong and it's gonna be modern shit. But the Horror Channel is still great. The only bad thing is the adverts. They don't run them for too long and at least they're mainly movie related. But no ad breaks would be better. The ads are over, so I should sign off. You know if you were here with me watching a Franco movie we'd end up doing rude things together. And guess what? We left a cat o' nine tails under Lola's bed. In her previous place I left some sexy knickers behind and a few other kinky things. And she's seen the photos her flatmate took of you naked, blindfolded and handcuffed on the bed. She must think we're a right pair of perverts.

Me: If we ever use another of Lola's rooms we'll have to think of something really strange to leave behind.

Maria: What about a cement mixer? I'll tell her you like to be immobilised in cement. But I wouldn't dare ask to use her pad again. She let us use two places and was kicked out of both of them. Can you guess what I'm fantasising about psychic twin??? And what fantasies do you want to act out with me?

Me: I think your fantasy is related to you saying how much you'd like to dress me up. And me? I still have to tie you up, and it's my turn coz I let you handcuff me last time.

Maria: I keep thinking about you wearing my stockings over your strong legs. I'm getting all wet just thinking about you stuffed into my very tight knickers. And I want to blindfold you and tie you to a chair. I want your arms restrained behind the chair and your feet tied to its front legs. I don't want to spoil it by telling you what I wanna do next, but you'll have as much fun as I will.

Me: I'll let you do that if you let me tie you up too.

Maria: Can I take some pictures of you dressed up in my underwear? And I really want more film of me tying and teasing you.

I parked my scooter close to Maria's Fortune Street block just before 10pm. I rang up and hung around outside until she came down. We kissed then walked hand in hand to the Masque Haunt. We bagged the sofa with the low table at the front of the higher level of the pub and sat down. We snuggled up close and kissed some more.

'Hey,' Maria said as she pulled cards from her bag and handed them to me, 'I wanted to show you this tarot.'

'It's a reprint of the *Jacques Vieville Tarot*,' I said, 'a 1650 cross between the *Tarot de Marseille* and later decks from Rouen and Brussels. Maybe it influenced those later eighteenth-century tarots, or maybe they were all just influenced by earlier tarots from northern Italy. Your deck is from Paris.'

'How do you know that?'

'I just do. And I don't even have to look at the cards to see Justice, The Chariot, Strength and The Hermit have been reordered. The Hanged Man is upright and even levitating slightly. The Tower has been replaced by a tree.'

'We don't need to talk about this, you remember everything

now. You get two versions of the major arcana in the set I bought. The second corrects the order and places the hanged man upside down, but it also reverses most of the cards because they look like they were made from a positive sheet rather than following the more usual procedure of tracing a negative copy.'

'So it's a Jean-Claude Flornoy tarot restoration.'

'Yes. Are you gonna choose a card?'

'The Lovers,' I said after shuffling the deck and taking a random pick. 'Judged on the clothes, it's women on either side of a guy with Cupid above them, but the three human faces all look kinda male to me and they all have shortish hair.'

'It's like we always say, the two sexes travel in the company of a third and together as The Lovers. You and me are gonna become that third sex.'

'Far out. Now it's your turn to choose a card.'

'But we know what I'll get.'

'Pick it anyway.'

'What you see is what you get.'

So after I'd handed Maria the deck, she shuffled it and pulled out The Lovers. We kissed, and the smooching didn't stop until we got out of the pub. I walked back to Fortune Street with Maria. I wanted to go into her flat, but she wouldn't let me in. Instead we had sex on the stairs.

Maria: Today I was wearing the scarf I blindfolded you with in Lola's room. It made me think of you. I wish you'd seen me today coz I actually looked pretty. That might have been coz I got plenty of sleep and have been eating wholefoods. You know I come from a poor family and most of what I know I've taught myself. I can't fly you to amazing places the way your rich clients do, but I hope you still have a great time with me even if it's always in the same few square miles of London.

Me: I don't care that you come from a poor family. I didn't come from riches either. I just wanna be with you coz we're perfect together.

Maria: Do you wanna go to King Henry's Walk tonight if I'm
well enough? I'm feeding the cat there. Any time is good for
me. We could do some sex magick if you're up for it. I'd
have to bring lots of sheets and towels coz we can't make a
mess and there are a lot of oils and potions we'd have to rub
into each other. The most difficult thing is making sure we
both come at the same time. Although the last time we were
together we more or less did. Only a few seconds difference.
Today I feel like shit. I couldn't do anything yesterday either.
I had a fever and it just got worse and worse. I had the worst
night ever. I was having panic attacks coz I couldn't breathe
properly and I still can't. My nose is blocked up, my throat
is inflamed and it's so dry it's difficult to swallow. If I'm not
better this evening I'm going to see a doctor. But if I'm well
I wanna fuck your brains out.

After running my clients through their routines in various
parks I called Maria. She was too sick to see me, and it was a real
effort for her to even talk. I didn't say what I was thinking. That
was better left unspoken. I believed Maria when she told me she
wanted to stop using shit, but I also knew that wasn't something
simple and that part of giving up smack was Maria saying she'd
done so. The claim was always gonna proceed the act because
after making the claim Maria needed to act on it to maintain face.
So I didn't ask her if she was sick because she was in withdrawal.
I may have been mistaken about what was wrong with her, so
that was another reason for not speaking my mind. I believed in
loving Maria as she was and that through her own efforts she'd
metamorphose into the best possible version of herself.

Likewise I didn't think Maria giving up junk was a straight
line with a full stop at the end. The way I saw it was she'd stop
and start, but what I hoped was that the gaps between stopping
and starting would get longer and longer until finally she never
started again. I knew Maria had been making an effort to stop

since I'd started seeing her and she sometimes succeeded for weeks at a time. The important thing was that she was trying to kick smack. So when she told me she was in control of the drugs, rather than the drugs controlling her, I could run with that. Maria needed me to accept her claims about this if they were ever gonna come true. I really believed that one day she would put her addictions behind her if I loved and supported her unconditionally. Sometimes I might need to push her a bit but only gently. It was up to Maria to tell me what she was going through, and if she didn't I would observe but not speak. Besides, Maria's addictions weren't the reason I loved her. She was so smart, funny and loving. She had so much more in common with me than anyone else I'd ever met.

Maria: How much I love you. I can't believe I'm saying this to you. Coz I really mean it. And now I don't know if you told me you loved me near the end of our phone conversation this afternoon or if just dreamt it. Anyway, tiger, I love you madly. Please don't get frightened and run away from me. I'm not used to feeling these kinds of things and it's even stranger to be saying them. Fuck. How sick I still am.

Me: You didn't dream it. I said I love you and I meant it. And you sounded so sick. It would have been crazy to meet. You need to rest.

Maria: I'm glad I didn't dream it. That's the first time you've whispered in my ear you love me, and it means so much. Do you know what else I was thinking today? How sad it is that junkies are only considered cool and interesting when they're dead. No one sensible wants to hang around with people who do smack. That's why smart users hide their habit from everyone. I don't like people to know I use shit. When I see Pete Doherty in the media saying and doing stupid things and telling everyone he's a junkie I can't stand it. And then the fucker complains about the cops stopping and searching him. What an idiot. I guess he thinks he's another Sid Vicious. I hate all those people.

Me: Don't think about other people. Think about us. And now you got me doing stuff with you that I've never done with anyone else – coz I want us to have fun. But if you enjoy it and it makes you happy, I'm happy.

Maria: You're amazing. Now you're saying that you're doing stuff coz it makes ME happy. Come on, you wouldn't do it if you didn't like it. Don't turn me on by making me think you're that submissive. You make me laugh with how manipulative you are sometimes. In fact you're just like me, coz I'm manipulative too.

Me: Now you're making me laugh. You brought those things you had in your suitcase, including the handcuffs, to Lola's room. They aren't mine.

Maria: You know what really cracks me up? It's the idea of forcing you to have sex with a really fat woman. A woman so obese that just by lying on top of you she might asphyxiate you. There are things we will never do together, and me forcing you to fuck a fat woman is one of them. But it's still something I like to think about. If you really were a submissive I'd make you do it.

Me: I don't even want to think about that. Now I'll be frightened if I ever see you with a blindfold again. I'll think you've got a morbidly obese woman hidden in the next room. Doh.

Maria: And I'll film it just in case you manage to survive, coz later I can torture you by making you watch the video and threatening to put it online.

Me: You really are sick and twisted. Is that why I love you?

Maria: I'm so happy I'm getting well again and I'm not sick. And you're making me laugh so much. Sleep well and think of all the crazy perverted things I'm gonna do to you when I have a chance. You drive me crazy.

XIIII

TEMPERANCE

TEMPERANCE

Maria had decided we were gonna go for a ride on my scooter, even if it was a 'fucking hairdryer'. I picked her up in Fortune Street. I drove east through Whitechapel and then headed into Limehouse. We got off the scooter and walked hand in hand along the river.

'Do you think we could find somewhere private to fuck?' Maria asked me.

'We can look.'

There were too many teenagers around for us to have sex without being interrupted. I suggested we head further east. We could find somewhere more secluded by a canal or the sewage outcrop. Maria said she still didn't feel well, so it would be better if I took her home. It was too early to have sex on the steps of Maria's tower block. Too many people were coming and going. Besides, Maria needed rest not physical love.

Maria: I wish I'd been feeling better yesterday. It was great to see you, but we really need to have a good fuck. I wanted you to hold me, but I was holding you. Don't get me wrong, the way you drive your scooter rocks, but I really know a lot more about bikes that you do. I learnt so many tricks from my brother and the Hells Angels. Next time you should let me drive and you can hold me. I was feeling all your muscles when you took me home and thinking it was so shit I was still sick and unable to fuck you. But when I'm well let's have some al fresco sex. I'll wear a dress just for you. I have so many that I never wear.

Me: I'd love to have you sitting on top of me in a park. If you wore a big dress you could spread it over my body and no one would really see what we were doing, although I guess it would be kinda obvious.

Maria: We'll fuck each other's brains out on a blanket. I want to roll around with you and wrestle you. I want to see how strong you really are and how easy it is for you to pin me down but without hurting me. Just playing. And of course you'll have to let me win at wrestling sometimes too. I bet you'll like it when I pin you down.

We were messaging in this way for the rest of the week waiting for Maria to get well. The following Sunday I called for her again. She was still sick but wanted to get out. We decided she'd take me back to Stoke Newington. I wrapped my arms around Maria's waist and pressed myself against her. She clearly knew how to ride a bike, and it wasn't until I got off that it occurred to me that she might not have a valid licence. Since we hadn't been stopped by the Old Bill there was no harm done. We went into the Parlour on Stoke Newington Church Street and sat in the garden at the back.

'Hey,' Maria said, 'I brought a tarot for you to look at.'

'What's this?' I asked as I shuffled through the deck.

'It's the *Mythic Tarot Deck*. It takes Greek legends and applies them to the tarot.'

I didn't like the illustrations. Some of the figures looked stiff. The major arcana were heavily influenced by *Rider-Waite-Smith*, but they weren't numbered. The deck didn't work for me.

'You know,' I said, 'the more you get me to look at tarot decks, the more I'm convinced that the *Tarot de Marseille* is the best and sticks most closely to the intentions of those who originally designed the cards. Even packs like the *Florentine Minchiate* seem like a deviation from true tarot.'

'You're such a traditionalist, but you've always been like that, so it makes me happy you're remembering who you really are and what you really like.'

'What have they added to this deck? It looks like Gods and Goddess in the major arcana and something a bit more complex in the suits.'

'Cups is the legend of Eros and Psyche. Swords graphically depicts Orestes and the house of Atreus, pentacles the tale of Daedalus. Finally Wands gives us scenes from Jason and the Argonauts.'

'I don't like it.'

'Pick a card anyway.'

'I have the Golden Fleece. My Golden Fleece is you,' I said as I pulled the six of wands, which showed the triumphant capture of this prize.

'Am I really your symbol of authority and kingship?'

'You're my queen. Now it's your turn to pick a card.'

'You must be right about me being your Golden Fleece,' Maria laughed as she pulled the queen of cups.

'Queen of love.'

'You're my prince even if you're my king and emperor too. That's not me saying it, the tarot says it.'

Maria leant over and kissed me. For a split-second she grabbed my cock and instantly gave me an erection that wouldn't go away. The tarot deck was forgotten and we talked about films and music. I took Maria home after an hour coz she felt too sick to stay out.

Maria: I just watched a crazy film called *Post Coitum,* directed by Juraj Jakubisko. There's a scene in which a guy is tied to a tree with a girl giving him a good hard fuck. We should try that. And I was amazed to see Franco Nero playing an old hippie photographer in it. Parts of *Post Coitum* really suck and the music is terrible. But the cinematography is great and the mise en scène is pretty good too. The set-ups for Franco Nero taking photos of half-naked girls are amazingly beautiful and classy. It even features a brothel where the girls are dressed like Greek goddesses. It looks like the fantasy brothel I want to run but with different themes.

Me: You watch so many flicks it amazes me you find time to do anything else.

Maria: Aside from movies I'm currently doing this Australian TV series *Underbelly*. It's loosely based on real Mafia stories. I saw the first series ages ago. Series two is even better coz the stories date from 1976 onwards and all the guys have sideburns. Yesterday I watched eight episodes in a row. That's about seven and a half hours' viewing. When I got home from work today I sat straight down and watched three episodes. I've only got two more to go and I'm done. I just took a break to write a quick message. I'm such a television addict I'm gonna go watch more now.

Me: Wow, so much TV. Hey, can you meet tomorrow night? It's the solstice.

Maria: We've done sex rituals on so many solstices in our past lives. Can we go to one of the Indian restaurants near you tomorrow? Afterwards we can fuck at King Henry's Walk.

I got to Rasa before Maria. She ordered moru kachiathu, mangoes and bananas cooked in yoghurt with green chillies, ginger and fresh curry leaves. I had rasa kayi, a hot curry with mixed vegetables. I had brown rice and a salt lassi; Maria coconut rice and a sweet lassi.

'You can see from what we eat that I am the all woman and you are the all man,' Maria observed.

'You're the only woman for me. No one else is all woman enough.'

'Before the food arrives I've some cards I want you to look at.'

When Maria handed me the pack it felt as if it was gonna jump out of my hands. There was an electric charge to the deck. I knew even before I checked them out that I was gonna love the pack. When I did look through the cards I could see that they were a restored version of Nicholas Conver's *Tarot de Marseille* of 1760. The imagery was traditional but had been cleaned up to reflect modern tastes and look good when reproduced on a contemporary printing press. The feel was crisp with no unnecessary additions to the artwork. The lines and colours were clear and unbroken.

'You knew this deck was gonna groove me, didn't you.'

'Of course, that's why I'm showing it to you. This pack is a *Tarot de Marsella* restoration done by Yoav Ben-Dov, an associate of Jodorowsky. You're such a traditionalist but at the same time you have modern tastes, so I knew you'd dig it.'

'What I really like is that the trumps are in the right order and that there are no fancy embellishments.'

'How do you know the cards are in the right order?'

'Intuition.'

'I like that, you are the all man, but I'm turning you into the all woman. Pick a card.'

'You know I'm gonna pick you.'

'That's cool. Find The Empress without looking.'

I did as I was told, then Maria pulled me in the form of The Emperor from the pack. Our food arrived, so we talked about tarot as we ate. I asked Maria if it was just chance that both times we'd come to the restaurant we were in she'd shown me classic decks?

'Nothing is by chance,' Maria assured me. 'It isn't chance we met, it was destiny. We are meant to be together and it was my task to help you recall who you were. I've done that, but there's no harm in me giving you further reminders.'

Neither of us wanted pudding. Maria had fruit for us when we got to King Henry's Walk. I pushed Maria's cycle and she had an arm around my waist as we headed down to Dalston. Our conversation had moved on from tarot to Jodorowky's films. Maria was more of an expert on them than me, she'd done her film-school dissertation on the man. Given this it surprised me that she didn't know movies by Jodorowsky's colleagues such as Fernando Arrabal's *I Will Walk Like A Crazy Horse* and *Long Live Death*; or Juan López Moctezuma's *The Mansion Of Madness* and *Alucarda*. When we got to the flat we went into the kitchen where Maria offered me blueberries and put out food for the cat.

'You know you can't fuck me because it's my period, it isn't safe. Did you mean what you said about letting me fuck you?'

'Yes.'

'I've got a strap-on in the bedroom, but I don't think your arse is ready for it yet. The sex toy is too big. I could get a small one for an anal virgin, but I want to loosen you up with my fingers and then use a regular strap-on for our first bum fuck. As your arse loosens you'll be letting go of the negative emotions your body is holding, so it might be a roller-coaster. I'll give you a finger-fucking tonight. I'm gonna show you the strap-on so that you can start preparing yourself mentally for taking it inside you. For now I'm just gonna put it in your mouth, and I know you're gonna love going down on me. I've got candles and incense too.'

We did a whole load of things that were new to me but not Maria. Ritual magick to cement our love, then sexual magick. Maria dictated what happened, I just followed her instructions. After the serious stuff was over and closed down, we just had fun. Because it was her period, Maria kept her pants on the whole time. Her pussy was a no-go zone, but as well as taking two of her digits up my backside at the same time, I had my cock and balls slapped around, sucked and manipulated in many other ways. We stopped messing around about 5am, and I got an hour's sleep curled up against my girlfriend before I had to get up and see a client.

Maria: After I made you come and we'd finished with the magick, do you know how much you teased me? I so wanted you inside me. God, just to think about it is too much. But when it's my period it isn't safe, not even to have the tip of your cock inside me, which I'd have liked so much.

Me: I so wanted to come inside you. There are so many things I want to do with you. And you know I got a mark on my shoulder?

Maria: I bit your ass too but not as hard as your shoulder. If I'd let myself go with your butt I'd have gone to town tearing it up. After spending the whole night driving you mad, I still feel like I could play with you all day. I wanna do a lot more Tantric work with you. What do you wanna do this weekend? I'm getting paid on Friday and I'm taking you out. I don't wanna do drugs, I wanna spend my money on something better. At the end of every month on payday it's always really tempting to buy shit. I know I'm weak. But when you're with me I can be strong.

I got to Maria's at 9pm. While I was waiting for her at the bottom of her block I noticed the gates to Fortune Street Park hadn't been locked. When Maria came down she kissed me. I put my arm around her and with her head cradled against my shoulder we walked into the park.

'I've got a blanket so we can lie on the grass or we can sit on a bench,' Maria said.

'Let's sit on a bench and see what it's like in here before we lay out the blanket.'

We walked past the children's play area to the west side of the park. There were benches close to the school on the south side and more on the Fortune Street edge to the north. We opted for a bench screened by trees and bushes. Maria put her bag down beside the bench. Soon we were kissing, our hands undoing each other's zips and buttons. Then Maria froze.

'I can't stand the sound of that teenage gang.'

'They're on the kids' play equipment and the bushes pretty much hide us from them.'

'Not entirely.'

'Enough.'

'No, not enough, let's go somewhere else.'

'You tell me where.'

'Quaker Gardens, it's only a few minutes' walk.'

When we got to the next park it wasn't locked either. Again we opted for an area of greenery behind the kids' play equipment. There was a sports pitch but that was further from us. There were youths on the podium of Braithwaite House, a big tower block behind us. Luckily they were being as furtive as we were because they were doing drug deals. We sat on a bench facing the block and returned to doing what we'd been up to before. This time we began having penetrative sex with Maria sitting on top of me. But before I reached orgasm she stood up and adjusted her clothes.

'See up there?' Maria said pointing to a darkened window in the middle of the tower block.

'See what?'

'Can't you see that pervert with a pair of binoculars watching us?'

'Your eyesight is better than mine.'

'Look and you'll see him.'

'I saw movement but there's no one there now.'

'Yeah, he ducked down. I can't stay here. Let's go to the stairs on my block.'

So we moved on again. I managed to orgasm, but I could tell by then that Maria was no longer one hundred percent into what we were doing. She cleaned me up with tissues and was much more relaxed when we were just kissing afterwards.

Maria: I'm still feeling sick and tired. The only time I went out in the last week was to see a Harley Street doctor. I know you've told me you think my face is perfect and I don't need cosmetic surgery, but you're looking at me through your eyes and not objectively through mine. But don't worry, I won't have anything done immediately coz I can't afford it and I've changed my mind about whether or not to have a little filler around my eyebrows a hundred times over the weekend. So I may not do it anyway.

Me: I'm not gonna say anything about plastic surgery. You'll do what you want and I'll love you regardless. But you look perfect to me, and you can't improve on perfection.

Maria: Hey, I'm not gonna have plastic surgery. I'm crazy but not that crazy. I only want a bit of Botox between my eyebrows coz I'm frowning all the time and that makes me look tired. I don't want to look younger, just refreshed, like I've had a good night's sleep. I just want to get rid of the frown. It won't be obvious. I'll still look like me but a little bit better. And I'm feeling well enough to go out. Let's hook up.

I arrived at the Rochester Castle before Maria. I was able to grab a booth that had just been vacated. When my girlfriend arrived I stood up to embrace her. We kissed for a long time. I drank in her smell. Drum tobacco and various beauty products. I loved to feel her hair against my face, always freshly washed. Maria's tight black military-style jacket with silver poppers showed her slim figure to full effect, as did her tight black trousers. Once I'd ordered coffee, I sat back down.

'Hey, I've got something to show you, and I know you're gonna like it.'

'Is it a tarot?'

'Yeah, and you're gonna love this one,' Maria said as she handed me the cards.

'Why are you so sure?'

'Because I know you better than anyone else you've ever loved in this or any other life.'

The cards were still in a sturdy box with *Miss Cleo's Tarot Power Deck* and *As Seen On TV* emblazoned on the front. I took the deck out, and it felt good in my hands. Flipping through I could see they were basically an Egyptian-themed *Rider-Waite-Smith* knock-off. The design was simple with roughly drawn figures and flat, coloured backgrounds. I liked the very masculine energy the designs gave off. They were simple, but I knew they'd work for me.

'Wow,' I said, 'I do love this deck. It's weird and it grooves me. I really dig the painted nails on the female hands holding up three of the aces. Obviously swords had to have male fingers. At first I thought this pack was really male, but now I'm getting heavy feminine energy from it.'

'It's a truly hermaphrodite tarot, it switches.'

'What's the story? There's something strange about this deck.'

'The pack works, but Miss Cleo was a fraud.'

'What do you mean?'

'She claimed to be a Jamaican shaman but it turns out she was born in Los Angeles to American parents. Her real background was exposed when the Federal Communications Commission in the USA charged the businessmen promoting Miss Cleo with deceptive advertising, billing and collection practices.'

'What happened?'

'Steven Feder and Peter Stotz made a financial settlement to get the charge behind them, and Miss Cleo was ruined despite never facing a lawsuit like her backers. She'd appeared in a load of TV commercials advertising expensive telephone tarot readings and, although many were happy with her services, the American media wouldn't leave her alone. That pretty much ended her career as a psychic. *Miss Cleo's Tarot Power Deck* was withdrawn from regular sale and dumped into bargain bins.'

'But why does the deck work if Miss Cleo was a fraud?'

'The deck wasn't designed by Miss Cleo. Check the bottom of the box where it says the cards are the work of JF Lambert and Seth Stephens.'

'Oh, so she was just the celebrity face on the front.'

'Yes.'

'I like the way she looks.'

'She was born the same year as you.'

'But after me.'

'See you are psychic. Now I want you to pull a card from the deck.'

I did as I was told and chose The World. There was an Egyptian hermaphrodite figure on the card with streams of water running on either side of him or her.

'We're getting more like each other,' I observed. 'In fact we pretty much are each other.'

'We're even closer since we did our solstice sex magick. We're hermaphrodite psychic twins. We're ready to merge into a single being.'

I put The World back in the deck and handed the pack to Maria, who shuffled it. Like me she pulled The World. We didn't need to speak. We kissed. We were still caressing each other when we were thrown out of the Rochester Castle at closing time. We walked the streets of Stoke Newington arm in arm for another half hour before Maria got on her bike and cycled home.

Maria: Last night I started watching Pete Walker's *House Of Whipcord* on the Horror Channel, but I didn't see much of it because I fell asleep. The Horror Channel is doing a Lucio Fulci season at the moment too. I've seen all his horror films but they're well worth watching again.

Me: *House Of Whipcord* I don't like so much. I used to see it on double bills at the Scala. Too much of a women in prison flick, although there isn't a pukka jail in the movie, just nutters imprisoning girls. But Fulci is mostly great. His movie *The Beyond* is one of the best horrors ever made.

Maria: Yesterday I went to Umit & Son and bought three blaxploitation movies: *Darktown Strutters*, *One Down Two To Go* and *Three The Hard Way*. I'm sure you've seen them all already. When I got home I discovered the whole of *Darktown Strutters* is on YouTube. Doh.

Me: *Darktown Strutters* is one of my all-time favourite films. I have an old VHS. I don't think there's been an authorised DVD, but then Ümit sells grey-market DVD-Rs. Let's meet tonight. Do you remember a year ago you met me at my friend Pete's birthday do? I'm going to that again, but once you arrive we'll leave, I don't want him harassing you again.

So I went to the Eagle for Pete's birthday drinks at seven, and Maria turned up at nine. We were in the Sir John Oldcastle by 9.30pm. I was drinking water, and Maria had a cappuccino.

'I've got a tarot for you to look at,' Maria said as she took the pack from her bag.

I flipped through the cards. I'm sure Maria could tell from the look on my face I didn't like them. The imagery mixed the mystical and the modern. Everything from crystal balls and dice to a large passenger jet flying through the sky and a computer screen demanding a password. I could see the trumps were based on the *Rider-Waite-Smith* but the illustrated suits bore no relation to that deck. The Empress was a thin female with shoulder-length dark hair writing what I took to be a wish list. That might have been Maria, but The Emperor definitely wasn't me. It was some bearded dude in a light suit with a waistcoat that didn't match. He had a pocket or stop-watch in the palm of his left hand. He looked like the kind of guy who'd teach philosophy at some provincial university. I couldn't relate to him at all.

'This deck doesn't work. It's meaningless.'

'It doesn't work for you. It's the *Law Of Attraction Tarot*. It isn't designed for general tarot readings, just for the explicit purpose of realising your desires.'

'Well it won't help me realise mine. I can't dig it. Look at The Lovers. That's a close-up drawing of the faces of a couple kissing. I need both Cupid and another babe on that card.'

'What, representing me, you and Linda Lovelace?'

'Yeah, and I choose you.'

Maria laughed and we kissed. When we stopped kissing Maria said: 'I knew you wouldn't like the deck.'

'Why are you always testing me? You know who I am and you know I'm in love with you. Surely I don't need to prove anything?'

Maria laughed and we kissed some more. When we were thrown out of the pub at closing time we made out on the steps of Maria's tower block. I had trouble getting out of bed in time for my morning flight to Toulouse. I was the last passenger to board the jet.

THE DEVIL

XV

LE DIABLE.

Maria: Hey, I was looking at the praise you posted on your private profile for *Phantasm*. I was thinking about that film again after watching Fulci's *The House By The Cemetery* for the tenth time. I first saw *Phantasm* when I was very young. From the date on your post I can see you were thinking about it at the same time as me. That makes me tingle all over, psychic twin. We're so connected. Now you're back home let's have dinner somewhere new, somewhere we've never been before.

I got to Abi Ruchi on Stoke Newington Church Street before Maria. When she turned up she looked great in a cotton Ben Sherman black women's bomber jacket. It had white piping and a round collar that fastened with two silver poppers. There were plain black epaulettes on the shoulders. When Maria took off the coat you could see the lining was black too.

I'd seen Maria in the jacket before and the Los Perros T-shirt she was wearing beneath it. The image on the shirt was of a woman on her knees licking the boots of a figure cut off at the waist and dressed in a black German SS uniform. The background featured naked women huddled together behind a barbed wire fence, and near the bottom was the slogan: *German Tour 2002*. When I'd asked Maria about the shirt on a previous occasion she'd told me Los Perros were a Spanish garage band who'd toured Europe with Los Ass-Draggers two years into the current millennium. Moving down from the T-shirt, Maria was wearing tight black jeans and black leather boots.

We ordered the vegetarian set meal for two: various starters, then a main course of two curries, a dosa, rice and a cabbage-and-carrot side dish. When the waiter left us alone Maria passed me a tarot deck. The imagery was a postmodern mix of Renaissance and classical themes with flashes of surrealism. There were a lot of nude figures with simple outlines. The colours were muted pastels. There were decorative gold borders on every card and extra space featuring creatures and other motifs. There was a further white border beyond the gold one. The minor arcana were essentially traditional pip cards with figures added to the requisite number of suit symbols. Among the trumps the Wheel Of Fortune was titled Chance and Judgment became The Angel.

'There is a very male energy to these cards. I don't think they're gonna work for me,' I said.

'Of course,' Maria agreed, 'but that's precisely why they're good for me. I need to merge with you, so I need more male energy, you need more female. This is the *Renaissance Tarot* by Brian Williams.'

'I don't like the nude man holding open the jaws of a lion on the Strength card.'

'Williams claims it was the *Tarot de Marsella* that made the figure female, and that older Italian decks used a man, perhaps meant to be Hercules.'

'That can't be right because the tarot is about the mystical marriage of yin and yang.'

'I agree, I don't dig this deck.'

'That's good to know. Were you testing me again?'

'Yes.'

'You don't need to.'

'I do when I'm worried you're too good to be true. Then I start wondering if I'm dreaming. Testing you is how I pinch myself and make sure I'm awake.'

The conversation was interrupted by the arrival of our main

courses. As we ate, our conversation moved away from the tarot to punk rock.

We didn't want desert. We moved on to the Rochester Castle because it was easier to kiss there. When the pub closed we found an alleyway to have sex in.

Maria: Do you remember what I told you about guys eating me out?

Me: Of course, that you hadn't liked guys going down on you coz you'd endured that for hours when you were sexually assaulted as a little girl. Before me you'd only had one other boyfriend you allowed to do that. With the others it didn't work for you.

Maria: It's true. But I really like you to lick me out. When that creep who raped me did it, I was screaming I had to go back to my mamma, and when I did that he told me to shut up or he'd smash my brains out. And you know what else the fucker told me? He said he wanted to expel the evil from inside me. And this morning in the paper I read about a guy who raped a girl and said the same thing to her. The same. Unbelievable.

Me: Scumbags.

Maria: I'd rather think about you. It's so nice the way you work your tongue around my pussy. With most of my other boyfriends I didn't like it. I can't control how I feel. You doing it turns me on. With most guys I've just frozen when they've tried it. Can we meet tonight?

I got to Fortune Street shortly after 8pm. When Maria appeared at the entrance door of her block she was wearing a Women's Superdry Boyfriend Lumberjack twill shirt with a navy-mix peyton check. She had another of these shirts in the same check but with a blue, white, black, grey and yellow colour mix. She looked great in both, but the one she'd donned – which was mostly navy and red with a bit of white thrown in – was the one I liked most. We kissed before walking arm in arm to Sedap on

Old Street. The food was billed as Malaysian/Chinese fusion, and it was cheap. Mary Khoo, who owned the restaurant, was from Singapore. I ordered sayur lemak, or vegetable curry, while Maria had black-bean tofu. I had steamed rice, Maria egg-fried rice. We both drank green tea.

'Guess what?' Maria said.

'You've got a tarot deck to show me.'

'Yeah,' she replied, and we both laughed.

I could tell as soon as Maria handed me the pack that she liked the deck. The cards had her energy in them. She'd used them a lot. The scenes were non-traditional. The minor arcana were identified at the bottom of the card by suit and number. The main part of each card was given over an image. The nine of swords, for example, showed a man looking in a mirror with the face of a monster reflected back at him. It really was a nightmare card. The deck explored the shadow side that was so important to Maria. The trumps featured Justice as card VIII and Strength as card XI, the traditional *Tarot de Marseille* ordering. Justice showed a voodoo doll with pins stuck in it placed in front of a pagan idol. Strength featured a petite woman taming a huge demon. The Fool was a man in a straitjacket. The Chariot looked like it had been lifted from a vampire movie with a hooded figure whipping crazed horses.

'You know,' I said, 'if you'd shown me these cards when we'd first met I'd have hated them, but now I can see and feel what you take from them and they make perfect sense to me.'

'That's because we've become so much more like each other – complete – the way we're meant to be.'

'You've brought out my dark side.'

'It was always there, I've just freed it from being buried and imprisoned deep within your rational mind.'

'Are we gonna pick cards?'

'I want you to pick The Lovers.'

'You're confident I can do it.'

'You will.'

I shuffled the deck and pulled out trump VI. The man didn't

look like me but there I was, in another life and a different time. I was in the foreground as was Maria, our hands clasped together. In that time past Maria was my true love, my reality, just as she was now and always would be.

'What's this deck called?' I asked.

'It's the *Dark Grimoire Tarot* created by Michele Penco and issued by Lo Scarabeo five years ago. The major arcana are based on the *Necronomicon* as described by HP Lovecraft in his horror stories. Each suit represents a different grimoire – chalices for dreams, pentacles shadows, wands light and swords demons.'

'It's far out.'

'But quite easy to read.'

'Are you gonna pick a card?' I asked Maria.

She picked The World, the end of the tarot sequence, from where one could only go back to the beginning. We'd finished our food so we moved on to the Masque Haunt, where we curled up on a sofa and got more intimate.

Maria: Time passes so quickly when I'm with you. I hate to keep banging on about the same thing, but I so want to go somewhere far away from London with you, even if it's just for a couple of days. But before we do that let's meet somewhere we've never been together. I just did a tarot reading, and somewhere close to London Bridge is the best place to see you in this city. There are better places, but they are further away.'

Me: Let's meet tomorrow at 7.30pm or 8pm.

Maria: That's great. I've located exactly the right place. Now I'm gonna tell you something I never told you before. In Spain I used to have my own radio show. I did it on and off for seven years. Can you believe it, someone as shy as me doing radio? The few people listening to it really loved it coz I played great records.

Me: Wow. If you had a radio show now I'd listen even if it was in Spanish and I couldn't understand a word, coz I'd get to hear your voice. I've told you before that one of the things I love about you is how shy you are. But it doesn't stop you knowing what you want, and you're very good at realising your desires.

Maria: I love you on top of me, fucking away like a feral animal. This afternoon I had to go into the West End for my work to film a client. That was boring, but while I was there I sneaked into the Liberty store. So I was paid for the hour I was trying perfumes. I found a scent I really loved, but it was nearly sixty quid for a tiny bottle. I couldn't afford it and it made me think how great it was to earn serious money when I did professional BDSM. You know I'm always dreaming about setting up my own dungeon. I'd need another woman to help me with the domination, but it would be great if we also had you as the master. I could teach you everything you need to know.

Me: Me as a master? You really would have to teach me what to do.

We met at 8pm on the corner of Borough High Street and St Thomas Street, just south and west of London Bridge Station. Maria was wearing a black leather biker's jacket, black jeans held up by an inch-wide brown leather belt and black baseball boots with white laces, toe caps and edging. On her left wrist was a broad black elasticised cotton band with a skull and crossbones on the outer forearm side. Maria habitually wore this wristband to cover needle scars at the bottom of her left inner arm. She had turquoise, white and black bangles on both her wrists, and she was carrying a large dark-green leather handbag with a gold-tinted zip. Under her jacket she was wearing a T-shirt for the band Johnny Throttle. The front of the shirt had the band's name blocked out in rough letters, which were in turn framed by a broken rectangular shape; the cotton fabric was black and the logo was red, with the words 'Johnny' and 'Throttle' ranged one above the other. Maria's naturally black hair was dyed dark red and spilt over her shoulders; at the front her recently cut straight cabello reached nearly to the middle of her small, pert and perfectly formed breasts. There were hints of make-up around her mouth and eyes but it had been discreetly applied.

We went for coffee at the Barrowboy And Banker on Borough High Street, more or less opposite the entrance to London Bridge tube. We sat upstairs. I shouldn't have had a double espresso so late, but when I was with Maria it didn't seem to matter. We hadn't been seated for long when Maria took a tarot from her bag.

The artwork was postmodern primitive, simple and light and clearly influenced by the more representational strands of modernism including surrealism. There was even a touch of Egyptomania in the pictorial designs. The suits had become the four elements, with earth representing pentacles, air swords, fire wands and water cups. The court cards were named Father, Mother, Son, Daughter, and the aces were simply ones. Some of the trumps had been renamed too, with I becoming Trickster, II Virgin, VI Choice, VII Victory, IX Shaman, X Fate, XI Law, XIV Peace and XXI Aeon. V was the more traditional Pope as featured in the *Tarot de Marseille*. It disappointed me that Strength was card VIII and Justice card XI, the mistaken reordering found in the *Rider-Waite-Smith* and many subsequent decks. The trump numerals were all Arabic.

'There's astrological symbolism all over these cards, and I don't understand it,' I told Maria.

'You've just forgotten it, but I'm gonna sort that out. I'm gonna teach you astrology again.'

'This deck confuses me.'

'You don't like it?'

'I do like it, and I especially like The Empress.'

'Why?'

'Because that card features both of us. I'm your tiger and it shows you riding me.'

'I love you,' Maria said before kissing me.

'I love you too,' I replied.

'This is the Elemental Tarot. All the key words and symbols on the cards are there to help you understand the meanings.'

'But what about all the crazy bits of text on the sides of the trumps, like "I am the knowledge of my inquiry" on The Hanged Man?'

'Those words are taken from a Gnostic poem called 'Thunder Perfect Mind', and you'll find bits of it on all the major arcana.'

'Wild.'

'After a while you'll see the quotes make perfect sense in relation to the card they are set on.'

'Are we gonna pick cards?'

'You go first.'

I shuffled the deck and pulled out Fate, what would have been The Wheel Of Fortune in a conventional deck. On the bottom was the key word 'change' and along the sides of the card: 'do not be ignorant of me – be on your guard, I am control and the uncontrollable'. In the RWS deck this card upright would have represented good fortune. It was more ambiguous in the Elemental Tarot, although for me the slender figure in a yin-and-yang wheel represented Maria, while I was the person above her trying to hold her upright. The words from 'Thunder Perfect Mind' were about my girlfriend, not me.

'That's us on the cards,' I observed.

'I know,' Maria said, 'we don't have long.'

'I want you to be with me until the day I die,' I told her.

'We don't have long,' she repeated.

'It's your turn to pick a card.'

Maria shuffled the deck and pulled out the seven of air, what would have been the seven of swords in the RWS. The card showed me as a tiger, with my jaws around Maria's head, a reversal of what was shown on The Empress. Maria was simultaneously depicted lying on a cloud observing what was going down between us on earth. At the top of the card was the word 'wind', and at the bottom the name of Bunjil, the eagle creator deity from Australian aboriginal mythology. Bunjil was a key ancestral being alongside the trickster crow and took us back to the first trump in the tarot.

'You know,' Maria said, 'if this was a traditional pack, this card would be telling me I've taken what I don't own.'

'But it's not a traditional deck. I'm the tiger eating you but you're also floating above this scene. What does it mean?'

'What do you think it means?'

'That we're becoming each other and becoming complete in ourselves,' I replied.

'That's one way of looking at it.'

'But what's the other interpretation?'

'That it means the same as your card, we don't have long.'

'But why not? I want to be with you forever.'

'Let's forget about the cards. Do you remember I told you I could teach you how to be a master?'

'Yes.'

'Imagine if we had our own BDSM dungeon, then we could make money while we had fun.'

'Would you really operate with another girl and me?'

'It's better to have two girls, but you know how jealous I can get, so you'd have to behave yourself.'

'So there would just be three of us?'

'Yes, apart from a butler or maid.'

'How would we find slaves to pay us?'

'We'd set up a website. In my bag I've got some notes I wrote on the subject. I'm gonna read them to you.'

'You're crazy.'

'Yeah, and I hope you're crazy enough to do this with me.'

'Are you sure?'

'Yeah, now listen to what I wrote. "Two beautiful and perverse mistresses, and one unforgiving, strong and unbelievably handsome master, offer you the ultimate in the art created by the Marquis otherwise known as sado-masochism. At your request, by you writing to us, we'll select the most suitable submissives, and in time they could become our favourite slaves, receiving all kinds of delightful treats."'

'Why do they need to write? Why can't they just phone?'

'We don't want to waste time on people who'd call and wank while speaking to us,' Maria explained. 'We're professionals. We won't put up with shit like that.'

'Okay.'

'Now I'm gonna read more from my notes, so try not to interrupt,' Maria mock scolded. '"When you visit us for the first time, you'll have told us in advance in writing the best course of action to take with you – and using your secret code word is the only thing that can save you from any undesirable pain. You'll be received by a butler or maid and then the fun will begin. We'll give you a new name, and in a special ritual you'll be handed a dog collar to place around your neck. This symbolises what you have become – OURS."'

There was a lot more. Maria had written a dozen pages. When she'd read everything I asked: 'Is this a fantasy or do you think you can make this work?'

'It is hard to make money from BDSM now, there's so much competition. I'd love to do this, but we'd have to invest in a dungeon first.'

XVI

LA MAISON DE DIEU

THE TOWER

Maria: I haven't been in touch because I had a bike accident yesterday. The chain came off. I didn't want to fall into the traffic. I aimed for the pavement and hurt my face and knee. I'm covered in scratches and my nose is a mess. It was close to home, so I went back there. When I called my boss to say I'd be late he told me to rest for a couple of days. I really am in pain. Shit.

Me: I hope you recover quickly. But if you've still got wounds when I see you then I'll kiss them all better.

Maria: Hey, handsome, I've recovered, but unless you bring a balaclava I cannot let you fuck me with my face looking the way it does. Doh. I don't want you to see me like this. What a shame. My period still hasn't come and my tits are big and round and really nice. The flat in Dalston is free. Maybe I should turn all the lights off and have some fun with you. Or you could fuck me from behind – but not in my arse. I'll never let anyone do that, not even you. Why are we so unlucky? We've got a comfortable bed to screw in, but I'm embarrassed by how I've fucked up my face. I just want to cry.

Me: I'm sure you're as sexy as ever. The scratches will just highlight your beauty.

I sent Maria a series of messages saying I loved her regardless of how much she'd messed up her face. I also told her it was a shame not to make use of the flat in Dalston. It took me most of the evening, but eventually Maria relented and agreed to meet. I got to King Henry's Walk just before midnight. I had to sit on the step because my girl wasn't there. She arrived a bit flustered twenty minutes later. Her face looked fine to me. There were just some small cuts that she'd hidden well with make-up. We kissed before going into the flat. We talked as Maria made tea. Once the brews were ready we went through to the bedroom. When Maria went to clean her teeth in the bathroom, I took off my clothes and lay on the bed. Maria returned in her stockings, suspenders, pants, bra and a chemise. All the garments were black. She was also wearing a huge black strap-on and had a very naughty smile on her face.

'Wow, you look so good I could eat you,' I said.

'Do you remember what I said about teaching you to be a master?' Maria asked.

'Yes, you said I'm a natural for it.'

'But do you know the first thing a master has to know?'

'No.'

'What it's like to be a slave.'

'Are you sure?'

'Of course I'm sure. Before you can dominate effectively you have to understand what it is to be submissive.'

'Okay, I'm happy for you to peg me.'

'You're not ready to be pegged with this strap-on, it's too big. I don't want to force things coz this ain't about kicks. I want to release your emotions and turn your all man into all woman. Tonight I want a good fucking from you, but first you have to go down on me and take my huge black rubber cock all the way down your throat.'

'I don't know if I wanna do that.'

'Are you gonna go down on it? I want you on your knees.'

I pulled Maria onto the bed and started kissing and caressing her. I had no desire to suck a plastic cock. But I really wanted to fuck Maria. That said she wasn't a girl who liked to rush, so there was just a lot of gentle touching to start with. That night in Dalston, Maria got to bite me and scratch me and I did the same to her, but there was no master-and-slave action. The strap-on wasn't used. Maria told me if I didn't have it in me to role-play a bottom, I'd never become a top. But I didn't care, and I suspect she didn't either. We had each other, so we didn't need a BDSM dungeon with paying slaves.

Maria: I'm sorry I made you wait, but I was so paranoid about my face being a mess, I didn't want to leave home. The wounds are healing now. I really had a great time with you. You always make me so happy.

Me: Hey, you always look gorgeous to me, even when injured.

* * *

Maria: I've just got my period. I didn't want to mention it but I was worried I got pregnant that night we fucked in the alleyway.

Me: If I ever get you pregnant I hope you'd have the baby. I'd want you to have it, although it's not for me to tell you what to do.

Maria: I couldn't have an abortion. I lost a baby when I was much younger. I can't even talk about it because it was one of the worst things that ever happened to me. But I don't think I'm destined to be a mother this time around. I just took two ibuprofen coz I have a terrible headache. When the weather is hot like this I get pain at the back of my skull because of my rheumatism. It hurts so much. I don't think I'll be well enough to see you tomorrow. Maybe you could drop by on Saturday.

I got to Maria's block shortly after 2pm and had to wait for her to come down. When she appeared we kissed. We walked arm in arm to the Masque Haunt, where we ordered vegetarian roasts. While we waited for our food Maria produced a tarot pack from her bag.

'Check this out.'

The cards were quite big with the titles at the bottom in Spanish. The scenes were lino prints that had been hand coloured afterwards. The deck was obviously influenced by Rider-Waite-Smith, while attempting to cram all eras of history into seventy-eight illustrated cards. El Ermitano was a hermaphrodite and El Sol featured the head of a man on the body of a baby beneath a golden orb. The Fool was a woman. There were Aztecs, Egyptians and what looked like Native Americans alongside modern hipsters and medieval Europeans.

'This is crazy. It's Spanish, right?'

'It's a Spanish version of an American deck. *Tarot Mistico Universal*, or *World Spirit Tarot*. Do you like it?'

'I'm not sure. I like its weirdness, but it's so mixed up, I don't think I could use it for divination.'

'I just like looking at it. The deck is very light, and you know that isn't what moves me psychically.'

'You like the shadow side, and this ain't gonna take you there.'

'It's too cute to use for anything serious, but I still like it.'

'How many decks have you got?'

'I lost count.'

'You told me about thirty but you must have shown me forty.'

'I underestimated, I've still got more you should look at too.'

'Let's take it slowly. I don't want this occult merging to stop.'

We laughed and kissed. We didn't stop kissing until our food arrived.

* * *

Me: I'm helping out with a fitness promotion in Manchester on 26 and 27 October. I'd love you to come with me. I've got a double room booked in a hotel. It would mean getting up early on Saturday if you're gonna come on the train with me – you could come later, but I'd like you to come with me. I'll buy the tickets and the hotel is paid anyway. We'd get home late Sunday night, so you wouldn't be away from Sidney too long.

Maria: Are you really serious? Just one night away and the next day I can be back home looking after my cat? Now you're talking. At last. I'll go on the train with you. I don't care about getting up early. I'm so happy we're going to Manchester together. I've never been there, but I'm told it's a great city.

Me: I'll book the train tickets.

Maria: You make me so happy. You know I've been so bad in my life that I need to make up for it. I wanna tell you about some of the evil things I did. I can't bring myself to write them down and I don't want to say them to your face. So talking on the phone is gonna be best. Tell me when you're free to talk. Because of the life I led when I was younger, I'm trying to give something back to the world. I donate over £100 to charities every month and I feed every stray cat I come across. I was so bad in my teens and twenties, I still don't think I'm doing enough to make up for it. The thing I most regret is that my father didn't live long enough to see how I've changed for the better. At least my mother saw that, but there are so many things I wished I'd said to my father before he died.

Me: I'm sure your dad is proud of you. Let's speak in thirty minutes. I bet I won't think you're as bad as you say. But let's talk about it.'

We had a long conversation. Maria talked about the beatings the skinhead gang she led dealt out, then the more serious crimes connected to her time with the Hells Angels in Valencia.

Me: I can understand why you don't wanna write those things down. But I don't think you did anything too terrible. So many people have similar stories to tell but they don't feel guilty about their past. The stuff with your parents so many of us go through, and when your biker friends went out and did gang killings you didn't know anything about the murders until afterwards. So you're not implicated. Really you're a good person.

Maria: You're more forgiving of my past than I can be. I didn't want to say anything about it on the phone, but tomorrow I'm going to the hospital to have lots of tests done. My rheumatism is playing up. They're gonna check my heart. I had pains last week and my doctor wants to make sure the problems I had in the past haven't come back. I had more than ten years of treatment in Spain. But it's not contagious so don't worry. The worst possibility is that my heart valves are damaged. Sleep well.

Me: I really hope the results are good. Stay well, gorgeous, but even if you're sick I'll always love you. I guess you have to wait a while for the hospital to get you the results, but I wanna know what they are as soon you do, okay?

Maria: I love you. I've already got the results of the electro-cardiogram test I had this morning. They were good. But they also told me you can be in cardiac arrest and still have a normal ECG.

Me: I'm glad the first result is good.

Maria: After the electrocardiogram, they took an X-ray of my heart and needed blood. The nurse who was supposed to take the sample gave up because she couldn't get any, so another sister made me spread my arms like Christ on the Cross, but it still took her six attempts before she found a good vein. It was really painful. I have to wait three weeks for the results. I have to see my doctor to get them. I don't know what you've heard about rheumatic fevers. They say they're mainly found in underdeveloped countries with overcrowding and bad sanitation, but that doesn't match my situation. It's not a contagious disease but it can be hereditary. My brother had it too but not my parents. I was eight when it was first diagnosed. I had to stay in bed and rest for four months. Then I had penicillin shots in my arse for nine years. Imagine how many injections I had. Then I got fed up and stopped having them, that was when I first left home and everything was crazy and unstable for me. I'll tell you more about the symptoms when I see you. Right now the doctor's main concern is my heart valves. But I don't want to think about that. Do you know what I'd really like to do? I'd like to spank you. That arse of yours is such a delight. So white and round and firm. I want to bite your glutes and sodomise you too. I'm gonna give you a good bum fuck but only when you're ready, because I'll be doing it to release you as well as for our pleasure. Anal sex magick will clear your blockages and afterwards you're gonna have perfect recall of our past lives together. But before I can do that I have to prepare you for it. That said, I can give you a good spanking right now.

Me: What about we meet at the Wetherspoon's pub the Angel in Islington tomorrow night and discuss whether I'm up for a spanking?

I got to the Angel ten minutes early. The lighting was too bright, and it was smaller than many other pubs in the chain. It wasn't as nice as the Rochester Castle or the Masque Haunt. That didn't matter because I was seeing Maria, who was an hour late.

Maria looked great dressed all in black. Her usual black boots and jeans with a black flight jacket. When she took the jacket off I could see she was wearing her cotton William Burroughs T-shirt. It too was black, with an image of Burroughs in a suit and grey fedora hat screenprinted onto it. Burroughs was holding a pistol in his right hand, which was partially raised. *William S Burroughs* was printed sideways beside his left arm. Over his right shoulder were the words: 'Cut word lines, cut music lines, smash the control images, smash the control machine'. The garment was made by Skinnifit, and despite the fact it was a medium, it was tiny – there was no way I could have worn it.

Maria insisted on ordering us both vegetarian roast. We kissed until the meal arrived. We ate and made small talk, and when we'd finished our food Maria got out a deck of tarot cards. Like everything Maria owned, the deck smelt of Drum tobacco and exotic perfumes. The cards showed the usual figures in traditional costumes. The illustrations were primitive with turquoise, red, green and yellow dominating the colour palette. The minors were pips and the cards were trilingual.

'I recognise the English and Spanish but the third language is a mystery to me. What is it?' I asked.

'It's Basque,' Maria explained. 'This is the *Basque Mythical Tarot.*'

'So are those Basque costumes the figures are wearing?'

'Yeah.'

'It's crude, but I like it. The Devil is fantastic with those two horned animal figures chained up beneath him instead of humans.'

'This is a powerful deck. Tarot traditions in the Basque Country and Spain are different to France and Italy. We're more eclectic in our choice of imagery but different correspondences are used too. It's a distinct tarot tradition.'

'Are we both gonna pick cards?'

'Let's use our psychic powers, and after shuffling we'll both pull out Les Enamorados, coz that's who and what we are. Unless you want to go for El Emperador and La Emperatriz.'

'We'll do The Lovers.'

'Look,' Maria said after we'd both pulled out the desired card. 'In this version you've become me and I've become you. I've got fair hair and yours is dark.'

My hair had been fair as a child, but now it was brown, still I took Maria's point. There was a dark-haired man on the card with a fair lady on either side. The smaller one was Maria, the taller my ex Petra. My face was set straight ahead, but that was just for show. I knew in reality I'd turned towards Maria, the smaller woman on my right (but the left of the card). Cupid, who was framed by the sun and its rays, had his arrow pointed towards her head. And although my face was pointing neither one way nor the other, my eyes were slanted towards Maria.

Maria: I'm preparing things for Manchester. My period still hasn't come, but I don't care coz if you can't fuck me when we stay in the hotel, then I'm gonna make you my sub. I wanna send you into a sex shop to buy some anal toys. I wanna be there, but you have to pretend to be alone. I wanna see and hear you asking the shop assistant lots of questions about the best way to get your arse fucked. I'd like you to be a little scared about buying the bigger size of butt plug. I want you to feel humiliated, but just a little bit.

Me: If that turns you on we can do it.

Maria: A big butt plug would be a great souvenir of Manchester. When I go on trips I buy lingerie for myself rather than tourist stuff. I've told you before about how I got three whips in Dundee. Maybe I'll bring one to Manchester. I'm so tired today. I fell asleep several times at my computer. This biker Juan who I haven't seen since I came to London eighteen years ago just found my profile on Facebook. I sent him my number when I was at work this morning and he called me tonight. He just had to hear my voice apparently. He rang just as I got in, so I told him to call me back in fifteen minutes. I was still feeding my cat when he belled again, so I told him to hold the line. Then I sat on the sofa, and after five minutes of listening to him confessing he loved me, I woke up to find the handset on the floor and the line dead. Fuck. I fell asleep while I was talking to him. So embarrassing. He doesn't understand women at all. It hadn't occurred to him that I knew back in the early nineties he was in love with me. It was so obvious. Oh wait, I just got a message from him now. Gonna see what he says. Poor Juan.

Me: Wow, you really know how to twist men around your little finger. That's too funny.

Maria: Good grief, Juan got back to me and talked for hours. I'm only just off the phone. He's completely nuts. How can he think it's okay to reappear in my life after an eighteen-year gap and tell me he's always been in love with me? He told me that as time passed he loved me more and more, although he had no idea what had happened to me. He thinks this can only mean one thing, that it is TRUE LOVE. He's on holiday somewhere remote and had to travel seventeen kilometres just to call me. He didn't realise I'd fallen asleep. He thought I didn't want to speak to him because being showered with his affection bothered me. I told him I had a lover I was really into, and he claimed I'd change my mind if only I'd meet him. He also wanted my permission to fight you for me.

Me: You ought to make a movie about this. Instead of me fighting him, how about we have a competition to see who can hold a headstand for the longest time while simultaneously declaring their love for you? In the meantime maybe you could get him to buy you a Harley – or what about him bringing you a Triumph from Spain to London – that would be funny.

Maria: My ex Matias had the three different Triumphs – Bonneville, Tiger and Trident. And I've known Juan since we were both eighteen years old. I met him on a Sunday morning when some guy was trying to make a movie about bikers in Valencia. When we're on the train going to Manchester I'll tell you some funny stories about the time I spent with the bikers in Valencia. There were two rival gangs, the Centuriones and the Dracs. Although they were enemies I used to hang out with both gangs. I was also good friends with the only three redskins in Valencia back then, I really loved them, but I knew the right-wing skinheads too.

Me: When I was a teenager I knew a few kids with Bonnevilles – it was kinda a British obsession. But some also had BSAs. I was never into motorbikes myself, I'm happy with my scooters. It didn't matter much in London anyway. Biker gangs were always more of a small-town thing. But I'd still really like you to tell me your stories on the train.

Maria: One of the bikers I went out with who I haven't told you about was extremely handsome. His name was Felipe and all the girls were gagging to shag him. He's still good looking and quite charming but he's barely literate. So apart from fucking, fighting and riding his bike, there's not a whole lot he can do. I was the only girl, maybe the only person, he let ride his bike. But even then, if I was driving, he insisted on sitting behind me so he knew exactly what I was doing. He really wasn't bright, he never read a book in his entire life. Shame. Coz I always needed lots of mental stimulation, which is why you're so perfect for me. You have everything I need. Brains and a violent streak too. Don't deny it. You control yourself very well and you've put your past behind you, but I know if someone pushed you too far you'd go apeshit. That's why people don't mess with you. I understand that you wanna stay away from violence precisely because once you start hitting someone you can't stop until they're out cold or worse. I know you as well as you know yourself, and when I've removed your blockages you'll remember you know me that well too. I can't wait to go to Manchester with you. I need a break from Juan too. He sent me three messages tonight. I haven't answered them. He needs to back off and let me breathe. Sleep well, handsome.

THE STAR

I was nervous Maria wouldn't get up in time to make our train to Manchester. I had her ticket, and if she was late I was gonna have to go without her. I'd told Maria the train left half an hour earlier than its real departure time. She arrived ten minutes after me. She looked great with her hair dyed red, black T-shirt, black jacket with silver poppers, black jeans with a tear in the left knee and black Chelsea boots with three-inch heels. I felt elated and relieved that when it mattered she could be reasonably punctual. We caught the train with two minutes to spare.

Once Maria's pull-along suitcase was stashed away, she had both her hands all over me. As promised she told me stories about her time with the Hells Angels, and while some were funny, others were violent, and many involved drug dealing. Maria hadn't had breakfast, so she went to the buffet and bought food. When we'd consumed this, out came a tarot pack. The cards were done in a naïve but humorous psychedelic style. The dog on The Fool, if it was a dog, had pulled his master's pants down. The Chariot was dragged along by what I took to be a goat and a turkey. The Hanged Man was suspended upside down from what looked like a cello. And the female figure representing The World held flowers in one hand. The German name of the card was incorporated into the picture design, with the English and French equivalents underneath. The trumps had their Arabic number on the bottom left, with the corresponding letter from the Hebrew alphabet on the right. Justice was eight and Strength was eleven.

'Wow, these are a trip,' I said.

'What are they?' Maria asked me.

'It's the *Gipsy Tarot Tsigane* by Walter Wegmüller. He also lent his name to a krautrock album entitled *The Tarot*,' I replied. 'This pack looks like it's from the sixties, but I'm guessing they're from the seventies.'

'You're right and you're not guessing. You know coz I know.'

'Okay, so are we gonna do our usual trick and pull out The Lovers?'

'You go first.'

The card showed Cupid shooting his arrow from above a rainbow. I liked the fact that the two women on either side of the hippie male figure appeared to be touching him. We were The Lovers, so it wasn't hard for us to accomplish the trick of pulling it from the pack. We spent the rest of the train journey laughing, joking and touching each other.

Mike Henderson was waiting to meet us at the train station in Manchester. He whisked us off to a shopping mall where I had to stand on my head while he ran through what he could do for people if they signed up as members to his gym. Although Mike hadn't coached me, we pretended that he had. He got me to do various hand balances and other flash exercise tricks. Once he'd signed people up we went and did the same thing elsewhere. Then it was time for a lunch break. I couldn't eat too much coz I'd be standing on my head a couple more times that afternoon. Maria never ate much. The three of us split a plate of cheese sandwiches, with a coffee each – two double espressos and a cappuccino for Maria.

'So why did you get Martin to come all the way from London to help you?' Maria asked.

'The local woman I was using just moved to the US but didn't tell me she was going. I'll find someone else in Manchester to work with as soon as I can, but I needed a fill-in at short notice, and since I've been on fitness instruction courses with Martin I knew him and knew he could do what I wanted. It ain't easy to do all those balances he can do; it impresses people.'

'You should see what we get up to when he stands on his head with me.'

'Tell me.'

'No don't,' I put in.

'Tell him,' Maria instructed.

'Well, she's given me blow jobs.'

'We can't use that in fitness,' Mike observed, 'but maybe you've got a new career ahead of you making blue movies. I'm sure there are not many porn stars who can do that.'

We all laughed. Soon I was back on my head and Mike was giving his sales pitch. Maria had a copy of Terry Taylor's novel *Baron's Court, All Change* with her, but I was gratified to see she preferred looking at me. After two further demonstrations and more people signed up for Mike's fitness business, we called it a day.

'Four down, two to go tomorrow,' Mike observed as he drove us to our hotel, the Premier Inn, Piccadilly.

Mike headed off and we checked in. We were gonna meet him later for food. I thought we'd just drop our bags and then go out shopping – but Maria wanted to wash, change and redo her make-up. I lay on the bed reading her book while she was in the bathroom. Our suite was what you'd expect, with dark carpets, wood-look doors and furnishings, white sheets. In a word, generic. Once Maria was ready we walked to the Ann Summers sex shop in the Arndale Centre. The place seemed to be aimed principally at women since there was a lot of lingerie and some sex toys. It was the sex toys we were interested in.

'Go on,' Maria encouraged, 'ask the assistant about strap-ons. And I want you to tell her you're an anal virgin.'

'Okay,' I replied.

I had to wait until another man interested in the same items had been served. He bought a vibrating dildo and lube to go with it.

'Can I help?' a woman in her early forties asked me.

'I'm an anal virgin looking to take it up the backside for the first time, so I want a strap-on for my girlfriend that won't hurt me too much.'

'You'll need something small to start with.'

'Should I get some butt plugs too?'

By the time I said this, Maria's sniggering in the background was quite loud, and I found myself looking over to her.

'Is that your girlfriend?' the assistant asked. 'If she's the one who'll be giving you anal pleasure I suggest you get her to come over to help you choose.'

'Maria,' I shouted, 'are you gonna come and help me?'

'Okay.'

'Do you have any ideas about what you'd like?' the assistant asked Maria.

'I want something with curves in it. I've seen them online. It's like a series of hard balls joined together. I really wanna make Martin squirm when I fuck him. I want him to feel just a little bit of pain, so he knows I can dominate and humiliate him.'

'We don't have the type of device you're describing. As it seems you want to hurt your boyfriend and he doesn't want to be hurt, the two of you should discuss what you really need. I'll come back later if you need me.'

We looked at the sex toys, and Maria observed we'd probably get more bang for our buck if we shopped online. Besides, Maria insisted I still had a way to go in terms of emotions and muscle stretch before I was ready to be bum fucked. So we figured we'd leave buying the strap-on for now.

It had been raining quite heavily, and the seam down the side of my black Everlast bomber jacket had come undone. I needed a new coat. As we were already in the Arndale Centre we moved on to Sports Direct. I looked at jackets while Maria took in other clothes. In the end I picked out some Everlast items on a sale rail and asked Maria which one she liked best. We both agreed a blue-and-orange number was the business. It wasn't bad value for twenty quid, although that was twice what I paid for the coat I was wearing. There wasn't anything as nice as my old plain black bomber with a discrete Everlast logo, but nonetheless I liked the jacket I bought. I walked out of the shop with Maria on my arm and the old coat in a Sports Direct carrier. As soon as we passed a bin, I headed for it.

'What are you doing?' Maria asked.

'Throwing my old jacket away. It's no use now.'

'You like it, right?'

'Yeah, I like it, but it's come apart at the seams.'

'Don't you know how to fix that?'

'It's not worth mending.'

'I'll sort it. I'm good at sewing.'

'You don't need to.'

'Well if I don't you're gonna throw the coat away, right?'

'Yeah.'

'That's a waste. I'll take it home and fix it for you. There's nothing wrong with the jacket, it's just a broken seam.'

'I've had it for years, it's worn and it only cost a tenner.'

'Don't throw it away, I'll fix it.'

'Thanks,' I said.

By this time I was hungry, and I was happy when Mike belled me on my mobile saying he was ready to eat. We hooked up with him in the Waterhouse in Princess Street. It was only a few minutes' walk from where we were. Being a Wetherspoon's, as soon as we entered the pub it seemed familiar. Mike had a table. He bought our vegetarian roasts and a curry for himself. Maria had her usual coffee, but Mike insisted I have a beer to accompany his drinking. I hate beer, but what could I do?

'I don't understand the economics of Martin coming here to help you out. Can you explain it?' Maria addressed the question to Mike as we ate.

'You'll have to ask Martin about it. I sent an email to all my fitness contacts asking if they knew anyone who could work with me in Manchester this weekend. Six hours' actual work for sixty quid, I didn't include the travelling time between gigs. I didn't expect Martin to offer because he must have lost a bundle of money on it, I'm not paying his expenses. I guess he wanted a weekend in Manchester.'

'That's about it,' I confirmed.

'How long have you two been together?' Mike asked.

'A couple of years,' Maria told him.

'What happened to Petra?' Mike asked.

'It didn't work out,' I said. 'But then I met Maria, and I've now found my soulmate.'

'Don't ruin it by getting married,' Mike laughed. 'That was the biggest mistake of my life.'

'Where's your wife tonight?'

'Playing bingo.'

'You're kidding.'

'I'm not.'

As we ate the conversation went around in circles. Maria and I talked about how happy we were together, while Mike bitched about his marriage. Before we finished, Mike got up and bought more drinks. When we'd consumed these my girl said she wasn't feeling well and wanted to go back to the hotel. I said I'd go with her, but she insisted I stay with my friend. Mike stuck with the pints, and because he was insistent I keep drinking, I had shots of Laphroaig whisky. Mike wouldn't stop going on about how his marriage had gone cold but he still loved his wife. I got away when Mike's wife phoned him to say she was coming home from bingo.

When I got back to the hotel Maria was lying in the bed with the lights out. I said hello, kissed her, then cleaned my teeth and took my clothes off before snuggling up under the sheets. Once I'd run my hands all over her beautiful body I realised she was wearing sexy lingerie beneath an oversized T-shirt. I was nude. We spent a long time touching and kissing, but eventually this turned into love-making. We took things slowly, changing positions every now and then. Maria was on top of me when I finally came. I was a bit drunk. I wasn't used to boozing any more, and I'd had a few with Mike. Still everything felt good and Maria seemed to like the way I was, a bit loose.

'Did you really feel sick when you left, or was it just an excuse to come back before me and put on something sexy?' I asked Maria when we were both lying flat on our backs.

'You know my health isn't good. So I needed to get away, but of course I wanted to look good for you too.'

That made sense, and maybe it was unfair, but I still wondered if Maria had come back to the hotel and changed then had a bit of smack. If she had it wasn't important. What defined Maria was her incredibly smart and funny personality, not whether or not she took drugs. And I'd told Maria I couldn't stop her taking shit even if I preferred her not to do so. It was her life, and I knew from observing my mother it could be hard to get over a drug habit. My suspicions may have been unfounded, but even if they weren't it would have been wrong of me to let Maria know I had them. She had to trust me enough to tell me what she was doing, and for that to work I had to avoid being or seeming judgemental; just saying I suspected she might have been using was always gonna sound wrong. I really didn't want to force her into a defensive position where she felt she had to lie to me about her drug use.

'Did you feel okay by the time I got back?'

'Yeah, I'd had a shower and time to rest. But now I wanna ask you about this work you're doing. It isn't really work if you're losing money on it, is it?'

'No, but it seemed like a good way to get a weekend away with you.'

'It's so great to be with you,' Maria whispered, 'but I'm still missing Sidney.'

We laughed and kissed and talked some more before falling asleep. It was fabulous to wake up in the morning with Maria beside me. I knew she didn't like sex first thing, so although I felt like a fuck I didn't try it on. I was happy I didn't have a hangover. I couldn't eat too much for breakfast coz I was gonna be standing on my head later. After several cups of coffee in a café down the street and not much else, we went back to our room and packed our bags. Then when we'd checked out we wondered where Mike was until we realised the hour had changed. British summer time had ended while we were making love that night and the clocks had gone back an hour. We had time to kill, so we left our bags at the hotel and went for a wander around the deserted streets of Manchester. It was so great to have Maria on my arm and laughing in my ear.

When we returned to the Premier Inn, Mike was waiting for us in the lobby. We put our bags into the boot of his car and headed off for Hyde and then Glossop. It was the same routine as the day before, and Mike was happy with the number of people he signed up either to his bare bones gym mini-chain or as personal-training clients. He dropped us back at the station with just enough time to catch our train. I was so happy to be alone with Maria again. We'd bought takeout falafel wraps on the way to the station; we didn't need to use the buffet. When we'd eaten, Maria got out a tarot deck.

'These are big,' I said as I took the cards from Maria.

'Not as big as some of the other decks I've shown you. Do you remember the first tarot we looked at?'

'Of course, the *Giger Tarot*, when we were in the Masque Haunt.'

'Yes and that was bigger than this. Do you remember the deck we examined in the Slice Of Life?'

'The mysterious Spanish major-arcana-only tarot, 1980s drawings but based on a traditional *Tarot de Marseille*. The inspiration was of Renaissance Provençal design, which in its turn was allegedly based on a now lost Gothic Catalan prototype.'

'That's right, and although those cards were slightly narrower than these ones, they were also considerably taller, so they have the same or perhaps even a greater surface area.'

'But neither of those were full decks, they were just trumps without pips.'

'I know, but I also have full decks that are bigger than this one. I have some giant *Rider-Waite-Smith* cards that I don't shuffle, I just use them for meditation on the tarot. I have other big decks too, but I'm not gonna tell you about them now. I want you to concentrate on these cards. Have a look through and tell me what you think.'

It was another hippie gypsy deck, like the one we'd looked at on the way up to Manchester by Walter Wegmüller. This pack more obviously drew from the *Rider-Waite-Smith* tradition, with some *Crowley-Harris-Thoth* influences thrown in for good measure. In the trumps, Strength was eight and Justice eleven. It was wrong, but the followers of the Golden Dawn tarot system would never change their ways. There seemed to be a lot of clowns in this deck, even The Hanged Man had a painted circus face. There were too many hippies, punks and rock-and-roll hipsters for my taste, although I could see Maria digging them. The colours were garish, and the inclusion of figures like the Mona Lisa and what I took to be Marilyn Monroe also put me off.

'I can tell you don't like The Magician being renamed The Juggler and appearing as a clown. You didn't like The Fool as a clown in the *Royal Tarot*. But surely The High Priestess being renamed The Wise Woman grooves you?'

'The overall shape of The Wise Woman has more than a passing resemblance to a giant pussy. I can get into that. She's the all woman and what fundamentally differentiates a woman from a man.'

'Do you like me as Lilith?'

'No, I like you as The Empress. You're gorgeous, there's no way you're a night hag, a female demon.'

'I quite like the association.'

'When The Empress is Lilith and The Emperor becomes Osiris, they don't make a pair. They're from different mythologies, one Jewish and one Egyptian.'

'But the mythologies aren't from distant parts of the world, they originate in the same region.'

'They are distinct,' I insisted. 'But why has The Pope, who *Rider-Waite-Smith* transmogrifies into The Hierophant, become The Grand Master?'

'In past lives we were both Templars. It's our Grand Master. Never forget Hugues de Payens or Jacques de Molay.'

'I haven't forgotten the Hospitallers' Grand Master Foulques de Villaret either.'

'You must like The Lovers. There're two chicks on it.'

'Neither of whom are hot enough to be you, and the guy is a hippie too.'

'Do you like the half-angel, half-demon towering behind them?'

'I'd prefer to have Cupid.'

'You're such a traditionalist. So what's your opinion of the six of wands? Some people think it depicts Jimi Hendrix.'

'No,' I said after shuffling through the cards and finding the six of wands, 'that couldn't possibly be Hendrix.'

'Why not?'

'Well, aside from the fact that the main figure on the card doesn't look like him, it shows a right-handed guitar player, and Hendrix was left-handed. For the figure to be Hendrix the guitars would have to be the other way around.'

'That makes sense to me too. I can't make myself see this figure as Hendrix either.'

'Six guitar necks to represents the six of wands makes the picture look kinda psychedelic, but I'd prefer more hands. What the hell does this mean?' I added after shuffling the deck and pulling out the five of cups.

'It's your card,' Maria insisted. 'Look, there's a naked man on it doing a handstand.'

'But what about the masked men and the infinity symbol made out of a snake?'

'It's you in the future. You're gonna go through a lot of self-examination after a major loss.'

'Now that I've found you, I ain't gonna lose you.'

'I'm not gonna live forever.'

'I don't like where this is going. Why don't you tell me something about the artist who made this deck?'

'Her name was Birgit Boline Erfurt, and when she worked on these cards she was living in the alternative community of Christiania in Copenhagen. So a lot of the subjects are just people around her in that hippie paradise. A few of the cards were created while she was on a gypsy caravan trip through Denmark. She also fronted a band called Boline. So she was an artist and a musician to boot.'

'You really go for some crazy tarots.'

'Yes, but the ones I most usually carry with me are quite

traditional,' Maria insisted. 'And those are the tarots and rune stones that work best when I want to see my future with you.'

'How often do you use them to help you understand our relationship?' I asked.

'Most days,' Maria replied.

I pulled Maria towards me and we kissed. I didn't want the train journey to end, but it seemed that all too soon we had arrived in London. We spent another hour in the Euston Flyer, a Fuller's pub near the station. Then Maria went south with my old jacket, which she'd said she'd mend, and I headed north to Stoke Newington.

XVIII — LA LUNE

THE MOON

Maria: Sex with you always feels good, but in Manchester I had the best orgasm ever. It was amazing. You made me feel so incredible and my weekend was more than great. You're a catalyst for making everyone I know love and praise me. You fill me which such happiness that I just spread all the good energy I've got around, and that makes everything happen in this perfect way. How much I love you. You make me laugh, you make me come and you make me feel like I'm seventeen again. I've got so many great friends but none of them do what you do to me. I never felt the way I do about you with anyone else.

Me: I love you so much too. And now I've got a busy week with clients when I'd rather be with you. Doh.

Maria: I did a lot at work. I had a fourteen-hour editing marathon. I stopped for half an hour to get some food and had four five-minute breaks to give my eyes a rest. But I was sitting so long that when I stood up I couldn't walk. My work paid for a cab to get me home. My boss was really happy with me. He'd have lost an important account if the editing hadn't been done on time. Our clients loved the video, and I'm having today off in exchange for the extra hours I did yesterday. I'm gonna go to bed soon, but first I'm gonna light some candles for our dead loved ones. I've got candles for both our mothers so they'll come to us. Last night I had a nightmare in which I was trying to convince a serial killer that if he let me live he could have fun with me.

The fucker kept saying: 'Hey, girl, that just doesn't cut it. I'm gonna have my own personal fun torturing you to death.' The dream was so real and horrible that I woke up screaming. That won't happen tonight coz my mother will be here to look after me.

Me: I should be at your place taking care of you.

Maria: I'd really like to go somewhere with you and a bunch of other people, escape for a bit so we can fuck, then go back to our friends as if we hadn't done anything. The idea of it really turns me on. Would you like to do that?

Me: You've got me so horny now.

Maria: My fantasy is we fuck and both come in three minutes, so no one can even guess what we've done. Well you know how easily I come with you. And I really want to fuck you on my staircase again.

Me: Sounds like a plan. We can do it next time I come to Fortune Street.

Maria: Now you're making me horny. You're so naughty and so highly fuckable. I want to fuck you forever. I just love you fucking me. I'm quite dominant. But it really turns me on when you grab me roughly and get me to do things your way. I love it when you're pressing down on top of me making things go the way you want. Coz you're so much stronger than me, you make me feel vulnerable and I like that. I'm not into being humiliated in a sado-masochistic way, I just like the fact you can so easily control me physically. I don't want to be hurt. And I won't be coz we're so very good together. It's some kind of alchemy. Something that happens when we smell each other and I feel your flesh against mine. Nobody else ever made me feel the way you do. I really would do anything for you. I can't believe I haven't got involved with someone else given how long we've been seeing each other now. You're the first man I've ever been faithful to. When will we meet next?

We hooked up in the Rochester Castle. Our plan had been to

have a coffee then find a restaurant we'd never eaten at before. Of course once we'd found a booth and cuddled up together we were more interested in each other than going somewhere else.

'I brought a tarot deck,' Maria said.

'It's a deeply occult set of cards.'

'How did you know?'

'We don't have any secrets, what you know I know.'

'Psychic twin,' Maria laughed as she kissed me.

Eventually the deck came out of Maria's bag. I looked through the pack. It was a curious mixture of systems. The pips were unillustrated and done *Tarot de Marseille* style. They were clearly identifiable as coins, swords, cups and batons – but they were also marked French suit style as diamonds, clubs, hearts and spades. The deck was numbered from one to seventy-eight, the major arcana came first with the The Madman AKA The Fool being both zero and twenty-two. The cards had upright and reverse meanings printed at the top and bottom, loosely lifted from Etteilla's first deck. The trumps were marked with the twelve signs of the zodiac and various planets, with the moon on The Popess and a skull and crossbones on Death. These were Egyptian-themed cards drawn in an art deco style, and the symbolism owed a lot to Papus and his book *The Tarot Of The Bohemians*. Justice was eight and Strength was eleven.

'You could use this deck for anything,' I told Maria. 'Even for a game of cards. They're designed to multi-task.'

'It's the *Cagliostro Tarot*.'

'The eighteenth-century freemason and adventurer?'

'Yes.'

'He didn't put this together. I can see the influence of Papus in it and the trumps are of early-twentieth-century design.'

'It's only named after Cagliostro. It was first published in Italy in 1912 by Modiano.'

'Are we gonna pick cards?'

'You go first.'

I pulled out card thirty-six, the ace of batons, or the ace of clubs, or the ace of wands. My card was one of two pips influenced by the *Rider-Waite-Smith* deck, with a hand holding the suit symbol. Aside from swords, the other aces and the rest of the pips looked much more like traditional *Tarot de Marseille* cards. The royal cards were done as mirrors. My pick had a slender hand holding a huge branch in a humanoid shape. The upright meaning given at the bottom was: 'BIRTH – LETTER'.

'Since I met you,' I said to Maria, 'I've been reborn. We don't have to take the word "letter" literally, it just means I'll be receiving important news in the near future and coz you're so important to me it'll be about you. It's not gonna be this year. It'll be next year, 2014. Now you pick a card.'

Maria pulled out a trump, card fifteen, The Devil. It showed a voluptuous naked woman tethered to a nude man. Satan floated above them like Cupid on The Lovers. A caduceus, two serpents entwined around a rod, was also in evidence. The card Maria had chosen was marked with her star sign too, Sagittarius, the archer who was half man and half beast. The key words on this card were: 'DESTINY – PHYSICAL LIFE – FATALITY'.

'Okay,' Maria took a deep breath. 'It was our destiny to meet. The carnal must act as the basis for our spiritual marriage and merger, transforming what is base into something elevated.'

'What about the fatality?'

'We've got a fatal attraction.'

Neither of us wanted to address the last prompt word on the card in terms of death. The idea of bondage represented by the tether between the male and female figure seemed appropriate for Maria. We didn't spend long talking about trump fifteen because a Spanish couple who knew my girlfriend came up to our table. I was introduced, and a few minutes later I went to get more coffee so that everyone else could talk in Castilian.

'Hey,' Maria said when I returned, 'there're a load of my friends here, we must have come in after most of them. They're all at the back.'

'Do you wanna go and talk to them?'

'When we're ready to leave. Let's drink our coffee first. I'm gonna go order food too. We ain't going anywhere else now.'

When we'd finished our meal we went to the back of the pub. There we found a huge group of Spanish skins and punks. They'd put a lot of tables together so that they could all talk. I was taken around and Maria introduced me as her boyfriend. There were smiles and a lot of greetings. We didn't sit down, so there wasn't any serious conversation. Maria said we had to go.

'That was so nice,' Maria said as we left the pub and headed north, 'to see all my friends and for them to see you.'

Maria walked me to the corner of Manor Road. We kissed and whispered sweet nothings in each other's ears. Finally Maria turned around to go and get her bike. I wanted to take her into my cousin's flat, but I couldn't in case we woke my niece.

Maria: Last night I had a horrible nightmare. I was in a very big squat in a city in the Middle East. There were lots of flats with missing doors and even parts of floors and walls had disappeared in some places. I was exploring the entire building, going through the bedrooms and seeing all these sleeping children in deplorable conditions. Then I realised some of the children weren't sleeping, they were dead but still in bed lying next to siblings who were alive. I had pictures of these dead children in my handbag, so I took them out and started to stick them on a wall. Every time I looked in my bag I'd find more photos of dead children. I really wanted to get all the pictures on the wall so that I could count them and there were hundreds of them. I was reassuring children who were awake that nothing bad was gonna happen and that I'd take care of them, but I had to get all the pictures on the wall before I could help. I spent ages putting photos on the wall and listening to the cries of children calling out to me. What a weird dream.

Me: Wow, that's whacked out. But given how much time you spend feeding stray cats and rescuing snails, it's probably just an extension of your desire to make the world a better place.

I was seeing Maria that night, in a flat she'd borrowed close to where I lived. From my cousin's place it was a short walk to Stamford Hill. I ran into Maria as I was wandering around the Summit Estate looking for the right stairwell. We kissed. My girlfriend took me by the hand and led me to a one-bedroom pad with nothing much in it. Maria made tea in the kitchen, then we went through to the living room. Like the kitchen this space had white walls and posters for various punk rock events stuck on them. There was a sofa and two chairs, a small table with a portable radio/CD player on it and a dozen CDs. We cuddled up on the sofa with our drinks.

'Whose pad is this?' I asked.

'Freda, you met her on Sunday in the Rochester Castle. When I was going to get my bike after I left you I ran into her again and told her about our situation. She said we could use her place tonight coz she'd be out late.'

'What time will she be home?'

'Not before 3am, maybe later.'

'We'll be gone before then.'

'That's what I told her.'

'There isn't much in here,' I observed.

'Yeah, but Freda is so lucky to have a room more than me. I have so much stuff in my place and it's only a bedsitter. I really need more space.'

'I don't think I know anyone with a big pad in London. Sometimes people in provincial towns have big houses. But I'd rather be in London with less space.'

'I really need another room or two, just so I don't have to be in the same one all the time.'

When we finished our tea we went to the bedroom and did all the things we'd talked about doing together. Around 1am Maria and I took a bath, then we cleaned up the flat before we left.

Maria: Did I ever tell you when I was younger I made three different men come just by kissing them? I swear they never got to fuck me. Each time it was just frottage with our clothes on and kissing. One of them tried to pull my knickers off but I didn't want him to, so I made him come before he got my pants down. Afterwards he was so apologetic. Poor boy. He's dead now. I'm gonna make you come just by kissing you, I want that so badly.

So we met every day and just kissed. I wasn't allowed to touch myself and Maria didn't give me any form of relief. I'd call on Maria in the evening, and if I didn't have much time we'd sit and kiss on the stairs in her block. If I'd seen my last client and the pub was still open then we'd head either to the Sir John Oldcastle or the Masque Haunt. We'd been doing this for a week, and I couldn't believe I hadn't jerked myself off when I called on Maria again. We kissed, and I wasn't expecting anything to happen coz we were just greeting each other and planned to go on to the Masque Haunt to continue our experiment, but I came in my pants.

'Oh fuck,' I said, 'that felt great.'

'Did you come?' Maria asked.

I didn't need to answer because she already had her hands in my briefs and was fingering the sticky mess down there. There was a huge smile on Maria's face and she kissed me some more. In the Masque Haunt we got tap water and a cappuccino before sitting down on a sofa.

'Hey, I want you to look at this deck,' Maria said pulling cards from her bag.

'What's this?' I asked.

'*Tarot Genoves.*'

'You mean a *Genovean Tarot*?'

'You make me laugh, you're so monolingual. You turn everything into English.'

'It makes me happy to make you happy.'

XVIIII — THE SUN

LE SOLEIL

Maria: I've been meaning to tell you about a boxing champion I knew in Valencia called Fernando Riera. I'd just escaped five years of junkie hell with my biker boyfriend Matias. It was December 1993, and I was getting out again after years of not socialising. I met Fernando, and it was love at first sight for me. We became close, but he already had a girlfriend. She was clever and knew I was a potential rival, so she befriended me. Because I liked her, I couldn't bring myself to hurt her. She was a traditional Spanish woman who lived for her man and wanted a marriage with kids. I couldn't take him from her. If Fernando had your intelligence and wit he would've been the most perfect guy to ever walk this earth. But he was a man of few words and wasn't into reading. He'd just say things like this week I'm gonna work on this muscle, he'd show it to you and he'd work on it. The following week it would be bigger.

Me: Better to work on your muscles than read books, but best to do both.

Maria: Fernando worked as a bouncer in the Villa Adelina, next to Barraca in Les Palmeres near Sueca. Although everyone who went to those clubs was drugged up to their eyeballs, Fernando never took anything. He'd train for hours every day. I met him on New Year's Day. I'd had an argument with some tosser who'd tried to get fresh with me and asked my friends to sort him out. I told everyone I wanted this cunt beaten up. When people saw the guy who'd pissed me off nobody would fight him. This surprised me since my friends were all hard as nails. I found out later the big man was a killer who'd just got out of jail and had a reputation for violence that left my bad boy mates looking like kindergarten kids. Since nobody would take care of the fucker, I grabbed his hair and pulled his face down so that I could ram my knee into it, but he was so tall my blow didn't connect. My friends were yelling at me to stop. A mate who worked for security tried to restrain me, and in the heat of the moment I bit his arm. When security managed to separate us, the killer told me he was gonna make me kneel on the floor and beg for my life with a gun at my head. No one dared say anything to the cunt. Security put the killer in a car and took me inside and told me I was crazy. They said that no one was gonna help me as I'd picked a fight with the meanest motherfucker they'd ever come across.

Me: That's crazy, but what's it got to do with Fernando Riera?

Maria: Sorry. I just got carried away remembering that night. A bit later Riera showed up, and my mates told him about the fight. So he sought me out and we discovered we had a lot of friends in common. He knew the Dracs Motorcycle Club but not my ex Matias who'd belonged to that MC before it disintegrated.

Me: So what about the big man you had the fight with? Was he a biker?

Maria: No, the killer was just a jail cunt. Riera was the only person who said he'd help me with that big bastard if he showed up again, which is how he won my heart within minutes of us first meeting. But I never saw the killer again. After that whenever Fernando had a prize fight I took along as many of my biker friends as I could. That made Fernando so happy and it was great for all of us. His girlfriend Cristina couldn't watch him in the ring. She'd be with Riera's mum waiting for the result like a good girl. Me and the bikers went on a ride to celebrate when he became Spanish super welterweight champion.

Me: Would you believe my former professional boxer friend is now a Buddhist monk?

Maria: Is that true? A Buddhist monk?

Me: Yeah, and he'd been a really promising fighter, but he did an opponent some serious damage in the ring, so he gave it all up and eventually became a monk.

Maria: Wow, I'm sure he's a great guy. But I want to finish my story. So I had a friend called Julia, and she was the only person I confided my love for Riera to. Julia knew Cristina, and she used to say to me that if he left her she might kill herself. So Julia told me to behave myself with Fernando. When Riera started to hold me I wanted to kiss him, but I told myself, no I can't. We never kissed but we were always touching. He used to come and clasp me tightly from behind just to see how long it would take me to escape. Usually I ended up hurt because he held me too hard, then I'd hit him and run behind some trees outside the club. But he always found me and put me in a bear hug again. We were like four-year-olds when we were together. This went on every Sunday for a whole year. Meanwhile, Julia split up with her partner of eight years and found a new boyfriend called Leonidas. He didn't go to the same clubs as us and he played in a punk band. Julia was very excited about her new relationship, and I was very happy for her. One day I was gonna go to Barcelona to visit a friend. Julia thought it would be a good idea if Leonidas went with me. He had to book a few gigs there and I could take care of him. So she put me on a bus to Barcelona with this guy I'd never met. Poor sod. I was on speed and spent the whole trip talking non-stop about Riera. But we did have a really good weekend and bonded as friends. Leonidas is an Aries like you. When we got home, Julia accused us of liking each other too much and said we weren't allowed to spend any more time together. We couldn't believe it and met secretly just to be able to talk.

Me: Oh no. Funny and sad.

Maria: Sad for Julia coz we fell in love. I guess when you're assumed to be guilty of something but you're innocent, it makes sense to act out the transgression.

From what had been said at other times, it was clear to me there was another boyfriend called Pedro between Matais being dumped and Maria getting it together with Leonidas. Maria's relationship with Pedro and friendship with Riera must have overlapped. Pedro was a drug dealer, and he and Maria bought a big flat right by what became the Science Park in Valencia. In the end Maria lost her flat to the bank before the mortgage was fully paid off because rather than selling most of the heroin he was getting wholesale Pedro was pumping it into his own arm. As far as I could make out, losing the flat was what finally ended Maria's relationship with Pedro. She'd hooked up with Leonidas around the time she'd lost the flat, and he was the boyfriend who'd arrived in London a few weeks after her.

I was seeing a lot of Maria and I won't recount all the details. For a week I was training a client every evening in a private gym on Chiswell Street, a few minutes' walk from Maria's flat. So we were going out every night and then having sex on the stairs in her block when we came back from the pub. We had alternate nights at the Masque Haunt and the Sir John Oldcastle. One night in Old Street as Maria came back from the bar, we caught a junkie opening her handbag, which she'd left on our table. I grabbed the guy while Maria checked to see if he'd taken anything. She kept her credit cards and cash in her phone case, so they were always with her.

'Okay, cunt,' I said as I spun the guy around and gave him a hard shove in the direction of the door, 'you better go. But if I catch you trying to rip shit off me or my girlfriend again, you'll regret it.'

Quick as a flash, Maria got between me and the geezer I'd given the warning. She grabbed the would-be thief from behind and deployed her knee as weapon. He took a direct and very painful hit right under the coccyx. After that the guy couldn't get out of the pub fast enough. I used to think I'd left my violent temper behind in my teenage past, but Maria could bring out the street fighter in me when she was in need of protection, and she clearly liked to see this side of me. That said, mostly we had good times without any aggression kicking off.

Time passed quickly, and before I knew it I was buying birthday presents for Maria and dressing up to attend her office Christmas party. For that I put on a nice Ben Sherman and jeans, which Maria liked much more than the sportswear I habitually donned. Maria's workmates were lovely, and we stayed at the party longer than planned. We'd only intended to go for thirty minutes before catching a gig. By the time we got from Mare Street to the Shacklewell Arms in Dalston, Los Chicos had played. This was a band from Spain that Maria really wanted to see. We were in time for headliners the Cannibals, but while enjoyable they were past their prime and did too many crowd-pleasing covers of well-known sixties garage rock songs like 'Sometimes Good Guys Don't Wear White', that one originally by the Standells. More curious was being introduced to Maria's ex Steve, who'd grown up on other side of London to me. He was funny but very drunk.

'So you like foreign birds, do you? You'd better coz Maria's great but takes a lot of looking after,' he told me.

'From what I've seen she can take care of herself.'

'She's the toughest girl on the punk rock scene and will start a fight with anyone, just look out you don't have to finish it for her.'

Maria knew so many people that every time I turned around she was talking to someone I hadn't seen before. Among her friends there seemed to be a division between those into booze and others who favoured different highs. Maria took a long break in the toilets with some girlfriends who favoured illegal kicks.

Me: Your friends were nice. The English ones were funny, reminded me of the kids I knew at school, same working-class humour. The guys were all handsome, but none of the girls were nearly as pretty as you. Now I can't wait to see you on your birthday.

We had Maria's birthday meal in Pho, a Vietnamese restaurant in St John Street, close to her flat. I gave her some DVDs and books. She was most immediately intrigued by Toshio Matsumoto's *Funeral Parade Of Roses,* a movie she didn't know. We ate and somehow the conversation turned to José Ramón Larraz, a Catalan director we both appreciated more for his horror films than his sex comedies. We were no longer talking about cinema by the time we moved on to the Sir John Oldcastle and found ourselves a booth in the pub.

'Hey, I've got something to show you,' Maria said as her hand moved from my leg to her bag.

'Another tarot deck?'

'It's a really crazy one, and you're gonna tell me why.'

'It's the *Royal Tarot* from Taiwan published by Kuo Kau Paper Products in 1995,' I said. 'There's supposed to be another version of it with the same cards but different backs known as the *Mystic Tarot.* It's our deck because we have to complete each other, just as these cards join up two different tarot traditions. The *Royal Tarot* really does split the difference between the *Tarot de Marseille* and *Rider-Waite-Smith* tendencies.'

Maria leant over and kissed me. When we'd finished our soft drinks we got more, and when we'd downed those we walked arm in arm around the City of London. Eventually we were on Fortune Street. We played around on the steps inside Maria's tower block. My girl wouldn't let me have penetrative sex with her. She was suffering her monthlies and said it wasn't safe. She made me come even if I wasn't allowed to do the same for her. If anyone had been watching us they'd have thought it was my birthday rather than Maria's.

Maria: Today I got some top-quality snow from Antonio. I met him at lunchtime. I thought some coke would get me through work this afternoon. I just made a speedball, I snorted half the snow earlier. There are days when doing speed or snow are the only things that fire me up to finish my editing. I'm in the toilets and I just sorted myself out, so I'm really high and you can't imagine what filthy things I'd do to you if you were here. But you ain't. Doh.

Me: Speedballs are not my thing, but being with you and doing naughty things is.

Maria: Now I'm waiting for the rain to stop so I can cycle home. Today I'm sad, that's why I needed the snow, it's the anniversary of my father's death. Fuck. I wanna go home.

Me: I could pick you up on my scooter and we'll get soaked together.

Maria: Don't be silly. I'm just gonna sit at work watching the Swedish vampire movie *Frostbite* until the rain stops.

Our Christmas plan had been to stay in the Dalston flat vacated over the holiday by Maria's friend whose cat needed feeding. That didn't work out because my girlfriend was using smack to blot out the still unprocessed pain of her father's death. I'd told my cousin and her family I was having Christmas lunch with Maria and I didn't want to impose, so I walked the streets alone rather than tell them I'd been blown out. My family knew I had a girlfriend. I'd talked a lot about how great Maria was and how happy she made me but had skipped over her drug use. My cousin wanted to meet Maria, but my girlfriend always made excuses whenever I tried to arrange a date. She wasn't ready to meet my cousin. She said she was worried my cousin wouldn't like her.

Maria wasn't up for seeing me until Boxing Day, the last night the Dalston flat was free. First we went to a party in Stoke Newington where, among others, we met Thurston Moore from Sonic Youth. I was more interested in getting to King Henry's Walk. It was late when Maria used her phone to film us fucking in front of the big mirror in the bedroom. She wanted me to appreciate how good my arse looked. I told her it was nothing special considering the amount of squatting and lunging I did.

Maria told me her nephew was renting Olga's flat for a New Year holiday, so we could go there and use the spare room.

Maria: I rang the guy with Olga's keys a hundred times today and all I got was his messaging service. Eventually he returned my calls and now everything is sorted. I just need to meet my nephew off the plane. We can go to Olga's flat as soon as he's settled in. I'm gonna cook something Spanish. We can have dinner with my nephew and his girlfriend. Afterwards we can fuck and then watch TV, and then fuck some more. My nephew won't mind, he's got the big bedroom and we'll have the small one. I can't wait to have you in my arms. Can you come around 9pm?

Me: I might even get to you for 8pm.

Maria: I've told my nephew you and me are gonna watch some films in the little room after dinner. He'll probably go to the pub with his girlfriend. Don't come at 8pm coz my nephew and his girlfriend probably won't be home. They've gone into the West End. I've come back to my flat and they've got the keys, so they're gonna have to let me in when they return. I have butterflies in my stomach coz I know I'm gonna see you. I love the feeling coz it shows all the years when I numbed myself with shit to avoid dealing with my emotions are behind me. Isn't it great? The only time I get this feeling is when I'm gonna see you or when I'm gonna get smack...

Me: Wow.

Maria: I shouldn't have said getting smack gave me the same feeling as seeing you because it isn't really true. What I feel for you is much stronger.

Me: My love for you grows every day, which given how deep it is already is almost unbelievable.

Maria: Not a word from my nephew. Maybe he's on the tube or somewhere with no coverage coz when I call I get a message saying he's unavailable. Don't come until we know he's at Olga's place. The minute I hear from him I'll let you know. My nephew isn't like me. He's very sensible and responsible. I can only think he's lost as he doesn't know London too well.

Me: I'll hang on till I hear from you.

Maria: Strange I still haven't heard from my nephew, not even a text. Do you think his phone battery is dead? He had trouble with Olga's adaptors. But if he's home he could have sent me a message via Facebook. Please bear with me and when I know what the fuck is going on I'll send you a message.

Me: I'll wait to hear from you.

Maria: Still no news from my nephew. This is so out of character that I'm sure that he's at Olga's with a dead phone and no way to contact me. Can you meet me at the Daniel Defoe in forty-five minutes and we'll go there together. And if my cousin and his girlfriend aren't around we'll find somewhere secret and I'll give you the best blow job ever.

Me: What a mess. I'll see you in forty-five minutes.

Maria: I'm on the bus. Earlier my tummy was full of butterflies but now there's a big lizard in there. Can't wait to see you.

I was standing on Stoke Newington Church Street waiting for Maria, and I heard her before I saw her. She was on the phone shouting angrily in Spanish. Her screaming attracted a lot of attention. I'd never seen Maria so agitated, and I didn't have to wait long to find out why. She ended the call as she approached me.

'My fucking nephew is being led astray by his girlfriend. He's the straightest guy in the world and he's gone to the West End and got stoned. He says he doesn't feel like coming back right now and is gonna stay out. He fucking promised me he'd have dinner with us and he's got the fucking keys so we can't get into the fucking flat. He never takes drugs, he's into sports, so what's with smoking the skunk? It's his fucking girlfriend. And what's with the fucking girlfriend anyway? He's nearly thirty and he's never had one before. *¡Joder!*'

'It doesn't matter,' I reassured Maria as I put my arms around her, 'I'm just happy to see you.'

'It matters to me,' Maria said. 'I was so looking forward to slowly cooking you a Spanish omelette and then fucking around in Olga's little bedroom. I'm so angry I need some shit to calm down.'

'Please give me a little time first. Let's get a drink. We can go in the Defoe or walk down to the Rochester Castle.'

'I'm too pissed off to go to the pub. I need smack. I promised you the best blow job ever if we didn't get to Olga's flat. And with you I always keep my word.'

'You don't need to do that, it was just a flippant comment.'

'I wanna make you come, then I'm gonna leave you and get high. There's a little park by the council flats in Yoakley Road, we'll be there in no time.'

I could see there was no point in arguing, so we went to the small garden. I lay on my back on a park bench in the darkness with Maria kneeling beside me. She didn't rush things because she'd promised me the best blow job ever, and she was as good as her word. Afterwards I said I'd go to the bus stop with her if she didn't want to go to the pub. Maria told me she wasn't going straight home. She knew a dealer who lived nearby and wanted to score. She didn't want me with her when she did that.

Me: Hey, it was great to see you yesterday. I wish we were together now. I know you were disappointed not to get into Olga's flat, which would have been great, but it really didn't matter to me. I love you but if you need time out that's okay, just contact me when you're ready to connect again.

Maria: I've been feeling very anti-social for the last few days, sorry. That's why you haven't heard from me. Today I felt okay. I've even made peace with my nephew. I haven't done too well staying away from shit this Christmas. Sorting that out once I go back to work is my New Year's resolution. Antonio said I should see in the New Year with him coz he has loads of gear. The temptation is too much so I'm gonna finish my binge and you'll see me once I'm clean again. I know how tonight is gonna go already. I wish I was strong enough to be with you instead. In case I'm too stoned to talk on the phone later very Happy New Year! I love you.

Me: I love you too.

* * *

Maria: This holiday has been so lonely. I've hardly seen anyone and I've avoided talking to my big sister coz she's gonna ask me how her son was when he was here and I don't want to tell her lies. Can you believe he sent me a message listing all my faults.

Me: Better not to get into it with your sister. If you tell her your nephew was getting stoned she'll probably blame you, although it's not your fault. Don't say anything, just pick up with your sister where you left off. No mother wants to hear criticism of their son, so please don't tell your sister anything about the visit.

Maria: I feel like shit. You're the best thing in my life.

Me: Can I see you tomorrow?

Maria: What the fuck is happening to me? I've been so moody lately. If I saw you I wouldn't be good company, although seeing you never fails to improve my mood and make me happy. Having been home so much doing drugs I realised my life revolves around my blind sick cat and trying not to give in to the temptation of getting high. I haven't been to Spain for more than three years, and I have a lot of stuff to sort out there. But I can't leave Sidney. I tried to spring clean, and every time I moved a box or a bag Sidney went mental. I've told you I made a corridor from the bedsitting room to the toilet at the end of the flat so she could get there and back. I can't let anyone into the flat because of all the things I've had to do to accommodate Sidney. I can't even let you inside. And I often think how nice it would be to have you here with me. Imagine. No more hassle when we want to fuck each other. I feel so guilty for resenting Sidney. And I can't resent her coz she loves me no matter what I do. Can you see how sad and helpless this situation makes me?

Me: You need somewhere with a garden for Sidney and someone you could really trust to look after her so you can go away.

Maria: I'm on the verge of a mental breakdown. Sidney's so important to me. I really love her. When we snuggle up and she makes her little noises – I don't know the English word but in Spanish it's *ronronear* – I forget about everything. Then I know I'm doing what I should be doing coz it comes from my heart. I never knew what unconditional love was until Sidney showed me. That's why I'm so delighted with our relationship too. So not everything's bad. I'm trying to see the positives here so that I don't go mad.

Me: The word you're looking for in English is purr. I told you I had another friend who has no social life coz she has to look after her sick cat, all she does is go to work and go home. That unconditional love you feel is worth more than anything else you could have in life, so even if life is hard, remember it's also very worthwhile. I know I'm writing platitudes, but what else can I do when they're so true. Can we meet tomorrow?

Maria: I've been offline because I was high. I was finishing some coke I had. But soon I'm gonna clean up my act and spend lots of time with you. I'm so sorry I haven't seen you or arranged to meet you because I've been off my box.

Me: Hey, it's alright. I'm just happy to hear from you. Let's meet in a day or two. Whenever you're ready. Should I send you some BDSM tunes by Adam And The Ants to remind you of your dominatrix days?

Maria: Sometimes I miss being a dominatrix and I really miss the money I got from it. It was such a good deal for me. All my anger was productively channelled, and back then I was very angry with the whole world. I was treated like a goddess and I got paid for having fun. The first afternoon I did it I earned £450 in four hours. Coz it was the first day

Cindy, the owner of the dungeon, didn't bleed me dry in commissions. I like punk-era Adam Ant but the best tune I discovered from your Facebook postings is 'You Got To Crawl To Me' by Johnny Davis, that could be a BDSM title, and the song is amazing, it sounds different every time I hear it.

Me: I think maybe you are happier doing what you do now – but if you wanna be a dominatrix again I'm sure you could do it and be really good at it.

Maria: I could do it after work when I'm tired and pissed off. I could do it at weekends too. Tomorrow Kristina is putting my name on the guest list for Dirty Water, if you can come it would be great. I think it's in Whitechapel.

JUDGEMENT

I arranged to meet Maria at Hamilton Hall on Bishopsgate, so we could have a quiet drink before we went to Rhythm Factory on Whitechapel Road. Liverpool Street Station was heaving, so the pub was busy too. Maria was late, and as soon as she arrived we headed south-east. We held hands as we walked.

'I wasn't at home,' Maria told me, 'I was close to where you live. That's why I'm late.'

'Were you seeing Olga?'

'No a different friend.'

The last time I'd seen Maria it had been close to my cousin's flat, and she'd left me to see a dealer. If that's where she'd just been I didn't want to get into it, I wanted to bond and only when things felt good address any difficulties in Maria's life.

'Some guys tried to start a fight with me while I was waiting for you,' I said to change the conversation.

'So what happened? Why didn't you cream the geezers hassling you?'

'There were fifteen of them. Outside a fictional kung fu film there's no way one person could have beaten them all.'

'You were practising the art of fighting without fighting?'

'That's what everyone should do when they know they can't win.'

'Tell me what happened.'

'I was drinking a double espresso, and a guy from the group came up and tried to knock my hat off. I ignored him so he started calling me names. I downed the remains of my coffee and walked out the pub. I thought that would be the end of it, but the whole lot of them followed me out. They'd been to football and were drunk. The same guy tried to knock my baseball cap off again, but I ducked so he didn't connect with it. By this point he was very riled up and his mates were making wanker signs at me. I noticed there was a line of coppers drinking coffee by a stall, so I went and stood right in front of them, then turned and looked at the football gang with a big grin on my face.'

'What did they do?'

'They looked really pissed off, and since the rozzers obviously weren't going anywhere fast, the gang left coz they didn't wanna get nicked. You turned up just after.'

Before we got through the door of the Rhythm Factory I was thoroughly patted down and Maria had her bag searched. The bouncers missed her garrote, and if she had a knife then it must have been well hidden too. I assumed Maria also had concealed gear. As she'd been searched Maria engaged the bouncers in conversation, commenting on their huge muscles and how much she liked men to look the way they did. I took this to be a diversionary tactic to put them off doing their job properly, and one that worked.

MFC Chicken got on stage shortly after we arrived. I paid more attention to the audience than the band. There wasn't a teenager in sight; most were younger than me but still in their thirties and forties. A good percentage of them looked Spanish and spoke that language. MFC Chicken had a 1950s take on music with Las Vegas Grind leanings. Tight and entertaining but nothing I hadn't heard before. King Salami And The Cumberland 3 didn't have the purist approach of the opening act, being unabashed garage revivalists with a touch of the more energetic pub rock bands of the seventies – more Hot Rods than Ducks Deluxe. The Dustaphonics were retro-futurists too and mixed some soul into their rock-and-roll and garage influences.

The bands were loud enough to prevent a coherent conversation with Maria. She ducked into the toilets and left me on my own for quite a long time. When Maria came back she'd been visibly enhanced by a stimulant. After the entertainment finished we hung out and talked with Maria's friends in the barroom we'd passed through to get to the hall in which the groups played. It took a while to leave because my girlfriend was clearly in two minds about what she wanted to do next. The choices were to head off with me or go and do drugs with friends who had some high-quality cocaine. I had no wish to snort my way to a temporary nirvana, but if that turned Maria on I wasn't going to be judgemental about it. Without me putting any pressure on her she decided to stay by my side, but as we headed north she picked a fight and before long had stormed off.

Me: Hey, you've gone all quiet on me and everyone else. No sign of you on social media. But it's better to see you than just catch you online. Can we meet?

Maria: I need a break from social media sometimes. Do you know what I really need right now? You to fuck me good and hard. I want you to blow my mind as you always do. That would make me happier than anything else. And it could do miracles for our relationship too coz you know that if I'm happy and content, then you can do whatever you want with me. But I'm sure you figured that out long ago. So when are we gonna meet???

Me: Is tomorrow night or Sunday gonna be best? Whichever it ain't gonna be that early, after 8pm coz I got clients. I could do with a really good fuck too. From my point of view seeing you both days would be ideal, but you've probably got gigs lined up and I didn't think I mixed too well with your friends at the Rhythm Factory.

Maria: I promise this weekend will be better than last weekend. It was okay to start with, but after I'd had some gear in the toilets and wanted more I behaved really badly. Don't think I don't know it. I gave you a hard time for no reason at all. I got angry because I'd left the people with the lines and gone off with you. Sadly you now know what I'm like when I want drugs and I haven't got them. I was too embarrassed to contact you and I was also worrying myself silly that you wouldn't want to hear from me. This week I'm back on track. It's stupid for me to get all wound up and give you a hard time. What a waste of an evening. I didn't have any money of my own, and the agreement was if I went and bought gear for those that wanted it with cash they'd given me they'd let me have a generous share of the supply, coz I know all the best dealers. There are plenty round my way but for super pure the best is close to you.

Me: You have all the top connections, and I don't mind what you do. But when I see you I just want you to myself. So when will we hook up?

Maria: Saturday is better for me. Sunday I'll restart my medication cycle, and I know I won't feel so good. Guess what? In a secret corner in my work building someone has left a big round leather seat for a group of people, like you'd find in a hotel lobby. It's very comfortable because it has no arms or legs. I was using it this afternoon and thinking what an interesting place to have a fuck or to get licked or sucked... you can sit on it but you can also lie on it. And of course we can film ourselves making use of it. When I was lying down there during my break I was thinking I could film you giving me oral sex. You could lie back and I'd sit on your face and shoot you from above as you licked my pussy.

Me: Sounds great to me.

Maria: That's my boy, I've been missing you so much. You haven't even fucked me yet and already I'm willing to do anything you want. Just by saying the things I wanna hear you exercise so much power over me. You're so Machiavellian and I love it. I wouldn't wanna do it with anyone else, but I wanna make dirty movies with you. I have a samurai sword and many daggers and big knives. We could put a bit of a story into what we're doing. I like the idea of me taking out a shotgun and then forcing you to strip and lick my pussy. That would look great on film. If I can't get

a shotgun by tomorrow night we could use my samurai
sword instead. What do you think?

Me: I'm up for anything.

Maria: My period is starting. We can't make a porn film while
I'm bleeding, but I still want to see you. What do you want
to do instead, handsome?

We met at the Angel in Islington. It was halfway between us and
made a change from the Masque Haunt, the Sir John Oldcastle and
the Rochester Castle. I'd been trying to get a client to master the
kettlebell swing, and in the hope he'd grasp it had gone over his
allotted training time. Despite more than half an hour of extra
tuition, he was still failing to do a satisfactory hip hinge and I was
late for Maria. I wanted my client's swing to resemble a deadlift; it
was so common to see it performed as if it was akin to a squat, but
that was not what I wanted. I insisted on a snap at the hips as the
bell went up to shoulder level only; the arms were to be used simply
as a lever.

'I like you to be late,' Maria assured me. 'It's usually me, but
I'm glad that sometimes you aren't punctual.'

'You make me laugh. No one is supposed to like other people
being late.'

'Well I do, but only if it's you.'

Shortly after, two roast dinners appeared. Maria explained
she'd pre-ordered them. The waitress apologised and said they
were short of hash browns for one of the roasts, so she'd given us
extra potatoes and veg. It wasn't just a little bit more of these
things, it was a mountain of them. It was the end of the day, and
if we hadn't been given this super-sized meal I guess the extras
would have been thrown away. Maria insisted I have the hash
browns, and when the waitress had gone she tipped half her plate
onto mine.

'Hey,' I said, 'you know there were 1,010 calories in my meal
before you added more.'

'How to you know that?'

'If you're a fitness instructor you have to access all the websites with that kind of information, so you're on top of diet as well as exercise for your clients. There are places that provide nutritional information on the food sold by chain restaurants and pubs. If I was training you the way most women want to be trained, you're eating about half your calories for the day right now, so I hope you had a light breakfast and lunch.'

My words had an effect because Maria heaped more food on my plate and told me I could eat it because I'd been working out all day. It was a shame Maria had her period coz otherwise I might have fucked the extra calories off that night.

Maria: How handsome you looked yesterday. I want to shag you on the stairs in my block. I know it isn't the best place to do it, but when I'm there with you it feels so bad it's super good. It's like being a teenager again.

The next time we got it on was in Mare Street on a night Maria worked late. The cleaner came in while we were at it. I had to hide. Maria spent ten minutes talking to him. Once he left we were back at it.

Maria: I'm enjoying myself so much fucking you. You shouldn't let the cleaner turning up bother you. He didn't know we were there. It's such a thrill being naughty like that. I had such great orgasms after he arrived to do his chores. You make me come so good. I love fucking with other people around as long as they don't know what I'm doing.

Me: I had to wait until after the cleaner went to have an orgasm. I was worried I'd make too much noise and alert him to the fact I was there. You dealt with him so well, but I wish he hadn't come in.

Maria: I've fed the feral cat that hangs out in the garden behind my work. She's had her kittens. Yesterday afternoon I took Sidney for her annual check-up coz the vet won't give her tablets if he hasn't seen her for a year. I had to spend £70 for nothing coz when he saw her he said she was fine.

Me: Glad Sidney and the feral cats are good. I just heard my friend Pete Sudden died in a motorcycle accident. I had to cancel my clients and go to the gym on my own for three and a half hours. I couldn't deal with people after getting that news.

Maria: Good friendships transcend time and place, as we both know. I'm sorry for you. I'm sure your friend doesn't live in London coz you've never mentioned him to me.

Me: He emigrated to Australia fifteen years ago. I last saw him in 2010 when he was over here doing a DJ tour. I saw a lot of him in the nineties. I was so cut up when I heard. I still loved him although he was so far away.

Maria: I wish I could help you. Why don't we meet up? My tits are getting bigger so I'm sure my period is coming. If we don't use this chance then I'll have to wait too long to have sex with you again. I know now is not the right time to talk about shagging but I want and need you to fuck me. C'mon.

Me: I'll come to your work tomorrow night. After I've seen my last client. I hope the cleaner isn't there.

Maria: Not too late please. I have to spend the whole day at work. But do you wanna fuck or are you just trying to please me?

Me: Right now I'm a bit down, but you'll excite me and I'll be happy to shag you tomorrow.

Maria: Sleep well and don't be too sad. Just think of all the good times you had with your friend and maybe he's somewhere better than we are.

I got to Maria's work not long after 9pm. We had missionary sex, and after Maria had her first orgasm she gave me an anal fingering. The cleaner didn't show, so we had several hours of uninterrupted pleasure. But one thing surprised me: during the anal action and afterwards Maria was more brutal than I'd ever experienced her during sex.

Maria: I was so tired when I got in from work I couldn't even stand up – all because of you and your cock. I'm a bit sore, are you?

Me: No, I'm not sore – just happy.

Maria: I'm very lucky getting to see the expression on your face before you have sex, it's something that only happens if I've teased you quite a bit or you're teasing me, and you've been made to wait. You look like a cat and I so love it. That's why I like to get you really steamed up and ready for sex and then pull away for a bit. I'm not normally a cock tease, but I so like seeing that look on your face when you know I'm finally gonna let you fuck me having made you wait and wait and wait. That smile is so unique and I'm sure hardly anyone has seen it. A lot of guys wouldn't be able to take what I do to you and they certainly wouldn't smile after I'd done it, they'd never be able to smile like you anyway. I love the way you patiently play along with my games and never get mad at me or try to force me to fuck you before I'm ready.

Me: I don't mind you teasing me coz I know there will be pleasing eventually, and having to wait is such a great way of building expectations and excitement.

Maria: I'll always fuck you in the end, but that isn't the case with everyone. When I was a dominatrix I'd drive guys crazy and not allow them any release. They paid me a lot of money to do that too. Whereas we are really connected. You don't know how amazing it makes me feel when you say you love me. But if a john said that to me it would just make me angry.

Me: I really love you.

Maria: This morning when I was at work I got a call from a number I didn't recognise. A woman with a Latin American accent asked if she could speak to Maria. She introduced herself as Erica from Venezuela. She'd got my number from this young guy Fernando. He has the most amazing six-pack, his chest is completely hairless and his skin looks like caramel. He's moved away now, but he used to live in a big house in Islington. He was gonna let me use one room as a dominatrix dungeon. When Erica said Fernando gave her my number I couldn't remember who he was, but after she hung up it came back. Erica wanted to ask me a big favour, but she was on a bus and couldn't speak freely in case she was overheard. She was in London and we were talking in Spanish. She said she'd call again when she got home. I'm sure you know by now what she wanted to ask me. And it was weird coz I hadn't seen Fernando for at least a year. She belled me when I was at Tesco this evening. She wanted my advice about becoming a dominatrix. Unbelievable because as you know I haven't done anything in that line since 2007. That's seven years ago, and I only did it for seven years. Erica said she'd done a workshop with a woman who runs a fetish website. I laughed when she told me about what she'd been taught. It was really stupid, and she paid £70 for it. But she's single and has a young daughter and is really desperate for money.

Me: Wow. Someone teaching a BDSM workshop for £70 sounds like desperation. If they were good they'd be getting more doing it rather than talking about it. Did you agree to help Erica? You're always saying you wanna get back into being a professional dominatrix. Of course, you'd need a dungeon, and if she has a kid around you can't do it at her place.

Maria: I don't know what I want any more, but she knows about dungeons you can rent for £50 an hour. Which would leave us with £100 profit on an hour's session. I told Erica how fierce the competition is and that she's an amateur. What else can I say? That's the truth. She begged me to meet her, even if it's just to talk. So I told her to call me at the end of next week and she's gonna invite me for lunch. All that dominatrix stuff makes me think about us having sex. Something weird happens to me sometimes, especially the last time I gave you some anal training. It's like I go back to when I was working in the dungeon and that isn't really about sex.

Me: We shouldn't do anything you feel ambivalent about.

Maria: I like to give you pleasure, and there are magickal dimensions too. When you're ready to have your arse properly fucked it's gonna be great. Coz I'm gonna release your inner woman and I'll have some fun with you at the same time. I wanna be the first person to peg you, and once I've done it I'm gonna get some other witches to gangbang you. I'll blindfold you first so you'll never know who they were, and I might tease you a bit by telling you there's a man among them whose also gonna bum fuck you.

Me: I can believe you'd do more than tease me about that.

Maria: Don't say that, I might do it. Yesterday I was looking at that gay novel I told you about, *Entertainment For A Master.* This is sounding so wrong. I wouldn't want you to go totally gay on me. I guess at most you'd be bi. I think everyone is bi-sexual but most are afraid to explore or admit it.

Me: Well I'm into you, and even if I liked being fucked by men, it wouldn't stop me digging you. Right now I'm only attracted to you.

Maria: That's great, but I've gotta avoid what occurred the last time we had sex. It hadn't happened since I was a dominatrix. I became someone else. It's never happened before with anyone who wasn't a john. I always switched into that other personality when I went to the dungeon and dragged up in my fetish gear. I didn't expect it and I couldn't control it, that's why I was so rough with you. When I was with those men who paid me to hurt them it wasn't me doing it, it was someone else.

Me: The way you've described your work at the dungeon you sound like someone else. Someone really angry. I like playing around and experimenting, but I want your love too.

Maria: I haven't told many people about my dominatrix years. And I don't tell many about my smack and crack festivals either. But you know pretty much everything about me.

Me: Well no one knows as much about me as you.

Maria: Carolina asked me if I'd like to do some dominatrix work with her on webcam. I don't like anonymous people watching me, so I said no. But then we came up with the idea of the men she does escort jobs for paying for me to make a porno movie with them and Carolina, not for distribution, just for the john to keep. Carolina will take the escort money, and we'll split what the john pays for the film. Carolina says loads of the City types she works for will pay £400 to be in a movie that will take me twenty or thirty minutes to shoot. Of course, I'll have to edit it afterwards, but that shouldn't be a big job. I could really do with the money. I'm a voyeur but that doesn't mean this will get me all horny and excited. It's a business venture. Hopefully it will give me practice at making blue movies coz maybe one day I'll become a porno director. I've always wanted to change the way dirty movies are done. To add some plot and make them more classy.

Me: Your film ideas sound great. Go for it if you can. Happy Valentine's Day too.

Maria: Happy Valentine's. I got your Valentine's card today. That made me so happy. And when we meet tomorrow please wear tight trousers, not your gym gear. Guess who wears sportswear in Spain when it's obvious they haven't worked out in years? Junkies of course. They look so funny, so totally out of condition in gym clothes. I'm gonna wear my furry zebra trousers for you. You'll love them. I haven't worn them in ten years. Really. I got too fat and couldn't get into them. But I washed them and tried them on again the other night, and now I've lost weight they fit. I've got butterflies in my tummy coz I'm gonna see you.

Maria arranged to meet me at the Shacklewell Arms in Dalston at 10pm. She wanted to see the Thee Tumbitas who were on at 9.15, but getting her hair right took priority over top-flight Galician garage rock. I arrived at 10pm and decided to wait outside for Maria coz the place was packed. Eventually I received a call. Maria had got halfway to the club on her bicycle when her trousers split and now she was going home to change them. She told me to catch the support acts, but I stayed outside looking at shit on my phone. While I was doing that I missed Sonic Angels and the Hypnotic Eye. When Maria showed more than an hour late we went inside.

'You should have gone in to see the bands.'

'I came for you, not the music.'

'But the groups are really good.'

'They're not as groovy as you.'

A mystery all-girl band were playing when we went in. I never did find out who they were. They were rough and unrehearsed and possibly only existed for that one night. The group were on stage to honour Maria's friend Jimena because it was her birthday. I was introduced to Jimena and got her a drink. She'd started celebrating her birthday the night before at Garageland in Camden and looked like she'd had a good time. She asked me if I'd come along for her final birthday shindig with a bunch of live bands on Sunday, but one night of rock and roll at the weekend was enough for me. Before long the Revellions from Dublin were on stage. They were hyped as arriving via a time machine from 1967, but to my ears they were closer to U2-style stadium rock. They fell far short of my ideals of psychedelia and garage rock. It was a shame I'd missed those lower down the bill, but then I'd only myself to blame.

After the show everyone hung around for the DJs and to socialise. Maria introduced me to dozens of mostly Spanish rockers. I stayed for another hour but then thought it best to split. I had to get up early to see a client, but I also left because I didn't want to cramp Maria's style. If I did we were bound to have a bust up like the ding-dong we'd got into after going to the Rhythm Factory. Every time Maria came back from the toilet I could see she'd got even more chemically enhanced. We had so much in common, but drugs were her world and not mine.

Maria: I just came out of the Shacklewell Arms to smoke. I also wanted to tell you how much I love you. I'm really high.

Since you went I've had a lot more coke. I'm gonna get sick coz the doctor told me my body can't take the abuse I'm giving it. I'm gonna go home once I've said goodbye to my friends. Everyone is asking where you are. Wish you were still here with me coz if you were I'd stay up and continue with the party. Love you.

Me: Wish I could have stayed too, but I have to get up early for work and I won't give my clients a good session if I don't sleep. It was great to see you. I love you.

*   *   *

Maria: I haven't slept yet.

Me: You ought to sleep soon. If we were together I could crash out with you.

Maria: I'm going to Leonidas' place now. He's making some lunch.

Me: Have fun, gorgeous. Get some sleep when you can. You need to rest. Then when you wake up can we meet?

Maria: I feel like shit. I put the heating on and I'm too hot, I turn it off and I'm too cold. It's always like this the first day I take my anti-addiction tablets, if I haven't taken them for a while. I don't like telling you this, but I'm not in a fit state to see you. I'm sorry.

Me: I'm glad you're taking the pills so no need to apologise. I love you and wanna see you at your best. Let's meet tomorrow.

Maria: I'm gonna go and lie down coz I'm very dizzy. Do you remember that night I had dinner with you after I took my pills? I felt so bad coz I really wanted to be with you but I had to go home. Today I feel the same. I can't stay on my feet for more than ten minutes. But tomorrow I'll be good again.

The following day I met Maria in Beyond Retro and we had a coffee there. We felt like finding somewhere new to hang and so we walked around for a bit. At the Dalston end of Stoke New-ington Road we saw a sign for a vegan café with the unlikely name of Mandelbrot Set Of Love. We descended the stairs, which were painted red, and it was as if we'd entered the underworld. The walls, ceiling and various shelving units were red, and the lighting reflecting off the fake-wood floor gave it a reddish tinge, although when I looked at it closely it seemed to be brown. There were red leather sofas, weird in a vegan place, as well as all sorts of dolls, books, talismans, and other strange knick-knacks. There was a massage table and signs offering yoga and neuro-skeletal realignment. The selection of teas was bewildering. After we'd hit on a tailored mix we had to choose a pot. We took a teapot in the shape of a bear. There was only one woman working in the place, and flowered curtains prevented us from seeing whatever was in the back of the basement.

'This is unreal,' I said once we'd sat down.

'It's got to be a front for a brothel,' Maria shot back.

'Do you think so?'

'Look at it.'

'It's strange for sure. Doing vegan food and selling used leather gloves is wacked out.'

'I don't think they're really selling those gloves and antique dolls.'

'What the fuck are all those giant stuffed toy bears and rabbits on the wall?'

'To cater for those with a schoolgirl fetish. This has to be a knocking shop.'

'You know there are some pretty weird businesses set up by those with an income who can afford to lose money. This could be one of them.'

'Come on, this is too kooky for that, and if it was a money-laundering front it would be more swish. It's gotta be selling illicit sex.'

We didn't get to finish our conversation because a vegan anti-fascist I knew wandered in with his girlfriend. They'd obviously been to the place before because they made their tea-and-cake order super fast. I introduced Maria to my friend, and he presented his better half. We talked for a bit, but I cut the conversation short because I could see Maria was bored by the bash-the-fash direction it took. I was happy enough to listen to tales of Nazis being done over, but I wanted my girlfriend to enjoy herself, so we split. Once we were outside we decided to see if we could find anywhere else for coffee that was even half as weird as the place we were leaving. We didn't but had fun checking out some Dalston caffs.

Maria: I'm making my first professional porno film this week. I'm gonna film it but not be in it. Carolina is doing it with an actor from Italy with a huge cock and six-pack. I'm attaching a photo of him. He's called the Stallion.

Me: I'm so glad you got your blue movie director thing going with Carolina. That picture you sent is too much. The Stallion looks like John Holmes on steroids. Hilarious.

Maria: Carolina is gonna meet the Stallion tomorrow, but I think he's totally gay. I know he's new to the porno scene in London, and I figure he needs work, so he can't be too choosy about doing straight action. He asked Carolina if I could film them doing twenty minutes of muscle worship and only ten minutes of sex. C'mon. All the muscle worship I've seen online with a hunky guy doing bodybuilder poses is gay. Now I'm borrowing porno movies from my male friends to get some fresh ideas about how to put them together. They're done badly if you ask me. The stuff I edit at work is much better than anything I've looked at. No wonder my boss' clients love me.

Me: If it's for Carolina's site, which I guess it is, her pay-to-view fans are not gonna be at all interested in muscle worship.

Maria: The Stallion is gonna pay us £300 coz he wants it for his own website and Carolina will use it on hers too. She's clever making him pay for everything.

Me: That's cool. If the Stallion is paying I guess he can do what he wants. Maybe Carolina will just want the ten minutes of sex. But if the Italian has a gay audience I don't understand what he thinks he's doing. Straight muscle worship is more sub men being dominated by bodybuilding and wrestling women. Of course their actual sexual orientation has nothing to do with what the actors do. Maybe he wants to shock his audience.

Maria: I think you're on the right track. In porno anything goes and the more shocking the better.

Maria: Now Carolina only wants me to take £100 of the Italian's money. I'd hoped she'd split it but I think coz she's having sex she wants more. Maybe when she sees it's more work to edit than film she'll realise I deserve half the cash. But if not, £100 ain't bad. On an hourly rate it's more than I get paid for editing porn at work. At least I'll have a good laugh too as I never get to film sex. And before I forget, a few hours before we shoot that crazy girl is going to some place she does sex parties to have more Botox put in her lips. I told her no. She's gonna look horrible if we film straight afterwards, her mouth will be so plump it will look utterly unnatural. And she told me, no Maria, only a little bit, I don't want to look like a duck. *¡Joder!* She already looks like a duck.

Me: Crazy. But maybe porno fans like a freak show.

Maria: Carolina said she'd ask the doctor if he thought she'd looked like a duck with more Botox. He'll say no because she's paying him for the lip job. I told her she doesn't need that shit and if she has it she's gonna look like a duck and all the fish in the aquarium rolled into one coz she's got a small face and her lips are already too big. But it doesn't matter what I say, she's gonna do it, and that's why she wants two-thirds of the Italian's money. Coz the doctor wants £200 for the lip job. She's really excited about the Italian guy, so as a joke I told her I could leave the camera running on the tripod and join them, and she told me we could both lick his dick at the same time. I wouldn't do that in a million years. But porn stars are so addicted to sex they get higher than a junkie on an unlimited supply of pure smack just talking about shagging.

Me: Crazy. High on hormones.

Maria: You know you get more and more attractive as you age. I really don't know how you do it, but you're more handsome and sexy every time I see you. Which is the opposite of me. I don't even recognise myself when I look in the mirror. I'm old and tired and washed up. What a horrible vision. But my skin is getting better now I'm using a very expensive moisturiser. It is amazing. It doesn't make me younger, nothing can, but the cream is improving the texture of my skin. And, best of all, it wasn't tested on animals.

Me: Hey, I love you and the way you look. We all looked better at twenty-one.

Maria: Carolina just sent me a text saying the guy is sick and can't do it today. But she says she already has the money, so we'll do it another day. I hate this. I don't like to accuse anyone without proof, but I wouldn't be surprised if Carolina cancelled the shoot so she could have her lips done today. I shouldn't have made her self-conscious about them by telling her she'd look like a fish.

Me: Can we meet at the Angel at 9pm tonight?

Maria: Hey, handsome, meeting at nine will be impossible for me. Ten will be much better coz I wanna wash my hair before I see you, and it needs to be completely dried, otherwise my fringe curls at the sides and I don't like it. Also I'm remembering how brightly lit the Angel is, and I don't like the seats either. So can we find somewhere else please.

Me: Okay let's meet at 10pm at the Masque Haunt. Catch you later.

Maria: Can we meet at 10.30pm instead please? Shit it's nearly 10.15, give me an extra half an hour.

I'd been in the Masque Haunt for three-quarters of an hour when Maria got there at 10.45pm. Fortunately I wasn't left all alone coz there were some people in the pub I knew from the Highbury Fields gym. I introduced Maria, and then we found a table to ourselves. I'd looked for one at the other end of the pub, but there weren't any free there, so my acquaintances could see us.

'This is so frustrating,' Maria said, 'I can't touch you the way I want when we're in your friends' line of vision. I so want to squeeze your legs and arse. You know how much I love to do that when there are lots of people around us, but I can't when people you know are looking. It would be too much.'

'You amaze me drinking coffee this late. I couldn't sleep if I did that,' I told Maria to change the subject.

'My sleep patterns are fucked, so I might as well enjoy myself.'

'Hey, you know what?' Maria said as she pulled *Baron's Court, All Change* by Terry Taylor from her bag. 'This book is brilliant.'

'Have you read it again?'

'No.'

'But you were reading it six months ago.'

'I know, but I just finished it. If I really like a book I leave the last few pages and come back to it months later so I can savour the story for a long time.'

'If I like a book I just wanna get to the end to see what happens.'

'I want to get to the end too, but making myself wait means I really appreciate what I've read and I remember it for much longer.'

'I've read that book a couple of times, and I liked it even more the second time.'

'Why was that?'

'Coz I'd found out that an editor made Terry Taylor add in all that kitchen-sink stuff about his family background and sister Liz. That slows the narrative down and makes the book more conventional. When you know the author's original vision was just to write about the early London mod scene and drug dealing you appreciate he was a far greater writer than the publishing industry allowed him to be.'

'That would be like if I wrote a novel based on our relationship and then some editor said I had to put in lots of details about you sofa surfing with your cousin and describe her kid going from being a baby to a toddler.'

'Exactly. It would get in the way of the real story, which is you and me.'

'So now I'm gonna have to reread *Baron's Court* with that in mind.'

'It's a great book, but it would have been even better without editorial interference.'

'Changing the subject, you look like an angel, but I know you aren't and that makes you even more adorable,' Maria laughed.

'Neither of us are angels.'

'If you don't fuck me soon I'm gonna end up shooting shit.'

Shortly after we were having sex on the communal stairs in Maria's block.

Maria: On your birthday you have to meet me at Tower Bridge. We're going somewhere special but it's a surprise. When we get there we're gonna be able to fuck, and I'm gonna bring at least a small camera. The place is having new carpets fitted tomorrow, so maybe you could pin me down on the clean floor. There's a glass roof so we can look up at the stars too. And I've got sexy new black-and-red stockings to show you.

I met Maria at 10pm on the north side of Tower Bridge. She led me down to St Catherine's Dock. I wondered if she'd booked a hotel. It wasn't until we were at the edge of the water I discovered we were staying on a boat. Seconds after descending into the living quarters we were fooling around on a double bed. Maria had me naked in no time and was biting hard at various parts of my anatomy. An hour into the fun she still had her clothes on. I was so steamed up I pinned her to the bed and pulled down the zip on her flies.

'No, no, no,' Maria screamed, 'I wanna have a shower before I fuck you!'

So I let her get up, and she didn't come back for at least thirty minutes. I lay naked on the bed feeling all turned on and trippy. When Maria reappeared she had a camera in her hand and was filming me. I was told I had to beg her to fuck me, and as I did this she videoed me. Then Maria insisted I let her spank me. Later she told me the boat belonged to a friend, so she'd got it for free. The timing was perfect for my birthday because it had just been done up and in a few days the new couple who were renting it would move in. The boat was amazing and so was my birthday.

Maria: Can we go and see *Under The Skin* this weekend?

Me: Let's see it at the Barbican on Sunday. No point going to the West End when it's on so close to your flat.

Maria: I've really wanted to see *Under The Skin* since I first read they were making it a couple of years ago. Could you buy the tickets? I have to pay Antonio for the drugs we bought at New Year. Yeah, I'm still paying for that two-week slumber party I had with him. He bought me hundreds of pounds' worth of gear, but I promised to pay him back. I'll clear the debt at the end of this month. Until next year anyway. Hopefully I won't need drugs next Christmas and New Year. I felt so low and lonely after all the bollocks with my nephew. Even when I was high I was having a shit time. It's been tough to be on such a tight budget for three months, but I really gotta pay Antonio back. Fuck it's already 4am. I better sleep.

I called for Maria at 8pm, and she came straight down. We wanted a little time together before the film started. We sat by the Barbican's artificial lake holding hands and whispering sweet nothings until the conversation got serious.

'I'm surprised you haven't shown me a tarot,' I said.

'I don't need to show you any more now you've recalled what you need to on that front. Very soon I'm gonna give you a tarot, and I want you to work with it. I'm also gonna give you a sex magick grimoire. I want you to read it very carefully and commit all the important passages to memory.'

'Why?'

'Because I've told the coven about you, and we're gonna initiate you. I'll be the first to peg you, but you're gonna give yourself up to all the witches as part of a Great Rite. It will really open you up, and afterwards you're gonna be so in touch with yourself and your past lives.'

'When.'

'Autumn equinox.'

'But that's six months away.'

'I have to prepare you.'

'Why?'

'Do you think you're ready to be fucked up the arse by twelve witches, one after the other?'

'I can dig it.'

'It's not about pleasure, there needs to be focus. You have to be tied down and blindfolded and stay quite still. Only when all the rites have been observed will the blindfold be removed so that you can see the light.'

The conversation shifted to music before it was time to make our way to the cinema. I hated *Under The Skin*; Maria loved it. Scarlett Johansson plays an alien disguised as a woman who seduces men and kills them. That might make for a good exploitation flick, but as art house it just made me yawn. I wasn't surprised the movie flopped at the box office but got good reviews. Maria was with the critics who loved it; I rarely agreed with their opinions. Fortunately I didn't mind sitting through bad movies if I was holding Maria's hand for the duration.

XXI

LE MONDE

THE WORLD

Maria: I nearly died of embarrassment today. A woman at work saw a clip I shot with my hand around your cock. I was showing her something I filmed yesterday, and she took my phone to get a better look and clicked on the wrong icon. I took the phone from her as fast as I could. She didn't see anything with our faces in. But if I hadn't taken the mobile she'd have watched everything.

Me: That's funny and no harm done if she wasn't offended.

Maria: She was fascinated and asked me if it was my boyfriend and whether I had lots of videos like that? I think she wanted to see more of your dick. No way. Those clips are only for me. Do you think there's any chance of you coming to my work tomorrow? I'm just asking coz I really wanna fuck you. I want you to do some bad and dirty things to me. I can't wait for you to eat my pussy. I'm gonna make you to do it for hours. Ten minutes is not long enough, and you've never done more than that.

Me: I can come, but I got clients in the evening so it wouldn't be until around 10pm.

Maria: I don't wanna hang around that long. I was hoping you could get here by 7pm. Let's leave it for another night.

Me: Doh. Let's go to the cinema soon. Parts 1 & 2 of *Nymphomaniac* are on at the Prince Charles over the next few days. My clients clash with the weekend screenings, but I could do Monday.

Maria: Monday works best for me. If *Nymphomaniac* is

boring we can always amuse ourselves in the dark by doing what they're doing on screen but better. And it'll be good for me to see how he's filmed the scenes with real sex. I can finish work at 4.30pm on Monday. Part 1 starts at 6.30pm and Part 2 at 9.00pm. I'd like to see both parts but I suspect you don't. I've heard that watching them together is very repetitive. All sex, sex and sex. There isn't even a story, just sexual encounters that ain't erotic. You tell me, shall we see Part 1 or Part 2 or both? I'm doing porn homework all weekend. I'm gonna watch as much of that trash as I can for two whole days in case Carolina and the Italian Stallion want me to make something modern and on trend for them. But I'd rather go for a retro-seventies feel. I wanna shoot them fucking from some unusual angles. If I can get a glass table I'm gonna film them from underneath while they fuck on top of it. All the modern porn I've seen is so fucking boring and predictable. Antonio keeps telling me that I must use the zoom a lot and keep my distance from them. If that's what Carolina and her Stallion want, then that's what I'll have to do. But I'll try to convince them to let me do something better. I'm going to watch *Deep Throat* and *The Devil In Miss Jones* again.

Me: Let's just see *Nymphomaniac* Part 1. Both would be too much. Enjoy your seventies porn.

Maria: My porn shoot ain't happening. I'll focus my anger on the Italian Stallion coz I don't wanna get upset with Carolina. Even if she's the one I should tell to fuck off. I got a text an hour ago saying they've got a porn producer who'll film them for free and he's not even their friend. So they're gonna do it with him. Great. I just wish Carolina hadn't asked me three times in a row to be ready to do it, then later cancelled the whole thing. How can they be so unprofessional? What I told her is that the porn producer should not only film it for free but he should pay them. Coz obviously he's gonna give them copies of the footage and sell it himself too. So if they paid me £100 to do it they'd be getting better value coz their short wouldn't be so over-exposed. Really she's working for free. This all started coz I said I needed money to get my teeth fixed and she thought we could work on something together. First films for the men who hire her as an escort, then she shifted it to professional porn for distribution. It's been nothing but false promises and bullshit. Now I don't care about it. Thank God I have a good day job coz if I had to rely on people like the Italian Stallion I'd be going hungry. I'm a bit pissed off. Fuck them. Can't wait to see you on Monday.

Me: What a wind-up. It wouldn't surprise me if the porn producer drags his feet over giving them copies so he gets to run it into the ground as his personal money-maker without them queering the pitch at the same time. Sounds fucked. So fuck it. Sleep well, gorgeous, I'll dream of you.

Maria: I wanted to tell you about an amazing thing that happened this afternoon. I had a wank coz I wanted to come and of course I was thinking of you. Then an hour later my period came at last. I hadn't had one for six months, since November. I must be getting strong again and that's good. And poor Carolina, I think you're right and that porno producer is really gonna shaft her. ¡Joder!

Me: Can we meet at the Prince Charles at 6.15? For *Nymphomaniac* Part 1 only. If you're late we'll have to see Part 2 only.

Maria was on time, so we kissed, got a seat in the front row and held hands throughout the movie. The Lars von Trier flick bored me shitless – still, it was better than *Under The Skin*. Maria didn't like it as much as that last movie we'd seen, but she still dug it a lot more than me. When it came to trash our tastes were perfectly matched, but Maria had a soft spot for mainstream art house that I didn't share. But since we were holding hands in the dark I was happy. Afterwards we went to eat in Gaby's Deli in Charing Cross Road. We both had the hot mixed-vegetable plate.

'I'm sorry I keep dragging you to movies you don't like,' Maria said.

'Don't worry, I'm happy to see anything with you.'

'Next time we go to the cinema it has to be something you like. Maybe we can see a martial arts flick or an old horror movie.'

'Is *The Raid 2* out yet? I'd like to see that.'

'It's out soon. What else do you wanna catch?'

'I'd like to see some good horror movies. But all the new ones seem to be shit. A few years ago I could still find horrors I liked but not now.'

'What was good then?'

'Shit like the Bruce Campbell movies. I really dug *My Name Is Bruce*, that was classic horror comedy.'

'What about revivals?'

'You know there's so much I'd like to see at the cinema. A few years ago at Tate Modern they did free screenings of a load of Italian genre movies paid for by a sponsor to go alongside an Italian art exhibition. It was great. They showed loads of my favourite directors on the big screen including Fernando Di Leo, Lucio Fulci and Mario Bava. But it's never been easy to see that stuff or old Spanish horror movies at the cinema in London. I'd love to see some Paul Naschy projected on 35mm.'

'Any titles in particular?'

'Well his greatest hit *Werewolf Shadow* would be a good place to start.'

'What's that in Spanish?'

'How would I know? It has a bunch of different English titles like *Blood Moon* and *The Werewolf Vs. The Vampire Woman*, but you must know it, Naschy's best Waldemar Daninsky flick.'

'You mean *La Noche De Walpurgis* from 1971.'

'Yeah, strangely I did know the Spanish title was *Walpurgis Night*.'

'It's a great movie.'

Maria: I can't stop looking at the footage I shot on the boat on your birthday. I was enjoying what you were doing before I went to take my shower. I really liked the way you took control. You should keep pushing me sexually like that, it's fun but I find it hard to accept that submissive role. I can only do that with men I really love, like you. It always takes me a while to get used to not being dominant sexually, which is why I disappeared into the shower and when I came out told you to beg me for a fuck and then spanked you. I hope you liked it and I didn't hit you too hard. I just wanted to make it painful enough to be thrilling. The video I made of your fine white arse transitioning to a bright shade of red turns me on so much. I often wank off watching it. I wouldn't intentionally hurt you. I just like to assert myself a bit. It's such a contradictory thing coz I really like it when you take control, but on the boat it became a bit too much and brought out the dominatrix in me. Let's work on it coz I also want you to pin me down and fuck me hard, while I fight you off and scratch you. But I won't struggle enough to prevent you getting your way with me. I just want to play and pretend you're forcing me to fuck you. I can leave my camera on a tripod and film it. What I can't figure out is a good way to shoot us doing penetration in close up. We'll have to practise with a big mirror, but if you're fucking me it's gonna be hard for me to film it exactly the way I want. Sometimes I think about making you screw another woman so I can capture some hardcore sex exactly as I want it, but then I know it won't work coz I'll get jealous and mess up with the camera. Doh. Right now I really want to squeeze your cock and capture it on video as I make it grow. Maybe I'll do that when I see you tonight. You'll know what's coming if I have my camera.

I got to Maria's late in the evening. We walked around for a bit and then fooled about on the communal stairs in her block. Before we did that she went into her flat to get a good movie camera. Afterwards we sat outside the Slice Of Life with soft drinks.

'I'm giving you a couple of tarot packs and my coven's grimoire. Our *Book Of Shadows* is secret, so you have to promise to keep it to yourself and not show it to anyone or discuss it with anyone but me.'

'Of course.'

'You promise?'

'I promise.'

'You can only read this in private, don't look at it now,' Maria said as she handed over a thick manuscript that I discovered later was a computer printout.

'Are you going to help me learn tarot reading?'

'No, from now on you need to practise alone with the decks I've given you.'

'But can I show them to other people?'

'Of course, but don't let just anyone touch them; you want them charged with your own vibes, not other people's energy.'

After that we talked about movies, most specifically those of Amando de Ossorio, viz. *Tombs Of The Blind Dead*, *Return Of The Blind Dead*, *The Ghost Galleon*, *Night Of The Seagulls*, *The Loreley's Grasp*, *Fangs Of The Living Dead* and *The Night Of The Sorcerers* – coz those were the flicks by this director we'd both seen. We were getting good at matching up Spanish and English titles. Maria was clearly very happy because she cheerfully discussed with me how the reanimated and very evil Knights Templar in the four *Blind Dead* movies were clearly intended as representations of Franco's fascist forces.

Maria: I wanted to be offline for a few days, that's why I haven't answered your messages. I slept all day Saturday but yesterday I was fixing up my flat. I'm gonna paint the kitchen and bathroom. I'd decorate the whole pad, but I can't because of Sidney. It was fabulous to see you on Friday. It was more than great you were so happy to see me and let me film you every which way I wanted. Just imagine the trouble you'll be in if I ever decide to blackmail you.

Me: You're the kind of trouble I like. Can we meet tonight?

Maria: I'm feeling anti-social. I've been like this for a few days. The anniversary of my mum's death made me feel very sad. I'm not sure if I'll be able to go out tonight. I really want to see you, but I'm so tired. Although I'm down I'm very proud of myself because this is the first year since my mum died that I didn't use shit to get through the anniversary. I just thought fuck it, if I never let myself really feel the pain then I'll never get over it. But because of that I'm in a state and I really can't see you now. I'll meet you any day next week, and because I'll be on holiday I can meet you any time too.

Me: I'm so proud of you. It's so great you didn't take any shit and worked through your feelings about your mum's death. It's hard but so much better to do that than blot it out. If I can't see you as soon as I want it'll make me appreciate it even more when we do meet. Let's figure something out next week.

Maria: The sadness is fading and I'm feeling so well now. Yesterday I made a promise to myself that I won't shoot any shit until Xmas. I'm going to live much more healthily. I've got an appointment to get a new passport, and I have to go all the way to Chelsea to sort it out.

Me: I ain't been to Chelsea in years. I've got no reason to go, everything moved east ages ago.

Maria: I actually made it to the Spanish embassy on time. I'm waiting to find out if they're gonna fine me coz my passport ran out two years ago. They say it should be renewed within six months and that because I'm living abroad I should renew it before it expires. I tried to sweet talk them out of penalising me.

Me: Surely they know you're committed to living in London and don't wanna move back to Spain? Did you tell them all you wanted was a little visit home? Maybe a week or two seeing your family and friends in Valencia.

Maria: I really needed to talk to you but you weren't picking up your phone. It's alright now.

Me: I just found your texts. I went to the cinema between clients and turned my phone to silent then forgot to put the ring back on. Can't believe Sidney is dead. I'm really sorry I didn't find your messages earlier. I called but you were engaged every time. I'm gonna call again and again until I get through. I should have been there for you. It's such a horrible thought, Sidney just bolting out the door when you left it open and diving off the balcony to her death. I'm so sorry.

* * *

Maria: As you know I talked to lots of people but talking to you was best.

Me: Do you wanna meet tomorrow afternoon? I've got clients early and late in Lincoln's Inn Fields, at 3pm I'm free for ninety minutes.

Maria: It would have been wonderful to meet you today but I only slept for a few hours. When I did crash out I had this weird dream in which you'd got a job at my work and a desk beside mine. I haven't slept much since Monday, but every time I get a few hours' shut-eye I dream of you and not my dear cat Sidney. I'm still grieving and I look horrible, tired and very old, so it is better if I rest today and meet you later in the week. Also I'm still spring cleaning and don't have much of my holidays left. I wanna use the daylight hours to sort out my flat, so it's gonna be better if we meet at night. I can't wait to see you, but I need to look better than I do now.

Me: Let's meet Sunday night. Everywhere will be quieter then and you'll have plenty of time to recover. I'm gonna check what's on at the cinema.

Maria: I don't wanna go to the cinema, not so soon after Sidney dying. I'd rather you came to my place. I want to show you the grave I made for Sidney. See you Sunday.

Me: Is 9pm okay or should I come by earlier if I can? I could blow out a client or two.

Maria: 9pm is great if it doesn't rain. I'm still not feeling good. I'm glad you've given me some time to recover.

Me: I don't care if it's raining. I just wanna see you. I don't mind getting wet.

Maria: Please forget about tonight. I have a fever and I'm still crying a lot. So I'm not good company at the moment. Just forget me for a day or two and don't be upset with me. I love you.

Me: I can't wait to see you, but I'll catch you when you're feeling better.

Maria: Thank you. Next week I'll be much better. I just need time to grieve properly.

Me: I'm fretting about you and hoping you're okay. Love you.

Maria: Don't worry about me. I'm just sad most of the time. I took shit the night Sidney died and the next day when I buried her, so I'd feel a bit better. But then I know shit solves nothing, it just stops me dealing with my feelings, so I haven't taken any more. That's why I feel so anti-social. I'll see you soon, but right now I can't.

Me: I'm glad you're not doing shit. I can understand why you're sad and anti-social, but it's good you're dealing with the pain and not freezing it. Can I see you next Monday night? That's nearly a week away, so I'm sure you'll be more gorgeous then ever by then.

Maria: Thanks for giving me space. Monday night will be great, and if you want we can go and see *The Raid 2*.

Me: That's Monday sorted then.

Maria: Which cinema do you want to go to?

Me: There are only three places we could see it after you finish work without travelling miles into the sticks: Empire Leicester Square at 20.20 or 22.15, Cineworld Shaftesbury Avenue at 20.40 and Aubin Cinema Shoreditch at 21.15. I'd say 20.20 or 20.40 are the best times. Aubin is small and has bad seating, but they do have sofas. The West End is better for seeing the film properly and also better times as I have to get up early the next day for a client. Can we meet in the West End at 7.30pm?

Maria: Hey, handsome, I've been so busy that this is the first chance I've had to reply. Did you know there's a tube strike beginning at 9pm tonight? The late buses are gonna be crazy busy. I'll meet you 7.45 to 8pm wherever you tell me to go. Did you know the Sci-fi Film Festival starts this week and next Saturday evening there's a martial arts double bill? You might like it. The films are called *Tai-Chi Zero* and *Tai-Chi Hero*. Tell me where we'll meet tonight.

Me: See you at FOPP off Shaftsbury Avenue at 7.45pm. We'll see *The Raid 2* at either 8.20 or 8.40pm. I've seen *Tai-Chi Zero* but not the follow up. Can't wait to see you, it's been too long.

Maria was fifteen minutes late, but we still had time to catch the earlier show in Leicester Square. It was nearly sold out, and the seats we were given were absolutely shit ones jammed up right in front of the screen. We walked in during the ads, but there were a couple of prime seats at the back that were empty so we took them. Just as the film was starting a couple of thirty-something men in business suits came to the end of our row.

'Those are our seats,' they shouted across to where we were sitting in the middle of the row.

'You've made a mistake,' Maria told them. 'These are our seats. I can show you the numbers on our tickets.'

The suits asked people at the end of the row to get up so they could get closer to us to argue about it.

'I'm not getting up,' a man told them. 'The foreign lady says those aren't your seats, and you're disturbing my enjoyment of the film. Go down to the front and sit where there are empty seats.'

The suits gave up and slunk to the front. I sat holding Maria's hand through a rollercoaster of simulated violence. We'd found a film we could both enjoy. A martial arts showcase about an undercover agent exposing bent coppers colluding with Jakarta's criminals. Afterwards we walked around Soho and talked mostly about the film we'd just seen. I brought up Sidney, but it was obvious Maria didn't want to talk about her, so I didn't press the subject.

Me: Hey, great to see you tonight. You looked as stunning as ever. I wanna see you again very soon.

Maria: You looked super fit. I just wanted to touch you all over. I didn't want to talk about Sidney because I didn't want to start crying again. And guess what? I gave you the Sci-Fi Film Festival programme for last year. So those tai-chi movies were on in 2013. This year it's different films and it finishes on Sunday. I can't believe that I was looking at the old programme.

Me: That's funny. The films in this year's Sci-Fi Festival don't look too good.

Maria: I don't like this year's selections either. I thought *The Creep Behind The Camera* might be interesting, but I saw the trailer and it sucked. It was really great to see you. You know what made me laugh? Towards the end of *The Raid 2* I put my hand on your leg and you trapped it. I liked that. When the film started I kept thinking how easy it would be to turn it into a gay porno movie with a jail setting, orgies and fighting in mud.

Me: Can I see you tomorrow? I'll come to your place coz I know you wanna show me Sidney's grave.

Maria: Of course.

I had to wait for Maria to come down. It was late, but the gates to Fortune Street Park were unlocked because the council didn't want to pay for someone to go around closing parks. Local residents were complaining about this because it meant after dark Fortune Street was transformed into a shooting gallery, and the needles left behind were a danger for their kids. The park was empty except for a few junkies, Maria and me. She'd buried Sidney in a fenced-off shrub area close to her flat. The grave was well hidden by greenery. Maria got tearful talking about her cat. Afterwards we took a stroll around the Barbican Highwalk and then down to the Thames.

'Now that I've lost Sidney,' Maria told me, 'you'll be able to come into my flat once I've sorted it out.'

'There's no rush,' I told her, 'and besides I don't really care what it looks like.'

'I'd be embarrassed for you to see it as it is now, but once everything is sorted you can come in.'

'I could help you sort it out. It might be quicker that way.'

'I'll do it myself and have it ready for you by the summer. I know it's only April now, but I own so many things and I need to paint, so it will take a while. I'm always so tired when I come in from work, so I'll only have the weekends.'

Me: Despite your sadness over Sidney, it was great to see you last night. Sorry I was so tired. Blame my client who's getting me to do *Insanity* with them. They're crazy, they don't need someone to do it with, it's a set of DVDs – but I'm not going to turn down money for it. And they were my last job of the day before I called on you.

Maria: I've been reading *Body For Life For Women* by Dr Pamela Peeke. It's taught me a lot about diet, and now I understand what you've been saying to me about food. The book tells you what's gonna happen to your body and mind as you age. I found it at the dump ages ago, so I don't know why it took me so long to start reading it. My house is full of stuff I've found at the dump. So many books and DVDs. In other news, the postman delivered my new passport this morning. Now I can go wherever I want, which means I'm gonna show you where I grew up. You'll come with me, won't you? I can't afford to go before Xmas, but I'm sure you can take time off from your clients then. It's a shame I went to sort out the passport on the day Sidney died, coz whenever I see it I'm gonna be reminded of that.

Me: We're going to Valencia as soon as we can afford it. I can't wait to go with you. I'm glad you got your passport, but I'm sorry it reminds you of Sidney's death. That book you read is part of the *Body For Life* series published by Rodale. It's a good place to start, but once you've really got going with that stuff I'm gonna move you on. However, I'm thrilled you're working on your health and fitness. It's the move from no exercise to a little that makes the biggest difference. But if you can take it further it's better. Diet is seventy percent of good health.

Maria: I love it when you explain your work and how it applies to me, but later I can never remember everything you said, so it's good to have books. I promised my friends I'd go to the Parkinsons gig, but I stayed home coz I know I'd have got as high as a kite. And if I start Friday night like that then I'll be doing gear the whole weekend. I wanted to stay drug-free for you. Instead of indulging in rock-and-roll excess I watched a movie called *The Paperboy*, a completely mainstream film in which the actors all look horrible and ugly. There's even a scene with Nicole Kidman pissing on someone.

Three months passed during which I met Maria at the same circuit of pubs and cafés. Sometimes we'd meet other people, but there were no gigs because the blatant drug use at them was too much of a temptation for my girlfriend who wanted to be clean. One night when we were in the Rochester Castle and Antonio was there too, Maria's old friend pulled me aside for a few words.

'How have you done it?'

'Done what?' I asked.

'Changed Maria,' he said. 'She doesn't want to do drugs any more. And she's become much more punctual. She's like the girl I first knew eighteen years ago and such a great friend again. That said, when I met her she liked doing drugs. But she's happy again now, not bitter and resentful. You've transformed her.'

'I didn't do anything. She changed herself.'

'You did something no one else could do.'

'All I did was love her, but then she loves me too.'

I wondered if Maria and I were gonna have a summer of a thousand Julys. Of course not everything was perfect, but things seemed as close to that as real life could ever be. There was a screening of the old Jackie Chan kung fu comedy *Drunken Master* at the Prince Charles, and I arranged to meet Maria there. I was waiting outside when I got a text saying she was late. Maria wanted me to buy her ticket and leave it at the desk. She'd find me in the front row when she got there. Maria arrived at the cinema as I was leaving after the screening. We laughed and decided to go to Gaby's Deli. It was a Sunday night and this restaurant was already closed. We ended up in Bar Italia on Frith Street.

'I've got something to ask you,' I told Maria after I ordered our food and drinks.

'Why I was late for the film? I just took too long doing my hair.'

'I don't care about that.'

'What is it then?'

'I've paid off my wife's debts at last, so if you like the idea I wanna look for a one-bedroom flat so we can live together. Would you move from your place? I think your bedsitter is too small for both of us. We need two rooms to be together.'

Maria didn't speak, I don't think she could, but she threw her arms around me and we started to kiss. I'd paid off my ex-wife's debts through a lot of hard work and too many long trips to Toulouse. Now there was nothing to stop me living with Maria. I was so in love with her it was way too late to worry about her addiction issues. In the past few months she'd handled them so well, but that didn't mean I thought we were entirely out of the woods; relapses were highly likely, but I had my fingers crossed they'd be minor.

'This is more than great,' Maria eventually managed to sob through tears of joy. 'I'm so happy.'

'You're never gonna be late for me again, coz we'll always be together,' I said.

'That's the way we're meant to be.'

'I don't think we can afford to live as centrally as you are now.'

'We can. I can get a decent rent if I sublet my council flat. I wouldn't wanna give up the tenancy. It was so difficult to get. I've told you about being homeless and sleeping on friends' sofas. It took a year to get that tenancy, and I had to fake some heavy domestic violence at the place I said I was staying to bounce me up the waiting list.'

'Living off Old Street would be great.'

'And that way I'd be able to keep an eye on whoever was subletting my flat and make it look to the council like I was still living there.'

We made so many plans for our future that night. Maria didn't want to go looking at places after work, and the next weekend I was in Toulouse with my ultra-high-net-worth clients. We'd start checking out flats the following weekend when I was back. I wanted to see Maria before I left on Thursday. At the start of the week she needed to work late. Maria had been invited to some literary event at the top of Old Street roundabout on Wednesday night, and we agreed to meet there. On the day she sent a message saying she was sick and couldn't make it. Her rheumatism was always worst when it was hot, and that week there was a heat-wave.

I was only in Toulouse for a week, and I couldn't wait to get home to see Maria. Given we'd committed to making our future together, I was expecting a constant exchange of messages while I was gone. There was a flurry from Thursday through to Friday evening, then nothing. From then until Monday I was sending increasingly frantic messages asking Maria if everything was alright? I knew in my heart something was wrong. On Monday afternoon I heard from Maria's boss, who asked if I knew where she was because she hadn't turned up for work. I explained I was away and Maria wasn't answering my messages. Her boss said that was really odd because despite being sick the previous week, she'd been so happy. She'd been telling everyone at her work about how we were going to live together. On Tuesday evening I got a phone call from Maria's boss. He told me to brace myself. The police had broken into Maria's flat and found her dead. I got more details in a phone call with Antonio, who confirmed my suspicion Maria had overdosed on smack.

THE FOOL

LE MAT.

The cops had to smash the door to get into Maria's flat. Now I had the keys to the new locks that had been fitted. It was odd going in coz Maria had denied me entry for so long. The place had been turned upside down by the fuzz. Antonio and I sorted through Maria's possessions. Some things were to go to charity shops, others to her family, there were mementos for friends. I was taking Maria's collections of weapons and tarot cards. Antonio was getting her records and complete run of *Maximum Rocknroll*. I couldn't believe some of the things I found. Maria had printed out, preserved and annotated every conversation I'd ever had with her. I also learnt more of her medical history.

There were letters about her failing to turn up for treatment for hepatitis C. Maria always told me she had negative results when tested for HIV and hep C. Documents in her flat showed she'd always tested negative for the former but not the latter. I'd suspected she had hep C for ages and for all sorts of reasons, including both her over-the-top statements about not having it and the fact she absolutely would not have sex with me when she had a period. Unlike HIV, hepatitis C was not thought to be transmitted through sexual activity; there might, however, be a slight danger of this happening when an infected woman had her monthlies. Needle sharing was how many of those living with hep C contracted it, although I'd also heard stories about people getting it from blood on shared notes used for snorting cocaine. If I'd known for sure Maria had hep C while she was alive it wouldn't have made any difference to me. She hadn't needed to hide it from me. I loved her.

Maria had preserved all her film-school course handouts and every letter she'd received in London, regardless of whether it was from her family or the Department Of Health And Social Security. She even had an extensive collection of art-opening invitations stolen from a critic who'd lived in the same block in Brixton as she had in the late 1990s. And then there were the needles. It was as if Maria couldn't throw anything away. She went to a needle exchange, but it looked like she'd kept every syringe she'd brought to the flat from there. The spikes were supposed to be safely disposed of, but Maria hadn't even put them in the safety boxes they were supplied with; they were loose all over the flat. She'd been a hoarder, and there was a lot to be disposed of including all the presents I'd given her – Antonio took most of them. One night I was in Maria's flat alone. I locked up, and as I came out of the block a woman approached me.

'You're Martin, right?' she asked in an American accent.

'Yeah.'

'I'm Cheryl from Maria's coven.'

'She told me about the coven.'

'She told us about you. When she died she came to me and wanted me to be her walk-thru, so she could continue her relationship with you, but I refused.'

'Walk-thru?'

'A dead person doesn't have to be reborn, they can occupy a living person's body if the host agrees to vacate their physical frame.'

'I don't know about that.'

'You do, you just don't remember it right now, but it will come back.'

'You sound like Maria.'

'Although I refused to be Maria's walk-thru, I agreed to look after you for her, until your next life together. I'm your girlfriend now. Are you ready to come home with me?'

'What's gonna happen if I agree?'

'One of my priorities is your anal training. You need to be prepared for the Great Rite at the fall equinox. Our coven is now short of a witch, and you're the best person to take Maria's place. You need to be prepared for initiation. The shock of Maria's death has blown you wide open emotionally, so now you're more than ready to become who you've always been.'

'I don't know who I am any more.'

'You'll find Maria again in another life, but for things to work out better next time you need help from me and the rest of the coven. Who you thought you were was just an illusion, so it's good you're over that now. Are you coming with me? It's just a short walk to my flat.'

'Okay.'

'This is what Maria wants.'

'What Maria wants, I want.'

'Stay with me tonight, we'll move your stuff in over the next few days.'

LONDON BOOKS

FLYING THE FLAG FOR
FREE-THINKING LITERATURE

www.london-books.co.uk

PLEASE VISIT OUR WEBSITE FOR

- Current and forthcoming books
- Author and title profiles
- Regular column by contemporary writers
- A lively, interactive message board
- Events and news
- Secure on-line bookshop
- Recommendations and links
- An alternative view of London literature

London Classics

The Angel And The Cuckoo *Gerald Kersh*
Doctor Of The Lost *Simon Blumenfeld*
The Gilt Kid *James Curtis*
It Always Rains On Sunday *Arthur La Bern*
Jew Boy *Simon Blumenfeld*
May Day *John Sommerfield*
Night And The City *Gerald Kersh*
Phineas Kahn *Simon Blumenfeld*
Prelude To A Certain Midnight *Gerald Kersh*
A Start In Life *Alan Sillitoe*
There Ain't No Justice *James Curtis*
They Drive By Night *James Curtis*
Wide Boys Never Work *Robert Westerby*

NEW FICTION

MALAYAN SWING

PETE HAYNES

Aidan is different. He is small, awkward and often silent, an easy man
to ignore, mock or exploit, yet on the inside he is intelligent
and thoughtful. He speaks to the reader in a way he can't manage
in everyday life, reflecting on the world around him with great insight
and an almost childlike honesty. This is the internal
life of an outsider.

We meet Aidan not long after he has moved into a room in a
shared flat, forced from the home in which he felt secure by a policy
labelled 'care in the community'. But the community is dismissive
and threatening. He becomes lonely and scared, his best friend
the radio he carries everywhere. An old shed offers a hideaway
during the day, while his evenings are often spent in the local pubs.

Aidan's physical and mental state starts to deteriorate, and when
he bumps into Joey from the home he comes to the notice of some
bad people. He wanders the streets and is attacked, his life quickly
spiralling out of control. The story ends in dramatic fashion, but it is
Aidan's decency and a sense of escape that remain with the reader.
Malayan Swing is a moving novel, a testament to those living on the
margins of society, and as such is a brave and important work.

London Books
£8.99 paperback
ISBN 978-0-9551851-6-8

New Fiction

BARRY DESMOND IS A WANKER

MARTIN KNIGHT

Barry Desmond is an only child. He's had a sheltered upbringing by ageing parents distrustful of the outside world. This leaves him ill-equipped to deal with the savagery of school, the trials of adolescence and the reality and politics of the workplace.

At school he is a figure of fun, excluded and picked on. At home he struggles with the eccentricities of his parents and is alarmed and confused as his hormones spring into life. He finds guilty pleasure in self-relief. Later, he follows his father into a career with the Empire Bank, a throwback organisation doomed to become extinct. In middle age, and following the death of his parents and redundancy, Barry ventures out into the wider world determined to live his life and strike up relationships. Unlike his parents Barry believes that people are fundamentally decent.
Will he find the fulfilment and interaction he craves?
Will society repay Barry's trust?

This novel from Martin Knight, author of *Battersea Girl* and *Common People*, explores and illuminates 21st-century suburban loneliness and the grim reality of having a face that doesn't fit. *Barry Desmond Is A Wanker* is a seductive and surprising book, laced with humour, shot through with poignancy and sensitivity.

London Books
£8.99 paperback
ISBN 978-0-9551851-9-9

New Fiction

SLAUGHTERHOUSE PRAYER

JOHN KING

When a boy realises the grown-ups are killing animals and that he has been eating their bodies, he gives up meat. But should he share the truth and break another child's heart? As a youth he wants to believe in the ability of words and peaceful protest to end the slaughter, while struggling to resist a desire for revenge. Now a disillusioned man trying to rebuild his life, he must choose one of two paths. Acceptance means security, but those meat-industry adverts keep taunting him and some familiar insults – *smelly pig, dirty cow, chick-chick-chicken* – fill his head.

Slaughterhouse Prayer deals in human invention and our treatment of non-human animals, the manipulation of language and the corruption of innocence. Society's pecking order is challenged as the story moves to its margins and beyond. A book of dreams, where visions are more real than reality and sentimentality is a strength, it asks a series of questions. Can a person honestly kill without emotion? Could a vegan soldier stay professional and humane? And will we ever confront the terror that surrounds us?

London Books
£9.99 paperback
ISBN 978-0-9957217-2-2